Retro PULP TALES

Edited by Joe R. Lansdale

SUBTERRANEAN PRESS 2006

First Edition

Trade Hardcover ISBN
1-59606-008-5

Limited Edition ISBN
1-59606-009-3

Subterranean Press
PO Box 190106
Burton, MI 48519

www.subterraneanpress.com

Table of Contents

Introduction

Short stories are a rare breed these days. The markets are evaporating, as they have been for years. At least that's true in the wider mainstream market, but, of course, there are still a number of reasonably large genre markets, and many more smaller ones, and as of recent, many internet markets. I dislike the latter because I like to hold the work in my hands and put it on my shelf, but I prefer it to no markets.

Still, there does seem to be a need for pure storytelling. It's coming back. And when I say pure storytelling, I don't mean it has to be raw genre or pulp. But that sort of storytelling is certainly the root for what is going on these days. Literature has gone back to storytelling more than ever before. And when I say literature, I include serious literature. Writers have begun to realize that a good story well told is what works. It's what the reader will come back to and pass along to others with enthusiasm.

Literary writers who would never have touched pulp ideas now embrace them. Philip Roth recently took a turn with the alternate history novel. It struck me as pretty bland tea, though for those mainstream reviewers who have no idea how much this has been done in the genres, thought it was a revelation. It's like the novel *Fatherland* a few years back by Robert Harris. A novel embracing a similar subject. They seem to have forgotten that already, and when Harris did it they were unaware then, as now, that it had already been done many times, and much better.

Compelling stories, that's what people want, and that's what the writers in this book have given you. And, you know what? In this book, we've embraced the pulps with open arms and slobbery kisses. Recently this sort of thing, a return to the pulps, has been done in a couple of volumes by another editor, a very good writer named Michael Chabon, but except for a story or two, the writers there tried hard to make sure no one thought they were really writing a pulp story, or even a literary pulp story. The result? Taking into consideration that exception or two, mostly boredom.

Here, however, you have storytellers being storytellers.

My rule for the writers as their editor was simple. Write a story in the vein of the old pulps, or digest magazines, something you think might have gone into a magazine back then. Something that takes place before 1960, and with the restrictions of those times.

Most writers stuck to this. A few cheated a little.

But, the results…magnificent. There's something for everyone here. Storytelling at its best. And the writers have offered up notes ahead of their story on their inspirations and sources.

So, don't let me hold you up.

Kick back. Dig in, and enjoy a trip to an alternate universe where these "pulp" stories were written and the world of the writer and reader was filled with adventure.

—Joe R. Lansdale

My love affair with the pulps goes back more than four decades, to that day in 1964 I picked up a copy of the Bantam reprint edition of the Doc Savage novel *Meteor Menace* off the paperback spinner rack in Tompkins' Drugstore. (As you can tell, the memory is still crystal clear in my mind.) I had been a pulp fan before that without even knowing it, reading and enjoying novels by Edgar Rice Burroughs, Max Brand, and Clarence E. Mulford. But that Doc Savage book was really the first time I was aware of the vast amount of entertaining fiction waiting for me in the slowly browning pages of the pulps.

Within a few months I had discovered the Shadow, first through the radio show, which played on a lot of stations during the nostalgia craze of the Sixties, and then the new paperbacks by Dennis Lynds writing under the Maxwell Grant house-name. It wasn't long until paperback publishers began reprinting the original pulp novels by Walter B. Gibson, and I read every one as it came out. The Spider, G-8, Operator 5, Jim Hatfield, the Rio Kid...It was a great time for pulp reprints, and I ate 'em all up. I even ran across a few actual pulps and bought them, the start of a collection I continue adding to even now (despite the fact that I'll probably never get around to reading all of them).

So when Joe Lansdale asked me to write a story for a pulp-oriented anthology, I was thrilled. There have always been pulp-influenced elements in my work, but this was one of the rare times when I could cut loose and write as if I were aiming the yarn straight at one of the pulp editors. When I settled on the idea of doing an air-war story, I wanted to produce something that could have appeared in the pages of *Daredevil Aces, Sky Fighters, Wings,* or one of the other aviation pulps. Of course, a little weirdness crept in (must have been all those reprints of *G-8 and His Battle Aces* that I've read over the years), but I still think "Devil Wings Over France" is a good pulp story.

—James Reasoner

Devil Wings Over France
A Dead-Stick Malloy Story

James Reasoner

CHAPTER 1
Night Patrol

With its Hisso howling, the Spad climbed steeply into the black sky. Bright lines of tracer fire clawed after it as a trio of Fokker D.VIIs gave chase. In the cockpit of the Allied fighter, which had taken off earlier in the evening from the aerodrome at St.-Mihiel, the pilot suddenly hauled back on the stick and sent his crate into a loop. The Fokkers tried to follow, but the Spad was quicker. It wound up above the last in the line of Boche planes.

Dave "Dead-Stick" Malloy grinned as he saw the flare from the exhaust stacks of the Fokker's engine through the ring of the Aldis sight. He had already fired a couple of bursts through his twin Vickers to warm the barrels of the deadly machine guns. Now his fingers punched the trips and sent leaden death flickering through the darkness.

He saw sparks as the slugs impacted the metal cowling of the Fokker's engine. The German pilot tried to veer away, but Malloy kicked rudder and stayed with him. The lines of tracer reached the cockpit and blasted the life out of the Hun. He slumped forward against the stick, sending the Fokker into a dive that would not end until the plane plowed into the earth far below.

It was a good victory, but there were still two more of the D.VIIs to contend with. Malloy couldn't let himself get carried away with excitement, or he would never return to the 'drome at St.-Mihiel. He sideslipped and looked around for the other two Fokkers.

Spandaus chattered somewhere behind him, and bullets tore through the canvas of the Spad's fuselage. One of the flying wires snapped. Malloy kicked rudder again and went the other way, but a second fiery curtain was there to turn him back. They had him boxed in, and the only way out was down.

A Fokker could outclimb a Spad, but not outdive it. Malloy pointed his crate's nose at the ground and poured the juice to the Hisso. The engine never missed a beat. Malloy's mechanic, Propwash Jones, was the best greaseball on the Western Front, and he kept the Spad's guts purring like a kitten.

The Fokkers came after Malloy, of course, but he didn't pull out of the dive until the Spad's trucks were brushing the treetops. He zoomed along, zig-zagging so swiftly that the tracers the German pilots sent down at him never had a chance to catch him. The Huns were having trouble pulling out. They had allowed the thrill of the chase to make them careless. The landing gear of one of the Fokkers clipped a tree, and that was all it took to make a wing dip far enough so that it struck, too. The plane went pinwheeling through the air, coming apart as it did so, before it finally slammed to the ground in a fiery explosion.

That left just one of the Fokkers, and Malloy was already looping up and around to go after it. Once he had disposed of that final fighter, he could go after the Gotha that the Fokkers had been protecting.

Malloy was flying night patrol as he often did, sleeping all day and then climbing into the sky when darkness fell to turn back any nocturnal mischief the Boche got up to. He was attached to the 87th Pursuit Squadron, but once he had demonstrated his knack for success flying alone, the Old Man let him fly when and where he wanted to. Malloy often limped back to the 'drome with his crate shot to pieces, and he had made more than a few landings with the engine completely conked out, hence the nickname "Dead-Stick". But he had walked away from every one of those landings, and he had enough kills under his belt that people were starting to talk about him in the same breath as that Hun, Richtofen. Malloy didn't really care about that. He just wanted to do his job, which was shooting down German planes.

Less than a half-hour after making his nightly venture over No Man's Land and into enemy skies, he had spotted the big Gotha bomber, flying high and heading west toward the front lines, escorted by the three Fokkers. Malloy was only one man; the Fokkers should have stayed in formation rather than coming after him, even after he had goaded them with a few bursts from his twin Vickers. But they had pursued instead, and now Malloy had done for two of them and was going after the third. Even if he failed to get the last Fokker, the Gotha was now unprotected, and more Spads and Camels would be waiting for it when it reached the lines, if it ever did.

Malloy intended to take care of it before then.

But first, he had that final D.VII to deal with. The German had managed to pull out of his breakneck dive, but he seemed to have lost sight of Malloy. The Fokker skimmed along above the treetops as Malloy looped back toward it. The set-up was perfect for a kill, almost too easy. Malloy sent the Spad angling down, and his hands reached for the Bowden trips, ready to fire.

Something slapped him in the face.

His head was protected by a leather flying helmet and thick goggles, but Malloy still felt like he had been punched. He was stunned for a second. He heard the propeller hit something, then again and again. The engine sputtered, fouled by whatever was smashing into it. The air around the Spad's cockpit was suddenly filled with the things. Malloy heard the fluttering of wings, even over the roar of the Hisso. Had he flown right into a flock of birds?

They were all around him, and he saw now to his instinctive horror that they weren't birds at all, but rather bats. In a burst of atavistic anger, he swept an arm at the ones closest to him, knocking them away. A horrible twittering and screeching filled his ears.

He flew out of the cloud of bats and realized at the last second that he was almost on top of the last Fokker. He slammed his hands on the trips and sent fire geysering from the muzzles of the Vickers. The lead chewed up the tail of the German plane, and then the line of tracers crawled up the fuselage until it reached the cockpit and ripped through the pilot. The Fokker nosed down and crashed into a field.

Breathing hard from excitement and horror, Malloy pulled up and flew level. He craned his neck as he looked around for the Gotha. He spotted the flare of an exhaust and climbed toward it. As he closed in, he saw that the exhaust flare indeed came from the Gotha, but the bomber had turned around and was winging its way back east, deeper into German-held territory. Malloy wondered if it had developed engine trouble or run into some other problem that had made the pilot turn back without completing his mission.

Well, it didn't really matter, he told himself. The Gotha was now alone, and Malloy intended to see that it never got back home.

He climbed steadily toward the bomber. Flame suddenly licked out from the Gotha's rear gun, which the second man in the two-man crew could reach by crawling back through a narrow tunnel in the plane's fuselage. Malloy darted right and then left to avoid the searching tracer. Unlike most of the forward-facing machine guns mounted on the planes of both sides in the great conflict, the rear gun on the Gotha was not fixed, but it still had a limited range of motion. Malloy made the gunner miss as he closed in.

The Vickers chattered as he fired, raking the bomber's belly. Malloy expected the plane's deadly cargo to explode as his bullets found it, but there was no blast. Maybe the Gotha *had* reached its destination and dropped its bombs, although Malloy didn't see how it could have had time to accomplish that. No matter; the Hun was going down either way. Malloy bored in until flames wreathed the Gotha's engine and it began to spiral out of control. A moment later, the big plane turned its nose down and plummeted toward the ground.

Malloy circled until he saw the Gotha slam into the earth with a burst of flames. Then he turned back toward Allied lines. Three Fokkers and a Gotha...not a bad night's work, even if he did say so himself.

CHAPTER 2
Winged Death

The tarmac wasn't lit up when Malloy reached the aerodrome, but there was enough moonlight for him to make a safe landing. The engine was still ticking over when he climbed out of the cockpit and dropped to the ground. He saw Propwash's lanky figure hurrying toward him.

"You all right, Dave?" the mechanic called to him.

Malloy pulled off his goggles and flying helmet, revealing a thick shock of sandy hair. "Why wouldn't I be?" he asked.

"The Old Man got word there was a big dogfight a few miles the other side of the lines, about where you were headed when you took off tonight."

"Yeah, I was there. Spotted a Gotha with three Fokkers escorting it, so I went after 'em."

Propwash swallowed, his Adam's apple bobbing up and down in his stringy neck. "You get 'em all?"

"Yep." There was no arrogance in the Texan's laconic answer. It was simple, matter-of-fact.

Propwash rested a knobby-knuckled hand on the canvas that covered the Spad's lower wing. "Any bulletholes in this old bus?"

"A few," replied Malloy. "You'll need to patch her up before I go out again. I don't think the engine was hit, though."

"I'll check it over anyway," said Propwash. "Better to be safe than sorry."

It was an old saying, but all too true, especially when it came to flying. Malloy grinned and said, "I leave it in your capable hands, Propwash."

"Better go report to the Old Man," said the lanky greaseball. "He'll be anxious to hear what happened."

Carrying his helmet and goggles, Malloy strolled across the tarmac toward the aerodrome's headquarters building. He glanced back at the mechanic as Propwash instructed some of the enlisted men to roll the Spad into a nearby hanger. Propwash was quite a character—skinny and grizzled, sometimes profane, often quite the mother hen despite his appearance—and in recent months he had become even more eccentric, refusing to set foot out of the hangers during daylight hours. Like Malloy, he saved his best efforts for the night, even though Malloy worried about the mechanic's growing pallor. They made a good team. Propwash kept the Spad flying, and Malloy kept the Boche going down in flames.

The Old Man looked up from the welter of papers on his desk as Malloy walked into the squadron's office. Despite what everyone called him, he wasn't really old. None of the men who soared into the beautiful, deadly skies were. The Old Man had busted a leg during a crack-up and the doctors said he couldn't fly anymore. He was stuck at a desk instead of in a cockpit, and he sent his brave young pilots out to die, rather than daring the Boche himself. That ate at him, Malloy knew, and the strain showed in the Old Man's lean face.

"Were you in the middle of that dogfight, Dave?" he asked.

Malloy propped a hip on a corner of the desk. "Yeah, I jumped a Gotha and its escort," he said. "Got the Fokkers to come after me, cleaned them up, and then downed the bomber."

"How many in the escort?"

"Three."

The Old Man let out a low whistle. "So four more kills overall. How many does that make for you?"

Malloy took out a cigarette, lipped it into his mouth, left it there unlit. "Twenty-four," he said.

And some of those had been two-man jobs, like the Gotha, so that meant he had sent over two dozen men to their deaths. That would eat on a fella, too, if he let it. Malloy tried not to think about it too much.

"Well, good job tonight," said the Old Man. He frowned up at Malloy. "Get creased by a slug?"

Malloy shook his head. "Don't know what you're talking about, Skipper."

The Old Man touched his cheek. "You've got a little scratch there, on your face."

Malloy reached up and felt the drying blood. "How about that? I didn't even notice it."

He hadn't mentioned the flock of bats he had run into. He didn't say anything about them now, but he wondered if the one that had hit him in the face had clawed him. That made more sense than blaming the nick on a bullet. As far as he knew, none of the German tracer fire had come that close to the cockpit.

"Have the medical officer take a look at it," suggested the Old Man, but Malloy shook his head.

"No, it's not worth worrying the m.o. with it. I've cut myself shaving worse than this. I'll just stick some plaster on it when I get back to my digs."

"Have a report on that engagement on my desk in the morning."

"Sure thing, Skipper." Malloy walked out of HQ and headed for the hut where he bunked.

When he got there he looked in the mirror over the basin and saw that he'd been right. He *had* cut himself worse shaving. The nick was a small one, less than half an inch long, and not deep. Nothing to worry about.

Still, the thought that it might have come from one of that bat's claws...

That was enough to make a little shudder go through a man.

The Boche kept Malloy hopping for the next ten days. Ten nights, rather, because he kept to his usual pattern of going on patrol only when the sun had set. The Germans were making a heavy push in the air, and Malloy sensed desperation in their increased flights. Since the Americans had entered the war, the tide had begun to turn, and Malloy was convinced it was only a matter of time until the Huns sued for peace. They had to know by now that they couldn't defeat the Allies, at least not by conventional means.

He had just landed from a patrol in which he had shot down an Albatross, when he saw a knot of men struggling near one of the hangers. As he dropped to the ground he heard the angry shouts that came from them. It was unusual but not unheard of for the pilots to fight amongst themselves, and the mechanics were a fractious lot, too. However, having been involved in a life-and-death struggle only a short time earlier, Malloy couldn't muster up much interest in a brawl. He would have bypassed it and gone on to his quarters if one of the men hadn't suddenly broken away from the others and raced toward him.

"Stop him!" shouted one of the men. "Stop him! There's something wrong with him!"

Malloy stiffened. Maybe they meant the guy was a spy. Something unusual was up, that was for sure, so Malloy moved quickly to intercept the running man.

In the light from the hangers he recognized the man as Ken Langley, one of the squadron's pilots. Malloy knew Langley, had flown and fought beside him, and knew that he wasn't a Boche spy. Langley's face was twisted into contortions of rage so extreme that he barely resembled himself. What in blazes could have made him so upset?

"Ken!" Malloy called sharply. "Langley, hold it!" He lifted a hand as if to stop the other flyer.

Langley snarled like an animal and swung a vicious punch at Malloy's head. Malloy's instincts took over and caused him to duck. Langley was a friend, but Malloy had never been the sort to let an attack go by. He struck back without thinking, slamming a fist into Langley's midsection.

Langley didn't even seem to feel the punch. He lunged into Malloy, clawing at him, and again Malloy was struck by the animalistic manner in which Langley was acting.

He grabbed Langley's arm, twisted, and threw a hip into the other man, pivoting in a wrestling move. Langley's feet left the ground and he flew through the air to land with a heavy crash. Before he could get up, the other men arrived on the scene, and one of them yelled, "Grab his arms and legs! Hold him down!"

They threw themselves on Langley, pinning him to the ground. Langley writhed frantically but could not free himself. His head jerked from side to side and spittle flew as he howled incoherent curses.

"Somebody get a doctor!"

"Hold him! Don't let him get away!"

Malloy stepped back, a little shaky from the ferociousness of Langley's attack. He and the other pilot weren't close, but Malloy considered him a friend and comrade in arms. He couldn't understand what would make Langley act so crazy.

The Old Man came running up, his attention attracted by the commotion, and the squadron's medical officer was with him. The m.o. took one look at Langley and gasped. "My God, be careful!" he warned the other men. "Don't let him bite you!"

"Doc, what's wrong with him?" asked one of the pilots as he struggled with the crazed Langley.

The m.o. was already preparing a hypodermic needle from his kit. "Hold him down," he said without answering the question. "Let me give him this sedative…"

He moved in and jabbed the needle through the sleeve of Langley's shirt, then shoved home the plunger. For a long moment, Langley continued to howl and struggle, as if he were in the grip of something even stronger than the drugs now coursing through his veins. Then, with a long, harsh sigh, he relaxed. His eyes fluttered and then closed.

"Pick him up and take him to the infirmary," ordered the m.o. He added, "Are any of you hurt? Did he...bite any of you?"

To Malloy's ears, it sounded like stark terror creeping into the medical officer's voice.

The pilots all said they were all right. Several of them hefted Langley's limp form and carried him toward the infirmary. The others trailed behind, including Malloy, the Old Man, and the doctor.

"Do you think it's the same as the others we've heard about?" asked the Old Man, directing the question at the m.o.

The answer was slow in coming, but when it did, it was couched in grim tones. "He has all the symptoms...the rage, the paranoia, the swollen throat and inability to swallow. I'll have to make a test, of course, to be sure, and even then I don't know if I have the facilities here to make absolutely certain."

"But if it is, you...you can do something for him, can't you?"

Malloy had never heard the Old Man sound quite so tentative, so shaken, not even in the darkest days of their fight against the Boche.

"No," said the medical officer. "Once a patient has exhibited the symptoms so strongly, there's nothing that can be done except to keep him sedated and under control until...the end."

"My God," said Malloy raggedly. "What are you talking about?"

The Old Man paused and turned to face the brawny Texan. "Rabies," he said. "The brass have tried to keep it quiet, so as not to cause a panic, but there's been a widespread outbreak of the disease along the front during the past twenty-four hours. They're not sure what's causing it, but their best guess is that it's being spread by bats."

Malloy's hand went to his face, to the little scratch, no worse than a shaving cut, that had been red and swollen and sore ever since he had gotten it.

CHAPTER 3
Horror From the Sky

Malloy didn't say anything, but a tiny voice in the back of his brain began to gibber in terror. He knew enough about rabies to know that the disease was spread by a bite from a rabid animal. If the scratch on his face had been made by one of the bat's fangs, rather than a claw, he could be infected without even knowing it. And from what the m.o. had said, he was already too far gone to be helped. The symptoms, the same hideous symptoms that Langley had exhibited, would probably begin to show up shortly, perhaps in the next few hours.

The Old Man and the medical officer were still talking quietly as they returned to headquarters with Malloy trailing them. Malloy took a deep breath and stepped forward to come alongside the two officers. He might be infected, but he wasn't sick right now. He could still do his job.

"Where did the bats come from?" he asked, breaking into the conversation.

The Old Man stopped and turned to look at him. "What do you mean? It's not unusual to find bats almost anywhere. They live in caves and under overhangs."

"No, I think I know what Lieutenant Malloy means," said the medical officer. "Just as there have been an unusual number of rabies cases reported, there has also been an increase in the sightings of bats, which makes us believe there's a connection."

"Wouldn't our men have reported being bitten by bats?" asked the Old Man.

"Some did, according to what I've heard. Others probably just shrugged it off as a minor wound, slapped some antiseptic on it themselves, and went on." The medical officer shook his head. "Probably many of them weren't even aware that bats can carry the disease, or if they are, they just didn't think about it."

The Old Man frowned at Malloy. "Why do you ask where the bats came from, Lieutenant?"

Malloy took a deep breath, knowing that he should have reported the incident as soon as it occurred, but knowing as well that now he had to plunge ahead. "Because a week and a half ago, when I shot down that Gotha and its Fokker escorts, I flew through a large cloud of bats not far from our lines."

The m.o. reached out and grasped Malloy's arm. "How many would you estimate?"

"Hundreds, at least," replied Malloy with a shrug. "Maybe thousands. I wonder if they came from that Gotha. It had already turned back east when I attacked it. I though it had abandoned its mission for some reason. But maybe instead of dropping bombs it released all those bats."

"That's insane!" said the Old Man. "You think the Boche were bombing us with rabid bats?"

"There's a chance Malloy may be right," said the medical officer. "The Huns could have rigged crates under the Gotha's wings, where they normally carry bombs, and the pilot could have opened them by some sort of wire arrangement when he reached a predetermined location. Bats are small creatures. You could put hundreds of them in a few crates."

The Old Man still looked skeptical. He said, "If the bats were released into the air, how could the Germans know they would fly over our lines and attack our men? What would stop them from simply turning around and flying back over the German lines?"

The m.o. rubbed his jaw and frowned in thought. "Despite the old saying, bats really aren't blind, you know," he said after a moment. "However, they don't see well, and most species navigate by sound...high frequency echoes. I wonder if it would be possible to rig up some sort of...echo machine, I suppose you could call it...that would attract them."

Malloy said, "That would mean the Boche would have to have an agent over here to operate the machine and lure the bats across our lines."

"The Huns have agents scattered through our ranks, just as we do in theirs," said the Old Man. He balled his right hand into a fist and smacked it into his left hand. "By God, you may be right! I still think it's a little crazy, but the Germans may be getting desperate enough to try almost anything."

"If the bats are rabid, they'll be more aggressive than usual," pointed out the m.o. "More likely to attack humans. There's a myth about so-called vampire bats sucking people's blood, but a rabid animal might certainly act like a penny dreadful vampire and come after a human being."

The Old Man nodded. "I'll get on the horn with Colonel Tremaine at Air Intelligence and see if he can get an agent on this. This was a probably a test run of sorts. Since it's been successful, the Boche may try to release more of the bats. Thousands of them, perhaps even millions..."

A shudder ran through the Old Man as his voice trailed off. Even his iron nerves were shaken by the prospect of millions of rabid bats swarming over the Allied lines. Such an attack would destroy morale and possibly weaken Allied forces to the point that a massive, last-ditch German push might be able to sweep them all the way to the sea.

Malloy knew all that, knew that the outcome of the war might be riding on what happened next. But at the same time, it was impossible for him not to dwell on his own situation. He might have less than twenty-four hours before he was a raving lunatic, frothing at the mouth like poor Ken Langley. He had to use the time remaining to him, had to somehow strike back at the filthy beasts who had done this to him.

"I'm going out on patrol again," he said.

The Old Man looked sharply at him. "But you just got back, Malloy."

"Yes, sir, but there's been enough time now for the rabies to start taking effect in our men. German agents could have already reported that the first attempt to infect us was successful. There could be Gothas loaded with bats on the way toward our lines right now."

Grim-faced, the squadron's commander nodded. "You're right. I need to get some crates up right away to patrol our lines."

"I'm ready to go now," Malloy said. He snapped a quick salute at the Old Man. "With your permission, sir…?"

"Go on, Lieutenant. I'll have more men in the air as quick as I can."

Without waiting for anything else, Malloy turned and ran toward the hanger where his Spad had been taken. Propwash would be in there now, going over the plane, making sure it was flight worthy for the next patrol.

He raced into the canvas-sided hanger a few moments later. He didn't see any of the greaseballs, which didn't surprise him. Propwash considered Malloy's Spad his own private property and often sent the other mechanics away while he worked on it. But as Malloy rounded the tail of the plane, he stopped short and stared at the figure huddled on the ground. He recognized Propwash's lanky form, but it was immediately obvious that something was wrong with him. Malloy's eyes widened with horror.

Rabies. His friend and mechanic had come down with rabies, thought Malloy.

"Propwash…?" he said tentatively.

Suddenly, the grizzled greaseball surged up from the ground and whirled toward Malloy. A hideous grimace contorted the weathered face. Propwash's lips drew back from his teeth.

His unnaturally long, fearfully pointed teeth.

With a snarl, Propwash launched himself at Malloy.

CHAPTER 4
Unholy Summons

Malloy's instincts and swift reflexes saved him, as they had countless times during dogfights. He twisted aside so that the bite Propwash aimed at his neck missed, the horrible teeth snapping together instead. Malloy slammed a punch to the mechanic's skinny chest and knocked him sprawling. Propwash rolled over on the ground next to the Spad, grunting and growling like a beast.

Something was even more terribly wrong here, thought Malloy wildly. Propwash exhibited some of the symptoms of rabies, but that disease, as dreadful as it was, didn't cause a man's teeth to grow longer and more pointed than normal. Something else, something far worse, was wrong with Propwash.

Rolling over, Propwash came to his feet and lunged at Malloy again. His eyes seemed to glow with a red, hellish gleam. Malloy grappled with him. The Texan was taller and outweighed his friend by a considerable amount, but he found himself forced backward and then thrown to the ground by Propwash's unnatural strength. Langley had seemed stronger than usual, too, but not to this extent.

Propwash leaped at Malloy, who had to roll desperately to the side to avoid him. Malloy came up on his knees and swung a punch that landed solidly on Propwash's jaw. The blow sent the mechanic sprawling again. Malloy caught up a wrench lying nearby, and for a second he was poised to bring it down in a blow that would crush Propwash's skull. He stopped, though, struggling to control his own frenzy.

"Propwash, you've gotta cut it out," he said breathlessly, hoping that his voice would get through to his old friend. "It's me, Dave. You don't want to fight me."

For a second, there was nothing human in the red eyes that glared up at Malloy. Then, abruptly, comprehension dawned in them, and a horrible shudder wracked Propwash's body. "Dave?" he croaked. "Davy boy, I'm sorry."

Malloy stood up, but he kept the wrench gripped tightly in his hand, just in case. He stepped back while Propwash climbed shakily to his feet. "Wh-what happened?" asked the mechanic.

"You attacked me," said Malloy bluntly. "It looked for all the world like you were trying to bite me in the neck. What happened to your teeth, Propwash?"

Propwash lifted a hand to his mouth, felt the inhuman canine teeth, and let out a groan that seemed to come from the very depths of his soul. "I'm sorry, Dave," he whispered. "I'm so sorry. I never meant to hurt you. I never meant for you to know…"

"Know what?" asked Malloy grimly, though a part of him feared that he already knew the answer, unbelievable though it might be.

"You remember when I had that leave in Paris a while back?"

Malloy nodded. "Yes, and I noticed that you acted a little odd when you got back to the 'drome. That was when you started sleeping all day and working at night."

Propwash swallowed hard. "Yeah, I had to. I couldn't stand the sun anymore. You see, Dave…when I was in Paris, I met a gal…a really pretty gal, who dressed and acted like she was rich…I didn't know what she'd want with a fella like me, with grease under my fingernails and not even close to what you'd call handsome…but she asked me to come back to her place with her, and I sure didn't say no. But then…then…" He covered his face with his hands and couldn't go on.

Malloy had to know. "What happened, Propwash?"

"She *bit* me!" spat Propwash. "She was some kind o'…monster! A creature of the undead, she called herself."

"A vampire," whispered Malloy, barely restraining his own horror.

"And when she bit me, she made me one, too!" said Propwash, his voice anguished. "You know me, Dave. I've always been a good guy, a hard worker. I never set out to be a monster!"

Malloy was torn. He wanted to step forward and pat Propwash's shoulder and try to comfort the mechanic, but at the same time his humanity made him pull back and clutch the wrench even more tightly.

"What have you done?" he asked. "How have you lived? You haven't…bitten people…?"

"God, no!" exclaimed Propwash, sounding just as horrified as Malloy felt. "When the cravings came on me, I slipped out and found a pig or a cow…one time even a horse…and I never took enough to kill even them, just enough to keep me from goin' mad. I never went after a person…until tonight!" He pressed his fists against his temples. "And I wouldn't have done that, if not for that infernal noise! All the screechin' and echoin', makin' me crazy—"

"Screeching and echoing?" Malloy cut in.

"Yeah. I don't hear it now, but it started a little while ago. I couldn't stand it. It…did something to me. Made me want to follow it…"

Malloy's pulse pounded heavily in his head as Propwash's words suggested a possibility to him. Like the Old Man had said earlier in the night, it was crazy, but sometimes, crazy was all that was left.

"Propwash, listen to me," he said. "Did you ever hear that noise before?"

The greaseball scratched at his jaw. "Yeah, a while back, maybe a week and a half ago. It didn't last very long, though. It bothered me for a while, but I got over it. Wasn't as bad as tonight."

"Have you been bitten by a bat since then?"

Propwash stared at him. "A bat? No, I ain't even seen any bats, let alone been bitten by one."

Was there some connection between rabies and the unholy affliction with which Propwash found himself cursed? Or between bats and…whatever Propwash had become? The medical officer had mentioned a myth about vampire bats, recalled Malloy.

Maybe it wasn't completely a myth. Maybe, like most legends, there was a kernel of truth at its core.

Before Malloy could say anything else, Propwash suddenly clapped his hands to his ears and let out a pained cry. "Oh, Lord!" wailed the mechanic. "There it is again!"

Malloy took a chance and grabbed Propwash's shoulders. He had to get through to his friend's fevered brain. "Propwash! Listen to me! Can you follow the sound?"

Propwash blinked bleary eyes and stared at Malloy. "What?"

"Can you follow the echoes?" Malloy asked again. "You have to take me to where they're coming from!"

"I...I dunno. That sound makes me crazy..."

Propwash's eyes began to get that red glow to them again. If this kept up, he was going to lose control once more. Then Malloy would have to defend himself and might even be forced to kill his loyal mechanic in order to save his own life.

The worst thing was that if Propwash died, the Allies' chance of stopping the Huns' evil plan might die with him.

Malloy's gaze suddenly fell on a spare flying helmet lying on a bench next to the canvas wall of the hanger. He sprang to the bench, snatched up the helmet, and turned back to Propwash, who was growing steadily more agitated. "Put this on!" Malloy urged, and without waiting for Propwash to comply, he started pulling the leather headgear over Propwash's head.

The greaseball tried to struggle, but he wasn't at the point yet where his strength could overwhelm the brawny Texan. Malloy pulled the helmet tight over Propwash's ears and fastened the strap under the mechanic's chin, making it as taut as possible. Propwash shuddered, but slowly his frantic breathing eased. The helmets were designed to muffle some of the racket from the airplanes' engines, so Malloy hoped it would shut out some of the devilish sounds now plaguing his friend. Evidently it worked.

"That's better," said Propwash in a shaky voice. "I can still hear it, but it's not near as loud."

"You can control yourself now," said Malloy. "You can lead me to where the sound is coming from without it driving you mad."

Propwash nodded. "I'll try," he said. "But why do you want to go there, Dave?"

"It's a long story," said Malloy grimly. "But you can rest assured that you'll be helping the Allies if you and I can find the source of that infernal noise."

"Do you hear it?" asked Propwash as they hurried out of the hanger.

"No, it's probably too high-pitched for human ears," replied Malloy without thinking of the implications of his words.

They didn't escape Propwash, though. He laughed hollowly and said, "Human...that's something I'll never be again."

"Don't say that," Malloy told him. "We'll figure out something. For now, just concentrate on figuring out where that sound is coming from."

They hurried along the tarmac and then Propwash cut through the woods that bordered the aerodrome. There was a small French village beyond the trees, Malloy knew, and a few minutes later they emerged from the shadows and saw the lights from the neat little cottages. Propwash stumbled a little and pressed his palms to his ears.

"It's gettin' louder," he said.

"That's a good sign," Malloy assured him. "Come on. Which way now?"

Propwash hesitated, then pointed to one of the cottages. "Over there."

Malloy reached down to his hip and drew his automatic from the holster there. He followed Propwash as the mechanic made his unsteady way toward the French dwelling. Malloy's nerves were tingling now, as if he could almost sense the high-pitched echoes that were emanating from somewhere nearby.

Propwash stopped abruptly and pointed to the sky. "Oh, my God!" he gasped. "Look up there, Dave!"

Malloy raised his eyes to the heavens and saw that they were darkened with more than the night. The stars and the moon were being blotted out by a myriad of dark, fluttering shapes.

Bats! More bats than he had ever seen before, maybe more than anybody had ever seen before in one place! And they were being called down on the Allied 'drome to spread their unholy contagion to everyone there!

CHAPTER 5
Hell's Fire

Malloy didn't waste any time. His boot crashed against the front door of the cottage, shattering the lock and ripping the door free from the jamb. He went through the opening in a rush, his eyes darting around the room. He spotted the man who had been crouched in front of a large, radio-like apparatus on a table. The man whirled toward Malloy, a snarl of hatred on his face, a gun in his hand.

Malloy fired first, the automatic roaring in the close confines of the room. The slug smashed through the shoulder of the German secret agent and sent him slumping to the floor. His gun fell from suddenly nerveless fingers and slid away from him. Malloy's automatic hammered out three more shots, but these were directed at the machine on the table. Sparks crackled and hissed wildly as the slugs tore through the apparatus.

The man on the floor howled, "No! You've ruined everything, you *verdammt* American!"

Malloy dropped to a knee beside the man and pressed the barrel of the gun under his chin. It was all Malloy could do not to pull the trigger and send a bolt of leaden death through the evil, treacherous brain. He recalled seeing this man around the 'drome. He had pretended to be a French farmer, had even from time to time sold apples to the pilots. And all the while he had been working for the Boche.

Vengeance had to take a back seat at the moment. Malloy leaned close to the man and said in low, menacing tones, "Tell me where the bats are coming from."

"*Nein!* I will not betray—"

"Dave?" Propwash stumbled into the room, tugging off the flying helmet as he did so. "Dave, that racket's gone. And so are the bats. I was watchin' 'em, and all of a sudden they just turned around and flew off back toward the east."

A groan of despair came from the wounded man. Malloy grinned tightly and said, "Yeah, your little pets are headed back where they came from, now that I busted up the gizmo that was calling them over here. You and your buddies have unleashed hell on your own troops tonight."

"It...it was not supposed to be this way," the German agent said through teeth clenched against the pain of his wounded shoulder.

"It never is when it backfires on the skunks who come up with plans like that," snapped Malloy. "Now tell me where they're gathering all these bats and infecting them with rabies, so we can wipe the place off the face of the earth!"

"*Nein,*" the Hun said stubbornly. "I will never betray my comrades!"

Malloy glanced over his shoulder at Propwash, who stood there looking confused and upset—and something else, too.

Propwash was starting to look hungry.

"Got the cravings, Prop?" asked Malloy.

Propwash's bony fingers pulled at his chin. "Yeah," he answered in a weak voice.

"Well, you can do something about it." Keeping the automatic trained on the German agent, Malloy stood up and moved aside. "See all that blood on this guy's shoulder?"

Propwash moaned. "Oh, Dave, don't...don't let me..."

"There's a lot more where that came from," Malloy said. "Rivers of it pumping through his veins, just waiting for you."

Propwash opened his mouth wider, revealing the inhuman, needle-sharp teeth. He made a hissing noise.

The wounded man's eyes grew wide with disbelief and then terror as Propwash took a step toward him. "*Lieber Gott!*" he screamed. "What...what is he? What sort of unholy creature—"

"You're about to find out, pal," said Malloy as Propwash continued to shuffle forward. "I'm going to step outside and leave my buddy here with you."

"No!"

"Then you'd better tell me what I want to know, and be quick about it."

"A castle, an old castle!" babbled the agent. "Across the lines near Montigny! You can't miss it! That's where the bats are kept, where they're infected—"

"That's the only place?" asked Malloy.

"Yes, the only one. The plan is still in the developmental stages. Tonight was our second test…if it proved as successful as the first, our goal was to blanket the Allied lines with rabid bats from one end to the other." The agent looked frantically at Malloy as Propwash loomed over him and started to lean down. "Please! I have told you what you want! Don't let him…please don't—"

A part of Malloy wanted to step outside and let Propwash have the wounded man, to do…whatever he wanted with him. But Malloy had found out what he wanted to know, and he was, after all, still human.

"Propwash," he said. "Don't do it."

The mechanic turned red, hollow eyes toward Malloy. The creature that now lived inside him had almost total control. But only almost. A semblance of human intelligence still lurked in Propwash's gaze.

"Dave," he croaked, "you don't understand how bad it is, how much I want to…have to…do this."

"I do understand," said Malloy. "I understand that you're Propwash Jones, my old friend and the best airplane mechanic who ever picked up a wrench and a rag. You can get over this, Propwash. You can be the boss of this thing, instead of letting it be the boss of you."

"I…I can't," agonized Propwash. "I ain't strong enough!"

"Yes, you are. I know it. I have faith in you."

Propwash stood there for a long moment, shuddering from the depth of the struggle that possessed him. But then, finally, he swallowed and nodded and turned away from the wounded man. "I got to get out of here," he muttered. "I can *smell* that blood…"

"Go ahead," said Malloy. "I'll see you outside."

He stepped past Propwash and bent over the wounded Hun. The automatic in Malloy's hand rose and fell, landing with a *thunk!* against the man's skull, cutting off his cry of protest. Malloy found some rope in a drawer underneath the table where the shattered echo machine sat and bound the man tightly, hand and foot. He wouldn't be going anywhere until Allied intelligence agents came for him. He might bleed to death from his wound, but Malloy doubted that. Anyway, the Texan was willing to take that chance.

He hurried out and found Propwash standing in front of the cabin. The mechanic was still shaken but back under control. "Now what do we do?" he asked.

"Go get my Spad ready to fly," said Malloy as he clapped a hand on Propwash's shoulder. "I'm going to lead the escort for the bombers that are going to wipe out that hellhole of pestilence over by Montigny."

"You…you still trust me?" asked Propwash in amazement.

"Of course I do," said Malloy with a grin. "Like I told you, you're still Propwash Jones, my best friend." He slapped the greaseball on the back. "Now go get that crate ready! We've got some bats and some Boche to blow to Hades!"

The Old Man had plenty of questions, of course, but he postponed them when Malloy said that he knew where the headquarters of the German rabies plot was located. Now that Malloy had destroyed the echo machine that had been calling the bats to the Allied lines, there was time to put together a flight of Handley Page bombers. Malloy led the large escort of Spads, Nieuports, and Camels, and in the dead of night, a torrent of bombs rained down on the old castle near Montigny. Malloy and his fellow pilots in the other fighters were kept busy dealing with the Fokkers that swarmed up from a nearby German 'drome in an attempt to protect the castle. For a short time, the sky was filled with fiery lines of tracer, billowing clouds of smoke from the exploding bombs, and towering columns of flame that climbed high into the sky from the ruined castle. Malloy was never sure how many Fokkers he knocked down during the fight and didn't care. All that mattered was that the Germans' hideous plan was smashed.

It was nearing dawn when the trucks of his Spad touched down on the tarmac at St.-Mihiel. He rolled to a stop and climbed out of the cockpit as Propwash, the Old Man, and the squadron's medical officer hurried out to meet him. Along the runway, the other planes in the flight began landing.

Malloy tugged off his helmet and goggles and grinned at the three men. "We flattened the place," he said. "It's over."

In more ways than one, he thought. Surely the deadly rabies germs swimming in his veins would soon destroy him, too. But he was willing to die, knowing that he had helped save the Allies from such a horror and perhaps even from an ultimate defeat.

The Old Man clasped his arm. "Good work!"

"What about that German agent?"

"Our intelligence boys have him in custody." The Old Man laughed. "He keeps telling some bizarre story about how Propwash here is a vampire!"

Malloy glanced at the mechanic. Propwash was pale in the lights that lined the tarmac, but he was in control of himself, and Malloy had no doubt that he would continue to be.

"Yeah," said Malloy with a grin. "That's plenty bizarre, all right. Nobody but some crazy Hun would ever believe that."

The m.o. suddenly frowned and said, "I never noticed that cut on your face, Malloy. When did you get that?"

Well, there was no getting around it now, thought Malloy. He said, "A week and a half ago...the night I first ran into those bats. One of them gave it to me when I hit him."

The Old Man drew a sharp breath. "You mean—"

"It's all right, sir," began Malloy. "I don't mind. I'm just glad I was able to help stop that Boche plan before it won the war for them."

The m.o. laughed. "You can stop being so noble, Lieutenant. You're not infected."

Malloy stared at him. "How can you know that, sir?"

"This is a very fast-acting strain of the disease. I wouldn't be surprised if the Boche scientists over in that castle tried to make it even more virulent than normal. You were the first one to encounter the bats, so if you were infected, you should have been the first one to develop symptoms. You don't have any, do you?"

"Well...not really," answered Malloy truthfully.

"We'll put you in the infirmary and keep an eye on you just to make sure, but I think you're safe," said the medical officer. "I'll put a little antiseptic on that cut, too, and see if it doesn't clear right up."

"Thank you, sir." Malloy felt relieved. He knew he wasn't completely out of danger, but at least now he knew he stood a good chance of living to fly again. He looked at the eastern sky and saw it growing light with the approach of dawn. "It's been a long night," he said with a meaningful glance at Propwash. "I think I'd like to turn in, get a little rest."

"And well-deserved, too," said the Old Man. "Congratulations, Malloy."

Malloy nodded his thanks and headed for the hanger. Propwash walked alongside him. When they were out of earshot of the officers, the mechanic said, "You ain't goin' to tell them the truth about me, Dave?"

"You heard how the Old Man was about what that German spy said. Nobody would believe me, either. They'd just think I was off my nut."

Propwash rubbed his grizzled jaw. "Yeah, I reckon you're right. But what am I gonna do?"

"Keep on being the best mechanic on the line," Malloy told him as they went into the hanger, before the sunlight of a new day could spread across the tarmac. "We've still got a war to win!"

My first pulp was a 1935 *Weird Tales* that I bought for four bucks from an old magazine store when I was in college. I'd been reading tons of pulp horror and SF in sixties paperback reprints, but once I had an actual old pulp in my hands, with its garish cover, its sense of age, and that *smell*, I was a junkie for life.

I collected ravenously from then on. My greatest coup was back in 1977 when I privately purchased from an estate a literal room full of pulp magazines that filled a flatbed truck. I kept them all (an incident chronicled in my story, "The Bookman," in Gary Raisor's *Obsessions*, and now in my own story collection, *Figures in Rain*, plug plug…).

I've read fewer pulps in recent years, however. As I get older, I'm reading the things I *should* have been reading when I was gobbling up dreck from *Terror Tales*. I've even started getting rid of pulps that I know I'll never read, something that would have been anathema to me several years ago. But will I ever want to peruse that *Front Page Stories* novel by C. S. Montayne? I don't think so…

I continue to love the pulps, and still get a tingle when I open a 1916 Burroughs *All-Story*. Also, some fine friendships resulted from my tracking down old pulp writers to talk to about those grand old days. I met the late Amelia Reynolds Long and my recently deceased pal, Lloyd Arthur Eshbach, in this way.

When Joe asked me to do a story for this anthology, I thought it might be fun to do a "back-of-the-book" story that used excerpts from the supplemental features of certain pulps. I recalled H. P. Lovecraft's idea of "the inability of the human mind to correlate all its contents," and decided to correlate the contents of disparate pieces from very different pulps over a 35-year period, bringing to light a story that would not otherwise be told.

All the departments and features I use are real ones, with the exception of the letter column in *Terror Tales*. (The weird menace pulps weren't real big on idea exchange—read, drool, and move on…) Even the taxidermy book is real. I love doing this kind of research, since it keeps me from actual *writing*. I hope you enjoy it, and that it gives a flavor of those great, long-gone days of cheap, tawdry, and utterly glorious fiction.

—Chet Williamson

From the Back Pages

Chet Williamson

From "Headquarters Chat," *Detective Story Magazine,* **July 15, 1919:**

"DEAR EDITOR: I am 13 years old, and I read every page of every story of your wonderful magazine. The stories have inspired me to want to be a detective myself when I am grown up. I like murder stories best, but what I don't like is when the villains get away and there are more stories about them later. I don't think it's good to show them getting away. They should be caught and then escape at the beginning of the next story.

"I want to get a tattoo of an open eye, like the Pinkerton Detective Agency has saying they never sleep, and like is on the dollar bill, but my parents say that I have to be on my own before I get one. Thank you for such terrific stories.

"Jim Shepard,
"134 N. Lincoln Street
"Omaha, Nebraska."

We can always use more detectives, Jim, so good luck to you! With you on the job, maybe those villains who get away at the end of every story will be captured. But your parents are right about that tattoo, and you may change your mind when you are older.

From "Ask Adventure," *Adventure,* **February 10, 1925:**

Good Book on Taxidermy

Always a handy thing to have around:

Question:—"I would like to know the title of a good book on taxidermy, with particular attention to tanning and preserving skins."

—B. D. WHITWORTH, Chicago, Ill.

Answer, by Mr. Belford:—A fine overall book on taxidermy, with a thorough chapter on tanning all types of animal skins and hides, is C. K. and C. A. Reed's *Guide to Taxidermy*, available at bookstores or directly from Mr. Chas. K. Reed, Worcester, Mass.

◆◆◆

From "The Camp-Fire," *Adventure*, September, 1934:

"The Camp-Fire" is usually filled with stories about our adventurer-writers, as it has been since its inception, but every now and again, we get some communications from some long-term readers who are pretty adventurous themselves. Such a reader is B. D. Whitworth, who we hear from every year or so. Mr. Whitworth is a hunter-adventurer who roams these great forty-eight states bagging big game, such as elk, mountain goat, and deer. He wrote us first in 1925 when he bagged his first trophy animal in the state of Washington, and later in 1926 (North Dakota), 1928 (Montana), 1929 (Wyoming), and 1931 (Idaho). Just this year he reports bringing down another prize in Colorado. Mr. Whitworth tells us that he never returns to any previous hunting sites, because of the many new and exciting vistas the country presents. The fortunate Mr. Whitworth is a traveling man whose business takes him all over, so that wherever he hangs his hat is home. He also reports that he has started to write fiction, and we hope that when he has something to offer, he will send it to *Adventure* for our consideration...

◆◆◆

From "The Madman Who Collected Women" by D. B. Worth, *Terror Tales*, January 1935:

..."Joan!" Dan cried, straining against his bonds, and just starting to feel them give way under his tight muscles.

"Yes, Mr. Beecher," cackled Dr. Schwarzenwald as he tossed the sheet aside. Next to him, the naked girl, her nubile body spread-eagled on the operating table, writhed in terror. The wires that held her cut into her pale flesh, and trickles of blood ran down her shapely arms.

"Don't worry, dear!" Dan called to his fiancée. "We'll get out of this!"

"*Nein, schweinhund!*" Dr. Schwarzenwald said, and the gibbering dwarf at his side capered up and down, his beady, piggish eyes drinking in the sight of the unclad beauty just an arm's reach away. "For once that Gunther and I have done our work with our instruments of art..." He held up what looked to Dan's horrified gaze like a scalpel. "...your lovely

Joan Simpson will be added to my collection, and what remains of her—and *you*—will be dissolved in the acid pit!"

Dr. Schwarzenwald flung back a trap door on the floor. Though Dan couldn't see into it, he could see the noxious green fumes rising from it, and knew that it would devour his body in seconds.

"And *then*," the crazed Prussian continued, "the *wunderschon* Miss Simpson will be with me forever, as are these other beauties! *Gunther!*"

The barked command sent the hideous dwarf scampering to a long curtain at the end of the room. He whipped it open, and behind it Dan saw a sight that set Joan screaming in horror and made his own heart pound like a piston in his manly chest.

A dozen glass cases held the skins of as many young women. They were each draped over a wire framework, roughly human-shaped. It was as though the women had been flayed in one piece, their flesh then preserved and put on display. Long hair hung from the tops of the heads, and Dan could see fingernails still attached to the dangling strips of skin that were the unfortunate victims' fingers.

"You, *Fraulein* Simpson, will now join my parade of beauties!" the madman crowed in dark triumph. "But for the best result, the procedure must be done while you still live! Gunther!"

Dr. Schwarzenwald bent with his scalpel over the girl's heaving chest, and the dwarf bounded to his side, placing his hands over Joan's lily-white breasts, as though to stretch the skin taut over her heart for the doctor's blade.

The perverse sight was all that Dan needed. In a frenzy of rage he burst apart the frayed leather strap that held his wrists, and in another second he had freed his legs as well. He raised his eyes to see the dwarf Gunther bolting toward him on his bandy legs, a huge knife raised over his head.

Dan quickly sidestepped and tripped the dwarf so that he fell headlong onto the stone floor, dropping his knife. Then Dan picked up the little man and threw the squirming bundle of muscle and bone directly at his master, Dr. Schwarzenwald.

The dwarf struck the madman in the chest, knocking him backward so that his feet went over the edge of the acid pit. In another second both the repugnant servant and his maniac master had fallen into the pit. Their screams lasted only seconds, but they were the second most welcome sounds Dan Beecher had ever heard.

The most welcome was heard a few seconds later, after he had freed Joan from the wires that had held her, wrapped her gleaming nudity in a sheet, and was holding her trembling body against his own. "Oh, Dan," she breathed, "I'm so glad it's all over. I...I love you, my darling..."

They were words that he knew he would hear again and again, every day of his life, now that their horrible nightmare was finally over.

From "The Friendliest Corner," *Street & Smith Love Story*, April 20, 1935:
Perhaps someone can help this gentleman.

DEAR MISS MORRIS: I know that your department usually helps people find friends and pen pals they don't normally know, but in this case I hope you will make an exception. I am looking for an eighteen-year-old young lady named Ruth Lundy of Sterling, Colorado. She has been missing for nearly eight months, and her parents are naturally very worried about her. If any of your readers are familiar with Miss Lundy, would they be kind enough to write to me at the Pierce Detective Agency, Denver, Colorado. Thank you.

J. W. SHEPARD

From *Best Detective Magazine*, July 1935:
CRIME SPOTS MAPPED

A series of murders of young women have taken place in the north-western part of the country over the past ten years, forming a triangle between Washington, North Dakota, and Colorado, where the body of Miss Ruth Lundy was recently discovered in a shallow grave a hundred miles northeast of Denver. The five bodies that have been found to the present time were all mutilated in the same way, leading police to believe the same person was responsible for all five killings. Police believe they will find the killer soon.

From "The Reader Writes," *Terror Tales*, August 1935:
Reader Wants More "Worth-y" Stories
"I think that D. B. Worth's 'The Madman Who Collected Women' in your January issue was one of the best stories you've ever published, right up there with corkers by Hugh B. Cave and Arthur J. Burks. But I've been waiting for months for another Worth yarn, and there's nary a one to be seen. Whatever happened to this great author?"

A Reader in Denver

Dear Reader,

We've been trying to find Mr. Worth ourselves to beg some more terror tales from his pen, but he seems to have vanished. If anyone knows him, please tell him our editorial doors are open wide to his kind of shocker!

The Editor

From "Ask Adventure," *Adventure*, November, 1935:

A good practical question for sportsmen from a long-time reader.

Request:—I do a great deal of hunting, and have recently been troubled by predators digging up the flayed carcasses of my kills after I have skinned them and taken my trophies. I don't wish to leave the carcasses to be discovered by others, but since I do not eat wild game, I would prefer to leave the remains in the wild rather than pack them out. How deep should one bury animal carcasses to ensure that they will not be dug up by predators?

B. D. Whitworth, Casper, Wy.

Reply by Mr. Ernest W. Shaw:—It is always advisable to bury carcasses at a minimum depth of three feet in regular soil, and at a depth of four feet when the soil is sandier. For further assurance, place a fallen tree limb or rocks over the area as well, to further discourage digging. With these precautions, the sportsman's leavings should remain undisturbed.

From "Lost Trails," *Adventure*, March, 1936:

WHITWORTH, B. D. Looking for my old chum, who has been "bumming" through the northwest for the past ten years or so. Any information of his whereabouts would certainly be appreciated. Address —J. W. SHEPARD, 428 W. 6th St., Denver, Colorado.

From "MISSING," *Detective Story Magazine*, October, 1936:

SHEPARD, JAMES W.—Formerly of Denver, Colorado. Thirty years old. Five feet nine inches tall, dark hair, gray eyes. May have been in the company of B. D. Whitworth. Kindly advise Grover F. Pierce, 310 S. Harlan Street, Denver, Colorado.

From "Around the Blotters," *Inside Detective,* **July, 1954:**

Denver, Colo.:

Authorities were horrified to find ten masks made out of dried human flesh in the cheap cardboard suitcase of a drifter. The man burned to death in his bed in a Denver transient hotel, apparently after having fallen asleep while smoking.

The body was rendered unrecognizable by the fire. The only identification found was a nearly twenty-year-old private investigator ID in the name of James W. Shepard, who vanished in 1936. Police are assuming that, in the absence of any other information, the body is that of former investigator Shepard.

"I don't know what this Shepard was up to," said Denver Police Lieutenant Randall Spotwood, "but you don't carry around dead people's faces just because you picked them up somewhere."

Police further informed *Inside Detective* that they believe nine of the ten victims are women, and that the single male victim had a bullet hole in the back of the head. Also found in Shepard's suitcase were a small stack of old magazines and a two-inch square piece of dried human skin tattooed with the image of an open eye.

Investigation into the positive identification of the corpse, as well as that of the ten victims, will continue.

Yellow Peril...how could a phrase that reeks so of racism and paranoia yield a body of fiction so...cool?

The term originated in the late nineteenth century. Asian immigrants were flooding our western shore and spreading throughout the country at a time when their homelands were growing more and more militaristic. Could this mass immigration be a silent first wave of an eventual invasion?

In polite conversation they were called Chinamen or Orientals (not "Asian," as political correctness now dictates). Down on the street they were chinks and coolies.

Chinese villains became regulars in the penny dreadfuls. In 1913 Sax Rohmer created the paradigm for all oriental evil: Fu Manchu. I became enthralled with the good doctor at age fifteen when I met him in the pages of the Pyramid reprint of *The Insidious Doctor Fu Manchu*. I became a fan of the pulps and particularly enjoyed the exotic yellow-peril stories they regularly featured. (Even the Shadow had an arch nemesis named Shiwan Khan).

So when Joe asked me for a pulp story, I said it had to be Yellow Peril. I decided it would involve a face-off between two fictional titans of the times. I came up with the most lurid title I could think of, and after that the story pretty damn near wrote itself.

—*F. Paul Wilson*

Sex Slaves of the Dragon Tong

F. Paul Wilson

"You'll find my Margot, won't you?" Mr. Kachmar said. "Please?"

Detective Third Grade Brad Brannigan felt the weight of the portly man's imploring gaze as Chief Hanrahan ushered him out of his office.

"Of course he will," the Chief told him. "He's one of our best men."

Brannigan smiled and nodded with a confidence as false as the Chief's words. He was baffled as to why he, the greenest detective in the San Francisco PD, had been called in on this of all cases.

When the door finally closed, sealing out Mr. Kachmar, the Chief turned and exhaled through puffed cheeks.

"Lord preserve us from friends of the mayor with wayward daughters, aye, Brannigan?"

As Hanrahan dropped into the creaking chair behind his desk, Brannigan searched for a response.

"I appreciate the compliment, Chief, but we both know I'm not one of your best men."

The Chief smiled. "That we do, lad. That we do."

"Then why—?"

"Because I know about Margot Kachmar and she's a bit of a hellion. Twenty years old and not a thought in her head about anyone but herself. Probably found a fellow she sparked to and went off with him on a lark. Wouldn't be the first time."

"But her father looked so worried."

"I'd be worried too if I had a daughter like that. Kachmar has only himself to blame. Rich folks like him give their kids too long a leash. Make it tough for the rest of us. You should hear my own daughter." He mimicked a young woman's voice. " 'This isn't the dark ages, Daddy. It's nineteen thirty-eight.' " He huffed and returned to his normal tone. "I wouldn't care if it was nineteen *fifty*-eight, you've got to watch your daughters every single minute. Watch 'em like a hawk."

While trying his best to look interested in the chief's domestic philosophy, Brannigan cut in as soon as he had a chance.

"Where was she last seen?"

"Washington and Grant."

"Chinatown?"

"At least that's what her girlfriend says." Hanrahan winked. "Covering for her, I'll bet. You give that one a bit of hard questioning and she'll come around."

"But Chinatown is…"

"Yes, Sorenson's beat. But I can't very well be asking him to look into it, can I."

Of course he couldn't. Sorenson was laid up in the hospital with some strange malady.

"And," Chief Hanrahan added, "I can't very well be pulling my best men off other cases and sending them to No-tickee-no-shirtee-ville to question a bunch of coolies about some young doxy who'll show up on her own in a day or two. So you get the nod, Detective Brannigan."

Brad felt heat in his cheeks and knew they were reddening. For a fair-skinned redhead like him, a blush was always waiting in the wings, ready to prance onstage at an instant's notice.

The chief's meaning was clear: I don't want to waste someone useful, so you take it.

Brad repressed a dismayed sigh. He knew this was because of the Jenkins case. Missing a vital clue had left him looking like an amateur. As a result the rest of the detectives at the station had had weeks of fun at his expense. But though the razzing was over, Chief Hanrahan still hadn't assigned him to anything meaty. Brannigan wound up with the leftovers. If he didn't get some arrests to his credit he'd never make second grade.

Stop feeling sorry for yourself, he thought. Your day will come. It just won't be today.

Brannigan took the chief's suggestion and called on Margot's friend Katy Webber for a few answers. Katy lived in her parents' home, a stone mansion in Pacific Heights.

Five minutes with her were all it took to convince him that she wasn't covering for Margot. She was too upset.

"One moment she was with me," she said through her tears, "and the next minute she wasn't! I turned to look in a jewelry store window—that was why we went there, to look at some jade—and when I turned back to point out a necklace, she was gone!"

"And you didn't see anyone suspicious hanging about? No one following you?"

"Not that I noticed. And Margot never mentioned seeing anyone. The streets were crowded with people and cars and…I don't understand how she could have disappeared like that."

Neither did Brannigan. "You must have seen *something*."

"Well…"

"What?"

"It might be nothing, but I saw this black car pulling away and I thought…" She shook her head. "I thought I saw the back of a blond head through the rear window."

"Margot's head?"

Katy shrugged and looked miserable. "I don't know. It was just a glimpse and then the car turned the corner."

"Do you remember the license plate? The make? The model?"

Katy responded to each question with a shake of her head. "I don't know cars. I did notice that it had four doors, but beyond that…"

Swell, Brannigan thought. A black sedan. San Francisco had thousands and thousands of them.

But Katy's story convinced him that someone had kidnapped Margot Kachmar. In broad daylight to boot. He'd start where she was last seen, at Washington and Grant, and move out from there.

But he'd move on his own. This was his chance to get himself out of Dutch with the chief, so he'd keep it to himself for now. If Hanrahan got wind that this was a real kidnapping, he'd pull Brannigan and put someone else on it for sure.

Someone in that area of Chinatown had to remember something. All he needed to do was ask the right person. And that meant his next step was good old-fashioned door-to-door detective work.

"Wah!" Yu Chaoyang cried. "Slow the car!"

Jiang Zhifu looked around, startled. He and Yu occupied the back of one of the black Packard sedans owned by Yan Yuap Tong. An underling Yu had brought from Singapore sat behind the wheel. All three wore identical black cotton outfits with high collars and frog-buttoned fronts, although Yu's large girth required twice as much fabric as Jiang's; each jacket was embroidered with a golden dragon over the left breast; each man wore his hair woven into a braid that dangled from beneath a traditional black skullcap.

"What is wrong?" Jiang said as the car slowed almost to a stop.

"Nothing is wrong, my tong brother. In fact, something is very right." A chubby finger pointed toward the sidewalk. "Look and marvel."

Jiang peered through the side window glass and saw a typical Chinatown scene: pushcarts laden with fruits and vegetables, fish live and dead, fluttering caged birds and roasted ducks; weaving among them was the usual throng of shoppers, a mix of locals and tourists.

Yu had come to America just last month on a mission for his father, head of the Yan Yuap Tong's house in Singapore; Jiang had volunteered to guide him through the odd ways of this strange country.

Yu was proving to be a trial. Arrogant and headstrong, he did not give proper face to his tong brothers here in San Francisco. Some of that might be anticipated from the son of a tong chief from home, but Yu went beyond proper bounds. No one expected him to kowtow, but he should show more respect.

"I don't understand," Jiang said.

Yu turned to face him. He ran a long sinuous tongue over his lips, brushing his thin drooping mustache in the process. His smile narrowed further his puffy lids until they were mere slits through which his onyx eyes gleamed.

"Red hair!" he cried. "Red hair!"

Jiang looked again and saw a little girl, no more than ten years old, standing by a cart, looking at a cage full of sparrows. She wore a red dress with white trim, but her unruly hair was even redder: a bushy flame, flaring around her face like the corona of an eclipse.

"Look at her." Yu's voice was a serpent, slithering through the car. "What a price I can fetch for her!"

"But she's a child."

"Yes! Precisely! I have a buyer in Singapore who specializes in children, and a red-haired child...aieee! He will pay anything for her!"

Jiang's stomach tightened. A child...

"Are you forgetting the conditions set by the Mandarin?"

"May maggots eat the eyes of your Mandarin!"

Jiang couldn't help a quick look around. He thanked his ancestors that the windows were closed. Someone might have heard.

"Do not speak of him so! And do not even think of breaking your agreement!"

Yu leaned closer. "Where do your loyalties lie, Jiang? With your tong, or with this mysterious Mandarin you all kowtow to?"

"I am loyal to Yan Yuap, but I am also fond of my skin. And if you wish to keep yours, you will heed my warning. Those who oppose his will wind up dead or are never seen again."

"Eh-yeh!" Yu waved a dismissive hand. "By tomorrow night I will be at sea with this barbarous country far behind me."

"Yes. You will be gone, but I will still have to live here."

Yu grinned, showing mottled teeth, stains from his opium pipe. "That is not my worry."

"Do not be so sure. The Mandarin's reach is long. He has never been known to break his word, and he has no mercy toward those who break theirs to him. I beg you not to do this."

The grin turned into a sneer. "America has softened you, Jiang. You shake like a frightened old woman."

Jiang looked away. This man was a fool. Yu had come to America for women—white women he could sell to the Singapore brothels. The lower level houses there and the streets around them were full of dolla-dolla girls shipped in from the farmlands. But the upper echelon salons that provided gambling as well as sex needed something special to bring in the high rollers. White women were one such draw. And *blond* white women were the ultimate lure.

Since nothing in San Francisco's Chinese underworld happened without the Mandarin's consent—or without his receiving a share of the proceeds—Yu had needed prior approval of his plan. How he had raged at the ignominy of such an arrangement, but he had been persuaded that he would have no success without it.

The Mandarin had set two conditions. The first: take only one woman from San Francisco, all the rest from surrounding cities and towns. The second: no children. He did not care to weather a Lindbergh-style investigation.

Jiang said, "We took a girl here only yesterday, and now a child from these same streets. You will be breaking both conditions with this act."

Yu smiled. "No, Jiang. *We* will be breaking them. We will watch and wait, and when the time is right, you will pluck this delicious little berry from her branch."

Jiang agonized as Yu had the driver circle the block again and again. Yes, he was a member of the Yan Yuap Tong, but he was also a member of a more powerful and far-flung society. And the Mandarin was one of its leaders. Jiang was the Mandarin's eyes within the Yan Yuap Tong, and as such he would have to report this. Not that he would mind the slightest seeing the worst happen to Yu, but he prayed to his ancestors that the Mandarin wouldn't make him pay too for his part in the transgression.

"Wah!" Yu said. "She has turned the corner. There is no one about! Now! Now!"

Fumes filled the car as Jiang poured chloroform onto a rag. He jumped out, the soft slap of his slippers on the pavement the only sign of his presence; he clamped the rag over the child's face and was dragging her back toward the car's open door when a ball of light brown fur darted across the sidewalk. Jiang heard a growl of fury, saw bared fangs, and then the thing was upon him, tearing at the flesh of his arm.

He cried out for help and received it in the report of a pistol. The dog yelped and tumbled backward to lie twitching on the sidewalk. The child's wild struggles—she was a tough little one—slowed and ceased as the chloroform did its work. Jiang shoved her into the back seat between Yu and himself. The car lurched into motion. Jiang glanced back and saw a pool of blood forming around the head of the sandy-haired dog.

He looked at the now unconscious child and saw Yu caressing one of her pale, bare thighs.

"Ah, my little quail," he cooed, "I would so like to use the trip home to teach you the thousand ways to please a man, but alas you must remain a virgin if I am to take full profit from you."

Jiang closed his eyes and trembled inside. He had to tell the Mandarin of this. He prayed he'd survive the meeting.

"I've run into a blank wall," Brannigan said.

"And so you've come to me for help."

Looking at Detective Sergeant Hank Sorenson now, Brannigan wished he'd gone elsewhere.

He'd had a nodding acquaintance with Sorenson at the station, but the figure pressed between the sheets in the hospital bed before him was a caricature of the man Brannigan had known.

He tried not to stare at the sunken cheeks, the glassy, feverish eyes, the sallow, sweaty skin as pale as his hospital gown. The slow smile that stretched Sorenson's lips and bared his teeth was ghastly.

"You mean to tell me you walked up to Chinatown residents and asked them what they saw?"

The whole afternoon had been a frustrating progression of singsong syllables and expressionless yellow faces with gleaming slanted eyes that told him nothing.

"I didn't see that I had any other option."

"You can't treat chinks like regular people, Brad. You can't ask them a direct question. They're devious, crafty, always circling."

Brannigan bristled at Sorenson's attitude, like a teacher chiding a student for not knowing his lesson.

"Well, be that as it may, no one saw anything."

Sorenson barked a phlegmy laugh. "Oh, they saw all right. They're just not going to tell an outsider. Not if they know what's good for them."

"What's that mean?"

"The Mandarin. You do not cross the Mandarin."

Sorenson went on to explain about Chinatown's lord of crime. Then added, "If this Kachmar girl is a blond, you might be dealing with a white slave ring. The Yan Yuap Tong—also called the Dragon Tong because their symbol is a dragon—has been involved in that before. The tong-sters probably have your missing girl's photo on its way back to Singapore already, to get the bidding started."

Brannigan had heard of Oriental rings that abducted white women for sex slaves, but he'd never expected that Margot Kachmar—

"Check Oakland and Marin and maybe San Jose," Sorenson was say-ing. "See if they've had a blonde or two gone missing recently."

"Why there?"

"Because police departments don't communicate nearly enough. Someday they will, but with things as they are, spreading out the abduc-tions lessens the chances of anyone spotting a pattern."

Oakland...San Jose...that seemed like a lot of legwork with slim chance of turning up anything useful.

"Why don't I go straight to the source? This Mandarin character... where do I find him?"

Sorenson began to shake with ague. His head fell back on the pillow. When the tremors eased...

"No one knows. He hides his identity even from his fellow Chinese. Just as well—you don't want to find him. I came close and look what it got me."

"I don't understand."

"I was homing in on the Mandarin's identity, getting closer than anyone before me, and then, a week ago, something got into my house and bit me."

"Something?"

"A giant millipede, bright red, at least eight inches long, crawled into my bed and bit me on the shoulder. I managed to smash it with a shoe as it raced away, but only got the back half. The front half broke off and escaped. Bug scientists over at the university says it only exists in Borneo."

"But what's that got to do—?"

"It was *put* in my house, you idiot!" he snapped, a faint tinge of color seeping into his cheeks. "By one of the Mandarin's men. And look what it's done to me!"

He pulled the hospital gown off his left shoulder to reveal a damp dressing. He ripped that off.

"It's due for a change anyway. Have a look."

Brannigan saw an ulcerated crater perhaps two inches across penetrating deep into the flesh of Sorenson's shoulder. Its base was red and bloody. A quick look was more than enough for Brannigan, but as he was turning away he thought he saw something move within the bloody fluid. He looked again—

And jumped back.

Many little things were moving in the base of the ulcer.

"What—?"

Sorenson's expression was bleak. Brannigan could see he was trying to keep up a brave face.

"Yeah. The bug didn't poison me. I wish it had. Instead it laid a bunch of eggs in me, a thousand, maybe a million of them. And they keep hatching. I think they're getting into my system, eating me alive from the inside."

"Can't the doctors stop it?"

He shook his head. "They've never seen anything like—"

He clasped a hand over his mouth as he broke off into a fit of coughing. The harsh barks seemed to be coming from somewhere around his ankles. With a final wet hack he stopped.

A look of horror twisted his features as he stared at his palm. It was filled with bloody phlegm, and Brannigan could swear he saw something wriggling within the glob, something with many, many legs.

"Oh, God!" Sorenson wailed, his composure finally broken. "Call the doctor! Get the nurse in here! Hurry!"

Brannigan turned and ran for the hallway. Behind him he heard the wrenching sound of a grown man sobbing.

Jiang could not keep his body from shaking as he knelt with his forehead pressed against the cold stone floor. The Mandarin stood over him, eerily silent. Jiang had told him what had transpired on the street. It had been hours ago, but he had come as soon as he could get away.

At last the master spoke, his voice soft, the tone sibilant.

"So...Yu Chaoyang has disobeyed me and endangered all we have worked for here. I half expected this from such a man. The Japanese are overrunning our China, slaughtering its people, and Yu thinks only of adding to his already swollen coffers."

"Venerable, I tried to dissuade him but—"

"I am sure you did your best, Jiang Zhifu, but apparently it wasn't enough."

No-no-no! cried a terrified voice within Jiang. Let him not be angry! But Jiang's outer voice was wise enough to remain silent.

"However," the master said, "I will allow you to redeem yourself."

"Oh, Illustrious! This miserable offspring of a worm is endlessly grateful."

"Rise."

Jiang eased to his feet and stood facing the Master, but looked at him only from the corner of his eye. The man known throughout Chinatown as the Mandarin—even Jiang did not know his true name—was tall, lean, high-shouldered, standing bamboo straight with his hands folded inside the sleeves of his flowing turquoise robe; his hair was thin under a brimless cap beaded with coral. He had a high, domed forehead and thin lips, but his eyes—light green, their color intensified by the shade of his robe—were unlike any Jiang had ever seen.

"Where is the child now?"

"Yu has her in the tonghouse, but soon he will head for his ship and set sail. Shall I stop him? Shall I see to it that he suffers the same fate as that bothersome detective?"

The master shook his head. "No. Did the child see you?"

"No, Magnificent. I took her from behind and she was soon unconscious."

"Then she cannot point a finger of blame at a Chinaman. Good. You will return to the tonghouse and light a red lamp in the room where the child is kept. I will send a few of my dacoits to see that she is returned to the streets. You must be present so that no suspicion falls on you. Then let Yu go to his ship and set sail with the rest of his cargo. He will never see home. He—Jiang, you are bleeding."

"It is nothing, Eminent. The child's dog bit me as I pulled her into the car. It is nothing."

"The red-haired little girl had a dog, you say? What kind of dog?"

"A scruffy mongrel. May this unworthy snail ask why such an Esteemed One as you would ask?"

When the master did not answer, Jiang dared a glance at his face and saw the unimaginable: a look of uncertainty in those green eyes.

"Exalted…did this miserable slug say something wrong?"

"No, Jiang. I had a thought, that is all…about a certain little red-haired girl who must not be touched…ever." He turned and stepped to the single high small window in the north wall of the tiny room. "It could not possibly be she, but if it is…and if she is harmed…all the ancestors of all the members of the Yan Yuap Tong will not save it from doom…a doom that could spread to us as well."

☯

Brannigan leaned against the center railing of the hospital's front steps and sucked deep draughts of the foggy night air.

Sorenson…a tough, no-nonsense cop…reduced to a weeping child. It gave him a bad case of the willies. Who was this Mandarin? And more important, was he involved in Margot Kachmar's disappearance?

Feeling steadier, Brannigan stepped down to the sidewalk and headed for his radio car. He needed to call in. A catchy song by Frances Day, "I've Got You Under My Skin," echoed unwelcomed in his head. From somewhere in the fog a newsboy called out the headlines of the evening edition. As he passed a silver Rolls Royce its rear door opened and an accented voice spoke from the dark interior.

"Please step inside. Someone wishes to speak to you."

Someone? That could very well be the Mandarin. Well, Brannigan damn well wanted to speak to him too, but on his terms, not in the back of a mysterious limousine.

"Have him meet me down at the station," he said, backing away. "We'll have a nice long chat there."

Brannigan jumped at the sound of another voice close behind him, almost in his ear.

"He would speak to you now. Into the car please."

Brannigan reached for his pistol but his shoulder holster was empty. He whirled and found himself face to face with a gaunt Chinaman dressed in a black business suit, a white shirt, and a black tie. A black fedora finished off the look. His expression was bland, his tone matter of fact, but his features had a sinister, almost cruel cast.

He held up Brannigan's .38 between them but did not point it at him. He gestured to the car with his free hand.

"Please."

Brannigan's first instinct was to run, but figured all he'd gain by that was a slug in the back. Probably better than a millipede in his bed, but he decided on the car option. Maybe he'd find an opening along the way to make a break.

With his bladder clenching, he ducked inside. The door slammed behind him, drenching him in darkness. He could sense but not see whoever was seated across from him. As the car began moving—the thin chink was also the driver, it seemed—Brannigan leaned forward, straining to see his host.

"Are you…?" His mouth was dry so he wet his lips. "Are you the Mandarin?"

A soft laugh. "Oh, no. I would not serve that one."

"Then why do you want to speak to me?"

"It is not I, Detective Brannigan. It is another. Hush now and save your words for him."

The glare from a passing streetlight illuminated the interior for a second, leaving Brannigan in a state of shock. The other occupant was a turbaned giant who looked as if he'd just stepped out of Arabian nights.

The car turned west on California, taking them away from Chinatown. A few minutes later they stopped at a side entrance to the Fairmont Hotel, perched atop Nob Hill like a granite crown. The driver and the giant escorted Brannigan to an elevator in an empty service hallway. Inside the car, the driver inserted a key into the control panel and up they went.

After a swift, stomach-sinking ride, the elevator doors opened into a huge suite, richly furnished and decorated with palm trees and ornate marble columns reaching to its high, glass-paned ceiling.

An older man rose from a sofa. He was completely bald with pale gray eyes. He wore black tuxedo pants and a white dress shirt ornamented with a huge diamond stickpin. Brannigan spotted a black dress jacket and tie draped over a nearby chair. A long thick cigar smoldered in his left hand; he extended the right as he strode forward.

"Detective Brannigan, I presume. Thank you for coming."

Brannigan, flabbergasted, shook the man's hand. This wasn't at all what he'd expected.

"I didn't have much choice," he said, eyeing his two escorts as they took up positions behind his host. The driver had removed his hat, revealing a bald dome; glossy black hair fringed the sides and back of his scalp.

"Oh, I hope they didn't threaten you."

Brannigan was about to crack wise when he realized that they hadn't threatened him at all. If anything they'd been overly polite.

He studied the bald man. Something familiar about him…

"I've seen you before."

The man shrugged. "Despite my best efforts, my face now and again winds up in the papers."

"Who are you?"

"Let's just say I'm someone who prefers to move in and out of large cities without advertising his presence. Otherwise my time would be consumed by a parade of local politicians with their hands out, and I'd never get any work done."

"What do you want with me?"

"You were in Chinatown today asking about a missing girl, Margot Kachmar."

The statement startled Brannigan at first, but then he glanced at the Oriental driver and realized he shouldn't be surprised.

"That's police business."

"And now it's *my* business." A sudden, steely tone put a knife edge on the words. "My daughter was abducted from that same area this afternoon."

"She was? Did you tell the police?"

"That's what I'm doing now."

"I mean an official report and—never mind. Are you sure she was abducted?"

The bald man hooked a finger through the air and Brannigan followed him to the far side of a huge couch. Along the way he glanced out the tall windows and saw Russian Hill and San Francisco Bay stretching out below. This had to be the penthouse suite.

The man pointed to a sandy-furred mutt lying on a big red pillow. A thick bandage encircled its head.

"That's her dog. She goes nowhere without him. He was shot—luckily the bullet glanced off his skull instead of piercing it—and that can only mean that he was defending her. He almost died, but he's a tough one, just like his little owner."

Two in two days from the same neighborhood…this was not the pattern Sorenson had described.

"How old is your daughter, and is she blond?"

"She's a ten-year-old redhead—her hair's the same shade as yours."

Cripes. A kid. "Well, I'm sorry about what happened to her, but I don't think she's connected to the Kachmar girl. I—"

"What if I told you they were both dragged into a black Packard sedan? Most likely the same one?"

Katy Webber had described a black sedan. Maybe there was a connection after all.

The bald man said, "I have men out canvassing the neighborhoods right now, looking for that car."

"That's police business. You can't—"

"I can and I am. Don't worry—they'll be very discreet. But I'll make you a deal, detective: You share with me, I'll share with you. If I locate Miss Kachmar, I'll notify you. If you find my daughter alive and well I will see to it that you never have to worry about money for the rest of your life."

Brannigan felt a flush of anger. "I don't need to be bribed to do my job."

"It's not a bribe—it will be gratitude. Anything of mine you want you can have. I've made fortunes and lost them, gone from living in mansions to being penniless on the street and back to mansions. I'm good at making money. I can always replace my fortune. But I can't replace that little girl." The man seemed to lose his voice and Brannigan saw his throat work. When he recovered he added, "She means everything to me."

The nods from the turbaned giant and the driver said they felt the same. Brannigan was touched. He couldn't help it. And from the looks on all three faces he knew that if they were the first to discover the child's abductor, the mugg would never see trial.

He couldn't condone or allow the vigilantism he sensed brewing here. And for that reason he couldn't tell them what Sorenson had said about the Dragon Tong. He'd keep that to himself.

"I promise you," he said, "that if I find her, you'll be the first to know."

The bald man put his hand out to the Chinese driver who placed Brannigan's pistol in it, then he fixed the detective with his pale gaze. "That is all I ask. Can my associates offer you a lift?"

"No thanks." He'd seen enough of the old man's chums for one evening. "I'll grab a cab."

He took the elevator down to the lobby level, but before going outside, he stopped at the front desk.

"Who's staying in the penthouse suite?" he asked the clerk. He flipped open his wallet, showing his shield. "And don't give me any malarkey about hotel policy."

The man hesitated, then shrugged. After consulting the guest register he shook his head.

"Sorry. It's unoccupied."

"Baloney! I was just up there."

Another shake of the head. "No occupant is listed. All I can tell you is this: The penthouse suite is on reserve—permanent reserve—but it doesn't say for whom."

Frustrated, Brannigan stormed from the hotel. He had more important things to do than argue with some hotel flunky.

Ten minutes later Brannigan stood in the shadows across the street from the headquarters of the Dragon Tong. Its slanted cupola glistened with moisture from the fog. A few of the upper windows were lit, a pair of green-and-yellow paper lanterns hung outside the front entrance, but otherwise the angular building squatted dark and silent on its lot.

What now? Sorenson had told him how to find it, but now that he was here he couldn't simply walk in. Much as he hated to admit it, he was going to have to call Hanrahan for backup.

As he turned to go back to his radio car he noticed movement along the right flank of the tonghouse. Three monkey-like shadows were scaling the wall. He hurried across the street and crept closer to investigate. He found a rope hanging along the wall, disappearing into a third-story window lit by a red paper lantern.

Apparently someone else was interested in the tonghouse. He knew the three he'd seen shimmying up this rope were too small and agile to have been the bald guy and company.

He looked at the rope, tempted. This was one hell of a pickle. Go up or get help?

The decision was taken out of his hands when the rope snaked up the wall and out of reach. He cursed as he watched it disappear into the window.

But then he noticed a narrow door just to his right. He tried the handle—unlocked—and pushed it open. The slow creaks from the old hinges sounded like a cat being tortured. He cringed as he slipped into some sort of kitchen. He pulled his pistol and waited to see if anyone came to investigate.

When no one showed, he slipped through the darkness, listening. The tonghouse seemed quiet. Most of the tongsters were probably home at this hour. But what of the hatchetmen the tongs reputedly used as guards and enforcers? Did they go home too? Brannigan hoped so.

He stepped through a curtain into a small chamber lit by a single oil lamp, its walls bare except for a black lacquered door ornamented with gold dragons uncoiling from the corners. The door pulled outward and Brannigan found himself in an exotic, windowless room, empty except for a golden Buddha seated in a corner; a lamp and joss sticks smoked before it, their vapors wafting toward the high ceiling.

Something about the walls…he stepped closer and gasped as he ran his fingers over what he'd assumed to be wallpaper. But these peacock plumes weren't painted, they were the genuine article. And all four walls were lined with them.

Dazzled by its beauty, Brannigan stepped back to the center of the room and turned in a slow circle. No window, no door other than the one he'd come through. The room appeared to be a dead end.

But then he noticed the way the smoke from the joss sticks wavered on its path toward the ceiling. Air was flowing in from somewhere. He moved along the wall, inspecting the plumes until he found one with a wavering fringe. And another just below it. Air was filtering through a narrow crevice. He pushed at the wall on either side until he felt something give. He pushed harder and a section swung inward.

Ahead lay a long, dark, downsloping corridor, end-ing in a rectangle of wan, flickering light. The only sound was his own breathing.

He hesitated, then took a breath and started forward. He'd come this far…in for a dime, in for a dollar.

Pistol at the ready, he crept down the passage as silently as his heavy regulation shoes would allow, pausing every few steps to listen. All quiet.

When he reached the end he stopped. All he could see ahead was bare floor and wall, lit by a lamp in some unseen corner. Still hearing nothing, he risked a peek inside—

—and ducked back as he caught a flash of movement to his left. A black-handled hatchet whispered past the end of his nose and buried itself in the wall just inches to the right of his head.

And then a black-pajama-clad tongster with a high-cheeked, pock-marked face lunged at him with a raised dagger. His brutal features contorted with rage as he shouted rapid-fire gibberish.

The report from Brannigan's pistol was deafening as it smashed a bullet through the chink's chest and sent him tumbling backward. Another black-clad tongster, a raw-boned, beady-eyed bugger, replaced him immediately, howling the same cry as he swung a hatchet at Brannigan's throat. He too fell with a bullet in his chest.

But then the doorway was filled with two more and then three, and more surging behind them. With only four rounds left in his revolver, Brannigan knew he had no chance of stopping this Mongol horde. He began backpedaling as the hatchetmen leaped over their fallen comrades and charged.

Brannigan fired as he retreated, making good use of his remaining rounds, slowing the black-clad gang's advance, but a small, primitive part of him began screeching in panic as it became aware that he was not going to leave the tonghouse alive. Not unless he reached the door to the joss room in time to shut it and hold it closed against the swarm of hatchetmen.

After firing his last shot he turned and ran full tilt for the door. His foot caught on the sill as he rushed through and he tumbled to the floor. The horror of knowing that he was about to be hacked to death shot strength into his legs but he slipped as he started to rise and knew he was done for.

As he rolled, tensing for the first ax strike, preparing a last stand with his bare hands, he was startled by the sound of gunfire, followed immediately by shouts and screams of pain. He looked up and saw the old man's turbaned Indian wielding a huge scimitar that lopped off heads and arms with slashing swipes, while the driver hacked away with a cutlass. The old man himself stood in the thick of it, firing a round-handled, long-barreled Mauser at any of the hatchet men who slipped past his front line.

Brannigan pawed fresh shells from his jacket pocket and began to reload. But the melee was over before he finished. He sat up and looked around. More than joss-stick smoke hung in the air; blood speckled the feathered walls and pooled on the floor. The old man and the Indian were unscathed; the driver was bleeding from a gash on his right arm but didn't seem to notice.

"What...how...?"

The old man looked at him. "I sensed you weren't telling us everything you knew, so we followed you. Good thing too, I'd say."

Brannigan nodded as he struggled to his feet. He felt shaky, unsteady. "Thank you. I owe you my—"

"Is she here?" the old man said. "Have you seen her?"

"I have her right here, Oliver," said a sibilant, accented voice.

Brannigan turned and raised his pistol as a motley group filed into the small room: a green-eyed, turquoise-robed Chinaman entered, followed by a trio of gangly, brutal-looking, dark-skinned lugs dressed in loin cloths and nothing else; one carried a red-haired girl in his arms; two black-pajamaed tongsters brought up the rear, one thin, one fat, the latter with his hands tied behind his back and looking as if he'd wound up on the wrong end of a billy club.

The lead Chinaman spoke again. "I feared you might have been drawn into this."

"So it's you, doctor," the old man said. At least Brannigan knew part of his name now: Oliver. "Striking at me through my child? I knew you were ruthless but—"

"Do not insult me, Oliver. I would gladly cut out your heart, but I would not break it."

The doctor—doctor of what? Brannigan wondered—removed a bony, long-fingered hand from within a sleeve and gestured to the loin-clothed crew. The one carrying the little girl stepped forward and handed her over to Oliver. She looked drugged but as the old man took her in his arms, her eyes fluttered open. Brannigan saw her smile

A word...a whisper: "Daddy."

Tears rimmed Oliver's eyes as he looked down at her, then back to the doctor. "I don't understand."

"This was not my doing." Without looking he flicked a finger toward the fat, bound tongster. "This doomed one broke an agreement."

"I thought I left you back in Hong Kong. When was it...?"

"Three years ago. I understand you recently closed your factory there."

He nodded. "The political climate in the Far East has accomplished what you could not. I'm gathering my chicks closer to the nest, you might say. A storm is brewing and I want to be properly positioned when it strikes."

The doctor's smile was acid. "To profiteer, as usual."

Oliver shrugged. "Nothing wrong with doing well while doing good."

Who were these two? Brannigan wondered. They stood, each with his own personal army, like ancient mythical enemies facing each other across a bottomless divide.

"And what of you, doctor?" Oliver continued. "With your homeland being invaded, why are you here?"

"You heard what the Japanese dogs did in Nanking?"

"Yes. Ghastly. I'm sorry."

"Then you can understand why I am here. To raise money from the underworld for weapons to repel the insects."

Oliver's faint smile looked bitter. "And all along you thought the enemy was people like me."

"You still are. My goal remains unchanged: To drive all foreigners from Chinese soil. I will admit, however, that I singled out the white western world as the threat, never realizing that a yellow-skinned neighbor would prove a far more vicious foe."

Something the doctor had said rang through Brannigan's brain: *To raise money from the underworld*...that could only mean—

He pointed his pistol at the green-robed chink. "You're the Mandarin! You're—"

The green eyes glanced his way and the pure malevolence in them clogged the words in Brannigan's throat. Before he could clear it, Oliver spoke.

"I'll take him from here," he told the doctor and pointed at the bound chink. "My associates and I have a score to settle."

"No, he is mine. He broke his word to me. I have experts in the Thousand Cuts. He will die long after he wishes to, I promise."

Brannigan couldn't believe his ears. These two acted like laws unto themselves. It was like listening to two sovereign nations states argue over extradition of a prisoner.

"Hey, wait just a minute, you two," he said, stepping closer to the Mandarin. "Neither of you is going to do anything." The green eyes turned on him again. "I'm arresting you and your tongster buddy here for—"

Something smashed against the back of Brannigan's skull, dropping him to his knees. He tried to regain his feet but the edges of his vision went blurry and he toppled forward into darkness.

Jiang Zhifu poised his fist over the fallen detective's neck and looked to the master for permission to finish the worm. The master nodded. But as Jiang raised his hand for the deathblow a shot rang out and a bullet plowed into the feathered wall beside him.

"That will be enough," said the man called Oliver.

The master motioned Jiang back toward Yu and he obeyed, albeit reluctantly. He was confused. Who was this white devil to give orders in the master's presence, and have the master acquiesce? Although this Oliver and the master seemed to be old enemies, the master treated him as an equal.

Something became clear to Jiang. It must have been because of this man that the master had sent Jiang to the Fairmont Hotel where he'd been instructed to ask a certain question of the kitchen staff. When Jiang returned with word that yes, meals were indeed being delivered to the penthouse suite, the master had changed his plans.

Jiang looked at the little red-haired girl in Oliver's arms. Yu had brought all this to pass by abducting her. The master had hinted that consequences most dire and relentless would befall anyone even remotely connected with harming that child.

Jiang had doubted that, but looking around the joss room now, he believed. So many of his tong brothers dead, shot or hacked to pieces. He and Yu were the only two members of Yan Yuap left alive in the house. Jiang would have to leave and return at dawn with the rest of the members, feigning shock at the carnage here.

"As I was saying, Oliver, before we were interrupted, this worthless one is mine to deal with, but if you wish I can have some expert seamstresses stitch his skin back together and make you a gift of it."

"Thanks for the offer," he said but did not look grateful. "I think I'll pass on that."

"Then I shall nail it to the wall of this tonghouse as a warning."

Jiang jumped as a slurred voice said, "The only thing you'll be doing is looking the wrong way through the bars of a jail cell."

Aiii! The detective was conscious again. He must have a skull as thick as the walls of the Imperial Palace!

"You have at most six shots, detective," the master said without a trace of fear. "My dacoits will be upon you before you can shoot all of them."

The detective leveled his pistol at the master's heart. "Yeah, but the first one will go into you."

Yu started to move forward, crying, "Yes! Arrest me! Please!"

But Jiang yanked him back and struck him across the throat—not a killing blow, just enough to silence him.

The master only smiled. "You may arrest me if you wish, detective, but that will doom the ten women this bloated slug collected for export."

The detective's eyes widened. "Ten? Good Christ, where are they?"

"In a ship in the harbor, moored at Pier Twelve. A ship wired to explode at midnight."

"You're lying!"

"He doesn't lie, Brannigan," said Oliver. "Over our years of conflict I've learned that the doctor is capable of just about anything, but he never lies."

"If you look at your watch," the master said, "you will see that you have time to bring me to your precinct house or rush to the harbor and save the women. But not both."

Jiang could see the detective's resolve wavering.

The master continued in a silky, almost seductive voice. "May I suggest the former course? Think what bringing in the mysterious and notorious Mandarin will do for your career. It will guarantee you the promotion you most surely desire."

The detective looked to Oliver. "Will you hold him here until—?"

The older man cut him off with a quick shake of his head. "This is your show, kid." He looked down at the child stirring in his arms. "I have what I came for. You choose."

"Damn you all!" he said, backing toward the door.

He turned and ran.

Jiang knew that if the young detective broke all speed records, he might reach the docks in time. Fortunately for him, he would meet little resistance aboard ship; most of the crew had deserted once word leaked out that Yu had displeased the Mandarin.

When the detective was gone, Oliver smiled. "Dear doctor, you never fail to find interesting ways to test people. I'm glad he chose what he did, otherwise I'd have had to send my associates to the waterfront. As it is, I've got someone here who needs attending to, and I have a call to make."

He turned to go, then turned back.

"Oh, and those weapons your people need...if you have trouble buying through the usual channels, call me. I'm sure we can work something out."

And then the master shocked Jiang by doing the unthinkable. He inclined his head toward this man named Oliver.

There's still a chance, Brannigan thought as he jumped behind the wheel of his radio car. He'd call the station and send a squad of cars to the docks while he returned to the tonghouse and collared the Mandarin.

But when he snatched the microphone from its holder he noticed the frayed end of its coiled wire dangling in the air.

"Damn!"

He tossed the useless piece of garbage against the passenger door. No options left. He started to car, threw it into gear, and floored the gas pedal. He didn't think he could make it, but he was going to try.

Traffic was light and with his siren howling he reached the docks in five minutes. He found Pier Twelve and raced up the gangplank of a rust-bucket freighter, his pistol held before him.

He reached the deck and, with only that wash of light from the city behind him for illumination, looked around. The tub looked deserted. Two of the three cargo hatches lay open. He ran to the third and rapped on it with the gun butt.

"Hello! Anyone in there?"

The muffled chorus of female voices from below was a sweet symphony. He found the fasteners, released them, and pulled off the cover.

"Detective Brad Brannigan," he said into the square of darkness below him, and the words had never sounded so good on his tongue. "Let's get you gals out of there."

As the captives shouted, cried, and sobbed with relief, Brannigan grabbed the rope ladder coiled by the hatch and tossed it over the edge.

"Squeeze the minutes, girls," he called. "We haven't got much time."

As the first climbed into view, a rather plain blonde, he grabbed her arm and hauled her onto the deck.

"Run! Get down the gangplank and keep going!"

He did this with each of the girls—amazingly, all blondes.

"I thought there were ten of you," he said as he helped the ninth over the rim.

"Margot hurt her ankle when they grabbed her. She can't climb up."

Hell and damn, he thought. Margot Kachmar, the one who started all this for him. He wished he could see his watch. How much time did he have left, if any?

Didn't matter. He hadn't finished the job.

He directed number nine to the gangway, then leaned over the rim and called into the darkness below.

"Margot? Are you near the ladder?"

"Yes, but—"

"No buts. Put your good foot on a rung and hold on tight."

"O-okay." He felt the ropes tighten. "I'm on. Now what?"

"I bring you up."

Brannigan sat on the deck, braced his feet against the hatch rim, and began hauling on the rope ladder. The coarse coils burned his palms and his back protested, but he kept at it, pulling rung after ropy rung up and over the edge until he saw a pair of hands grip the rim.

"Keep coming!" he shouted, maintaining tension on the rope.

When her face was visible and she had both elbows over the rim, he grabbed her and hauled her onto the deck.

"Oh, thank you!" she sobbed as she looked at the city. "I'd given up hope of ever seeing home again!"

"Don't thank me yet." He lifted her into his arms and carried her toward the gangway. "C'mon, kiddo. Your daddy's waiting for you."

His haste gave him a bad moment on the gangway as he slipped halfway down and nearly fell off. He was just stepping onto the dock with his burden safe and unharmed when a bright flash lit up the night.

"Hold it!" a man's voice said. "One more!"

The purple afterimage of the flash blotted out whoever was talking. "What?"

A second flash and then another voice saying, "Joe Stenson from the *Chronicle*. You're name's Brannigan, right?"

"Yes, but—"

"That's with a double 'n,' right?"

"Get out of here!" Brannigan shouted as he began carrying Margot away from the ship. "The ship's going to blow at midnight!"

"Blow?"

"As in explode!"

"But it's already after midnight," Stenson said.

Brannigan slowed for a few steps. Had he been duped? Then he remembered what Oliver had said about the Mandarin always keeping his word and resumed his frantic pace.

"Just get away from the ship!"

"If you say so." Stenson was pacing him to his left. A photographer ambled on his right.

"How come you're down here?" Brannigan asked.

"Got a tip. Guy didn't give his name, just told me to get down to Pier Twelve if I wanted to catch a hero cop in action, and am I ever glad I listened. The girls told me what happened to them, and that picture of you carrying this little lady down the gangplank—hoo boy, if that's not front page stuff, I'll quit and open a flower shop."

Ahead Brannigan could see the rest of the girls waiting near the street, cheering when they saw he had Margot. He set her down on the curb and they all gathered around, hugging her, hugging him, while the photographer flashed away.

"What was that about the ship exploding at midnight?" Stenson said. "Were you—?"

And then the pavement shook and the night lit up like day as huge explosions ripped through the old freighter, rupturing her hull and shooting hundred-foot columns of flame up the hatches.

"Are you getting this, Louie?" Stenson was shouting to his photographer.

"I'm getting it, Joe. Am I ever getting it!"

The adrenaline began seeping away then, leaving Brannigan fagged. He'd missed collaring the Mandarin, but looking at these ten girls, all alive and well because of him, he couldn't help but feel on top of the world.

But who in the world had called the *Chronicle*?

He sensed motion behind him and turned to see a Silver Rolls Royce gliding by. A little red-haired girl smiled and waved from the rear window before the car was swallowed by the fog.

For a while I had been wanting to write a story about the Purple Gang, Detroit's contribution to the gangster pantheon of the Roaring Twenties. The Purples were apparently so mean that they kept control of the rum-running trade in Detroit because Al Capone didn't want to take them on, and if they never achieved the glamour of Siegel or Capone or Rothstein, it wasn't for lack of trying.

Also, there's something about the tale of the isolated group on a winter night, and the intrusion of a stranger into that group—the shape of that story has always interested me, and I got to thinking about pool, and what a shame it was that there aren't pool halls like there used to be, and the germ of "New Game in Town" was there. After that, it was just a matter of adding a double-cross here and there, together with strange lights in the sky.

—*Alex Irvine*

New Game in Town

Alex Irvine

There was a foot of snow on the ground, with more coming, and the Bavaria Club was quiet. Cornell was brushing the three-rail table at the back, Rudy Szetela and Phil Glaubman were rolling balls around the short table near the door labeled MANAGER that led to the card room, where Abe Bernstein was playing Hi-Lo with a group of guys that in another, better, life I would have been arresting. Two of Abe's boys were playing railbird on Rudy and Phil's game, mostly out of meanness since they knew kibitzing drove Phil crazy. Back in the corner, where the lights mostly didn't reach, Barney Steeple sat fat and patient as a spider—waiting for a mark, if any such were out braving the weather.

Phil made a sharp cut of the twelve down the length of the table, and one of Abe's boys started jumping around like a monkey while the other threw twenty bucks on the floor. From Barney's corner came a soft sigh, full of disdain. Only Cornell kept doing what he'd been doing, his brush moving in perfect even strokes out from the center of the three-rail table, building little ridges of chalk and lint under the lip of each cushion.

Cornell and me, I should say. I kept up what I was doing too, which was sipping uncut whiskey straight from King Canada and waiting for a word of my own. If it was the wrong one, I figured I might come up against the two railbirds. They were Abe's boys, and Abe was boss of the Purple Gang, and if I caught a break tonight the Purples were going to be out a lot of money.

Four guys came in, raccoon-coat types who might as well have carried a sign saying Slumming College Boys. One split off for the bar while the other three sifted through the house cues that lined the wall between Barney's perch and the three-cushion table. Nobody looked at them except me and maybe Barney, who betrayed his interest by crossing his left leg over his right, uncovering an inch of hairless calf between black silk sock and black trouser cuff.

"Whew! You see those lights?" the college kid at the bar said. "Someone's out there flying in this crazy weather."

Gunter behind the bar drew beer and called out to Cornell. "Rack up number three." Cornell left off his brushing and went to number three. There was no wasted motion about Cornell; he had the balls out and racked in the time it took me to get my pipe going, and they were as centered and level as if he'd used a chalk string and a square.

He was on his way back to the three-cushion table when Joe College with the beer said, "Why don't you brush this one, too?"

Cornell stopped and turned around. "Nobody's played it since I brushed it last."

"Well, brush it again, boy. This table looks like it's felted with pocket lint." The four of them laughed. I wondered if they knew what kind of place they were in. Gunter had no undue love for the colored man, but Cornell had been working for him since he'd opened the place in 1898.

Cornell looked toward the bar, and Gunter shrugged. "Do the college boys a favor, Cornell."

So Cornell went and took his perfect rack apart with the same fluidity and grace he'd displayed putting it together, and then he brushed the table until if it was a horse it would have fallen asleep. I thought that one of the college boys was going to say something else to him, but they had enough sense to know better. The little drama caught the attention of the two Purples, and as Cornell was mortaring together another rack one of them—a boy of about nineteen called Nate Cooley—said, "After all you put Cornell through, I hope you boys can play."

That caught their attention. "What's your name?" asked the one who'd bothered Cornell.

Nate identified himself, and the college boy said, "My name's William Jorgensen. You let me roll some balls around, Nate, and then how about we play a game?"

"You let me know, William," Nate answered, putting a little twist on the name. Then he went back to watching Rudy and Phil, both of whom might have liked to put their money up against William Jorgensen's but neither of whom were dumb enough to get competitive with a Purple. Rudy and Phil were automobile mechanics who did most of their business on cars shot up or otherwise marred by Purple business. They knew what went on.

I did too, which was why I was keeping quiet, up toward the front of the bar away from Nate and his comrade-in-arms Lester Greenbaum. Should only be an hour or so, I thought, before word comes down about the night's work. Until then I could let this little drama take my mind off things.

I should clarify some things here. My name's Ferris Terwilliger. I'm a cop. My beat is the area around Third and Fort, near the old Union Depot. I spend most of my time rousting drunks out of the station, and not much else goes on there except barrels of Volstead nectar being rolled down into the basement of a foundry on Fourth, and then rolled out again after the fellows in the basement cut it. I take ten dollars a week for making sure that the attentions of the Detroit Police Department are focused elsewhere while the barrels are rolling. I'm doing everyone a favor; people get their booze and there won't be any gunplay on my beat.

The liquor comes across the Detroit River from a fellow named King Canada. He has boys to row it across, or drive it across when the river freezes, and the Purples pick it up on the bank down toward Dearborn or even Romulus before trucking it down to Toledo or up to the foundry or the half-dozen other neighborhood hidey-holes they keep around town. The King also flies booze to Chicago for Al Capone, and that's what I was waiting to hear about.

I knew it was going to snow, and I knew that the King usually sent the Chicago plane at about ten o'clock so it arrived well after midnight. Capone had once thought about muscling into the Detroit rackets, but the Purples were so mean he had second thoughts. And he didn't trust Abe's boys to let truckloads of whiskey drive unmolested down Michigan Avenue toward Illinois, so he paid the King to fly the juice. The Purples knew this, and during my many nights in the Bavaria I'd heard them chew over the idea of taking off one of the planes if weather ever brought one down on their side of the river.

This is where it gets complicated. See, I knew what the Purples wanted to do, and the Purples had not long before rubbed out a guy I knew, a cop named Vivian Welsh. Vivian was in their pockets too, and made the mistake of trying to work a little protection racket on his own. They didn't like it, so they took him for a ride.

There wasn't much I could do about it, since if I rolled on the Purples they'd give me the same treatment. Still, I felt a need to take something from them even if they didn't know it was me who had done it. So I started talking in what you might call a low voice to some other cops I knew to be in my situation, and once we'd gotten four guys other than me together, we decided that if one of King Canada's planes came down in the neighborhood we'd be there when the Purples tried to annex the cargo. We knew some guys in Cleveland who would take the proceeds off our hands, and that would be that.

My only regret was that I couldn't be there because it was Thursday, and if I didn't show up at the Bavaria on Thursday to collect my sawbuck things would have seemed unusual. So when the weather got threatening and Abe's brother Joel made the call, I stepped out for a sandwich and made a call of my own on the way back.

What Joel said to King Canada was that the Purples would keep an eye on the plane if it had to set down at this particular airport down in Flat Rock.

What King Canada figured, or what I figure he figured, was that it was more in the nature of a suggestion than a hypothetical offer, and that if something was going to happen he was willing to go along if it led to open war between the Purples and Capone. That way the King would only have one guy to deal with from Detroit all the way to Chicago. It would simplify things. He also had to worry that if he didn't see the wisdom of cutting his flight short in such weather, he wouldn't be able to count on his trucks and boats making it across the river.

So what King Canada said was that he was going to send the plane if it could take off, and if it had to land because of weather, and the strip in Flat Rock was the closest place to land, well, that was an act of God. Wasn't it.

What I said when I called my boys was: Tonight.

When William the college boy talked about lights in the sky, I got a sinking feeling, but a peek out the door told me all I needed to know. No way was a plane flying in that. Young William had tippled a little too much before finding his way to the foot of Riopelle Street, behind the old Michigan Stove Company where speedboats came in under the pilings on summer nights.

I put it out of my mind and watched the next act of the little drama unfold.

It turned out that William knew his way around a pool table, and once he'd had a couple of frames to get loose he gave Nate Cooley the serious business. Nate couldn't back down because he'd asked for the game to begin with. All he could do was play and lose and look for a reason to dent William Jorgensen's skull with the butt of the .38 he carried in a tailored coat pocket.

And as they played, Barney Steeple leaned forward just a little more.

After he'd lost three games of fifty-point straight pool, Nate changed the game to nine-ball, which any self-respecting billiard player regards the way a big-league ballplayer considers fungo. William went with it, and beat Nate anyway, and things were just about to get ugly when Barney Steeple's feet hit the floor and his wheezy voice carried across the room to William.

"You care to play someone who knows a pool cue from a chopper?" he asked.

Nate Cooley froze in the act of chalking his cue, and even the unflappable Cornell, who had been born an Alabama slave and had seen more in his thirty years at the Bavaria than I'd seen in twenty years of policing Third and Fort, paused as he racked the balls for the next game. Maybe that was just because he didn't know whether he should be laying nine balls or fifteen. I get the feeling, though, that he was looking at Nate out of the corner of his eye and judging whether he should hit the floor.

The only people in the place who weren't worried were me and Barney, me because I knew I could take Nate Cooley before he got his shooter out of his coat and Barney because he was the only man I've ever known who honestly believed he couldn't die. When you can shoot pool like Barney, it's a natural assumption.

I never did find out what would happen because right then Killer Burke and Mickey Kreble walked in. They shook the snow off their coats and Burke said, "There's crazy lights in the sky. My uncle was in the merchant marine, he used to talk about St. Elmo's fire. All he could talk about once he got old. Must be some kind of lightning, because I don't think anyone is flying tonight. King Canada sure ain't."

I kept quiet, but he looked at me anyway, with Mickey behind him and a little off to his left.

"Something tells me you know a little about that, Ferris."

"Beg your pardon?" I said. Politeness is a curse I inherited from my mother.

I'd played it the best I could. From my seat at the bar, Nate and Lester would only have half of me to shoot at. The door wasn't too far away. And if I could take out the Killer, there was a small chance that Mickey wouldn't shoot.

"Reason I bring it up is that we just cooled off two cops down in Flat Rock," Burke said. "Normally that's a pretty good night, but the other two got away."

Which two, I wondered.

"Cat got your tongue, Ferris?" Mickey prompted.

"You haven't told me everything, Killer," I said evenly. "You killed two cops at the field, that's all I know. And Capone won't be getting his juice tonight. How does that lead to Mickey there waiting with his hand in his pocket?"

"Well, let me see how I can make it clear to you." Burke made a great show of thinking. He pushed his hat high up on his forehead so he could scratch at the exposed scalp; he twirled the swizzle stick in the drink Gunter put in front of him; he rubbed at his five o'clock shadow. When he'd gotten it all arranged to his satisfaction, which meant that Rudy and Phil, Nate and Lester, the college boys, Barney, and even Cornell were watching, he said, "I think I got it. You know we've been thinking about King Canada's planes. You were here when Joel made the call tonight. And when the plane came down, there just happened to be a jazz quartet in blue waiting for us. Waiting, Ferris."

Nate and Lester had moved away from the pool tables as Burke spoke, lining themselves up in case the conversation got adversarial. Nothing like a little shooting to liven up a snowy night, and they'd missed the fun out in Flat Rock. Willie Jorgensen and his buddies looked like kids on a pond who have just heard the ice start to boom under them. They were my wild card. Burke would have second thoughts about ventilating me with that many witnesses, and I didn't think he'd do all of them just to get me right then.

But I couldn't be sure. Truth was, I was playing for five lives.

"Sounds to me like King Canada might have made a call of his own," I said.

Which could have been true.

Burke looked terribly disappointed. "That's beneath you, Ferris. Trying to shift the blame like that. I had you pegged for a standup guy considering you're on the take. Now I got to reassess everything."

I wanted to ask whether the surviving cops had gotten away with the booze. If they had, and I survived, it would be a nice payday. Plus it would have been a useful bit of insight into exactly what Burke was assessing. If he had the booze, he was just trying to sniff out a rat. If he didn't, he was trying to sniff out a rat and figure how to explain to Abe how the job had ended up with dead cops. Too many variables.

So what I said was, "How stupid do I look to you, Killer? If I was going to take off a load of hooch, why wouldn't I wait until you only had the two guys in the truck out back of the foundry? If you and Capone get shooting, that just makes more trouble for us, and believe me, we don't need any more trouble. Me in particular—if Capone's boys move in, where's my saw?"

"I get it," Burke said. "You don't bite the hand that feeds you. That about the size of it?"

"Common sense," I said, even though I knew he wasn't buying it. The tone of his voice, the theatrical consideration, told me I was going to die.

Just then a kid blew through the door shaking off his tweed cap. "Say, I've heard that people play some pool in here!" he said in a voice that was pure Oklahoma. He was a big, good-looking kid with his story written all over him: farmboy come to Detroit to work for Henry Ford's dollar an hour after watching Daddy's spread dry up and blow away. He'd probably been shooting pool with his buddies down by the Podunk train depot while his old man signed the foreclosure papers, and now he was in the big city full of piss and vinegar, his first paycheck burning a hole in his pocket. I wanted to tell him to hit the bricks before he woke up tomorrow with knots in his head and nothing in his pocket but lint.

"Beat it, hayseed," Mickey said.

The kid looked at him with a big grin on his face. "Don't believe I will, sir. I've been hearing about big city pool shooters since I was a boy, and I reckon it's about time I found out for myself."

Mickey looked at Burke for a cue, but before anybody could say anything the door marked MANAGER clicked open and Abe Bernstein himself stepped out.

"You might be in luck, kid," he said. "As it happens, we've been talking business and I think maybe we could use a break to consider our positions." He produced a roll from his pocket and peeled off a hundred-dollar bill. "I'll back you the first game. Rudy, why don't you play the shitkicker? No disrespect intended, kid. You have kicked shit, right?"

"You bet I have," the kid said. "Only way to get my little brother out of the way sometimes."

Abe laughed. "Cornell. Set up Number One."

I let myself look relieved. Hell, who wouldn't be when a shitkicking angel from Oklahoma had just stopped the countdown on his life? Now I had the amount of time it took for Abe to get bored, and maybe that would be enough.

Cornell set the table and melted into the shadows near Barney. "Break 'em up, kid," Abe said. He'd settled at a booth between the bar and the first row of tables, including Number One, which was a beautiful nine-foot Brunswick with felt like fuzzy emeralds and pockets about as loose as a nun's hip sockets. Number One was center stage in the Bavaria, the big-money table, the only table that would draw Barney Steeple out of his corner.

"Aw, c'mon, I'm the new guy here. Don't seem right I should break right off the bat," the kid said.

Abe shrugged. "Rudy, break 'em. Gunter, get the kid a drink. And boys, my bet's getting lonely."

Phil knew his role. He put twenty down against Abe's hundred, and then Nate and Lester—who would bet on the sun setting in the west—

added something to Rudy's pile, and then one of College Willie's friends surprised me by putting twenty of his own on the Okie.

"Killer, Mickey, Ferris," Abe said. "Get a piece."

Burke shot me a glance full of murder. I shouldn't have, but I winked at him even as I was thinking about the two of my fellow cops he'd killed. I put down ten bucks on the kid. What the hell, it was bad money anyway. Abe pointed at the table when I put my money down, and I sat across from him. Burke and Mickey put fifty each on Rudy, and then we all let King Canada and dead cops and Al Capone drift out of our minds.

The game was straight pool, to fifty. A good quick game if the hands on the sticks are any good, but Rudy wasn't. His fingers were too busted up from turning wrenches, not to mention the prizefighting he'd done when he was younger. He broke, and it wasn't a bad break, the rack still pretty tight and only the left corner ball, the six, sprung loose with the cue all the way back down the table. The Okie kid picked up a cue without looking at it, scrubbed chalk on the end, and crushed the six into the corner with just a little English to hook the cue into the rack. I felt Barney move in his lair, and part of him came into view: a single pudgy hand finding the ashtray on its stand by his chair. Barney smoked when he thought about playing.

Rudy did what he could, but the kid chased him right off the table. He didn't play a great defensive game, but he could make shots, no doubt about it, and against Rudy that was enough. Shot-making, though, Barney was fond of saying when he was cleaning out the latest hotshot who'd heard about Riopelle Street, was the mark of the good second-rate player. Dodge Main and Rouge Steel were full of people who could make shots.

Abe watched with an expression on his face like a guy sitting through a mildly amusing picture with his girlfriend because he knows if he does she'll think better of him later in the evening. The look said *I don't mind this so much, but wait till later, that's when things get interesting.*

When the Okie had dropped number fifty, on a thin cut all the way across the table into a side pocket, Abe counted out the piles. I got my saw back plus another. "You bet on the kid because I did?" Abe asked. Cornell was already gathering the balls.

I shrugged. "Nah. I know how Rudy shoots, and figured I'd rather lose ten on an unknown."

"That's a good instinct. Sometimes." Abe's hundred was still on the table. "You gonna stay with him now?"

"He was good to me the first time."

"Yeah. Lester, you wanna play this kid?"

Lester didn't, but he'd burned up all of his brain cells trying to figure out why Abe wanted me sitting next to him. Was it a gesture of support, or was Abe just waiting for the right moment to take care of me himself? A question like that could keep a guy like Lester working for days.

Me, I guess I'm smart enough not to worry about where the bullet's going to come from once I know it's coming.

"You see that lightning tonight?" the kid said. "Man, is it something."

"It don't lightning when there's snow," Nate said.

"Well, it is tonight," the kid said. "Like I never saw before. Flashes, big balls, the works." He grinned at Nate. "Lightning strikes where you don't expect."

"Ain't that the truth," Burke said. "I would of thought there was airplanes out tonight. If Ferris and I didn't know better."

"Cut it out," Abe said. "Cornell, rack the balls."

Cornell had uncharacteristically paused in his ritual. He was looking at the Okie kid. At Abe's word, he got to it.

Lester broke badly enough that the Okie ran him right out. Fifty balls; not a bad run by any standard, and certainly more than Lester could handle. He pocketed balls as fast as Cornell could rack them, and he was lining up to shoot the fifty-first when Abe said, "Take it easy, kid. You won."

The kid straightened up. "I did? Well, shut my mouth. I lost count."

Lester didn't much like that, and neither did Nate, but Abe did. Abe liked it a lot. He laughed until everyone else joined in, even Barney. I wouldn't be surprised if Cornell cracked a smile just to be prudent.

"Hey, college boy. William," Abe said. "You and your friends want to get behind the Okie again?"

The college boys had shrunk back against the wall, leaning their cues against a bar stool and trying to make themselves inconspicuous. "Don't believe we do," William said.

"Okay. See you later," Abe said.

It took William a minute to catch up, but pretty soon he and his fraternity brothers had their raccoon coats on and were headed out the door. I was surprised they hadn't all rabbited when it looked like there might be shooting—but young William might have taken the situation to be something other than what it was. Any idiot out on a night like that one can't be credited with great observational skills.

"Now it's just us chickens," Abe said. Mickey started to laugh, figuring this was another cue, but nobody picked it up. He stopped and looked at his feet.

"Boys, we got an issue to decide. If I know King Canada, he's already talked to that wop Capone, who will be wondering what has happened to his goods. Maybe King Canada has suggested that the Purples took him off. If so, that greasy bastard will probably send a message our way.

If he does, we will send one back, and then things will be as they were, because Al Capone is a pantywaist wop in spats who fears us."

That last bit was true. I wasn't sure about the rest of it. I figured the King would be sitting tight until whatever dust the night's events had raised settled and he could see clearly again from over in Ontario.

"Whereas I am the meanest Jew in Detroit," Abe said, "and I am not afraid to kill a cop."

This was also true. Vivian Welsh had proven that.

Abe was looking at me, and I felt like I had to say something. So I said, "It's a good speech so far, Abe. Don't stop now."

For a minute there was dead silence. Then Abe winked at me and went on.

"I ain't afraid to kill a cop, but on the other hand I don't want to do it without reason. My boys killed two cops tonight, but I lost three boys, and Augie'll count four by morning. So the scales aren't even." He looked away from me. "Ferris here was in a position to know what was going to happen tonight. In other circumstances that would be reason enough to take action. On the other hand, I have no way of knowing that the boys in blue down in Flat Rock weren't just following the well-known gangster Killer Burke here, figuring he was up to some mischief, and then deciding to turn the situation to their advantage. It ain't outside the realm of possibility. But the fact is, I'm down four boys and a truckload of Capone's hooch. I gotta do something."

"Come off it, Abe," Burke said. "You know what you gotta do."

"Shut up, Killer. Cornell, rack Number One again. Brush it up first."

Cornell emerged from Barney's corner and began brushing. The evenness of his strokes calmed me a little.

There was a flash of light outside, bright as lightning. "See?" the Okie said. "I'll be damned if that ain't lightning."

"Kid," Abe said. "I'm going to ask you a serious question that's got nothing to do with lightning. Are you hustling?"

The silence that followed this question was as deep and tense as the pause when Abe had said he wasn't afraid to kill a cop. Meaning me. Lester had once cut the thumbs and pinkies off a pool hustler's hands on the dock behind the Bavaria. "There," he'd said when he was done. "A pool hustler ain't no better than a pigeon, and now you're a pigeon." I'd never pointed out to him that pigeons had four toes.

Lester liked to tell that story, and I guessed he was hoping for a reason to get his knife out tonight. The kid surprised us all, though. He looked Abe Bernstein right in the eye and said, "Mister, if you're calling me a hustler we're going to have to settle things."

Everyone lost their voices again. Then Cornell stood up from his brushing and said, "Son, that ain't a wise way to speak to Mister Abe Bernstein."

"Well, thank you, Grandpop," the kid said. "I never claimed to be wise."

Cornell racked the balls and walked up to the front of the bar.

"I'm gonna take that as a no, kid," Abe said. "What I was saying. Since I trust the Killer here, and I trust Ferris, I got to rely on instinct to tell me my direction here. And my instinct tells me to let you settle this."

"I didn't come here to settle anything," the kid said. "I came to shoot pool."

"That's what you're gonna do, is shoot. Here's the situation." Abe was speaking to all of us now. "The kid here shoots a good stick. Barney shoots a good stick. So the kid and Barney are going to shoot to find out if I have to shoot." He looked at me. "That seem fair to you, Ferris?"

Hell no, it wasn't fair. The kid was a good country pool player, better than I'd expected. But Barney played Cy Yellin on even terms. I'd seen the two of them playing to five hundred, all night long, and after that night Yellin had been back to Detroit half a dozen times, but he never came near the Bavaria again.

"Now wait a minute," the kid began. For the first time since he'd walked in, he seemed to realize where he was, and what was going on.

"Don't sweat it, kid," I said, and stuck my hand across the table. "You're dealing the cards, Abe."

We shook, and I got up to sit at the bar. Gunter brought me a schooner of beer. Burke and Mickey stared at me, but I didn't look back at them. I was giving the kid all my attention.

He saw me looking at him. It was the first time I made eye contact with the kid who was playing for my life, and he did something that flat astonished me. He winked at me, and he looked just like Abe doing it. You tell me how a nineteen-year-old farmboy can suddenly look like a Jewish gangster ten years older and half his size. I blinked, and the impression was gone. A trick of the light, I told myself, or your mind is saying uncle and everyone in the world is suddenly going to look like Abe Bernstein. God forbid. I nearly crossed myself even though I'd stamped the reflex out after quitting Most Holy in the tenth grade.

"Barney, come over here," Abe said. Barney did, and he and the kid lagged for the break. I was struck by the difference between them: the kid long and raw and vital, Barney fat and overdressed and marinated in his own ego. The balls both stopped an inch from the near rail, even enough that I couldn't tell the difference.

"Your call, kid," Barney said, in a tone of voice that made clear he didn't care who broke.

The kid squatted at the side of the table, one eye squinted shut. "Declare I can't tell a difference," he said. "Someone else look."

"Oh for the love of Christ," Abe said without a trace of irony. He got up and looked himself. "Hell with it," he said, standing up again. "Tie goes to the runner."

The kid and Barney looked at each other, and then Barney moved to a shooter's position and broke with a look on his face that said he was doing the kid a great favor even though the truth was just the opposite. His break popped one corner loose to bounce right back into the rest of the rack while the white ball came all the way back down the table.

"Just so I can remind myself," the kid said as he lined up his first shot, "what are we playing to?"

"What are they playing to, Ferris?" Abe grinned at me.

"Five hundred's a nice round number," I said. Long enough that one mistake wouldn't decide it, not so long that I'd come across like I was trying to postpone the inevitable. Nothing like the threat of death to make you consider the consequences of your actions.

"Five hundred it is," the kid said. "Four in the corner."

Crack! and the four jumped out of the rack and shot like an arrow into the pocket. Too hard, kid, I thought. Criminy, settle down a little.

The kid didn't have an ounce of settle in him, though. He hit every damn ball twice as hard as he needed to. A pure shotmaker, no sense of what he'd do on the next shot, except maybe a dim intuition that kept the cue out of the pockets. And nineteen balls in, even that failed him.

If all he could string together was nineteen, I was going to find myself in the river before I had time for another beer. I stood up and dropped my whole roll on Abe's table. "Kid's just getting warmed up," I said.

Lester laughed. "I always thought you was smart for a cop, Ferris." Smirking at me, he fanned five hundred dollars out next to my rumpled sixty.

"Sucker bet, Lester," Abe said. "Kid wins, Ferris has put up sixty to get five C's. Kid loses, doesn't matter what's in Ferris's pocket."

"You dumb gorilla," Burke added for emphasis. Me, I was wondering where a cheap trigger like Lester Greenbaum had laid hold of five hundred bucks. Cop instincts don't let up.

And meanwhile Barney Steeple was standing at the table with his lips pursed like Father Coughlin in a whorehouse. He looked at me as I went back to the bar, and I could tell that if he hadn't cared about the game before, he did now. The fat old spider in the corner wanted my juices now.

Which was fine. Barney's strength came from disdain. When he got mad, he forgot to be disdainful, and maybe I was playing dirty, but the

Marquess of Queensberry never had Abe Bernstein and the Purples to worry about.

Barney got even hotter when the lightning started up again. The Bavaria didn't have much in the way of windows, its main service being illegal and all, but whatever was going on in the sky lit the room up like flashbulbs.

"It don't lightning when there's snow out," Nate said again.

"Looks like it does, Professor," Lester snapped.

And all the while Barney stood there with his ears getting redder and redder.

"Shut up, the both of you," Abe said. "You're distracting Barney."

"The hell with Barney," Lester said. "What is he, an old woman, needs his peace and quiet to write poetry?"

"Lester." Abe was getting quieter as Lester got louder.

"All I'm saying is what the hell is it if it ain't lightning?"

Abe pinched the bridge of his nose. "Enough. Mickey."

At which Mickey shot Lester three times, right through the breadbasket.

"Gunter," Abe said. "Need Cornell to clean up a mess."

"Leave Cornell out of this, Abe."

Abe looked up at the ceiling. "Am I gonna get nothing but lip tonight? First the kid, then Lester, then Gunter. What have I done?" He waved at Mickey. "Okay then. Mickey, you made the mess. You clean it up."

Mickey got up and dragged Lester's body through the door marked MANAGER.

"We going to play pool any time soon?" Barney complained. All of a sudden I was worried. I had no idea what Abe would do if Barney just refused to play. He might decide to remove all of his irritants, including me and the kid. The last thing I needed was worries about the kid. He'd lipped himself into the situation.

"I was wondering the same thing," the kid said. Either he was the coldest farmboy I'd ever heard of, or his mouth was on automatic pilot from shock. I hoped for cold-blooded, then felt bad about hoping. Devil and the deep blue sea.

Barney shot the kid a poisonous glance, and then he bent to shoot.

Watching him, I started to wonder if I'd misjudged the situation. I'd been hoping to throw him off, but Barney played like he was divinely inspired against the flashbulb demons popping in the sky over Riopelle Street. The difference between Barney and the kid was that the kid shot pool to sink a ball, whereas for Barney the ball that went in the pocket was just something to bounce his cue ball off on its way to where he wanted it to go.

He ran off three hundred and ninety-six balls, and only missed when he spun the cue a little too heavy on a push down the rail and it ran away across the table, rattled in one of Number One's virgin-tight pockets, and fell.

"Holy Mother of God," Nate Cooley said. Barney had been shooting for seventy-eight minutes. Even if I live through the night, I thought, which isn't likely now, I'll never see anything else like that.

Barney went back to his corner and sat as Cornell got the cue from the pocket and spotted the ball Barney'd sunk on the foul. "Three ninety-six to nineteen ain't bad, kid," Barney said. "I've played lots of guys didn't get nineteen."

"Tell you what, fat boy, you're about to see more than nineteen," the kid said. He rolled the cue ball up to just shy of the second diamond, near the middle of the table, then looked like he was having second thoughts. "Ferris," he said. "What do you reckon I should do?"

I hated him for that. Hated him so much that I would have put a bullet in him just for rubbing my face in the fact that I'd put him in the situation, just as I'd put two of my fellow cops in the ground tonight by whispering about a plane that would be landing in Flat Rock.

Killer Burke leaned against me and said, "How you feeling, copper?" I smelled his cigar and wanted to stick it down his throat.

"Kid's got a trick up his sleeve yet," I said. Just words. I didn't believe it and neither did Burke.

"I like an optimist," he said, and left me alone to watch the kid bang away at the balls like his cue was a hammer and each ball was a nail in my coffin.

"You gonna give me some advice here, Ferris?" the kid prompted with a wink and a grin, and I not only hated him but was sure that he was in on the whole thing.

"You're a damn fool not to shoot the seven," I snarled, even though the seven was frozen on the far rail and I was taking up the hammer myself.

Abe burst out laughing. "Play nice, boys," he said, and added, "Kid, you make that seven I'll give you a hundred bucks."

"How many rails?" the kid asked.

Now everyone laughed except me. "Four," Abe said, and raised a C. "Let's see it."

"It's a tough shot, Mr. Bernstein," the kid said. I almost killed him. This was my life. Maybe I was just a cop on the Purples' take, but it was my life.

He didn't even move the ball, which was perfect to roll the thirteen in the side with good shapes on the last four and the rack beyond, but ridiculous for the seven. Four rails meant a backcut on a frozen ball that would straighten itself out coming off the rail and not have a snowball's chance in hell of wrapping the table to come back to the far corner.

The kid lined up, winked at me again, and shot—and I felt a crazy glimmer of hope when the seven ball shot off the far rail, hit left and near and right and plunked into the corner. He never even looked at Abe or the C; he just glanced over his shoulder and said, "You ought to try that shot sometime, Barney. It ain't easy, but it sure feels good when you make it."

And then he sank four hundred and eighty balls to save my life.

It took Barney seventy-eight minutes for his three hundred and ninety-six. The kid did four-eighty in an hour flat. Eight balls a minute, and that's averaging in the time it took Cornell to rack every time the kid got to the last of each. He talked the whole time—"Hoo, Barney, you see that?" he'd crow, or "Mr. Bernstein, how about another C for three rails into the twelve-four?"—and during the last rack a kind of paralysis descended on the Bavaria. Even Gunter and Cornell watched, and both of them hated billiards.

Me, I aged a hundred years with the ten balls of that last rack. Every shot lives in my mind like the first man I ever killed: eleven in the corner with a sharp kick off the side rail to loosen the rack, then the eight, five, and fifteen in the same corner, then the ten caromed off the seven into a side, then the seven in the same side, then the one and three into the near left corner with an inhuman draw from the three back to drop the twelve and fourteen in the far right corner. And then the kid stopped and said, "That's five hundred, ain't it?"

Four hundred and eighty balls, with a man's life on the line, and this kid was joking at the end like it was nickel-a-ball at the student union against Raccoon-Coat William. He'd saved my life, and I wanted to kill him.

The lights outside flashed without thunder. I stood, and couldn't decide whether I really thought I was going to live. As a test I said, "Lester doesn't need his five C's any more, does he?"

"No, he doesn't," Abe said. "You'd be a hard copper not to cut the kid in, though."

"Kid gets it all," I said. I took the whole roll, five hundred and sixty dollars, nearly four months' working wages at River Rouge, and held it out to the kid.

He turned it down. "I got my hundred from Mr. Bernstein, Ferris. What else does a country boy need?"

I shook his hand and turned to leave, and that's when I noticed that both Burke and Mickey had their guns pointed in my direction.

"Wait," I said. "You called the game, Abe."

"I also asked the kid if he was hustling," Abe said, with what passed for a regretful smile on his face. "Wish you hadn't lied to me, kid."

Behind the door marked MANAGER was a folding table with six chairs around it. Cards, chips, and empty glasses littered its surface. With Abe leading the way and Burke and Mickey bringing up the rear, we all went out the back door onto the dock behind the Bavaria. There wasn't much wind, and the snow had stopped, but it was cold as hell. The river looked to be frozen all the way to Windsor except dark spaces down-stream of the Ambassador Bridge's pilings.

Under that dock was a door that led into a basement under the Bavaria. The Purples moved a lot of traffic through that door, both human and liquid. In summer, a rowboat bumped against the dock posts; in winter Abe kept a nondescript Olds down there in case something had to be moved without much notice. I wondered if I'd be taking a ride in that car the way Vivian Welsh had.

"I guess I don't understand," the kid said when we were all outside. The strange lightning was still flickering in the clouds. "I didn't hustle anybody. I just played pool."

"Whatever, kid," Abe said. "It's a shame Lester isn't around, but I guess Nate can stand in for him. Right, Nate?"

"You bet, Abe," Nate said. He walked over to where Lester's body lay at the edge of the dock and squatted. When he stood again, he had Lester's knife. The kid watched him, still with that smile that I was deciding must mean he was retarded, and Mickey smacked him across the cheekbone with the barrel of his .45. The kid went down like a sledgehammered steer, and Mickey kneeled on his back while Nate sawed the thumbs and pinkies from both his hands.

It takes longer than you'd think to cut off a finger. Even if you find the joint and get some weight on your blade, there's always a little flap of skin or gristle that slows you down. The kid never made a sound while Nate worked; he lay with his face in the snow, and I watched knowing that I had done this. Just like I'd left two cops cooling in the snow down in Flat Rock, I'd put this kid from Oklahoma or wherever face-down on a Detroit River dock while a crazy Purple Gang hood carved away the digits that separated him from the animals.

When it was done, Nate bunched the fingers and thumbs in his hand and dropped them next to the kid's head. "I feel bad about this, Ferris," Abe said, "but it ain't fair that the kid was a ringer."

"You dealt," I said. I wasn't sure whether I was resigned or still arguing.

"I gave you a chance. The kid queered the deal. It ain't your fault." Which was what passed with Abe for sympathy.

Lights flashed in the sky. "That ain't lightning," Nate said.

"For the love of Mike, Nate," I said, "put a cork in it."

"No, he's right."

We all looked down, because it was the kid who had spoken. He'd gotten up to his hands and knees, face caked with snow that started to slide off as he stood and looked at his mutilated hands. There was blood on his face where Mickey had cracked him, and more leaking from the stumps of his amputated fingers.

Until it stopped. He rubbed a sleeve of his denim shirt across his face, and when the sleeve had passed, he'd wiped the gash from his face along with the blood and melting snow.

A flare from the clouds overhead made us all flinch. When I looked at the kid again, he was holding his hands up for all of us to see.

There were tiny buds of flesh at the knuckles of his missing fingers. The lights flashed again, and he wiggled the soft pink digits that were growing to replace those in the snow at his feet. Like baby's fingers, with little specks of nail at the tips.

All the while he had his farmboy grin splitting his face, and I started to realize just how we'd all been hustled.

Another flash faded from my eyes, and the kid stood in the alley with perfect five-fingered hands. He winked again, not just for me this time.

"There's a new game in town, boys," he said against a background of lightning that wasn't lightning at all. "Mr. Bernstein, I hope I can trust you to spread the word. I'll see you around."

And he went back into the Bavaria, shutting the door gently behind him, leaving four gangsters and a crooked cop and a body cooling on the corner of the dock over the frozen river.

And four fingers in small oblong haloes of melted snow.

Okay, so I don't know how to go tandem on a long board and all I did on the shores of Malibu when I visited there sixteen years ago, was, well, not surf. And maybe the Gidget flickering in my memory—like a golden but oh yeah—bitchen—eternal flame originated in an old black and white telecast and did not derive from a cool lifestyle as some Great Kahoona's babe. I can still dream though and that may very well be what this story is all about—that and the weird space adventures I used to make my Barbies star in, inspired by old *Superman* and *Lois Lane* comics as well as far too many wonderfully bad SF movies, *Twilight Zone* and *Outer Limits* episodes.

In researching this, I read many magazines of the period; the original *Gidget* by Frederick Kohner and *Cher Papa,* its sequel; *The Real Gidget* by Deanne Stillman in the very fine *Surf Culture: The Art History of Surfing* and other related material. I also watched and rewatched, with delicious nostalgia, a color copy of the fab film a friend found for me. I'd forgotten that Moondoggie actually sang to Gidget! And what a hottie Cliff Robertson was! And yeah, my sister Melody and I used to jump up and down on our beds re-enacting the surfing-on-the-bed scene until our Mother would scream!

Dig it—deeply, madly, truly—Sandra Dee was a childhood idol I never outgrew although technically she was more of my sisters'π eras—my oldest Michele's young adult period and Melody's pre-teen era, not my childhood's. But little sisters tend to like whatever their big sisters like and we all worshipped Sandra Dee, the neatest actress alive and saw all of her movies. I think Melody and I saw *Gidget* in a double feature with one of the subsequent and inferior GIDGET sequels in the early sixties, but I'm not certain. I do know we were captivated by the

California mystique complete with say, the Beach Boys' *Pet Sounds* playing in the background. Growing up in landlocked central Texas, we dreamed we could become the Malibu Barbies—tanned, blonde and sexy that we read about in *Teen* and *Seventeen*—you know—"making California dreaming a reality" á la the Mamas and the Papas? At the very least we could own a swimming pool. As an adult, luckily, Melody did have a home for awhile with a swimming pool and she traveled to Hawaii and California more than once but I don't think she ever tried out a surf board and although I don't even have a goldfish pond…I continue to lust after guys who remind me of James Darren or Cliff Robertson and can play the bongo drums. If they happen to be from California, so much the better, but I've never learned to surf (I can hardly swim); I have at least seen Malibu but haven't made it to Hawaii yet.

And I still love Gidget, her boundless enthusiasm, her spunk and goofy innocence that's also oddly wise. And as timeless as Sandra Dee who died in 2005. I dream of riding the Ultimate Wave. As for Melody, I can pretend she's doing just that or reading this story on a gorgeous beach in a heavenly version of Maui since she died in November, 2003 . I like to think she's as eternal as the Great Ocean God. And Gidget, that timeless late fifties' icon? She'd probably just say…"Shoot the curl! Let's ride!"

—*Melissa Mia Hall*

Alien Love at Zero Break

Melissa Mia Hall

"Shoot it!" That's what I yelled the day I did my first standing island on my twenty-five-foot-long board made of balsa and fiberglass. Just like Gidget, I shot out on a wave that blasted in all the way from outer space like a rocket ship from another planet, and then, wow, I humped that bitchen wave all the way back again, me, just sixteen, a green Telifornian (Texan plus Californian equals Telifornian). Okay, so maybe the boomer wasn't a twenty-foot-high wave rolling in from Makaha or Nanakuli and it was definitely not the Zero break that stole my virtue and made me learn there's a cost for taking the Ultimate Ride. But it was then I decided to go all the way by the end of the summer. I had to find out about the end of the whole blast.

But that would come later at Zero break in Malibu and that's what this true confession is all about—the Ultimate Ride I had to make in order to become a woman. Truth? There are consequences. I have to let other girls know, that there's a price, come hell or low tide.

I wanted to be Gidget in the worst way (or Sandra Dee—back then the two were pretty much the same) not just because I wanted a Moondoggie/James Darren (he's the creamiest) or a Great Kahoona/Cliff Robertson (he's the dreamiest) in my life to take me away on their long boards to discover the Ultimate Big Wave, the one that takes you into the Milky Way or what my dad, who loves to study world religions, would call Nirvana or a Zen state, and my mom, Inez, would call Pure-D-Heaven, a kind of down-to-earth Texas-sized Christian Holy Roller state in which everything is perfect but you also get to whoop, holler, speak in tongues and maybe drink a vodka martini with lots of green olives or a margarita with salt on the rim while square dancing or doing the cha cha cha. I know I was a little young to be so preoccupied with losing my virginity (my mother didn't lose hers until she was twenty-six and it was to my dad on their honeymoon) or being the best surfer girl since Gidget but we had just moved to California from Texas and all the California (mostly Breck models with perfect hair and Ipana-white teeth) girls in my school had me convinced that it was the only way I could be truly popular although you had to never let on once the deed was done, you could only hint at it because if anyone found out you'd be dirty or considered white trash and therefore unacceptable for proper society and just forget about getting a decent date for any respectable prom or garden party.

As for surfing the waves off Malibu Point? That just seemed my idea of sheer heaven, not to mention the second I saw the oodles of good-looking guys unloading their boards on my first trip to the beach. I just knew it would be the place where I could learn to use my wings or at the least learn how to go tandem on a long board. Okay, so I'm pushing it. I'd read the book. I'd seen the movie. Now I was ready to live my dream.

One of them had a bleached crewcut. I remember tugging at the pink and orange straps of my Catalina swimsuit and he winked at me while goose pimples popped out on my white virginal flesh and I began thinking about getting my own surfboard and riding beside him, his tan back rippling with muscle or, even better, with him, sharing his board while his body behind me was close so I could feel the bulge of his tight swim trunks. And then I saw a built, tall, dark boy with a wiry build, with flashing brown eyes and a profile like a Greek God's or Gary Grant's. At first, I couldn't move. It took awhile for me to get up the nerve to mix in with strange boys despite my Goal to Become a Real Woman.

It's not like I'm an ice princess, or a Fridget. Dog Boy (the blond with the crewcut) invented that term— He's a poet and boy, does he know it. He got it from goofing with these creative if not original word combinations: freak plus creep equals freep; girl plus midget equals gidget; freep plus gidget equals fridget! Dog Boy is a surf-rider who chases the fabled wetbacks past surf-line around Malibu Pier. He's called Dog Boy because his paddling looks distinctly doggish and no way could he shoot the curl of a Zero break. And he named his board "Lassie." He met the real Gidget last year. Her real name is Kathy or Kara and hey, maybe I've even seen her a couple times. One time Dog Boy pointed her out to me and she waved at us. If that was her and she looked a bit like the photographs I've seen—she is dark, short and tiny, really cute. Not a blonde star like Sandra Dee who's sort of like a blonde Elizabeth Taylor and began modeling at twelve. In two years she's made seven pictures! I read in *Coronet* that she makes $1000 a week and owns a Thunderbird. Can you imagine? That real Gidget, though, wow, she can ride those waves and I don't think Sandra can and the real Gidget has a boyfriend who's a dreamboat. I don't know if it's really that Jeff guy, the real Moondoggie. And I got the impression Sandra doesn't have a boyfriend. Isn't that sad?

I'm not as little as the real Gidget or the fab Sandra who weighs a mere ninety-nine pounds, although I do make an effort to drink Fizzles instead of Cokes, skim instead of whole milk and eat D-zerta puddings instead of Jell-O because I am determined to not get too heavy. Only now I've avoided my topic, as my English teacher Mr. Boone might say.

Dig it; I can cut the mustard. I'm not talking about making out in drive-in movies. This is beyond that. I had no idea that when I did let some guy on the make take me to the moon that it would be a wild surf-ride with (oh, this is so hard) a space monster!

Now, I must tell you more about Zero break so don't get your panties in a wad. I first read about that in the copy of *Gidget* by Frederick Kohner that Mom bought me before we moved here to L.A. so Dad could pursue his big dream of writing for Television. He used to work for an ad agency in Fort Worth but he has an uncle (Ken "Ace" Lowe) who works for Universal. He said he could get him a job even though he was in Accounting and it took my dad, Clarence "King" Lowe (they play poker a lot) about five years before he really believed him. And he did. He writes toothpaste jingles while he tries to get into writing all the witty words for game shows like "What's My Line?" or talk shows like Carson's but he really wants to write Audrey Hepburn movies. He met Mel Ferrer once at an espresso cafe. He just might do it but he says *Green Mansions* is a sink-hole mess, having scored a copy of the script from an agent buddy. It was not *Funny Face* (I wish we could all dance like Fred Astaire) or *Love in the Afternoon*. (Was it my love for Gary Cooper that drew me to the Monster in the first place? I mean the older man thing—I thought he had to be 20 at least and Coop is really OLD, like maybe over 40?!) I still can't wait to see Audrey as Rima, the Bird Girl, though, and next to Sandra, she's my favorite actress in the whole wide world but back to what's really important. Chastity. Virginity. Monsters. Space. Sex.

Zero breaks usually occur only once a year when there's an earthquake (one of the things I hate about living here except Mom pointed out, in Texas tornadoes are almost as bad. I pointed out that tornado seasons don't last all year round!) or a huge ground disturbance under the sea. They are more likely, however, to occur during a storm surf. They're like H-bomb blasts that are supposed to only happen in the islands. They can be as high as thirty feet, coming in over 30-miles per hour. That's fast. So think about it. The chances of riding one of those without spilling? Get my drift?

Now here we go. I'm going to be straight with you. Summer of '59. August. Tell it like it is. School was out. I'd been doing the surf-riding

and the beachcombing bit with my friends, Debbie and Suz. They preferred pouring fancy Ban-de-Soleil on their bodies and "laying out" with
their portable transistor radios, flirting with the guys more into girls than
surf-riding, to swimming or anything remotely athletic. They had the
car, a jalopy with peeling seat leather and belching mufflers. Top down,
my board fit in fine. They didn't care what I did. I had a Junior Learner's
driver's license so I could drive when Debbie was having cramps during
her time of the month. Debbie, a neighbor and high school grad, was
eighteen and a lifetime resident of Southern California and both of her
parents worked for Warner Brothers. She loved teasing me about my
accent and was kind of like a jazzy big sis. She was going to move into a
dorm at USC in the fall and her boyfriend, Bob, who was studying to
become a doctor, had already given her his fraternity pin. Her hair shone
raven black while her olive skin really didn't need a lotion to glow.
Debbie Muscante was Italian-American. That day she brought a big red
beach ball. That was the thing back then. Toss the ball around and catch
a man.

Suz O'Connor, sixteen, was my best friend in California. She had
curly strawberry blonde hair and she had fair skin that freckled easily.
She was really smart. That morning:

"Can you imagine, my dad says the X-15 program is more than about
man's first flight into the unknown, it's the first step into the domination
of the universe by the white man. He says we're just looking for Indians
to run off. My dad says it's Outer Space Manifest Destiny at work. My
mother says that's ridiculous. She says he's just jealous of her brother
who's a test pilot and he's determined to go to the moon and probably
will. My dad says you couldn't pay him to go to the moon. 'What if it's
not made of cheese,' he says, 'I'd be devastated.' My dad's such a kidder.
I thought my mom was going to flip him the bone she got so irritated.
Just think. What would it be like to fly so fast you could get to the
moon?"

"Scott somebody. Isn't he neat? Like a football hero? Yeah, his name
is Scott—he's supposed to break some record in space my dad said,"
I said.

"Yeah. Do you think there's life on other planets? Do you think we'd
kill them off if we found any? Could there be life on the Moon, or say,
Mars, for instance?" Suz delicately applied some suntan lotion on the tip
of her nose.

"Look at that curl. The waves are bitchen today. The pull-out will
be the ultimate. That's the only life I'm interested in today!"

"Jeez Louise, Tammy Jo, is that all you think about? I think you're
taking this Gidget thing far too seriously," Debbie groaned.

"Forget space; forget waves! Getting a guy, now that's what matters!" Suz said, slamming the door as she got out of the car. Heat radiated off the hood and the summer bright sky. Suz crinkled her nose and winked at Debbie.

"Yeah, you've already got Bob," I mumbled.

"Love that Bob!" Suz laughed.

"Did you bring some Midol?" Debbie said, frowning into the cavernous depths of her straw beach bag.

"Don't tell me—"

"Rocketing five times at the speed of sound…cramp attack!" Debbie laughed.

"Lord, give me a spaceman."

"Lord, give me some Midol."

"You're not going to leak?" Suz whispered.

Debbie shook her head.

"Praise the Lord for small favors," I said.

We unloaded, me tugging at my long board, my friends not helping as per usual, Debbie more intent on her beach bag and checking for Midol and Suz checking her bag of peanut butter sandwiches ("Maybe just one bite?") and potato chips which we'd probably end up giving away to Dog Boy and Lord Plato so Debbie could buy burgers and Coca-Colas instead from the cute guy named Tab at the "greasy grub" joint off the Pier.

Boy, the surf was bitchen but the beach was already getting crowded. I left the girls quickly, heading for a cluster of surf bums, surf semi-bums and pretenders like myself. I wasn't the only girl. It wasn't like it is in the movies now. It was 1959 and more than one girl wanted to be Gidget. Most of them couldn't surf-ride. I could.

My board had been waxed right. I had actually taken some informal lessons from Dog Boy and Lord Plato who liked to pretend he was similar to the Great Kahoona of Legend but was just a college student with a talent for surf-riding. The rumor he'd lived in Hawaii fascinated me. Maybe he'd actually experienced the Zero break but I still hadn't found out. Dog Boy had said he had. So did surf buddies, Kelly, a tanned tomboy girl who showed up once in a while in her cutoffs and bikini top, her golden hair cut in a very short bob that looked a bit like an abbreviated Prince Valiant; and Cool B, an easy-going short guy who had a darn good build and a sweet smile. I have never found out what the "B" stood for and he didn't stick around Malibu; instead, he preferred the waves at San Onofre. He said his pull-outs were better there. Dog Boy said he was a faggot, a flit—a homo. That his lover lived there. I think Dog Boy was jealous of Cool B. And I think he was jealous of Lord Plato, too. What reasonable boy wouldn't be?

Lord Plato was lordly, all right, with muscles that rippled royally beneath his golden skin while his honey-brown eyes danced and his exotic ancestry and worldly air combined to just blast any normal red-blooded girl straight into orbit.

"They're doing it to me," he said that day as we slid on our boards to head out to surf ecstasy.

I dug my hands into the green foamy water and paddled out, acting like I didn't hear him. Sometimes Lord Plato made me nervous. Like the first "lesson" when he showed me how to find my balance. We'd done the tandem ride more than a few times that summer. That day I felt the same tingle.

"Hey, Tammy, did you hear me?" he yelled over the sound of screeching seagulls and the fizz of the waves.

I got on my knees and pushed my shoulders up and slid my body back. I had to concentrate or find my chi as Dog Boy would say when he was attempting to sound Chinese Wise. I pretended not to hear him or see him, but I could see that handsome Surf God shooting like a rocket beside me.

Almost in sync, we sprang to our feet and put them the perfect distance apart in one fluid motion. We shot the curl simultaneously.

"Yeah!" we said in unison.

"Shoot it, Tammy!"

"Shoot it, Lord Plato!"

"Olé!"

"Olé!"

Bitchen rocket bombs exploding!

Afterwards, sprawled side-by-side like beached dolphins, we smiled at each other and stretched out on the sand in post-ride-orgiastic bliss.

"Tam—did you not hear me? They're doing it to me!"

My toes dug into the sand. I tightened my pony tail. Cue the bongo drums. Lord Plato was always pontificating about something. "They're always doing it to me. I love it, boy, do I. These are the bitchenest waves in the entire world!"

"These are nothing. If you really want to catch a wave, you need to go to Hawaii."

"What are you talking about?"

Lord Plato shrugged. "The sun is so bright today. You know, Plato once said the sun is God's shadow. I wonder what the ocean is. His tears?" He could be so intelligent it was scary. I felt so small and humble in his orbit. "His bathtub?" He snorted with a horsey laugh. "Sorry." Well, maybe not that intelligent. I wondered what his real name was. He'd never told me. I'd known him for over two years. I met him last summer when I first moved to L.A. and began my Gidget Quest.

He did something surprising then. One of his hands touched the top of one of my thighs and then one finger trailed over to my inner thigh. I almost died.

"You know how you get beyond surf-line and you can't see anything but the water coming at you, a wall of waves, and you shoot toward the first set of incredible humpers and you stand and it's like you're saluting the water, rising up straight, proud…and you're lifted up and you want to say 'I am'—you know, just 'I am' like a friggin' Ocean God Almighty. You stand it, Tammy Jo—you stand it like a man and say, Olé!? Well, I say…I AM! It's like, well, a giant—" Lord Plato's finger suddenly pressed on my skin and trailed upwards until it stopped at the cuff of my Catalina.

A beach ball suddenly plopped in my lap. I jumped and looked around to spot Debbie waving.

"A giant what?" I breathed. The girls would get p.o.'d at me if I didn't hurry up. I got to my knees. The sand fleas were biting.

"You know what I mean. You're doing it to me, now. I am and you are—so—" He touched me again, fingers like butterfly wings. My skin blistered.

"What?" I said, flustered.

"Well, do you want to do it with me?"

A sly smile slid across his sexy lips.

I was so gone on him at that moment I was shocked. I knew what he was talking about! I might've been just sixteen but I had been kissed by Tommy Snow back in Fort Worth when I was just thirteen. I blushed. Sometimes a surf-ride can last two minutes. This moment seemed to last two hours, before I could open my mouth.

"You make me feel so jazzed up. I never saw you before like this, you're all grown up. I never realized, you're such a sweet piece of—" His words faded off and he smiled again, slowly. I still couldn't speak.

He must've broken up with his girlfriend, Jayne.

Me? Jazzed about me?

"You said 'they were doing it to me'—they what?" I felt a little dizzy. Maybe I was getting sunstroke.

He boldly looked down at the V of my swimsuit. I swear, he did. It's very rude for boys to do that. It wasn't as if I was wearing falsies but I had recently graduated to a C-cup. The red deepened on my cheeks as I noticed that the shelf bra inside my suit didn't hide the embarrassing natural points of my nipples standing at attention. I looked down and noticed something else—Lord Plato was also very alert. I was mortified. Why? Had I not set out that summer to become a woman? Had I not been thinking about it non-stop since Debbie confided in me that she really had loved her Bob in May after her Senior Prom? And yet, honestly, chastity was so important. Did I not want to wait until I was married? Sexual intercourse should be a way of expressing true love. I suddenly thought I should give myself only to someone I belonged to—like Ozzie belonged to Harriet? This boy was really a man, probably at least twenty, dangerous like Wyatt Earp.

"Want to go out tonight? I could pick you up at seven if you give me directions to your house?"

He didn't say, "If your parents will let you go out with me."

"I don't even know your real name."

"Jack Cortez," he muttered, his hands flipping through his shiny wet hair. It stood up like a soggy mass of brown kelp.

"That's not Hawaiian." Another pretender.

"I know," he said softly. "My grandmother's the real Hawaiian. But I really did live there for three years when I was little."

"Oh." I held the ball to my breast and squeezed it till it squeaked.

"So, you want to go out with me, or what?" Maybe I should've said 'or what' but instead, I nodded my head and we made the arrangements. I wondered if he should write down the directions to my house. But his dark eyes held mine like a kid's hand gripping the string of a balloon. Don't let go, I thought, chest thumping to beat the band. This is it, I thought, oh yeah, this is what it means to be falling in love. In love with Lord Plato, my surfing teacher? How did it happen so fast? Before, I never thought, well, he was dating that awful brunette who was supposed to be a model or a stripper. And now, he wanted to be with me! But I worried. Cortez. Was he from Mexico? I knew my mother came from El Paso originally and one time went out with a boy from Mexico City when she was growing up. We ate Mexican food all of the time. Mother's Green Enchiladas were really delicious. And her breakfast burritos were to die for. I frowned. Why should it matter? Riding the really big boomers, did I not often shout, "Olé?"

Dog Boy came up to me as I headed off to the car where the girls were waiting with hamburgers. We needed to eat on the run because it was getting late and Debbie's boyfriend was supposed to call.

"Are you really going out with him?"

Dog Boy's blond eyebrows arched. He grabbed my hand.

"Lord Plato's trouble for girls like you."

"What?"

"You're just a kid!" Dog Boy barked.

"Get your hands off of me!" I said.

"Just be careful—the tacos might be a little too hard to handle. You might break a tooth," he said, shaking his head.

Just a kid! "You're just jealous!" I laughed, then frowned. And mean.

He raised his hand in a careless wave but wouldn't turn to look at me. "Confirm or deny, you yellow-bellied sapsucker!" I hollered, dredging up the worst Texan insult I could, to no avail, as the Freep just kept going. Who was he to tell me who I could or couldn't go out with? You'd think he was Moondoggie and Lord Plato was the Great Kahoona. Goose bumps popped out on my flesh as I arrived for my burger and fries.

What if they got into a fight over me? This was turning out to be the most incredible summer of my life! I had no idea of what was to come.

My parents said I could go but I'd have to be back by eleven. When school started my curfew would go back to ten. They trusted me. And when he drove up in a Corvette with red leather upholstery, they trusted him. Why, I don't know. Movie dads take one look at a fancy car with a handsome guy in it picking up their daughters and say, "No way my baby is going out with some big operator like that. My baby is only sixteen!" But my dad was preoccupied with making some deal with a director or producer. When Jack came in to meet them, old King just nodded his head, sucked on his pipe and went back to his study and the telephone, leaving my mother, the gracious Inez, asking Jack if he wanted some iced tea and was his family any relation to the Cortez family in San Antonio, Texas? And she didn't even know anyone in San Antonio. She was just making polite small talk. Jack wore a white summer-weight sweater with a pair of tight jeans and the moment he flashed his white teeth in a five-star grin, shook his head and said, "No, thanks, ma'am," Mom was a goner. As for Nancy, she waved her new Barbie in his face, willing to give it to him if he just patted her on her head. And even Buddy wanted him to check out his latest science project involving hamsters and a wheel that wouldn't stop moving unless they performed some tricky maneuver with a bell he swiped from Nancy's parakeet, Bobbie Sue—Buddy's idea of mad fun which is a little odd, if you ask me. Thankfully, my date didn't have eyes for anyone but me and Jack took my hand and we went out into the velvet night. I wore a turquoise sundress and a white sweater piped in pale yellow stars. I touched the gold heart locket my parents had given me for my birthday for luck. Beneath the dress I wore my tight white swimsuit that reminded me sometimes of mother's favorite girdle, just in case we did some night swimming. Be prepared is my motto.

I clutched my wicker basket tote. He opened the car door for me. As I got in I caught a whiff of his aftershave, Canoe. He got in and we tore off in his rocket job. He had to have rich parents. A Corvette? I felt like a movie star. All my dreams were coming true.

We drove and drove. We parked. We made out to Fats Domino on the radio until I got all goosey inside and then suddenly we tore off in his fantastic car, covering the pavement like hot oil. Slipping and sliding down the road.

Hollywood is a fairy land. All the lights. Looking down from the hills it was like looking at Vincent van Gogh's *Starry Night* made Modern, you know? Then it's like we were one mind and all we could say was, "Let's shoot it."

So we drove down to the water. To Malibu. "We need boards," I said.
"We'll get 'em," he said.

We started peeling our clothes. He had on a bikini suit. It was white. We matched. I started getting hot but the night air had a very faint chill, like it knew August would soon be a memory even if a hot Santa Ana might blow in, shocking the fall, but right now, it was like a North East wind all the way from some place like Canada.

Dog Boy was there. He loaned us his board and Jack's. It was like he knew we were coming. Jack gave him some cash to skedaddle and when I think back, maybe he'd paid him for something else. I don't know. He whispered something to Jack and nodded towards me. Then he left.

"What was that about?" I asked Lord Plato—because when he stood there stroking his board, he was no longer Jack.

"Nothing." He looked at me directly. "Let's share. Let's go tandem." I nodded. Since I didn't have my own board, it seemed safer. It just goes to show you how a girl doesn't always know what that word means.

Riding tandem is delicious. I got on my stomach while Lord Plato became my Steersman. He was in control, behind me. I could almost feel his breath on my bare skin. I paddled out into the water, in rhythm with him. It was like we were rowing a boat together. When we got clear, Lord Plato got to his feet and then when it was just right, he told me to stand. The waves were perfect, like electrified glass and I leaned slightly forward and placed one of my feet (toenails painted coral) ahead of the other so I could balance and we didn't spill. Not that time.

Seaside, we rested. The beach seemed mysteriously quiet and empty. I could see only one figure in the distance, walking away from us, not toward us. The stars beamed down abnormally bright. The moon seemed so full it was about to explode. My swimsuit straps flopped down. I started to pull them up and Lord Plato said, "No, leave them."

"It's getting late."

"Let's do it again," Lord Plato said softly.

This time we paddled out but didn't immediately get on the board. He was on one side; I was on the other. We rested our arms on it, our hands reaching out toward each other. Suddenly he let go, went under;

when he came up, he held his trunks up. I went under and tugged off my suit, not knowing how I did such a wickedly wild thing. I bounced up. His mouth fell open. I don't know if it was in appreciation or shock.

Then the undersea disturbance began. Our eyes went wide.

"Jack!" I tried to pull my suit back on, got it up about half way. Lord Plato managed to put his back on and we got on the board.

"Earthquake?" Lord Plato managed.

I didn't know what to do but hold on to the long board. I was terrified. He was terrified.

So much for sexual intercourse.

"DUKE KAHANA MOKU!" Lord Plato shouted. "I am!"

Lord Plato liked to invoke surfing legends when he was excited. Underneath us the sea seemed illuminated by searchlights. My pink skin burned white-hot. Lord Plato grabbed me. "BALANCE!"

I had just wanted to become a woman. Not die!

Tremendous sea spray doused our heads.

"Can we make it back—" I spluttered. I just wanted to go home!

The waves began to break behind us. We twirled around like a top.

"Get on your knees, Tammy—"

Weight toward the rear of the board, we shot the nose over the wild foam. We propelled ourselves forward with amazing grace. HUGE WAVES. Beneath us yellow-green lights flashed, practically blinding us. A piercing buzz sounded, more than the usual roar we expected. Unearthly, creepy. I felt more than saw a round disc split the darkness and dancing stars seemed to whirl around it.

"Save me, Lord Plato!" The ride kept going past the three-minute best Lord Plato said he'd only experienced once, in Hawaii. I felt a whooshing, rushing thrill. This was the biggest wave of my life and Lord Plato and I were one with the sea and salt spray. This was the Ultimate Ride, beyond anything I could believe. "I am! I am!" we shouted and we merged as one person. This wasn't Tandem riding this was Riding as ONE person. Then suddenly I was jolted by the fury of the ZERO BREAK'S cruel lesson. IT HURTS to ride a wave that BIG!

Suddenly we wiped out—I clung to the board in splitting pain and Lord Plato pinned me to the board and I saw the TRUTH. I screamed. That strange something from undersea had vaulted into the night air above us, spinning around and around, illuminating Lord Plato with an ultraviolet ray! I looked into Lord Plato's face as another light, a sickly green one, revealed his true identity! He was a monster with an alien face complete with sea gills and horny rubbery obtrusions sticking out of his head. One pale silvery tentacle drooped from his nether regions. I had made out with a space monster who had pretended to be a surfer!

"I am!" it bellowed weirdly, that long pole which had pierced me practically in two suddenly re-inflated! This was not what I expected at all.

Then the board chittered and shivered. The monster grabbed me and sucked me into the disc ship thingie, like no rocket I had ever seen. It was like a giant Corvette only more cigar shaped, rounder around the edges on the outside, with more knobby metallic and very sharp objects inside.

What remained of my cute white swimsuit was in shreds and I had bled like a stuck pig. Luckily it dried up quickly in the hot air of the ship, air that didn't smell normal at all, rather like a mix of Canoe and pizza. We were not in clear water. We were under the sea after a massive Zero break Event stole Lord Plato and turned him into a Space Monster who took my Virginity!

"Take me home right now!"

The creature consented grudgingly. He transformed, turning into Jack Cortez before we pulled up in front of my home.

My teeth were chattering.

"I'm sorry," the space monster said, pretending to be Lord Plato.

I smoothed my sundress and checked to see if my straps were in place. "Tell it to the Air Force," I said through clenched teeth. I felt a curious grief for what I had lost. To think such a thing can happen in America, in 1959.

"It wasn't me," Lord Plato said. "—I don't know what came over me. I just lost my head."

I stole a glance at his half-mast eyes. He looked at me slowly.

"I guess it's time I went back to Hawaii. You California girls are all alike. You say one thing but your actions say another."

"I am a Texan!" I growled. "And you're no Hawaiian. You're a monster!"

"I know," the thing said, his webbed fingers clutching the steering wheel, "and now it's time to get back home, my real home, under the sea—and then the stars."

"You—Freep!"

"I know," the space monster sighed, "but tell me, didn't you love it, just a little bit? Wasn't it—the Ultimate Ride?"

"Oh, yeah, sure. What if I have a little monster now? I suppose you'll take care of it on your space ship?"

At Pacific Ocean Park outside of Santa Monica, there's this "Flight to Mars" ride where you take a walk that explains what it might be like if you were a spaceman going to Mars and how, through a secret process, your body might be "disintegrated" then "reconstructed" after transmission back the Earth. My parents, my little sister Nancy, my brother Buddy, and I all took that ride not long after we moved to Santa Monica and I felt a weird foreboding of what was to come. That was in March of 1959. By August I had ridden the Zero break, the giant one that took me way past Mars and back to Earth and let me tell you, when you blow somebody apart and put them back together again you are never the same. I know because that's what happened to me when I made love with a spaceman, an alien creature pretending to be a surfer boy! He was not only from another country but from another galaxy! He "disintegrated" my body and "reconstructed" my soul and now, at heart, I am no longer the same person at all and my entire life is a wipeout. And here I am trying to make sense of it. Don't let it happen to you! I feel compelled to warn all young women that it's not worth it. You don't have to lose your virginity to be popular or even to be a woman, for that matter. But if you do, you may discover finding yourself may mean losing yourself. And when you come back together—if you can—you will learn you are not the same. You become one of them—alien.

And yeah, something grows inside me and I may have to drop out of school and I haven't heard from the monster. It's November. He's gone off on his rocket ship to his water land on some distant planet. Will he come back and take us with him so it can grow up saying "I am!" or will I just say "olé" when they come to take it away because it can't live without water? What do I say if it has gills instead of lungs? Or fins instead of hands? I mean look at me. I'm not the same. And that's the final destination. That's it. I'm a monster, too. The other night I had to go lick some humps. The middle of the night. And my skin shone with alien spangles.

I pearl-dived into the depths off Malibu Pier to see if I could find him or someone even more gifted at showing me just what I can do if I set my mind to it. Shoot the curl. Monsters! Boys! Men!

I keep doing it, praying for the next Zero break. So maybe I'll have to surf-ride all the way to Hawaii.

Get my drift? Girls, be careful! Don't lose your head over some sex hound who might actually be from outer space!

Oh, who am I fooling with this gag? The Zero break was the bitchenest thing I ever experienced in my whole dang life. And there's no monster inside me. The monster is you. If you make out with a spaceman from Planet Earth or Mars and he rockets off to Jupiter, get past it. Can you dig it? It's like that song, you just have to remember before you do the deed, that "there's no such thing as the next best thing to love"*, okay? That said, what's the *best* thing to do?

Let's ride.

Yes, girls, shoot the curl. Shoot it. Go all the way; ride the thirty-footers if you dare. Risk the monster wave. Spaceships come, spaceships go; but the Almighty Ocean God is Eternal. Makaha, here I come!

* Stanley Styne (from the lyrics of "The Next Best Thing to Love")
  Music by Fred Karger

I've always loved giants. Big, mean, frightening, impossible beasts of myth and legend, so terrifying because, mostly, they're just like us. Except a damn sight bigger. Whether they're jerky Ray Harryhausen creations, Roald Dahl's BFG, poor Gulliver with his size issues, or characters in a series I used to watch as a kid called 'Land of the Giants' (anyone remember that? I've never met anyone who ever saw it, and sometimes I wonder if I dreamed it all up...), these big folks have always fascinated me.

And so when Joe asked me to think about a story for this anthology, I instantly knew where I was going to go: I was going to go big. The giant buried down in the basement was already pulling me that way, I think, long before the story was a conscious thought. Maybe because he's so damn *huge*, he has a gravitational effect on my imagination.

It's true. He's in my basement and this story is, in effect, Chapter One of his authorised biography.

Well, maybe not...but it was great fun exploring what could happen if a giant was found sleeping beneath suburbia. After so long, I knew one thing for sure: he'd be hungry.

—*Tim Lebbon*

The Body Lies

Tim Lebbon

At first I thought I'd found an old ceramic pot buried in the cellar. I had been excavating the foundation for a new circular staircase, designed to rise from the cellar, up through the three floors of the house to the viewing cupola on the roof—the Denkins next door had spent a lot of money having solid timber flooring laid throughout their house, and I wanted something that would kindle such envy in their eyes as resided in my own—when my shovel threw back sparks. I took the opportunity to pause, go to the kitchen and open a bottle of beer. It was a lovely day outside, and so dark down in the cellar. I almost never went back.

But when I did return, the creamy white scar in the ground told me that I might have hit something valuable. I spent the next hour digging around the buried object, becoming more and more convinced that it was a jar that could contain anything. Buried money? Old secrets? A dead baby, hidden away after a still-birth a hundred years before?

And then, on either side of the jar, I found others. I concentrated on the first, more excited now. The ground not as compact as I had expected, especially the soil beneath the objects, but one end of the jar was buried deep in some sort of grey, slick clay, and when I scraped its surface it let off a foul odour that discouraged me from trying again. I found no opening into the ceramic container and two hours later, with Theresa due home and darkness starting to steal the light from the narrow cellar windows, I struck down hard with the shovel, determined to break my way in.

The tool rebounded, and for a second I thought that my entire body was vibrating with the impact. It was only when I heard Theresa's confused shout from upstairs that I realised the house was shaking from its foundations up.

The noise that accompanied it sounded like a deep, weary growl.

◆◆◆

"There's nothing on the radio," Theresa said. "Nothing about an earth tremor. There was one in South Wales when my mother was a little girl, it cracked a window pane in her parents' kitchen. It was still cracked when I went to visit them when *I* was a child." She was wearing her coat, sitting on a stool in the kitchen, twisting her scarf in her hands while she stared down at the broken cup on the floor. It had swung itself right off a hook and shattered on the tiles.

Whatever I hit with the shovel had done that.

"Perhaps it was very localised," I said, thinking of the white scar where I had struck the porcelain jar. "You know, just around here."

Theresa looked at me as if I was not there, so I made it so. The cellar was calling me. I mumbled something about checking the house for any damage, closed the cellar door behind me and hurried down the dimly-lit staircase. Our dog Nibbs had not accompanied me down, and I cursed her for siding with Theresa.

The cellar floor was cracked. Not badly, and I was not surprised, but the fact that the cracks radiated out from the thing in the ground confirmed my suspicions. To make certain I could strike it once more with the shovel...but that was folly. And besides, there were other ways to find out.

I continued to dig around the buried objects, excavating below them with the intention of eventually lifting them out. For some crazy reason, each time I glanced at the jars I thought of that broken cup on the kitchen floor directly above me. A stranger viewing one small shard of pottery would have no clue as to what its whole entailed.

It had grown fully dark now, and the only light came from several bare bulbs strung across the room from corner to corner. I cleaned them of dust and spider webs, but still the light was poor. It did not matter. By now I had uncovered evidence of further objects buried alongside the others, these slightly deeper, and consciously or not I had set my mission for the evening.

Theresa shouted down once, but I told her that one of the internal walls had cracked due to the tremor, and I had to shore it up before coming to bed. I sensed her standing at the head of the stairs for a few silent moments, perhaps imagining what I could really be doing down in the semi-dark, but in the end she shut the door and I heard her walk into our living room. She hated dirt, dust and spiders, and this place had always been my safe retreat.

Later, having lost track of time, with mounds of earth around my knees and the hole increasing in size, the things fully exposed and cleaned with an oily rag and impossible, I felt the first hints of the ground giving way. I leaped to one side—I suppose I had been prepared in a way, readying myself for this quick movement—and rolled across to the far wall.

The ground did not shake as much as I had expected, the house did not move, but the air shifted with a sudden, rattling breeze. An exhalation that came up out of the ground, past the half-dozen teeth I had already exhumed.

And the buried giant spoke in a language I should never have known.

When I woke up I was still sweating from the nightmare. Theresa breathed steadily beside me, ignorant of my soaked pyjamas, the electric feel of my skin, the panic that hung in the darkness above me like a shadow waiting to fall. I reached out to touch Nibbs where she slept at our feet, but she was not there. A warm patch on the blanket marked where she had recently been.

Earthquakes, teeth in my cellar, our village shaking in a precise, unbelievably distinct pattern...separately they were foolish ideas, but their memory brought something black and terrifying to me. I stood slowly so as not to wake Theresa and went downstairs for a drink.

Our dog did not trot out to greet me. That was unusual. Also strange was the mud under my fingernails visible when I turned on the kitchen light, and the dirty footprints heading back into the dark house, and the fact that the cellar door stood open like a sideways sneer.

Sleepwalking, I thought, but it was more, I knew that already. I was perfectly willing to believe that I had had a terrible nightmare, and the nearer I came to the cellar door the more I wished this to be the case. Because there was a breeze coming from down there. It came in gusts, evenly spaced, as if the house was breathing while its inhabitants were supposedly asleep. Perhaps it held its breath during the day, not wishing to be discovered for what it was. I paused in the centre of the kitchen and listened. In the silence of midnight, every sound was louder than usual: the refrigerator buzzing itself cool; the electric light hissing above me; the house settling, creaking, stretching as it...breathed.

Again, that exhalation from the cellar. This time it seemed to bring something with it, the reek of ages and rot and forgotten things, rich and moist like turned earth.

And then, beneath these sounds that were louder than they should have been, a single low whine.

"Nibbs!" I whispered, and the breeze from the cellar came faster.

I am not a brave man. I'm not a coward, but I have never had to delve the depths of my courage, never been faced with a testing situation. Now I only wanted to turn around, go back upstairs and sleep the night through. Let the dark complete its nefarious dealings without me. But a sense of responsibility weighed down heavy on my shoulders, and when the dog's whine came again I darted to the cellar door and descended quickly below ground.

I switched on the light and waited for a few seconds, my own breath held. Blood rushed through my ears, but behind that I was sure I heard a chuckle, a grumble like something shifting deep below my feet. The thought of turning back was unbearable now, so I walked around the corner and looked down at what I had uncovered.

Nibbs's rear legs and tail lay on the cellar floor next to my excavation, severed, the wound rough and ragged. The rest of her had vanished. Down the hole, I knew. Into the mouth. And those things I had so foolishly believed to be ceramic pots were smeared with my dead pet's gore.

"Too weak. Too deep." The whisper roared in my ears, shaking the walls of the cellar and lifting dust from the floor. Theresa would surely hear and come to investigate, but I could not move. I was rapt, held there by fear and a guilt so intense that I thought I could never let the light of day touch me again.

What have I uncovered?

"Only me," the voice rumbled. I think it was trying to whisper, but the effect was like standing next to a busy road. And if it knew what I thought…

"What are you?" I asked. I looked at the chewed parts of my dog that had been coughed out onto the cellar floor. Damp, bloodied earth clung to the ceiling. The huge jaw worked, widening the wound in the floor and causing one wall to bow in with every utterance. I wondered what would happen if the buried thing shouted, and then the true impossibility of what I was seeing struck home. I was not asleep and dreaming, of that much I was now sure. Whatever I had uncovered in the cellar was moving, and that movement insinuated words, and those words were making some sort of crazy sense to me. If madness had a part in this, it had come on covertly and left no signs. I knew that I should call Theresa…but then I saw Nibbs's head stuck in a clot of mud on the ceiling, dripping blood back down into the giant mouth.

I laughed out loud. There was nothing else I could do.

"Need help," the voice roared. "Need…food."

This is all unreal, I thought. *This thing in my cellar—this mouth—is impossible. Therefore, I am either imagining everything, or I'm having the worst nightmare of my life, or I'm mad.*

The mouth rumbled and shook. "None of them! And I am so much more than a mouth. I am a victim, wronged and left for dead. And you can help me rise."

"Don't shout," I said. "You'll wake my wife." And then I could only laugh again. Maybe this is how all lunatics felt when, in a moment of sane clarity, they realised their situation.

"Then listen to me," the voice said, and I thought that it was quieter. Perhaps whatever formed those words—out loud or in my head, I had not yet decided which was true—was acceding to my request. I stared at the mouth as it chewed, teeth fully uncovered now, lips indistinct and smothered with dirt, a shadowy thing that may have been a tongue rolling in the darkened depths. I stared, but I could not believe.

"Believe me," the voice said. "Or at least, do your best. I have a story to tell, and I would like you to listen."

"Do I have any choice?" I asked. Fear was still at bay, but presenting its face more and more. The dark, the blood, the smell brought it on.

"Yes," the voice said. "Live or die."

Tell me your story, I thought, and those lips cracked the earth to form a gruesome smile.

◆◆◆

"I know of the tides of time, the movement of history. I feel the skies pass by above where I am buried, and though I cannot see it, I know progress. I have laid here dreaming for eons, and what I dream is the truth.

"There was a time of giants. Not all ages are remembered, and many are lost in the mists of memory, the trials of evolution. There are more gaps in time than periods that are recorded and understood, and I and my kind inhabited those times. We dwelled in the hills, made our homes in the fledgling mountains of places which are now Scotland and Wales, and in those times there were fewer people. We never troubled the little folk, and they lived with the knowledge of our existence. Worried, perhaps. Nervous at times. But they accepted us, and in turn we protected them. Sometimes they were ignorant of that, but the wars we fought for them were many. Snow demons came from the north and the giants of the land united and faced them in the Highlands, dashing them down and diluting their essence in the seas. Wolf Men sailed in from the New World and we swam out to meet them, capsized their ships with tidal waves, swallowed those monstrosities whole and removed their evil from the land. And even internal struggles were sometimes settled with our intervention: in those cases the losers did not survive to tell of us, and the victors always chose to ignore our actions in their storytelling, because that would lessen their own achievements. We did not mind. We accepted that because it did not draw attention, and anonymity is something we craved. A strange desire for a giant, perhaps. But eventually, we knew, a time would come when we became too much of a threat, or an oddity, to exist in peace. Because even then there were only a few hundred of us, and we knew that our time could not last forever.

"I lived in the moorlands and forests of the south west, this place that is now Cornwall, eating horses and bears and deer, and other things that roamed these wild places, sucking mineral waters up from deep caves, carving my name in the land without anyone recognising my signature. Today you see standing stones and other monuments that you believe are naturally formed, but much across Cornwall is my own work. These places took weeks, months, sometimes years to build, and they were my art. I sculpted the story of my existence into the landscape, my history, my millennia as an inhabitant of those forgotten times, always in the misguided hope that the future would recognise me. It was a small enough desire, surely? A petty affectation? I am huge. I could not walk across the land without being seen. And times were changing. I was born at the end of the giants' reign, when humankind had found its feet and was hunting and killing any species that challenged it. There were others—many others—but we giants were the last to hold out. Arrows and slings were to us as gnat bites are to you. But if a million gnats bit you, you would die.

"By the way, I apologise for eating your dog."

There was little I could say so I simply stood there, breathing deeply. The voice had shaken the walls and ceiling, dust clouding the air, much of it particles of my own skin from where I had been down here week after week, year after year, for decades. And all that time I had had no idea of what lay beneath my feet.

"That's alright," I said. Nibbs grinned at me through bared teeth, her head slowly drooping down from the ceiling on a rope of blood and muck.

"And so there I was," the giant continued, "working the land, making my mark, keeping quiet because I was all I had. I was building a stone mountain as high as myself, stirring in a stew of sunlight and moonlight to give power to the rock. Did I mention that some giants had powers beyond the mortal? We were on the edge of natural as dusk is at the edge of day, and sometimes I found that my hand could manipulate more than the physical. With a wave of one finger I once brought down a lightning bolt and burnt a forest. Only once—I tried again many times, but conjured only rain. And sometimes I could feel the light or darkness around me without opening my eyes. Perhaps light was so heavy on a body so large that it weighed me down. Or maybe the dark stole something away.

"I was working hard when I heard what sounded like thunder coming down from the north. It rolled across the hills and filled valleys, and it took only a few heartbeats for me to realise that another giant was coming my way. The ground shook, the air shimmered from fear, and the clouds were illuminated as if harbouring the fires of creation in their depths. But the fire was not in the sky. It came from elsewhere."

The giant fell silent, and again and again I wondered whether I was truly mad. But the mouth was there, always moving now that it had found life again, moving even when it uttered no sound. Time passed— seconds, minutes—and for a moment I thought that this buried colossus had fallen asleep. When he spoke again it was a roar, something that shook me to the spine and set the walls of my house vibrating as if hit by a passenger train.

"The fire was coming for me!"

I collapsed to the ground, holding my ears and waiting for the slick heat of blood from ruptured eardrums. But though the pain was great there was no blood, and I nursed the agony as it slowly faded.

I heard my wife shouting my name from upstairs.

"The fire," the giant said again, whispering this time, so lightly that it was almost as if I imagined the words inside my head. "It was coming for me in the hair, the clothing, the flesh of another giant. He had already melted by the time he reached me. Do you hear? Do you *understand*? The little ones had grown covetous of our talents and gifts, and they set him aflame with some new, unknown magic of their own. Him and dozens like us. Perhaps he had come to warn me, seek me out. But I did the only thing I could."

Theresa screamed for me again, demanding that I go to her, tell her what her nightmare had been. I turned to leave, amazed at my courage.

"He reached me, and I kicked him down onto the ground."

I placed my foot on the first step.

"And then I dragged him across the landscape, scorching a line in the earth…"

I walked slowly upstairs. Theresa's voice lured me like sanity singing its song, while behind me the mad giant finished his story.

"…until I dropped him in the sea. The flames were gone. But I knew that my time was over. I found a cave and buried myself deep, and now time has eroded the land into new shapes and you have found me."

When I reached the door it took several attempts to open it, as if the giant's words held weight that kept it pressed shut.

"Do you plan on burning me, little one?"

I shook my head and opened the door.

"Good. Because I need your help to rise."

And then the light of dawn flooded through the kitchen window as I emerged, handing me back to normality for a while.

"There's nothing!" Theresa said. "Still nothing on the radio at all, nothing about the earthquake. Just what was it that shook our house like that? Should we call the police?"

"I didn't feel anything," I said again, buttering another slice of toast, hating my lie but trying to convince myself that it was for my wife's safety.

"But you must have!" she said. "The whole house shook, from foundations to roof! The blankets slipped from the bed, our china duck fell from the wall and shattered. You must have felt *something* down there?"

I took a bite of toast and shook my head, looking down at the table as if to fend off crumbs. I could not look her in the eye as I lied. "Nothing," I said. "Maybe because you were higher in the house you felt the effect more. It'll be on the news soon, don't you worry." I looked up and smiled, and the fear in her eyes seemed to echo my own.

Theresa went out to do the weekly shop and I said that I would remain at home to check the house for more earthquake damage. She did not believe me. I knew that straight away, but once uttered the lie would be even more damaging if retraced and analysed. She knew that too, and she left with both of us knowing that a falsehood hung between us. We had a good marriage. There had never been any reason for untruths. I vowed that by the time she returned home that would be the case again, and I would be able to tell her everything.

"I need to talk to everyone," the giant said. "I need to rise, but I am weak, the ground above me is weighed down with whatever you little folk have built up there."

"Homes," I said. "A school. Some shops." I tried to map out his position judging by the size and lay of the mouth, and the dimensions constructed in my mind were monstrous. His eyes were below our garden, Laurel Avenue and Sycamore Crescent may cover his legs, and the primary school could well be his torso. As for his arms, that would depend on where they were. If they were spread, he could well encompass the whole village in his primordial embrace.

"Ah," the giant breathed, "such weight. It's you who are the giants now. You who rule the day. I need to talk to your neighbours, to reveal, and to ask permission."

"For what?"

"To destroy their homes," the giant said. "How else can I rise? Bring them to me. Can you imagine the fame, the fortune? Can you?"

"But their *homes*?" I had lived in Skentipple my whole life. The thought of its old stone houses, church, school and winding, cobbled streets being destroying in an upheaval filled me with dread and sadness. With those buildings would go many fine memories, echoes of history that sight and sound and touch brought back every time I passed by. No pile of rubble or hole in the ground would replace such recollections.

"You *can* do it," the voice said, pre-empting my thoughts. "You have no idea of the wonders I can show you, *give* you. I'm not in any of your histories—the giants were wiped out, purged from the land, and the little folk back then would have ensured that no trace survived. I'm from out of time, as are my talents. Do you still use fire?"

"Yes, of course," I said.

"There are alternatives. I know of them. The root of a certain plant, the breath of a certain bird, a thought of sunlight, in combination they will give fire without flame. I used to cook horses whole like that, spitting them on trees and casting the spell at them. They would sizzle and roast within minutes. I listened to them die. They always tasted better, cooked alive."

I saw past that grotesque image to the benefits such an energy would bestow upon those with the right knowledge. "And you would share that?" I asked.

"And more, much more. I used to mix memories into the turn of tide, and it gave a sound to make you weep. Those final few waves that struck the shore and marked the turning, they whispered of everything good in your experience, or everything bad, depending upon your desires. With that knowledge—with the right touch—you can make someone love you, or drive them away under a cloud of fear or hate."

"*All* of that? Why would you share that with us little ones? We tried to burn you."

"That was an age ago, and the ones that did that are long gone. Not even their memory remains. I should have died along with my like, but here I am, buried and preserved by time. I will gladly give up *any* secret for the ability to rise, to *live* once more. But the weight is too heavy, the ground too laden. I can use the blessing of those above me to draw strength into my petrified muscles. Their approval will be a positive force…and I have spells which can give that potency!"

"I fear you," I said. "You terrify me." And yet the giant seemed sad and pathetic pleading with me like this, offering everything for the right to sit up and let the daylight of a new world touch his skin.

"That fear has always been the little folks' problem, not my own."

He sent me away then, saying that he was tired and needed to rest. I closed the cellar door, stood at the living room window and faced the real world once again. Neighbours were heading off to work or out to the shops, and children were walking along the street on their way to school. Somebody was exercising their dog…and I pictured Nibbs down there in the cellar, chewed up and spat out by the thing I had uncovered.

Maybe it was not a whole body at all? How could I trust something like that? Where were his eyes, his nose, his hands? If he had been lying just below the surface down there for all this time, how was he still alive?

The answer, of course, was that it was impossible.

And yet those things he offered…Even if the chance was slight, I could see no harm in entertaining the notion for an evening. It had been a long time since we had thrown a party.

The first house on Laurel Avenue belonged to the Jacksons. They had a television in both of their downstairs rooms, and a lush garden much larger than my own. I invited them to our house that evening, and although it was short notice they promised to come. George even pledged to bring some of his homemade wine. He was often complimented on its excellence, and that made me uncomfortable, but I could hardly refuse.

The next house was home to Mrs Singleton, the old spinster who had apparently lived in the village since time immemorial. As I knocked on her door I wondered blithely whether she had known the giant when he walked. She opened the door on my smirk and I blessed the fact that she was virtually blind. She had been left a huge inheritance by her late husband, and I craved the sort of means she lived by. I could smell the money on her like mothballed clothes. She too agreed to come along to our house, as long as the Jacksons gave her a ride in their new car.

Frank Marshall lived in the large stone house next door, its beautiful gardens surrounded by a high boundary wall and cast iron gates, gargoyles adorning the highest points. I had been inside his home only once, and his blatant wealth had kept me awake all night, staring at the cracks in my old cottage's ceiling and listening to the unmaintained building creak and groan around me. Frank would come, he said, if I had some good brandy. I lied that I had and moved on.

Of thirteen houses in Laurel Avenue I had eight commitments to attend our impromptu party. Skentipple was a small community, and any social gatherings were welcomed.

In Sycamore Crescent I found myself having to make promises. I would be revealing something of benefit to the whole village, I told one householder. I would be sharing a secret that could make us all rich, I told someone else. And though my claims seemed outlandish and were backed up by little more than my earnest expression, few suspected me of any shady dealing.

With every step I imagined the legs of that buried giant stretched out below me. Would drains have been buried in his old, old flesh? Were his bones cracked by the weight of the roads and buildings above? Could he feel me even now, a tickle on his skin like a fly landing on my own leg? Perhaps he was tracking my progress and planning the evening's revelation.

Few would believe. But that would not matter. A short trip to the cellar would slaughter disbelief and open their eyes to ages none of them had learned about in school.

In every home, with every couple or person I spoke to, I found something to covet. Peter Jones had a gorgeous young wife; the Petersons had a marriage that still seemed as fresh as the day they had wed; one house was four storeys high, another was an attractive bungalow. When I eventually arrived home late that afternoon and saw Theresa glaring angrily from the kitchen window, there was nothing there that made me feel good.

But I had something more special than everyone. And I looked forward to that evening when its disclosure would put me at the centre of everything.

◆◆◆

"They're coming," I said.

"I know." He was whispering, but still his voice sent a rumble through the house.

"What are you doing? Is it you causing that racket? Just what the hell are you *doing* down there?" Theresa was standing at the open cellar door staring down into the dark, as close as she ever came to entering its space.

"Later," I said, "I'll bring them down later."

"No rush," the giant said, and 'rush' came out like a waterfall with no end.

◆◆◆

"Honey, there's something in our cellar. Something wonderful. It will make us rich!"

"Rich, rich, is that all you think about? Money, wealth?" Theresa fussed over the remains of a joint of meat, picking off scraps to use for a meal the next day. I always hated leftovers; it made me feel so poor. "You really should be grateful with your lot. Don't you ever think about *us*, what *we* have? Which reminds me, where's Nibbs?"

"Of course, but—"

"So what is it?" She was really angry, and I wondered what revealing the secret now would achieve. But in a way the spiteful part of me relished that. She would be in a bad mood when I showed her what would make our future fine and secure, and she would be forever in my debt. I would prove to her that all my jealousies, all my desires had been worthwhile, because for the final half of our lives we would live like royalty.

I imagined a little island somewhere in the Mediterranean.

"It's a giant," I said. "He comes from a time we don't know about in history. He was hunted down so he hid himself away in a cave, and time passed and our house was built above him, and he has magic and knowledge that will…will make us…" I was losing her already, I could see that. And listening to myself I understood why.

"Oh for God's sake." She wiped her hands and walked upstairs.

Wait until later, I thought.

"Later," the voice hissed from the cellar, and if Theresa had turned around then I would have blamed it on the plumbing.

◆◆◆

Later, everyone was there.

Peter Jones and his beautiful wife stood decoratively by the mantlepiece, drinking wine and trying to catch everyone's eye. I smiled at Peter, looked his wife up and down and turned away. The Denkins from next door were smiling at the poor décor our house sported, nudging each other and pointing at peeled wallpaper, threadbare carpets, smug behind their wine glasses. Frank Marshall scowled at me as he drank the old brandy I had found for him in our pantry, and the Petersons held on to each other as if this was the last party they would ever attend. His hand was curved around her hip, ready to fight any man that looked at her in the wrong way. She was a beautiful woman, but then so was Theresa, and I did not feel the same protectiveness about my own wife. I liked to think that it was the maturity of our relationship, but in reality I recognised the growing apathy that had smothered us for years.

George Jackson was parading through the party with a cloudy green wine bottle in each hand, loudly exhorting the merits of his own homemade distillation over the cheap rubbish I had bought in bulk from the village shop that evening. Most guests succumbed to his persuasive manner, emptying their glasses into plant pots or draining them quickly so that they could sample what he had to offer. The glint in their eyes, the thanks, the nods of appreciation bit into me like serrated knives. When he turned to me and smiled it was all I could do not to curse him out of my house.

He would see. Later, he would know the true value of his petty talent, when everyone here forgot the smell and taste of his wine and inhaled the bouquet of the future from my cellar.

Theresa, bless her, gave the impression of being the finest hostess, parading through our small living room with trays of fancies and bottles of beer. She pointedly avoided me, and though the revelation to come stood my hair on end, that made me sad. This was something we should have been revelling in together.

"So where is this surprise?" Malcolm Culver asked. He was already half drunk, and the mockery in his voice was apparent. A few people turned and glanced at me; I had only mentioned a surprise to those who had not been keen to attend, and for many this was something new.

"I'll show you soon," I said. "Let's enjoy the party for a while, have a drink. Please, there's plenty of wine—"

"Robert found a giant living in our cellar!" Theresa said. Nobody reacted, even when she let out a shrill laugh. "He has! A giant that knows magic! Perhaps it's Merlin, buried away for all this time and grown fat on cave mushrooms!" She laughed again, and I knew she was drunk.

"A giant?" Malcolm muttered, shaking his head, spilling red wine onto our carpet.

A few smiles came my way, nervous, confused. Other faces were sterner, accusing me of time-wasting without uttering a word. Here they all were, better than me, richer, happier, more interesting, more attractive...and in front of them stood my wife, laughing at me.

"You thought it was an earthquake," I said, but I could not shame her. "Where do you think Nibbs went?" She could not even hear me above her cries of mirth. "There *is* a giant!" I shouted, eliciting another screech from Theresa.

"Robert, please," someone said, though I could not tell who spoke.

"I'll show you." They fell silent, staring. "I will. And when you see you'll all take back your ridicule, won't you? I'll show you and you'll realise that we all have a richer future than any of you could dream of, even you Marshall. Even you! Me, I'm buying an island, and I'll live there on my own. You lot can do whatever you want with your share, I don't care, but you should be grateful I even bothered to include you all. I could have let him...*rise up*. But he's polite. And he'll share—"

"Mister giant!" Theresa called. She had slipped into the kitchen and stood at the head of the cellar stairs, leaning drunkenly against the open door, calling down at the dark. "Hey, big guy, there are some people up here who—"

He stole her words away.

He must have drawn in a huge breath, larger than any he had dared take since I had uncovered his teeth and mouth. A wind tore through the house, tumbling crockery from cupboards, flipping pictures from walls, rucking the carpet and drawing rugs across the floor, tearing books from shelves and sending them flapping like drunken birds. My party guests fell or staggered, some reaching out for support, most of them missing. They slid towards the cellar door, Jackson's spilled wine easing their way across the cheaply carpeted floor. Their clothes rippled and tore, and I saw that Peter Jones's beautiful wife was not so beautiful naked. There were welts and burns on her pearly skin, and even *in extremis* there was rage in his eyes as he realised I had seen.

As I turned and darted for the door to the hallway, the last thing I saw of Theresa was her upturned feet as the hurricane sucked her down into the cellar. I slammed the door and listened to the noise inside the living room. Furniture crashed, wood splintered, screams erupted. And then came a shout I recognised. Theresa, her shriek filled with disbelief and terror, cut off quickly by a crunching, crushing sound I can never forget.

The wind abated for a few seconds before rising more violently than before, the walls of the house shivering under its onslaught. More screams came, more sounds of my party guests masticated to death, and each time the giant drew breath it was faster, healthier, *stronger*.

He had used me to ensure his place in history. I realised my mistake in trusting him. And yet as I felt the first vibrations of the final earthquake, I wondered whether it was really a mistake after all.

When I started reading science fiction in the 1950s, I fell in love as much with the names and the covers of the digest magazines, especially the low-end magazines, as with the stories: *Fantastic Universe*, *Imaginative Tales*, *Amazing Stories*, *Other Worlds*. There was lots of talk about flying saucers in those days, and all these magazines regularly featured them on the covers. In fact *Fantastic Universe* seemed to have one on just about every cover.

And then there were the monsters. A magazine called *Super Science Fiction* did at least three "Special Monster Issues," and the SF movies of the time were filled with monsters of every description, from crawling rugs to sentient tree stumps.

What I wanted to do was write a story about flying saucers and monsters while bringing in a couple of other favorite SF themes of the '50s, immortality and first contact. Putting all of that into one story would be, I thought, a fine tribute to the magazines and stories I loved so long ago.

—*Bill Crider*

'Zekiel Saw the Wheel

Bill Crider

Air Technical Intelligence Center
Project Blue Book
Wright-Patterson Field
Dayton, Ohio
28 July 1958
Interview Subject: Moses Bates
Tape Transcription Number: 636
This Document is Classified: *Top Secret*

Moses Bates: I live in a little town in East Texas. Never mind the name of it. No use in you looking for it, either. All little East Texas towns are pretty much alike. White folks live on their side of town, and we live on ours. They go to their schools and picture shows, and we go to ours. We shop in their stores sometimes. They don't mind. Our money spends just like theirs does. Mostly, though, they think they're better than us. It's not their fault, 'Zekiel says. Color of their skin does it to them.

'Zekiel's a friend of mine. He knows a lot of things, but that's only natural, him being right at a hundred and fifty-seven years old. You don't have to shake your head at that. That's how old he is, and I know it as well as I know anything. He doesn't look it, though, and he can mow two yards a day with a push mower and rake up all the clippings without hardly breaking a sweat. And still put a smile on a woman's face on Saturday night. That's the living truth. It's his story I'm going to tell you, just the way he told it to me, and you can judge for yourself what it means. I learned a long time ago that most white people never hear what you're telling them. They might listen and be polite about it, but they never hear. But I figure since you let me in to talk to you, maybe you want to listen. Be that as it may, this here is the story I came to tell you.

◆ ◆ ◆

They'd been doing all right, following the directions in the drinking gourd song, until they stumbled into a graveyard that had been ravaged by a flood sometime in the last year or so. The graveyard was down in a little hollow not far from a creek that ran into the Tombigbee River near where the Tombigbee joins the Tennessee, and because only slaves were buried there, nothing had been done about the damage.

The graves had all been marked with just boards and sticks, and these had floated away on the swirling, muddy waters. The coffins had been slapped together out of boards that were already half rotted, and sometimes the ones who did the burying didn't even bother with coffins at all. So the bodies had decayed rapidly in the rich, dank soil, helped along by the worms and the insects. When the water washed what was left of the bodies and coffin boards up out of the ground, the 'possums and 'coons and swamp rats and skunks and whatever else hadn't minded the smell had picked the bones clean as lye-soaped laundry. They lay there now, what hadn't been carried off by the scavengers, dry as dust, cold as stone, and gleaming in the moonlight like the light of a will-o-the-wisp. A skull sat on top of a little mound of dirt and looked off into the distance with empty black eyes.

'Zekiel and the others stood there and looked at the bones, their breath hanging like thin gray clouds in front of their faces. It was early in the winter, and Zekiel's rheumatism was bothering him a little. He had on a pair of linsey-woolsey pants and a heavy coat. His head was wrapped up in rag that made him look like he had a toothache. Some kinky white hair stuck out around the edges of the rag.

The dry bones didn't bother 'Zekiel any. He'd seen a lot worse in his time. But he thought they might bother some of the others.

There were eight of them left. The fever had taken Li'l Tom, and the paddy rollers had gotten Samuel. It had taken the rest of them a couple of months to get to that graveyard, holing up during the day and coming out at night when they could follow the drinking gourd star to the Ohio River. Winter was the best time to get there, they'd been told, because you could cross the river on the ice and find yourself in freedom's land.

'Zekiel believed in freedom. He'd heard his grandmother tell the stories over and over of the place she came from, where blue waves washed up on the sandy shore, where fierce tawny beasts roared at night and roamed the tall grass of the plains. He thought he'd like to see a lion and a place where there was water so wide you couldn't see across it, so he and the nine others had left Marse James' plantation quarters late one night and struck out, with nothing to go by but a song and a faith that they could somehow or another find their way to freedom.

"We got to pass by them bones?" old Franklin asked. He was stick thin and oak hard, but hard as he was, he didn't like the idea of messing with dead folks' bones.

"We not out of Babylon yet," 'Zekiel told him. "We can't let some bones be stoppin' us now."

There was some muttering, but nobody held back when 'Zekiel moved forward. They'd followed him this far, and they all knew they had to get to the Tennessee River and then follow it to the Ohio. 'Zekiel had told them that somewhere along the Tennessee, they'd be met by a guide who'd see them the rest of their way.

'Zekiel skirted around the graveyard as best he could. He wasn't afraid of ghosts or anything like that. He just didn't think it was respectful to disturb the bones. He would even have stopped to bury them if he'd had the time, but there were just too many of them, and he knew they dasn't linger for that.

The paddy rollers were back there behind them somewhere, looking to grab them all and take them back to Marse James, if not do something worse to them. Ghosts and bones didn't bother 'Zekiel hardly any at all, but the thought of the paddy rollers turned his insides to water and his knees to jelly.

They were almost past the graveyard when Leethy fell down. She was the youngest one of them, not more than seven years old, wore her hair in braids tied up on her head, and looked a whole lot like Marse James with those cornflower blue eyes of hers. The fact that she looked that way and was probably sprung from his loins didn't faze Marse James, though, one way or the other. A slave was a slave to him, just another piece of his property, one more nigger gal, no matter where she came from.

She rolled over once and came to rest right face to face with one of those skulls that had got washed up onto a little higher ground than the others. She let out a high-pitched scream like a dying rabbit.

'Zekiel got to her first and picked her up.

"No reason for you to be a-scairt, Leethy," he said, hugging her up against him, her little heart beating like a bird's.

But telling her that didn't do any good, and Leethy started in to crying. 'Zekiel handed her to Dinah, her mama, a short, coffee-colored woman who was probably half white herself.

"Hush, chile, you hush now," Dinah said, rocking Leethy in her arms.

Leethy finally calmed down to where she was just gulping in air and not crying at all. But the damage, if there was any, had been done, and everybody knew it. They were all standing still as the bones of the dead, listening. From somewhere away far off there was a screech owl cry, and then 'Zekiel thought he heard the nicker of a horse, cut off as if some-body had clamped a hold on its muzzle.

The others heard it, too, and they all looked at 'Zekiel. Some of the looks were accusing, and some were just sad and resigned, as if to say, "Well, you got us this far, 'Zekiel, but it looks like we won't be going any farther."

'Zekiel wasn't the kind to mope around and look on the dark side of things, though, so he put a finger to his lips and started tippy-toeing it along, trying not to step on any sticks from the limbs of the bare trees all around. The others came along after him. They didn't have much choice. It was either that or stay there with the bones and wait for their fate to catch up with them.

Turned out they didn't have to wait. Their fate was waiting for them right there in the trees in front of them. 'Zekiel saw them first, lined up beside their horses, all four of them holding pistols, big '51 Colt's Navy models with bullets that would put a little hole in the front of a man and keep right on going till it made a bigger one coming out his back.

"You can stop where you are," said a man who stood a little forward of the others.

His voice was hoarse like he had a bad case of the cattarah, but that wasn't what it was. He'd been stabbed in the throat some years before by a slave he'd been chasing, and his voice had never recovered. Neither had he. He hated slaves, every one of them, as much as he hated the man who'd stabbed him. 'Zekiel knew him. His name was Rankin, and his eyes had no more light in them than the empty eye sockets of the skull that had scared Leethy.

"You niggers're a long way from home," Rankin said. "We come to take you back."

One of the men laughed and cocked his pistol. Eb Etter. 'Zekiel knew him, too. He was a little man with bad teeth and worse breath, and he smelled like he bathed in vinegar, though the truth was, he never bathed at all. He had a cast in one eye, but he could still shoot with the best of them.

"What say we just kill 'em and take their ears?" Eb said. "Mr. James don't want no runaways comin' back. They'll rabbit again first chance they get. 'Sides, it's a hellva long way back there."

"We could always take 'em to the next town and sell 'em," another man said. "Be more profit for us in doin' that."

Rube Sellers. 'Zekiel had heard about him, mean as a snake with a mashed in nose and carbuncles that grew on the side of his neck like fiery anger ready to bust out of his skin.

Rankin scratched the tip of his nose with his pistol. The moon and stars were so bright that 'Zekiel could see a drop of clear snot that hung for a second on the front pistol sight and then dropped off.

"Kill 'em or sell 'em," Rankin said, sounding like it hurt him just to talk, and maybe it did. 'Zekiel sure enough hoped so. "Or take 'em back. I think we'd better take 'em. Mr. James wants to be sure they're punished, and dyin' ain't punishment enough."

"Hell," Eb said, "they're just niggers. Let's kill 'em."

"Might be more fun to take 'em back," said the fourth man.

His name was Clawson, and he was big and round, but there was no fat on him, or if there was, it was hard as a puncheon floor. His voice was big and round, too, like a preacher's, and 'Zekiel knew he did a little preaching on Sundays now and then, saving white folks' souls for Jesus when he wasn't out with the slave hunters, sending black folks to Hell or back to their masters, which amounted to the same thing.

"Fun?" Rube said. "How the hell could harryin' a bunch of niggers back down the river be fun?"

"There's one of 'em looks pretty good to me," Clawson said, pointing his pistol at Dinah. "I wouldn't mind harryin' her a little."

"Mr. James might not like that."

"He wouldn't care," Rankin said. "Not that he'd need to find out. Anyhow, he's done through plowin' that field, and we ain't about to start. Eb, you tie their hands together and hobble their ankles. Then we'll move their sorry asses out of here."

Eb uncocked his pistol and stuck it in a black sash he had tied around his waist, shaking his head sadly. "I still say we oughta kill 'em."

"I'll tell you what," Rankin said, "if any one of 'em sasses us along the way, or if any one of 'em tries to get away from us, you can kill that one."

Eb grumbled a little bit while he was getting the ropes out of his saddlebags and then said he guessed that'd have to do.

'Zekiel heard Sim take a deep breath. Sim had been beaten down by Marse James' overseer more than once, and his back carried the hard black ridges of the whip scars. 'Zekiel knew that Sim wasn't going to stick around and let Eb hobble him, guns or no guns. He was going to run for it.

"Don't you do it, Sim," 'Zekiel said out of the side of his mouth, trying to sound braver than he felt. "We got to let 'em take us. That way we still got a chance."

He heard Sim release his breath in a long, slow hiss.

Rankin laughed as if he knew what Sim had been thinking as well as 'Zekiel had.

"You ain't got no chance at all, nigger, no more chance than you got of makin' those bones over there live again."

Just as soon as he finished rasping out the words, there came a stirring in the graveyard, like an icy wind through the trees. There hadn't been any breeze at all before then. 'Zekiel turned to look, and he saw something that looked like a whirlwind spinning around. The next thing he knew the bones were gathered up off the ground into the whirlwind that spun them around and about, skulls and all in a crazy dance, touching and clicking until all at once they clacked together like living things, and skeleton men started walking across the graveyard with little points of light flickering in their dark eye sockets.

If 'Zekiel's knees hadn't locked themselves together in terror, he would have run, run so fast that even a bullet from Rankin's pistol couldn't catch him. But his fear froze him where he was.

Dinah screamed, looked up to heaven, and clutched Leethy, who started crying again.

Old Franklin dropped down on his knees, clasped his hands under his chin, and started to pray.

Sim broke and ran.

The paddy rollers started yelling and shooting, and 'Zekiel's knees unlocked, and he flattened himself on the ground, dragging Dinah and Leethy down with him. The others fell beside him as .36 caliber bullets flew over their heads, breaking off tree limbs and smashing into the skeletons.

Bones cracked and bone dust scattered.

Skulls splintered, and pieces of them flew off in all directions. Some of them shattered apart, leaving the bony bodies headless. But the skeletons didn't stop their clattery march until they were standing a few feet from where 'Zekiel lay. He could see their bony toes, and when he looked up at them, he saw that some of them had lost more than heads. One was missing a leg, and several were missing arms. But they all stood there, as if they might be waiting for somebody.

The paddy rollers were reloading their pistols, and judging from the smell that was mixing with the gunsmoke, 'Zekiel was pretty sure one of them had soiled himself. 'Zekiel didn't blame him. He felt like doing the same.

But he knew he ought to take advantage of what was happening, even if he didn't understand a bit of it, so he stood up and turned to Rankin.

"I guess I got a better chance than you thought," he said.

He could hear Franklin off to the side, still praying and calling on the Lord. Maybe it was helping.

Rankin looked at 'Zekiel with those dead eyes, rammed a last bullet home, and aimed his pistol at 'Zekiel's head.

"I don't know what you did, nigger, or how you did it. But you won't be doin' it again."

He cocked the pistol, and that was when the moon and the stars started to wink out, one after the other, like somebody was pulling a thick black curtain over them.

'Zekiel looked up and saw blackness moving above the treetops as quiet as a cloud, but it wasn't a cloud. It was too low and too solid for that.

Everyone was looking up now, even Rankin, who didn't fire his pistol, maybe because it was too dark for him to get off a certain shot.

'Zekiel turned his head to look at the skeletons. They were all standing right where they'd been, and they were all looking up, too, the ones of them with heads, their dark eyes raised toward the thing that was now hovering over the treetops, blocking out the light from the moon and stars.

It was about then that 'Zekiel discovered that he couldn't move any part of his body except his head. The rest of him might as well have been frozen in a block of winter ice on the Ohio River. He looked at Rankin, but it was so dark now that he couldn't see any of the paddy rollers. He could still hear Franklin praying, though.

Round about then, lights started to come on above them. They came on one at a time around the edges of the blackness, and 'Zekiel could see that the thing that hung over them was shaped like a big wheel. Inside that wheel other lights were coming on, and to 'Zekiel it seemed that there was a smaller wheel inside the bigger one.

A *wheel in a wheel*, thought 'Zekiel, *way up in the middle of the air, just the way it said in the Book.* Maybe he should be praying, too. It wasn't every day you witnessed a miracle. But 'Zekiel couldn't drop down on his knees. He was still stiff as a stick.

A beam of light came down from overhead and centered on 'Zekiel. Other beams picked out the others. The paddy rollers, too, but not the skeletons. They all collapsed at the same time, with a rattle and a clatter, and they didn't move again.

The light that engulfed him wasn't quite a pillar of fire, which suited 'Zekiel just fine. He'd long ago forgotten that he'd ever felt cold. He surely didn't need to be turned into any burning bush. He was still thinking about that when he blacked out.

'Zekiel came to in a place that was filled with light. The floor was white, the walls were white, the ceiling was white. Not bright. Just white.

So this is heaven, he thought, wondering where the pearly gates and golden streets were. And when he'd be getting his long white robe. He was still wearing the linsey-woolsey pants, and he still had the rag wrapped around his head. It didn't seem like a dignified way to meet the Lord. He hoped the robe wouldn't be scratchy.

He was lying on some kind of a floor, which wasn't exactly soft, but it wasn't hard, either. The others were all there, too, even Sim, who had run away when the skeletons started walking. Even the paddy rollers were there. They all looked like they might be asleep.

Rankin started to come around. He sat up, rubbed his head, and discovered that his pistol was still in his hand. He pointed it at 'Zekiel and pulled the trigger.

The hammer snapped, but the gun didn't fire.

"Your weapons are useless here," a voice said.

'Zekiel wasn't surprised. It was heaven, after all. A man didn't need a gun in heaven. And then it struck him that he hadn't heard the voice with his ears. He'd heard it in his head. Just like a man was bound to hear the voice of the Lord.

"I am not your Lord," the voice said. "I am Geebahs."

'Zekiel had never heard of a name like that before. It wasn't any angel name he'd ever heard, like Michael or Gabriel. Wasn't the Lord's name, either.

"You the one made those skeletons walk?" he said.

"It was just a trick. We've used it before, long ago in your way of measuring time."

"I thought it seemed mighty familiar."

"We thought your friend called Rankin might enjoy it."

"I don't know 'bout that, but I surely did," 'Zekiel said. "Anyway, he ain't my friend. What you goin' to do with us?"

"You will be judged," the voice said.

"That so? Judgin' is the Lord's business. You right sure you ain't the Lord?"

There was a noise to 'Zekiel's right, and he turned to see someone stepping out of the wall. It didn't look like an angel. Or the Lord, either. It was taller than a man, and wider, with arms that hung down farther than they should have. It had very large feet, with thick, hairy toes. In fact, it was covered with hair, or something like it, so that 'Zekiel could barely see its eyes. It smelled almost as bad as Eb, but different.

Rankin's pistol clicked three or four more times, but it didn't shoot. Rankin didn't learn very fast. He had a kind of a wild look in his eyes, and 'Zekiel saw that he was checking the charges.

"I seen you before," 'Zekiel said to the thing that had stepped out of the wall. "Out in the Big Woods one day when I was cuttin' firewood. You run off fast and hid, but I got a good look at you. Nobody b'lieved me when I tole 'em."

"That was not me," said the voice in his head. "That was one of the Watchers. There are several of them on your world. But it would be easy for you to make a mistake. We all look alike to your kind."

'Zekiel smiled at the last remark.

"What that watcher be watchin'?" he asked.

"You. Your friends. Everybody."

"He can see all that?"

"More or less."

"But you ain't the Lord?"

"No. I'm just different from you."

"And you ain't from around here."

"That is true. I'm from…a different place."

Rankin had finished checking the charges, and he pulled the trigger of his pistol again. The hammer clicked again.

"Some of us need watchin' more'n others," 'Zekiel said, with a look in Rankin's direction.

"Yes. Those are the ones we will examine most closely."

The wall opened and three more things that looked to 'Zekiel exactly like Geebahs stepped into the room. Geebahs made a motion with his hand, and they gathered Rube, Clawson, and Eb into their arms. Eb had been playing possum, and now he was weeping like a child.

"Don't let 'em eat me, Rank! Don't let 'em!" he whimpered.

Rankin aimed his pistol at Geebahs, cocked the hammer, pulled the trigger.

Click.

"I will take that one," Geebahs said.

He walked over to Rankin, who looked like he wanted to run. But he couldn't move. It was like his feet were stuck in deep mud. Geebahs slapped his pistol aside, and took hold of him. Rankin tried to bite him, but Geebahs just wrapped his big arms around him and held on. Rankin's arms waved and his legs kicked. He looked like a spider trying to dance. Then he went limp.

"We'll be back," Geebahs said, and he and the other three things walked through the wall, carrying the paddy rollers in their arms.

While 'Zekiel was waiting to see what would happen next, Leethy woke up and looked around. She didn't cry. She didn't even seem scared. But she didn't say anything.

Sim came to next, and all the others were awake soon afterward. 'Zekiel told them what he'd seen.

"You right sure 'bout that?" Sim said, and 'Zekiel said he was.

"I saw one of 'em once when I was choppin' wood. I tole you about him, but you just laughed."

"They be from the Devil," Franklin said, and started in to pray again. 'Zekiel didn't see any use in trying to stop him, but he did tell Franklin that he didn't think Geebahs was from the Devil. Or the Lord, either.

"Leastways he says he ain't. He's mighty peculiar, though."

After a while, the wall opened again. Clawson came through first. Eb and Rube followed right along behind him, and Rankin came next. Geebahs was last. The paddy rollers were all walking kind of bow-legged and careful, and they had a glazed look in their eyes, like they weren't really seeing what was in front of them. Rankin stumbled a little over his own feet. He let out a little moan and grabbed his backside.

"What'd y'all do to 'em?" 'Zekiel said.

"Examined them," Geebahs said. "They are fine, healthy specimens, except for this one." He jabbed Eb in the ribs with a thick, hairy finger. "He has trouble controlling his bowels. And he should wash more."

'Zekiel wanted to say that Geebahs could do with a wash himself, but he didn't think it would be polite.

"They have been judged," Geebahs said. "We are returning them now. They will remember very little of what has happened here."

"They'll wonder what happened to us, though," 'Zekiel said.

"They will not worry about that. They will simply be glad to be returned to live out the rest of their lives with the chance to become something other than what they are."

"I don't 'zactly like bein' what I am, either."

"You are no longer what you were, and you will never be again. But now these others must be returned."

Before 'Zekiel hardly knew what was going on, the floor opened up, and the paddy rollers sank right through it and were gone. Old Franklin's prayers got a little louder.

"They gonna be all right?" 'Zekiel said.

"Does that really matter?"

'Zekiel thought about it. "Not a whole lot. What about us?"

"You will be examined now," Geebahs said.

◆◆◆

There wasn't much to it. 'Zekiel went into another white room and took all his clothes off. He lay down on something that looked like a white marble slab. A light brighter than the light in the room came on in the ceiling right over his head, but for some reason it didn't hurt his eyes. It made him feel a little tingly all over, but that was it. After a short time, Geebahs told him he could get up, and he did. His eyes weren't glazed, and he wasn't walking funny. For some reason, though, he felt a lot better than he had when he'd lain down. He made a fist with both hands, then opened them. The rheumatism that had been bothering him earlier seemed to be completely gone. His eyesight was better, too, and his back didn't hurt the way it sometimes did.

'Zekiel put his clothes back on, but he didn't tie the rag around his head. When he was dressed, he and Geebahs went back into the big empty room, and all the others were waiting for them.

"You have been examined," Geebahs told them.

"What about the judgin' part?" 'Zekiel said.

"You were judged during the examination of the others."

"You gonna send us back down there to that graveyard, then?"

"No. Not unless that is what you want."

"You gonna take us with you somewhere?"

"No. We take no passengers. But we will take you anywhere you want to go."

"You really mean that? Anywhere?"

"Anywhere at all. In your world, that is."

"I always wanted to see that place I heard about, with those roarin' animals and blue water rollin' onto the shore."

"I know that place," Geebahs said.

But that's not where 'Zekiel went. He talked it over with Geebahs, who said that it might be a mistake. After all, 'Zekiel didn't know how to talk the talk in that place, and he didn't know the people. Geebahs had a better idea.

All the others were taken to the free states, where some were reunited with family and others started new lives. But 'Zekiel didn't go to the free states, either.

What he did was go to Texas, where he got him some papers that proved he was a freedman, and started living in a little tiny town right near where Geebahs took him in that wheel. I won't say where it is, but it's close to a place they call the Big Thicket. There are Watchers there, and 'Zekiel sort of works for them. He still goes to talk to them now and then, and sometimes one of those flying things shows up, a wheel in a wheel. You've seen them. Otherwise you wouldn't have set up this place to ask people about them.

'Zekiel says we're still being judged, black and white, according to how we treat each other. One day, sooner or later, there'll be a final judgment. It won't be like anything you're thinking, because it's coming from somewhere you can't even imagine, from beyond the stars.

You ought to tell President Eisenhower what I've said. Maybe he'd listen. Maybe it'd give him something to think about. That's all I got to say.

End of transcript.

"Well," said Major Robert Friend, "what do you think?"

Dr. J. Allen Hynek flicked a slender finger at the transcript.

"You've been with Project Blue Book only a short time, Major. We get tales like this quite often."

Friend didn't agree. It was true that he'd become involved with the project only recently, but he wasn't quite as naive as Hynek seemed to think. He said, "Not exactly like this. You told me that detail is one of the things we look for, and this story is very detailed. Look at the descriptions of the people involved, of the weather. Even the names."

"Some of the names are rather unusual," Hynek said. "You should be able to check on them."

"I did. There was a man named Ebenezer Etter who lived in Louisiana from 1837 until 1894."

"The right time period, I admit, but it proves nothing."

"I know. But there's more. Etter had a history. He was a fiery abolitionist, and after the Civil War, he worked tirelessly to improve the lot of the former slaves."

Hynek smiled. "Doesn't sound much like our man at all."

"No, not until you find out that rumors of his past as a slave hunter haunted him for most of his life."

"I see. But of course if he was so well known, it would have been easy for your Moses Bates to have heard of him and to have dropped his name into his story."

"Not so easy. Etter's not in the history books, or at least not in any that you'd find in an average school or public library. Not even in an above-average one. We had to do some digging."

Hynek seemed more interested now. He said, "And the others?"

"We didn't have first names for Rankin and Clawson, so we didn't try with them. We did find something about a man named Reuben Sellers, sometimes called Rube."

"What about him?"

"We found out about him more or less by accident. We were making inquiries in the same Louisiana Parish where Etter lived, and someone at the public library mentioned an unpublished family history that was shelved in a back room. In the years just before the Civil War, Reuben

Sellers became a circuit-riding preacher who spent his life telling people about the miracle he'd witnessed when the lord made the dry bones live and took Ezekiel up to heaven in a wheel within a wheel. Some people thought he was crazy. Others thought he'd seen what he said he'd seen."

"And you think this friend of Moses Bates might have seen it, too."

"The *friend* part is what I'm wondering about. How many times have you heard people tell about something that happened to a 'friend' to conceal that it really happened to them?"

"More than once," Hynek said. "But that would make Bates a hundred and fifty years old. Surely you don't believe that's possible."

"Frankly, I don't know what's possible and what's not anymore," Friend said. "The world of possibilities changed ten years ago when Kenneth Arnold saw whatever it was that he saw up there in Washington state and called it a flying saucer." Friend paused for a moment. Then he said, "Have you thought about what Washington state has in common with the area of Texas where this 'Zekiel is supposed to have taken up residence?"

Hynek shook his head.

"Bigfoot sightings, that's what. Now think about that creature Bates described. It's very similar to the supposed Bigfoot or Sasquatch that people tell of. And 'Zekiel is supposed to have seen another one in the Louisiana woods, another place where there are Bigfoot sightings to this day."

"Good Lord," Hynek said. "I think you believe the whole thing. You should bring this Bates back for another interview."

"I tried, but as soon as he left this office, he disappeared. We had the plate numbers of the car he arrived in, but they turned out to have been stolen from a car in Texarkana, Arkansas, a few days before Bates got here. There's no Moses Bates to be found in the 1950 census in any part of East Texas. Or in Arkansas, either." Friend drew a hand across his forehead. "What if his story's true? What if he was trying to warn us about something?"

"What would he be warning us about?" Hynek said.

"You know what's going on in Arkansas. It started last fall, with Faubus and that desegregation predicament. And it's not just the events at the Little Rock school. You know what else is happening there, since it involves you."

Hynek nodded. "The saucer sightings. That's actually what my job here is, to decide if there's an astronomical explanation for a UFO sighting, not to evaluate stories by people like Bates."

"Those Little Rock sightings are the reason I called you in to read Bates's story. Have you found any astronomical explanation for those sightings?"

"Well, no. Not yet. But Bates couldn't know about them."

"Couldn't he?"

"No. We've been very careful to keep them out of the papers. There haven't been any reports published as yet."

"I know it hasn't been in the papers," Friend said. "What if Bates didn't learn about the sightings from the papers? What if he had...other sources?"

Hynek leaned back and thought it over.

"If you think it's even remotely possible, we should send someone to investigate."

"Investigate what? A man who doesn't exist?"

"We could look for him."

"We'd never find him," Friend said. "Not in East Texas. If there's someone there who doesn't want to be found, he won't be. Believe me."

The two men sat in silence for several minutes. Then Hynek said, "Do you really think we're being watched by beings from out there somewhere?" He waved a hand toward the window to indicate the blue sky beyond. "Beings from an advanced civilization, say, who might be judging us to see how well we get along with each other here, as if it might make a difference in how we'd get along with them if they revealed themselves?"

"If Moses Bates is telling the truth, they do reveal themselves now and then. But not to men like us." Friend reached over and took the transcript from Hynek. He laid it in a blue folder on his desk and closed the folder. "And that's why I don't sleep so well at night."

It's late summer in East Texas. Outside the little town of Timpson, a dirt road loses itself in the trees. Hardly anyone ever travels the road. It's not much of a road, nothing more than ruts, really, and it's overhung by trees that throw it into deep shadow all day. It doesn't go anywhere, either, just dead-ends in the middle of a lot of trees. A car can get stuck in the deep sand if the driver's not careful. There aren't many houses along the road because hardly anyone wants to live that far away from civilization.

One man doesn't mind the isolation, however. He lives in a small shotgun house near the end of the road, where the ruts play out. He's a black man who looks to be about fifty years old, though looks can be deceiving. He likes to sit in an old chair out on his little front porch in the late afternoons, and that's what he's doing on this particular day as the shadows deepen in the tall pines. In a little while the lightning bugs will start to come up out of the grass and flicker around as the stars come out.

There's a woodpecker tapping somewhere far off, but the man can hear him just fine from the porch. Sound carries well in the country.

Maybe it's an ivory-billed woodpecker, he thinks. There might still be one of them living 'way back in the Thicket. Nobody knows what-all might be back in there, least of all people living in far away places like Washington, D. C., or even Ohio. The man on the porch knows things about the Thicket that no other man knows. After all, he's had a hundred years to look it over.

His name is Moses Ezekiel Bates, but that name isn't on any census record or any other kind of government list. For all practical purposes he doesn't even exist, though a few people around Timpson know he lives in the little house at the end of the road. They don't bother him, and he doesn't bother them. He goes into town when he feels like it, which isn't often. Most of the time he just keeps to himself.

He wonders if he did the right thing by talking to that man up in Ohio. It didn't hurt anything, he thinks, and maybe it did some good, though 'Zekiel doubted it. Maybe someday they'll catch on, he thought, though Geebahs told him that they probably never would.

"The people on your world have to learn to get along," Geebahs had said on that day long ago when 'Zekiel had been taken up into the wheel within a wheel. "It's that simple."

"Or that hard," 'Zekiel had told him.

"Yes," Geebahs said. "Or that hard. But you're going to live a long time by their standards. You'll be around if they learn."

"Or maybe even I won't last that long."

Geebahs didn't smile or frown or anything like that, but 'Zekiel thought he felt something like a smile in his mind when Geebahs responded: "Yes. You'll live a long time, but possibly not that long. They are slow learners."

Damn slow, 'Zekiel thinks as he sits and waits.

Now and then Geebahs, or someone like him, appears at the edge of the trees, and 'Zekiel ambles over to have a little talk with him. Sometimes Geebahs, or whoever it is, tells him a little about the lions and the blue water in a far-off land, but those stories are a lot sadder now than they were when 'Zekiel's grandmother told them. The lions aren't what they once were, and the land that 'Zekiel had thought of as an earthly paradise wasn't what it once was, either. Not even close.

So most of the time 'Zekiel sits on his porch in an old chair, smoking a Bull Durham cigarette that he's rolled himself while he waits for people to learn what they need to learn.

And he watches the skies.

Ray Bradbury is so established as an American literary icon today that it's hard to believe he started out in the pulps. But start out there he did. Before *Esquire*, *The Saturday Evening Post*, *McCall's* and *Collier's Weekly* there were *Planet Stories*, *Super Science Stories*, *Weird Tales* and *Thrilling Wonder Stories*. Before the smooth white finished stock of the slicks, his tales were appearing on paper that was yellowing even as its garishly covered magazines were sitting new on the newsstands. A cursory look at his first and famous collection *Dark Carnival* reveals that nearly all of the stories first appeared in the pulps.

Unless I'm mistaken, "Summer" presents one of the very few ideas that Bradbury never covered: namely, what if glorious summer never ended? Not to say that he's never touched on the season: his "Rocket Summer" and "All Summer in a Day" (you may notice my clumsy and roundabout paraphrase of that title in the first line of my story) are wonderful evocations of the warm months.

Regardless, I'd like to think there's a little salt and pepper of the Old Master in my tale. Perhaps if Ray had had that idea before me, it would have looked, in *Thrilling Wonder Stories*, a bit like what you're about to read.

—*Al Sarrantonio*

Summer

Al Sarrantonio

It was a summer day that was all of summer. Dry heat rose from the cracks in the sidewalks, brushing by the brown grass that grew there as it shimmered by. There was a hush in the stilted air, high and hanging, the sun like a burnt coin frozen in the pale and cloudless sky, the trees still, green leaves dried and baked, panting for a breeze.

Rotating window fans moved hot air from outside to inside. Newspapers rustled on kitchen tables, their pages waving until the artificial breeze moved on, then settling hot and desultory back into unread place. The breakfast plates sat unstacked, forgotten; lunch plates with uneaten lunch—curling pumpernickel, wilted lettuce, an inkblot of mustard dry as paper—sat nearby. Morning coffee milled in two mugs, still tepid from the afternoon warmth.

"My Gosh, Mabel, has it ever been this hot before?" George Meadows said from his easy chair; he sat arranged like a man who had eaten a great meal, with his shirt and trousers loosened, but only against the heat.

His wife Mabel, prostrate on the nearby couch, the faded sunflowers of her house dress clashing and merging in a wilted riot with the worn daisies of the sofa print, tried to say something but failed. Her right hand continued to weakly fan herself with its magazine and she tried again.

"Hot as it's…ever been," she managed to get out in a croak, and then closed her eyes and ears, discouraging further comment.

"Yep," George managed to answer before closing his own eyes. He couldn't resist, he never could, getting the last word in. He rallied to add, even though Mabel was already perfectly aware: "Man on the radio said it might get hotter still."

◆◆◆

Three twelve year old boys hated Summer.

They hadn't always. At one time, Summer had belonged to them. From the first day of school letting out, until the dreaded bell sounded again, they had ruled summer as if they owned it. There had been baseball and bad tennis, and miniature golf and marbles in the hot dust. There had been butterfly hunts with orange black monarchs big as pterodactyls and just as difficult to catch. Trips to the secret pond with jars, and pondwater drops under Lem's microscope to watch the amoebas within. And their own swimming, from dawn to dusk some days, emerging at the end waterlogged beings, raisin boys, to dry and unwilt in the setting sun. And Monk's telescope at night, the fat dry cold moon sliding across the eyepiece like a pockmarked balloon; Saturn hanging silent and majestic with its golden split ring. Backyard campouts, the walls of Shep's pup tent lit from within not with fireflies but with the flashlights of boys with comic books, the smell of Sterno and pancake batter the next morning, the metal taste of warm water in boy scout canteens.

Summer had been their time—the time away from schoolbooks and parents waggling fingers, the time to be boys. And this year it had started the same—the banishment of blackandwhite marble notebooks, pencils thrown under beds spearing dust bunnies, school clothes in the backs of closets.

And out with the baseball glove! Oiled, smelling like new wet leather, sneakers that smelled of dirt, short pants, the dewy morning giving way to a fresh hot feeling and late afternoon thunderstorms scattering the ballplayers with warm wet drops big as knuckles and the temperature dropping and making them shiver. And swimming, and more swimming, and more swimming still, and the cool-warm nights, the sharp cold taste of ice cream, of a bottle of cola drawn from an iced bucket, of a hot dog steaming, hiding under hot sauerkraut. A drive-in movie in Uncle Jed's pickup truck: two hiding under the tarp until they were in.

Morning noon and night it was summer.

Real summer.

Until:

Something…

…began to change.

It was Shep who noticed it first: in the dangerous treehouse on a mid-August afternoon. They had finished trading baseball cards, arguing over how many cards (always doubles!) to attach to bicycle spokes to make them clack and were halfway through another argument about who was prettier, Margaret O'Hearn or Angie Bernstein, when Shep's head went up and he sniffed, just like a hound dog might. His leg, swinging through one of the hut's many floor holes, pendulumed to a frozen stop.

"What's wrong?" Lem asked, and Monk looked up from his new copy of *Vault of Horror* with a frown.

"Turn off your brain, Shep," Monk growled. "It's summer."

"Just because you don't want to talk about girls or leg hair or b.o.—" Lem began, but he stopped dead at the look on Shep's face.

"Something's different," Shep said, and he still held that pointer-at-a-bird look.

Lem tried to laugh, but stopped abruptly, a hiccup of seriousness at the look in Shep's eyes.

A whisper: "What do you mean: different?"

Shep spoke without breaking his concentration. "Don't you *feel* it?"

Monk shook his head with finality and went back to his comic, but Lem's face had taken on a worried look.

Shep was never wrong about these kinds of things.

"I...don't feel anything..." Lem offered mildly.

Idly, still scanning his *Vault of Horror*, Monk kicked out his sneaker and caught Lem on the shin. A scatter of orange infield dust, dislodged from the sculpted sole, trickled down the other boy's bare leg.

"You feel *that*, Lemnick?"

"Be quiet—" Shep said abruptly, and it was not a request.

The other two boys were silent—and now Monk sat up, his butt easily finding the structure's largest hole, which they inevitably called "the crapper."

Something like a faint hiss, something like the eerie castanet sound cicadas make, passed by his ears and brushed him on one cheek, but there was not so much as a breeze in the early hot afternoon.

"What was—"

"It's getting hotter," Shep said simply.

"Maybe it's because of Hell Cave," Monk laughed, but nobody joined him.

◆◆◆

That afternoon it was too hot to swim. It stayed that way the next three days. They abandoned the treehouse, leaving it's lopsided open-work collection of mismatched boards and tatooed, badly nailed orange crates, and moved into Monk's cellar, which was damp but cool.

It had never been too hot to swim before:

Never.

They perused Monk's comic book collection, which after banishment to the basement was on the verge of mold. Monk had built, from boards too useless even for the treehouse, a lab table in one corner, and they fiddled with the chemistry set, trying to make things that were yellow and then turned red, others that made smoke. They toyed with the rabbit-ear anten-na on the ancient television, a huge wooden box with a tiny black and white screen the size of a tv dinner tin—for a while they brought in the monster movie channel, and watched, in a snowy and line-infested picture, the Man from Planet X rampage through the Scottish moors. Monk brought down a bowl of grapes, and they ate some of them, and spit the rest at each other out of their mouths, pressing their cheeks for cannonade.

But their eyes kept drifting to the cellar windows, and the heat and light outside.

"Maybe we should go swimming anyway," Monk said, finally, on the second day.

They made it halfway to the secret pond, and turned around, drip-ping and panting.

Overhead, the sun looked hotter, if not larger.

They played darts in the cellar, and set up plastic army men and knocked them down with marbles and rubber bands.

Lem and Shep talked about body odor and shaving their upper lips while Monk scowled.

And always, for three days, they kept looking to the cellar windows, up high, filled with light, and closed against the summer heat.

That night they took Monk's telescope to the secret pond, and Shep's pup tent, and Lem's dad's battery radio.

The radio played music, and talked about the heat. The air was dry as the insides of an oven. There was a cloudless sky, and a smile of moon tilted at an amused angle, and, after a while, there were stars in the dark but they looked faraway and dim through the hot air. The telescope went unused. They swam for a while, but the water, over the last three days, had taken on the temperature and feel of warm tea. Inside the tent it was as hot as outside, and they shifted uncomfortably as they tried to sleep. When they tried to read comics by flashlight, the flashlights dimmed and then went out.

In the dark, Lem tried to talk again about Margaret O'Hearn and Amy Bernstein, and about Shep joining the track team when they all started Junior High in the fall, but Monk told them to shut up.

Later Shep said, out of the blue, "What do you think about Hell's Cave?"

"What about it?" Monk sneered. "You think it leads down to hell?"

"That's what they say."

Lem was silent, and then he said, "You think that's why the heat won't end...?"

"I wonder," Shep replied.

"You really think—?" Lem began.

"Go to sleep!" Monk demanded.

◆◆◆

In the morning it was even hotter.

The sun came up over the trees the color of melted butter. Monk set up the griddle over two Sterno cans, but no one was hungry so he didn't even start breakfast. They spit out the water in their canteens, which tasted like warm aluminum.

It was getting even hotter.

"Ninety-nine today," the radio chirped, "and who knows how hot tomorrow. It only went down to eighty-nine last night, folks. Hope you've got those fans on high, or your head in the fridge!"

He went on to say the weather bureau had no idea why it was so hot.

"What does that mean?" Shep said. "Isn't it their job to know?"

As if in answer the chirpy radio voice said, "Apparently, folks, this heat has little to do with the weather! According to meteorological indications, it should be in the middle eighties, with moderate humidity! Fancy that!"

"Fancy *that*!" Monk nearly spat, in mocking imitation.

The radio voice, again as if in answer, chirped just before a commercial came on: "Hey, folks! Maybe it'll *never* be cool again!"

Shep looked at his friends, and there was a suddenly grim look on his face.

"Maybe he's right," he said.

◆◆◆

It didn't rain over the next ten days. Thunder heads would gather in the West, dark mushrooming promises of cool and wet, and then break apart as they came overhead, dissipating like pipe smoke into the blue high air. The grasses turned from moist green to brown; postage stamp lawns changed color overnight and died. In town, the few places with air conditioning—Ferber's Department Store, the Five and Dime with its brand new machine perched over the front door, dripping warm condenser water from its badly installed drain onto entering customers— were packed with customers who didn't buy anything, only wandered the isles like zombies seeking cool relief. The temperature rose into the low hundreds, dropping into the nineties at night. On the roads, automobiles like ancient reptiles sat deserted at angles against curbs, their hoods up, radiators hissing angrily. Buses, looking like brontosauruses, passenger-less, stood unmoving, their front and middle doors accordioned open, yawning lazily at empty white bus stop benches.

Birds stopped singing in trees; the morning dawned as hot as midday. Dogs panted in their doghouses. There were no mosquitoes, and house-flies hung motionless to window screens. Spiders crawled into shadows and stayed there.

Cold water came out of taps almost steaming.

It was getting even hotter.

Three twelve year old boys made one more pilgrimage to the secret pond. They were sick of Monk's cellar, had done every experiment in the chemistry manual, had recklessly mixed chemicals on their own until one produced in a beaker a roiling cloud of orange choking gas that drove them upstairs. It had become too hot in the cellar anyway, with the windows closed or open. In Monk's kitchen the refrigerator whirred like an unhappy robot, its doors permanently open to provide a tiny measure of coolness to the kitchen. Milk had spoiled, its odor battling with the sour stench of rotting vegetables. Dishes, unwashed, were piled in the sink. The radio was on, a background insect buzz. Monk's parents had gone to the five and dime for the air conditioning.

"And even hotter, with record temperatures reported now not only around the United States but in Europe and Asia as well, in a widening area…" the radio said, though the announcer sounded less chirpy, almost tired. "Locally, state authorities are warning anyone prone to heat stroke…"

Monk and Shep and Lem took whatever dry food was left, found Shep's pup tent, inexpertly rolled and abandoned in a corner, and set out for the pond.

"…forty deaths reported in…" the radio voice reported unhappily as the screen door banged behind them.

It was like walking through a bakery oven. The heat was not only in the ground and in the air, but all around them. They felt it through their sneakers, on their knees, their eyelids. Their hair felt hot. The air was dry as a firecracker.

Shep looked up into the sun, and his eyes hurt.

"I don't care how hot the water is," Monk said, "it can't be worse than this."

It was. When they got to the pond and stripped, there was vapor rising from the surface of the water, and fish floated dead, like flat plastic toys.

"I don't care," Monk said, and stepped in, and yelped.

He looked back at his friends in awe, and showed his retracted foot, which was red.

"It's actually *hot!*" Monk said.

Lem sat on the ground and put his head in his hands.

Monk was putting his clothes back on, his hands shaking.

Shep said with certainty, "Someone stole summer, and we're going to Hell's Cave to get it back."

"Ungh?" a weak voice said from the kitchen table. George Meadows sat staring at his half empty coffee cup, watching the coffee in it steam. He had poured it an hour and a half ago, and it was still hot.

He lifted his hand toward it, looked at the sweat stain it left in the shape of a hand on the table and lowered it again.

"Mabel?" he called in a raspy, whispery voice. The sound of fanning had stopped and when George Meadows made the extreme effort to turn his head he saw that his wife's house dress looked as if it was melting, with her in it, into the sofa. Her right hand, unmoving, still gripped her magazine and her eyes held a fixed, glazed look. Her chest barely moved up and down.

"Oh, Lord…" he breathed, closing his eyes, getting the last word in though she hadn't said anything. "Gettin' hotter still…"

Three twelve year old boys stood in front of a cave opening buttressed with rotting timbers. With them was Monk's rusting Radio Flyer, bursting like a Conestoga wagon with their supplies: the battery radio, two new-batteried flashlights (one of them worked); three boxes of cereal; six comic books, no doubles; a large thermos of hot ice tea; four cans of warm creme soda; a length of clothesline pilfered from Lem's mother's backyard; a mousetrap, over which they had bantered incessantly ("What if we meet up with rats?" Lem debated; "Why not a gorilla?" Shep shot back; in the end Shep got tired of the argument and threw it on the pile), a B-B gun, a kitchen knife with a broken handle, a crucifix, a bible. The last two had been added by Shep, because, he said, "We're heading down *there*," and would listen to no argument.

They headed in.

It was dim, and, compared to outside, almost cool in the cave. But as they moved farther in it got even dimmer and hot and stuffy. Their bodies were covered with sweat, but they didn't notice. There was a twist to the left, and then a climb that disappointed them, and then a sudden drop which brought them to real darkness and a halt.

Lem, who was pulling the wagon, rummaged through the pile and pulled out the bad flashlight, and then the good one, which he handed to Shep.

Shep switched it on and played the light over their faces.

"You look scared," he said.

"Can we stop here for the night?" Lem asked.

Shep consulted his watch with the light beam. "It's two in the afternoon!"

Behind them, they saw how steeply the floor had dropped; there was a circle of light leading out that looked hot and far away.

"I'm hungry," Monk said.

"Later," Shep answered, and turned the flashlight beam ahead of them.

There was darkness, and a steep descent, and Monk and Lem followed as the beam pointed down into it.

After twenty minutes that seemed like a day, the black wagon handle slipped out of Lem's sweaty hand and the wagon clattered past him.

"Look out!" he called, and Monk and Shep jumped aside as the wagon roared down the steep incline ahead of them.

They heard it rattle off into the bowels of the earth, then they heard nothing.

"Why did you tell us to get out of the way?" Shep asked angrily. "We could have stopped it!"

"We'll catch up to it," Monk shot back.

"Sorry..." Lem said.

"No matter. Monk's right." The flashlight beam pointed ahead, and down they went.

Two real hours went by. Lem was thirsty, and Monk wanted to stop, but Shep kept going. If anything it was hotter than above now, and Lem finally panted timidly, "You think we're almost...there?"

"You mean *hell?*" Shep replied, and then added, "If we are, we don't have the crucifix anymore to protect us. It's in the wagon."

Monk snorted, and Shep spun angrily toward him with the flashlight, which at that exact moment went out.

"*Ohhh,*" Lem mewled.

"Be quiet," Shep ordered, "it's just stuck." They heard him shaking the flashlight in the dark, but the beam didn't come on.

"Maybe the cover's loose—"

There was the rattle of loosened metal, a *twang,* and they heard flashlight parts hitting the floor of the cave.

"Uh oh," Monk said.

"Help me find them—" Shep ordered, but now there was a note of desperation in his voice.

"I hear rats!" Lem cried, and they all went silent.

Something was skittering in the dark ahead of them.

"Get down and help me find the parts!" Shep said, and for a few minutes there was only the sound of frightened breathing and the pat and slide of hands on the floor of the cave.

"I've got the lens!" Shep cried suddenly.

"And here's the reflector!" Monk added.

"What if there are *rats* on the *floor!*" Lem said, but Shep ignored him.

"All we need is the cover, and one of the batteries. The other one is still in the body."

"I've got the battery!" Monk exulted a moment later.

"I can't find the cover!" Shep said desperately.

"I'm telling you there are rats!" Lem whimpered.

"I can't find the cover either!" Monk said.

There was fumbling in the dark, heavy breathing.

A bolt of light blinded them, went out, blinded them.

"I don't need the cover—I'll hold it on," Shep said.

He pointed the flashlight, clutched together by the pressure of his hand, at his friends, Monk on the cave floor, still probing, Lem with his back against the wall, eyes closed.

The beam shot to the floor, moved crazily this way and that, then froze on a round red piece of plastic.

"The cover!" Monk yelled, and pounced on it.

"Give it to me!" Shep said.

There was more fumbling, darkness, then bright light again.

They stood huffing and puffing at their exertion.

Their breaths quieted.

The scrabbling sound was still ahead of them.

"*Rats!*" Lem cried, and then let out a wail.

The flashlight beam swung down and ahead of them, and caught the crashed remains of the red wagon on its side, a chewed-open box of cereal, and the long fat graybrown length of a rat as it put its whiskered, sniffing nose into the mouse trap.

There was a loud *snap!* which made the light beam shiver, and then, in the darkness behind Shep, he heard Lem laugh nervously and say, "See?"

◆◆◆

They stopped two hours later for the night. By Shep's watch it was 10 o'clock. The flashlight had gone out again, and this time it was the batteries but Shep took the batteries from the other unworking one. They were tired and hungry, thirsty and hot. The wagon was serviceable but now made a loud squeak with each turn of the front wheels. The handle had been bent, but Lem forced it back into shape. They'd found everything but one can of pop, which Monk promptly stepped on when they set out. He smelled like creme soda, and his friends didn't let him forget it.

"We'll need the batteries for tomorrow," Shep said solemnly. He had found a flat wide place to stop, a kind of hitch in the slope. Ahead of them was only darkness.

It was hot and close and sticky, and they felt a vague heat drifting up at them from below.

"What happens when the batteries run out?" Lem asked.

"We'll have to conserve them," Shep said.

"But what happens—"

"Be quiet," Shep said, at the same moment Monk snapped, "Shut up, Lem."

They ate in darkness, and drank warm soda and un-iced tea, and listened, but there was nothing to hear. No rats, no nearby roasting fires, no dripping water, no sound of any kind. Just the silent sound of heat getting hotter.

"I hope we're close," Lem said. "I want to go home."

"Home to what?" Shep answered. "If we don't find something down here…"

The rest went unsaid.

They sat in a circle, and moved closer, the flashlight in the midst of them like a doused campfire.

Shep laughed and said, "We never finished talking about Angie Bernstein, did we?"

Lem laughed too. "Or how your pits smell!"

"Or your mustache!" Shep shot back.

Monk was silent.

"Hey, Monk," Shep said, "you shaving your lip yet?"

"And using 'B-Oderant'? You smell like creme soda, but do you also smell like a *horse?*"

Monk feigned snoring.

"Hey Monk—"
The snoring ceased. "Leave me alone."
Lem hooted: "Creme soda boy!"
"Horse pit boy!" Shep laughed.
Monk said nothing, and soon he was snoring for real.

Shep woke them up at seven o'clock by his watch.

At first he couldn't move; it was hard to breathe and so hot he felt as if he was under a steam iron. He knew it was growing impossibly warmer. He could feel and smell and taste it, just like he had in the tree house.

"We have to find the end today," he said, grimly.

They ate and drank in the dark, just like the night before. Now there was no talking. Lem was having trouble breathing, taking shallow ragged huffs at the air.

"Feels...like...we're...in a...barbecue..." he rasped. "Hard... to...breathe..."

They turned on the battery radio and there was hiss up and down the dial until the one strong local channel came on. It was the same announcer, only now all of the chirp had gone out of his voice.

"...hundred and ten here this morning, folks," he said. "And it's September first! Local ponds are steamed dry, and the electricity was out for three hours yesterday. Same all over, now. Ice caps are melting, and in Australia, where it's the end of wintertime, the temperature hit 99 yesterday..."

They snapped off the radio.

"Let's go," Shep said.

Lem began to cry after a half hour.

"I can't *do* this!" he said. "Let's go home! I want to swim in the pond, and get ready for school, and look at the fall catalogs and feel it get chilly at night!"

"It's not much farther," Shep said evenly. He was having trouble breathing himself. "This is something we've got to do, Lem. If we do it maybe we can have all that again."

Shep pointed the flashlight at Monk, who was trudging silently, straight ahead.

The flashlight began to fail as they reached a wall of fallen rocks. Ignoring the impediment for the moment, Shep used the remaining light to rip the battery cover off the back of the radio and pull the batteries out.

They were a different size, so he put the radio on and let it stay on, a droning buzz in the background.

The flashlight went out, then flickered on again.

"Quick!" Shep shouted. "Check to either side and see if there's a way around!"

Lem shuffled off to the left, and Monk stood unmoving where he was.

Shep pushed impatiently past him, flicking the flash on and off to pull precious weak yellow beams out of it.

"There's no way around here," Lem called out laconically from the left.

Shep blinked the light on, off, punched desperately around the edge of the barrier, looking for a hole, a rift, a way through.

"Nothing…" he huffed weakly.

He turned with a last thought, flaring the flash into life so that the beam played across Monk.

"Maybe there's a crack! Maybe we can pull the wall down!"

"There is no crack," Monk said dully, "and we can't pull it down." His legs abruptly folded underneath him and he sat on the cave floor.

Shep turned the light off, on again; the beam was dull, pumpkin covered but he played it all over the rock barrier.

"Got to be—"

"There is no 'Hell's Cave'," Monk said dully. "It's just a myth. My father told me about it when I was seven. This is just an old mine that played out and then caved in."

"But—"

"*I* made it all happen," Monk said hoarsely, without energy. "The heat, the endless summer. It was me."

"What?" Shep said, moving closer. On the other side, Lem sank to the floor.

"It was me…" Monk repeated.

Lem began to cry, mewling like a hurt kitten, and the flashlight beam died again. In the dark, Shep flicked it on, off, on, off.

"*Me*," Monk said fiercely.

Shep hit the button one more time on the flashlight, and it flared like a dying candle, haloing Monk's haunted face, and then faded out again.

"I didn't want it to end." In the darkness Monk spoke in a whispered monotone. "I didn't want it *ever* to end."

"Didn't want *what* to end?" Shep asked, confused.

"This summer," Monk answered, sighing. "The three of us. I wanted it to last forever. I didn't want us to…change. Which is what we were doing. Talking about girls instead of baseball cards, hairy legs instead of monster comics, body odor instead of swimming and telescopes. We used to do everything together and now that was going to change. When we went to Junior High Lem was going to try to date Angie Bernstein and you were going out for track. Then you would go out with Margaret O'Hearn, and the baseball cards and comics would go in the back of the closet, along with the marbles and the pup tent and the canteen and butterfly net. The chemistry set would collect dust in the corner of the basement. I could see it coming. It was all changing, and I didn't want it to."

"But how…?" Shep asked.

In the dark, he could almost hear Monk shrug and heard him hitch a sob. "I don't *know* how I did it. I just wanted it, I fell asleep crying for it at night, I prayed for it every day. Every time you and Lem started talking about girls and body hair and growing up, I prayed for it louder. And then, suddenly, it happened. And then I couldn't make it go away…"

Lem cried out hoarsely, then settled into low rasping sobs.

It had become even hotter, and then hotter still. The radio, still on, blurted out a stifled cry of static and then was silent.

In the sweaty, close, unbearably hot cave, the flashlight went on with one final smudge of sick light, illuminating Monk's crying face.

"I'm so sorry…" he whispered.

"Mabel?" George Meadows croaked. He could barely talk, his words fighting through the heat, which had intensified. His wife lay unmoving on the sofa, her desiccated arm hanging over the side, fingers brushing her dropped magazine. Her house dress was now completely part of the couch's pattern, melded into it like an iron transfer. The window fan had given up. The sky was very bright. Puffs of steam rose from the floor, up from the cellar, from the ground below. Somewhere in the back of his nostrils, George smelled smoke, and fire.

"Mabel?" he called again, although now he could not feel the easy chair beneath him. He felt light as a flake of ash rising from a campfire.

His eyes were so hot he could no longer see.

He took in one final, rasping, burning breath as the world turned to fire and roaring flame around him.

And, even now, he could not resist getting in the last word, letting his final breath out in a cracked whisper even though there was no one to listen: "Yep. Hottest ever."

I suppose one of my earliest influences was *Weird Tales* contributor Joseph Payne Brennan, whose understated style and edge-of-the-eye terrors have probably influenced my own approach more than I realise. He got me young, did JPB. Less of a mainstream figure than H. G. Wells, who mugged me with *The Door in the Wall* and *The Magic Shop* at around the same time, but an influence nonetheless with tales like *The Calamander Chest* and *On the Elevator*.

Fast-forward three decades or more, and you find me at the poolside in the sea tank of a marine training college where our ex-babysitter, now a PhD student, needs someone to film a helicopter escape for her thesis on stress and survival. After the exercise, I found some excuse to go back to the poolside alone. The empty simulator was hanging there on its crane arm, as sinister as an empty coat.

I pretty much had the story by the end of the drive home.

—*Stephen Gallagher*

The Box

Stephen Gallagher

It was a woman who picked up the phone and I said, "Can I speak to Mister Lavery, please?"

"May I ask what it concerns?" she said.

I gave her my name and said, "I'm calling from Wainfleet Maritime College. I'm his instructor on the helicopter safety course."

"I thought that was all done with last week."

"He didn't complete it."

"Oh." I'd surprised her. "Excuse me for one moment. Can you hold on?"

I heard her lay down the phone and move away. Then, after a few moments, there came the indistinct sounds of a far-off conversation. There was her voice and there was a man's, the two of them faint enough to be in another room. I couldn't make out anything of what was being said.

After a while, I could hear someone returning.

I was expecting to hear Lavery's voice, but it was the woman again.

She said, "I'm terribly sorry, I can't get him to speak to you." There was a note of exasperation in her tone.

"Can you give me any indication why?"

"He was quite emphatic about it," she said. The implication was that no, he'd not only given her no reason, but he also hadn't appreciated being asked. Then she lowered her voice and added, "I wasn't aware that he hadn't finished the course. He told me in so many words that he was done with it."

Which could be taken more than one way. I said, "He does know that without a safety certificate he can't take up the job?"

"He's never said anything about that." She was still keeping her voice down, making it so that Lavery—her husband, I imagined, although the woman hadn't actually identified herself—wouldn't overhear.

She went on, "He's been in a bit of a funny mood all week. Did something happen?"

"That's what I was hoping he might tell me. Just ask him once more for me, will you?"

She did, and this time I heard Lavery shouting.

When she came back to the phone she said, "This is very embarrassing."

"Thank you for trying," I said. "I won't trouble you any further, Mrs Lavery."

"It's *Miss* Lavery," she said. "James is my brother."

In 1950 the first scheduled helicopter service started up in the UK, carrying passengers between Liverpool and Cardiff. Within a few short years helicopter travel had become an expensive, noisy and exciting part of our lives. No vision of a future city was complete without its heliport. Children would run and dance and wave if they heard one passing over.

The aviation industry had geared up for this new era in freight and passenger transportation, and the need for various kinds of training had brought new life to many a small airfield and flight school. Wainfleet was a maritime college, but it offered new aircrew one facility that the flight schools could not.

At Wainfleet we had the dunker, also known as The Box.

We'd been running the sea rescue and safety course for almost three years, and I'd been on the staff for most of that time. Our completion record was good. I mean, you expect a few people to drop out of any training programme, especially the dreamers, but our intake were experienced men with some living under their belts. Most were ex-navy or air force, and any romantic notions had been knocked out of them in a much harder theatre than ours. Our scenarios were as nothing, compared to the situations through which some of them had lived.

And yet, I was thinking as I looked at the various records spread across the desk in my little office, our drop-outs were gradually increasing in their numbers. Could the fault lie with us? There was nothing in any of their personal histories to indicate a common cause.

I went down the corridor to Peter Taylor's office. Peter Taylor was my boss. He was sitting at his desk signing course certificates.

I said, "Don't bother signing Lavery's."

He looked up at me with eyebrows raised, and I shrugged.

"I'm no closer to explaining it," I said.

"Couldn't just be plain old funk, could it?"

"Most of these men are war heroes," I said. "Funk doesn't come into it."

He went back to his signing, but he carried on talking.

"Easy enough to be a hero when you're a boy without a serious thought in your head," he said. "Ten years of peacetime and a few responsibilities, and perhaps you get a little bit wiser."

Then he finished the last one and capped the fountain pen and looked at me. I didn't quite know what to say. Peter Taylor had a background in the merchant marine but he'd sat out the war right here, in a reserved occupation.

"I'd better be getting on," I said.

I left the teaching block and went over to the building that housed our sea tank. It was a short walk and the sun was shining, but the wind from the ocean always cut through the gap between the structures. The wind smelled and tasted of sand and salt, and of something unpleasant that the new factories up the coast had started to dump into the estuary.

Back in its early days, Wainfleet had been a sanatorium for TB cases. Staffed by nuns, as I understood it; there were some old photographs in the mess hall. Then it had become a convalescent home for mine workers and then, finally, the maritime college it now was. We had two hundred boarding cadets for whom we had dormitories, a parade ground, and a rugby field that had a pronounced downward slope toward the cliffs. But I wasn't part of the cadet teaching staff. I was concerned only with the commercial training arm.

Our team of four safety divers was clearing up after the day's session. The tank had once been an ordinary swimming pool, added during the convalescent-home era but then deepened and re-equipped for our purposes. The seawater was filtered, and in the winter it was heated by a boiler. Although if you'd been splashing around in there in December, you'd never have guessed it.

Their head diver was George "Buster" Brown. A compact and powerful-looking man, he'd lost most of his hair and had all but shaved off the rest, American GI-style. With his barrel chest and his bullet head, he looked like a human missile in his dive suit. In fact, he'd actually trained on those two-man torpedoes toward the end of the war.

I said to him, "Cast your mind back to last week. Remember a trainee name of Lavery?"

"What did he look like?"

I described him, and added, "Something went wrong and he didn't complete."

"I think I know the one," Buster said. "Had a panic during the exercise and we had to extract him. He was almost throwing a fit down there. Caught Jacky Jackson a right boff on the nose."

"What was he like after you got him out?"

"Embarrassed, I think. Wouldn't explain his problem. Stamped off and we didn't see him again."

Buster couldn't think of any reason why Lavery might have reacted as he did. As far as he and his team were concerned, the exercise had gone normally in every way.

I left him to finish stowing the training gear, and went over to inspect the Box.

The Box was a stripped-down facsimile of a helicopter cabin, made of riveted aluminium panels and suspended by cable from a lifeboat davit. The davit swung the Box out and over the water before lowering it. The cabin seated four. Once immersed, an ingenious chain-belt system rotated the entire cabin until it was upside down. It was as realistic a ditching as we could make it, while retaining complete control of the situation. The safety course consisted of a morning in the classroom, followed by the afternoon spent practising escape drill from underwater.

The Box was in its rest position at the side of the pool. It hung with its underside about six inches clear of the tiles. I climbed aboard, and grabbed at something to keep my balance as the cabin swung around under my weight.

There had been no attempt to dress up the interior to look like the real thing; upside-down and six feet under, only the internal geography needed to be accurate. The bucket seats and harnesses were genuine, but that was as far as it went. The rest was just the bare metal, braced with aluminium struts and with open holes cut for the windows. In appearance it was like a tin Wendy House, suspended from a crane.

I'm not sure what I thought I was looking for. I put my hand on one of the seats and tugged, but the bolts were firm. I lifted part of the harness and let the webbing slide through my fingers. It was wet and heavy. Steadying myself, I used both hands to close the buckle and then tested the snap-release one-handed.

"I check those myself," Buster Brown said through the window. "Every session."

"No criticism intended, Buster," I said.

"I should hope not," he said, and then he was gone.

◆◆◆

It happened again the very next session, only three days later.

I'd taken the files home and I'd studied all the past cases, but I'd reached no firm conclusions. If we were doing something wrong, I couldn't see what it was.

These were not inexperienced men. Most were in their thirties and, as I'd pointed out to Peter Taylor, had seen service under wartime conditions. Some had been ground crew, but many had been flyers who'd made the switch to peacetime commercial aviation. Occasionally we'd get students whose notes came marked with a particular code, and whose records had blank spaces where personal details should have been; these individuals, it was acknowledged but never said, were sent to us as part of a wider MI5 training.

In short, no sissies. Some of them were as tough as you could ask, but it wasn't meant to be a tough course. It wasn't a trial, it wasn't a test. The war was long over.

As I've said, we began every training day in the classroom. Inevitably, some of it involved telling them things they already knew. But you can't skip safety, even though some of them would have loved to. No grown man ever looks comfortable in a classroom situation.

First I talked them through the forms they had to complete. Then I collected the forms in.

And then, when they were all settled again, I started the talk.

I said, "We're not here to punish anybody. We're here to take you through a scenario so that hopefully, if you ever *do* need to ditch, you'll have a much greater chance of survival. Most fatalities don't take place when the helicopter comes down. They happen afterwards, in the water."

I asked if anyone in the room had been sent to us for re-breather training, and a couple of hands were raised. This gave me a chance to note their faces.

"Right," I said. "I'm going to go over a few points and then after the break we'll head for the pool."

I ran through the routine about the various designs of flight suits and harnesses and life vests. Then the last-moment checks; glasses if you wore them, false teeth if you had them, loose objects in the cabin. Hold on to some part of the structure for orientation. Brace for impact.

One or two had questions. Two men couldn't swim. That was nothing unusual.

After tea break in the college canteen, we all went over together. Buster Brown and his men were already in the water, setting up a dinghy for the lifeboat drill that would follow the ditch. The students each found themselves a suit from the rail before disappearing into the changing room, and I went over to ready the Box.

When they came out, they lined up along the poolside. One of the divers steadied the Box and I stayed by the controls and called out, "Numbers one to four, step forward."

The Box jiggled around on its cable as the first four men climbed aboard and strapped themselves into the bucket seats. Buster Brown checked everyone's harness from the doorway, and then signalled to me before climbing in with them and securing the door from the inside. I sounded the warning klaxon and then eased back the lever to raise the Box into the air.

In the confines of the sea tank building, the noise of the crane's motor could be deafening. Once I'd raised the payload about twelve feet in the air, I swung the crane around on its turntable to place the Box directly over the pool. It hung there, turning on its cable, and I could see the men inside through the raw holes that represented aircraft windows.

Two divers with masks and air bottles were already under the water, standing by to collect the escapees and guide them up to the surface. Buster would stay inside. This was routine for him. He'd hold his breath for the minute or so that each exercise took, and then he'd ride the Box back to the poolside to pick up the next four.

Right now he was giving everyone a quick recap of what I'd told them in the classroom. Then it was, *Brace, brace, brace for impact!* and I released the Box to drop into the water.

It was a controlled drop, not a sudden plummet, although to a first-timer it was always an adrenalin moment. The Box hit the water and then started to settle, and I could hear Buster giving out a few final reminders in the rapidly-filling cabin.

Then it went under, and everything took on a kind of slow-motion tranquillity as the action transferred to below the surface. Shapes flitted from the submerged Box in all directions, like wraiths fleeing a haunted castle. They were out in seconds. As each broke the surface, a number was shouted. When all four were out, I raised the Box.

It was as fast and as straightforward as that.

The exercise was repeated until every student had been through a straightforward dunk. Then the line reformed and we did it all again, this time with the added refinement of a cabin rotation as the Box went under. It made for a more realistic simulation, as a real helicopter was liable to invert with the weight of its engine. To take some of the anxiety out of it, I'd tell the students that I considered escape from the inverted cabin to be easier—you came out through the window opening facing the surface, which made it a lot easier to strike out for.

Again, we had no problems. The safety divers were aware of the non-swimmers and gave them some extra assistance. The Box functioned with no problems. No-one panicked, no-one got stuck. Within the hour, everyone was done.

At that point, we divided the party. The two men on rebreather training stayed with Buster Brown, and everyone else went to the other end of the pool for lifeboat practice. I ran the empty Box through its paces yet again. Buster stood at the poolside with his students and ran through the use of the rebreather unit.

The rebreather does pretty much what its name suggests. Consisting of an airbag incorporated into the flotation jacket with a mouthpiece and a valve, it allows you to conserve and re-use your own air. There's more unused oxygen in an expelled breath than you'd think. It's never going to replace the aqualung, but the device can extend your underwater survival time by a vital minute or two.

Both men looked as if they might be old hands at this. Their names were Charnley and Briggs. Even in the borrowed flight suit, Charnley had that sleek, officer-material look. He had an Errol Flynn moustache and hair so heavily brilliantined that two dunks in the tank had barely disturbed it. Briggs, on the other hand, looked the non-commissioned man to his fingertips. His accent was broad and his hair looked as if his wife had cut it for him, probably not when in the best of moods.

Buster left them practising with the mouthpieces and came over to pick up his mask and air bottle. I was guiding the empty Box, water cascading from every seam, back to the poolside.

"Just a thought, Buster," I said, raising my voice to be heard as I lowered the cabin to the side. "Wasn't Lavery on the rebreather when he had his little episode?"

"Now that you mention it, yes he was."

"How many were in the Box with him?"

"Two others. Neither of them had any problem."

I didn't take it any further than that. None of our other non-finishers had been on the rebreather when they chose to opt out, so this was hardly a pattern in the making.

The rebreather exercise was always conducted in three stages. Firstly, the Box was lowered to sit in the water so that the level inside the cabin was around chest-height. The student would practise by leaning forward into the water, knowing that in the event of difficulty he need do no more than sit back. This confidence-building exercise would then be followed by a total immersion, spending a full minute under the water and breathing on the apparatus. Assuming all went well, the exercise would end with a complete dunk, rotate and escape.

All went well. Until that final stage.

◆◆◆

The others had all completed the lifeboat drill and left the pool by then. The Box hit the water and rolled over with the spectacular grinding noise that the chain belt always made. It sounded like a drawbridge coming down, and worked on a similar principle.

Then the boomy silence of the pool as the water lapped and the Box stayed under.

The minute passed, and then came the escape. One fleeting figure could be seen under the water. But only one. He broke surface and his number was called. It was Briggs. I looked toward the Box and saw Buster going in through one of the window openings. My hand was on the lever, but I waited; some injury might result if I hauled the Box out in the middle of an extraction. But then Buster came up and made an urgent signal and so I brought the cabin up out of the water, rotating it back upright as it came. Tank water came out of the window openings in gushers.

Buster came out of the pool and we reached the Box together. Charnley was still in his harness, the rebreather mouthpiece still pushing his cheeks out. He was making weak-looking gestures with his hands. I reached in to relieve him of the mouthpiece, but he swatted me aside and then spat it out.

Fending his hands away, Buster got in with him and released his harness. By then, Charnley was starting to recognise his surroundings and to act a little more rationally. He didn't calm down, though. He shoved both of us aside and clambered out.

He stood at the poolside, spitting water and tearing himself out of the flotation jacket.

"What was the problem?" I asked him.

"You want to get that bloody thing looked at," Charnley gasped.

Buster, who had a surprisingly puritan streak, said in a warning tone, "Language," and I shot him a not-now look.

"Looked at for what?" I said, but Charnley just hurled all his gear onto the deck as if it had been wrestling him and he'd finally just beaten it.

"Don't talk to me," he said, "I feel foul." And he stalked off to the changing room.

The two of us got the Box secure, and while we were doing it I asked Buster what happened. Buster could only shrug.

"I tapped his arm to tell him it was time to come out, but he didn't move," Buster said. "Just stayed there. I thought he might have passed out, but when I went in he started to thrash around and push me away."

So, what was Charnley's problem? I went to find him in the changing room. Briggs had dressed in a hurry in order to be sure of getting out in time for his bus. As he passed me in the doorway he said, "Your man's been wasting a good shepherd's pie in there."

Shepherd's pie or whatever, I could smell vomit hanging in the air around the cubicles at the back of the changing room. Charnley was out. He was standing in front of the mirror, pale as watered milk, knotting his tie. An RAF tie, I noted.

"Captain Charnley?" I said.

"What about it?"

"I just wondered if you were ready to talk about what happened."

"Nothing happened," he said.

I waited.

After a good thirty seconds or more he said, "I'm telling you nothing happened. Must have got a bad egg for breakfast. Serves me right for trusting your canteen."

I said, "I'll put you back on the list for tomorrow. You can skip the classroom session."

"Don't bother," he said, reaching for his blazer.

"Captain Charnley..."

He turned to me then, and fixed me with a look so stern and so urgent that it was almost threatening.

"I didn't see anything in there," he said. "Nothing. Do you understand me? I don't want you telling anyone I did."

Even though I hadn't suggested any such thing.

◆◆◆

There was a bus stop outside the gates, but Captain Charnley had his own transport. It was a low, noisy, open-topped sports car with a Racing Green paint job, all dash and Castrol fumes. Off he went, scaring the birds out of the trees, swinging out onto the road and roaring away.

I went back to my office and reviewed his form. According to his record, he'd flown Hurricanes with 249 Squadron in Yorkshire. After the war he'd entered the glass business, but he'd planned a return to flying with BEA.

Hadn't seen anything? What exactly did that mean? What was there to see anyway?

I have to admit that in a fanciful moment, when we'd first started to suspect that there might be some kind of a problem on the course, I'd investigated the Box's history. But it had none. Far from being the salvaged cabin of a wrecked machine, haunted by the ghosts of those who'd died in it, the Box had been purpose-built as an exercise by apprentices at the local aircraft factory.

It was no older than its three-and-a-half years, and there was nothing more to it than met the eye. The bucket seats were from scrap, but they'd been salvaged from training aircraft that had been decommissioned without ever having seen combat or disaster.

When I went back to the sea tank, Buster Brown was out of his diving gear and dressed in a jacket and tie, collecting the men's clocking-off cards prior to locking up the building. The other divers had cleared away the last of their equipment and gone.

I said, "Can I ask a favour?"

He said, "As long as it doesn't involve borrowing my motor bike, my missus or my money, ask away."

I think he knew what I was going to say. "Stay on a few minutes and operate the dunker for me? I want to sit in and see if I can work out what all the fuss is about."

"I can tell you what the fuss is about," he said. "Some can take it and some can't."

"That doesn't add up, Buster," I said. "These have all been men of proven courage."

Suddenly it was as if we were back in the Forces and he was the experienced NCO politely setting the greenhorn officer straight.

"With respect, sir," he said, "You're missing the point. Being tested doesn't diminish a man's regard for danger. I think you'll find it's rather the opposite."

We proceeded with the trial. I found a suit that fit me and changed into it. I put on a flotation jacket and rebreather gear. No safety divers, just me and Buster. Like the tattooed boys who ride the backs of dodgems at the fairground, you feel entitled to get a little cavalier with the rules you're supposed to enforce.

I strapped myself in, and signalled my readiness to Buster. Then I tensed involuntarily as the cable started moving with a jerk. As the Box rose into the air and swung out over the pool, I looked all around the interior for anything untoward. I saw nothing.

Buster followed the normal routine, lowering me straight into the water. The box landed with a slap, and immediately began to rock from side to side as it filled up and sank. It was cold and noisy when the seawater flooded into the cabin, but once you got over that first moment's shock it was bearable. I've swum in colder seas on Welsh holidays.

Just as it reached my chin, I took a deep breath and ducked under the surface. Fully submerged, I looked and felt all around me as far as I could reach, checking for anything unusual. There was nothing. I wasn't using the rebreather at this point. I touched the belt release, lifting the lever plate, and it opened easily. There was the usual slight awkwardness as I wriggled free of the harness, but it wasn't anything to worry about. I took a few more moments to explore the cabin, again finding nothing, and then I went out through a window opening without touching the sides.

I popped up no more than a couple of seconds later. When Buster saw that I was out in open water, he lifted the dunker. As I swam to the side it passed over me, streaming like a raincloud onto the heaving surface of the pool.

By the time I'd climbed up the ladder, the Box was back in its start position and ready for reboarding. I said to Buster, "So which seat was Charnley in? Wasn't it the left rear?"

"Aft seat on the port side," he said.

So that was the one I took, this second time. Might as well try to recreate the experience as closely as possible, I thought. Not that any of this seemed to be telling me anything useful. I strapped myself in and gave Buster the wave, and we were off again.

I had to run through the whole routine, just so that I could say to Peter Taylor that the check had been complete. It was second nature. In all walks of life, the survivors are the people who never assume. This time I inflated the rebreather bag while the cabin was in midair, and had the mouthpiece in by the time I hit the water. Again it came flooding in as the cabin settled, but this time there was a difference. Almost instantly the chain belt jerked into action and the cabin began to turn.

It feels strange to invert and submerge at the same time. You're falling, you're floating...of course people get disoriented, especially if they've never done it before. This time I determined to give myself the full minute under. Without a diver on hand to tap me when the time was up, I'd have to estimate it. But that was no big problem.

The cabin completed its turn, and stopped. All sound ended as well, apart from boomy echoes from the building above, pushing their way through several tons of water. I hung there in the harness, not breathing yet. I felt all but weightless in the straps. The seawater was beginning to make my eyes sting.

I'd forgotten how dark the cabin went when it was upside down. The tank was gloomy at this depth anyway. I'd heard that the American military went a stage further than we did, and conducted a final exercise with everyone wearing blacked-out goggles to simulate a night-time ditching. That seemed a little extreme to me; as I'd indicated to the men in the classroom, the Box was never intended as a test of endurance. It was more a foretaste of something we hoped they'd never have to deal with.

I found myself wondering if Buster had meant anything by that remark. The one about men who'd been tested. As if he was suggesting that I wouldn't know.

I'd been too young to fight at the very beginning of the war, but I joined up when I could and in the summer of 1940 I was selected for Bomber Command. In training I'd shown aptitude as a navigator. I flew twelve missions over heavily-defended Channel ports, bombing the German invasion barges being readied along the so-called 'Blackpool Front'.

Then Headquarters took me out and made me an instructor. My crew was peeved. It wasn't just a matter of losing their navigator; most crews were superstitious, and mine felt that their luck was being messed with. But you could understand Bomber Command's thinking. Our planes were ill-equipped for night navigation, and there was a knack to dead reckoning in a blackout. I seemed to have it, and I suppose they thought I'd be of more value passing it on to others.

My replacement was a boy of no more than my own age, also straight out of training. His name was Terriss. He, the plane, and its entire crew were lost on the next mission. I fretted out the rest of the war in one classroom or another.

And was still doing that, I supposed.

How long now? Thirty seconds, perhaps. I breathed out, and then drew warm air back in from the bag.

It tasted of rubber and canvas. A stale taste. The rebreather air was oddly unsatisfying, but its recirculation relieved the aching pressure that had been building up in my lungs.

I looked across at one of the empty seats, and the shadows in the harness looked back.

That's how it was. I'm not saying I saw an actual shape there. But the shadows fell as if playing over one. I turned my head to look at the other empty seat on that side of the cabin, and the figure in it raised its head to return my gaze.

The blood was pounding in my ears. I was forgetting the drill with the rebreather. Light glinted on the figure's flying goggles. On the edge of my vision, which was beginning to close in as the oxygen ran down, I was aware of someone in the third and last seat in the cabin right alongside me.

That was enough. I didn't stop to think. I admit it, I just panicked. All procedure was gone from my head. I just wanted to get out of there and back up to the surface. I was not in control of the situation. I wondered if I was hallucinating, much as you can know when you're in a nightmare and not have it help.

Now I was gripping the sides of the bucket seat and trying to heave myself out of it but, of course, the harness held me in. My reaction was a stupid one. It was to try harder, over and over, slamming against resistance until the webbing cut into my shoulders and thighs. I was like a small child, angrily trying to pound a wooden peg through the wrong shape of hole.

Panic was burning up my oxygen. Lack of oxygen was making my panic worse. Somewhere in all of this I managed the one clear thought that I was never going to get out of the Box if I didn't unbuckle my harness first.

It was at this point that the non-existent figure in the seat opposite leaned forward. In a smooth, slow move, it reached out and placed its hand over my harness release. The goggled face looked into my own. Between the flat glass lenses and the mask, no part of its flesh could be seen. For a moment I believed that it had reached over to help me out. But it kept its hand there, covering the buckle. Far from helping me, it seemed intent on preventing my escape.

I felt its touch. It wore no gloves. I'd thought that my own hand might pass through it as through a shadow, but it was as solid as yours or mine. When I tried to push it aside, it moved beneath my own as if all the bones in it had been broken. They shifted and grated like gravel inside a gelid bag.

When I tried to grab it and wrench it away, I felt its fingers dig in. I was trying with both hands now, but there was no breaking that grip. I somehow lost the rebreather mouthpiece as I blew out, and saw my precious breath go boiling away in a gout of bubbles. I wondered if Buster would see them break the surface but of course they wouldn't, they'd just collect and slide around inside the floorpan of the Box until it was righted again.

I had to fight not to suck water back into my emptied lungs. Some dead hand was on my elbow. It had to be one of the others. It felt like a solicitous touch, but it was meant to hamper me. Something else took a firm grip on my ankle. Darkness was overwhelming me now. I was being drawn downward into an unknown place.

And then, without sign or warning, it was over. The Box was revolving up into the light, and all the water was emptying out through every space and opening. As the level fell, I could see all around me. I could see the other seats, and they were as empty as when the session had begun.

I was still deaf and disoriented for a few seconds, and it lasted until I tilted my head and shook the water out of my ears. I had to blow some of it out of my nose as well, and it left me with a sensation like an ice cream headache.

My harness opened easily, but once I'd undone it I didn't try to rise. I wasn't sure I'd have the strength. I gripped the seat arms and hung on as the Box was lowered.

I was still holding on when Buster Brown looked in though one of the window holes and said, "What happened?"

"Nothing," I said.

He was not impressed. "Oh, yes?"

"Had a bit of a problem releasing the buckle. Something seemed to get in the way."

"Like what?"

"I don't know."

He looked at the unsecured harness and said, "Well, it seems to be working well enough now."

I'd thought I could brazen it through, but my patience went all at once. "Just leave it, will you?" I exploded, and shoved him aside as I climbed out.

I never did tell Buster what I'd seen. That lost me his friendship, such as it was. I went on sick leave for three weeks, and during that time I applied for a transfer to another department. My application was successful, and they moved me onto the firefighting course. If they hadn't, I would have resigned altogether. There was no force or duty on earth that could compel me into the tank or anywhere near the Box again.

The reason, which I gave to no-one, was simple enough. I knew that if I ever went back, they would be waiting. Terriss, and all the others in my crew. Though the choice had not been mine, I had taken away their luck. Now they kept a place for me amongst them, there below the sea.

Wherever the sea might be found. Far from being haunted, the Box was a kind of *tabula rasa*. It had no history, and it held no ghosts. Each man brought his own.

My days are not so different now. As before they begin in the classroom, with forms and briefings and breathing apparatus drill. Then we go out into the grounds, first to where a soot-stained, mocked-up tube of metal stands in for a burning aircraft, and then on to a maze of connected rooms which we pump full of smoke before sending our students in to grope and stumble their way to the far exit.

They call these rooms the Rat Trap, and they are a fair approximation of the hazard they portray. Some of the men emerge looking frightened and subdued. When pressed, they speak of presences in the smoke, of unseen hands that catch at their sleeves and seem to entreat them to remain.

I listen to their stories. I tell them that this is common.

And then I sign their certificates and let them go.

This slots into a loose series of stories I've been doing about various generations of characters involved with the version of Conan Doyle's Diogenes Club I developed (poaching a lot from Billy Wilder and I. A. L. Diamond's *The Private Life of Sherlock Holmes*) for my *Anno Dracula* novels; readers are referred to my collection *Seven Stars* for various pieces which play with some of the characters who appear in "Clubland Heroes", though I've been writing about Catriona Kaye and Edwin Winthrop off and on since my 1982 play *My One Little Murder Can't Do Any Harm* and they get another work-out in the novella "Angel Down, Sussex".

Though characters like Sherlock Holmes, Fu Manchu and even James Bond have left cultural footprints, there were a huge number of other British pulp characters, appearing from the early Victorian era until well after World War Two in a great many fiction magazines. With this story, I was trying to play with the types of hero (or even superhero) who came to typify this tradition: Sexton Blake (sort of an equivalent of Nick Carter), Bulldog Drummond, the Blue Dwarf, Zenith the Albino, Biggles (a long-running heroic aviator on the Captain Midnight mould) and so on. We even had characters called the Shadow and the Spider—though one was a masked blackmailer from a 1930s play and film and the other a Spock/Namor-eared Diabolik-type super-thief from '60s comics. I first tackled this area in my story "The Original Dr Shade", whose dark avenger type character pops up for a cameo here.

Of course, much as we all love these pulps and their characters, times move on and there are many, many aspects of their adventures which can't help but raise a cringe: Bulldog Drummond's impersonation of a black man in the last chapter of *The Female of the Species* is amongst the most offensive scenes in literature, and a whole range of similar failings is covered in Colin Watson's brilliant 1971 study of the field Snobbery *With Violence*—a major influence on this piece and much more in my work.

—*Kim Newman*

Clubland Heroes

Kim Newman

Catriona Kaye would always remember the first time she looked up and saw one of them. In her case, it was the woman—the Aviatrix—swooping from a cloudless sky. An unhooded hawk, the Aviatrix was tracking quarry through holiday crowds who were beneath her.

Like the 20th Century, Catriona was nineteen years old. On an unseasonably warm Spring Bank Holiday, she had motored down to Brighton in a charabanc with a rowdy group of nurses and their quieter patients. Most of the party were about her own age, but the girls, in flapping white uniforms, seemed a different species from the haunted-eyed men, all veterans of the Great War. In theory, she was researching an article for the *Girls' Paper* on angelic latterday Florence Nightingales aiding the recovery of shell-shocked officers. The commission had devolved into an outing to the seaside. The mostly tiny nurses, strong in the upper arm as wrestlers, got behind wheelchairs and pushed mind-shattered men along the promenade like babies in perambulators. They even held races, which made Catriona fear for fellows who had come through the War whole in limb but might here take a nasty spill.

Between the piers, she observed human behaviour. Fellows in striped suits and straw boaters loitered, eyeing each passing ankle, calling out cheerful impertinences. She had already fended off several propositions, and would have been more flattered had supposedly heartbroken suitors not instantly recovered to press their attentions on the next girl to twirl a parasol. Old ladies occupied deckchairs, snoozing or staring out to sea. Families shared fish and chips. Boys built sand-castles and conducted sieges with tin soldiers. Hardier types in bathing costume dared the still-freezing sea and, through wracks of shivers, proclaimed their dips most invigorating. By the West Pier, a knot of children gathered around a tall thin striped box, looking up with mouths open as Punch and Judy went through their eternal ritual of bloody farce. A cheer rose from the audience as the crocodile clamped long jaws around the policeman's wooden helmet.

A news-vendor sang "Have You Seen Him?", promoting the *Daily Herald*'s competition. Among the teeming crowds at the resort supposedly lurked that master of concealment, Lobby Ludd, whose silhouette was printed on the front page (in Fleet Street, Catriona had learned the expression "slow news day") and on circulation-boosting posters. Keen-eyed readers brandished *Heralds* and barked "you are Mr Lobby Ludd and I claim my five pounds" at bewildered local characters, sometimes tugging genuine whiskers in an attempt to unmask the elusive gent. She had witnessed several scuffles, with indignant non-Ludds battered by rolled-up newspapers, and one genuine fist-fight.

Floss, who could have boxed for Lancashire, trundled Captain Duell up to the guardrail and locked the brake on his wheelchair.

"Mind the cabbage, would you, love? I've got to spend a penny."

At first, Catriona had been shocked to hear nurses say such things, but she'd soon seen they were ferociously devoted to their gentlemen. When a Member of Parliament touring the convalescent hospital refused to visit the shell-shock ward on the grounds that the patients there were all shamming cowards, Floss had rolled up her mutton-chop sleeve and personally punched his head for him. Captain Duell, twice sole survivor of his battalion, had served twenty-eight months in the trenches.

Floss tripped off in search of a convenience.

Catriona looked into the Captain's watery eyes. He was in a near-permanent dream-state. He didn't flinch at loud noises—those cases were left behind at the Royal Vic, since Brighton on a Bank Holiday wasn't where they'd be at their most comfortable—or stutter to the point of incomprehensibilty. He just seemed used up, forever on the point of falling asleep or starting awake, head hung loose on his neck, lolling forwards. Always tired, never resting. She couldn't imagine what he'd seen.

A middle-aged woman carrying a *Herald* stared at Captain Duell, comparing his face to the front page silhouette. Catriona tensed, sure the Captain was about to be harangued as a probable Lobby Ludd, but the woman thought better of it and passed by, looking for another suspect character.

Catriona shrugged a smile at Captain Duell, forgetting momentarily that he had little idea she was there. Then, she saw something *spark* in his eyes. She knew better than to believe in miracle cures, but had learned every tiny interaction with the world outside their minds was a triumphant step.

The Captain looked upwards, eyes rising. He lifted his head, detaching his chin from his breast.

"Yes," said Catriona, "look at me."

His gaze passed up over her face. She tried to encourage him with a smile, but he didn't focus on her. She was puzzled as Captain Duell looked up higher, above her head, into the sky.

The crowds hushed. She had a *frisson*, almost of fear, and twisted away from the man in the wheelchair, following his eyeline. All along the sea-front faces were turned upwards. Fingers pointed. Breaths were held. Then, thunderous applause rolled over the sea. A cheer went up.

A woman flew out of the skies, towards the prom.

Catriona had, of course, heard about the Aviatrix.

Since her stunning debut, the *Girls' Paper* had three times pictured Lady Lucinda Tregellis-d'Aulney—"Lalla" to her friends and an Angel of Terror to her foes—on the cover. Shortly after the armistice, distracted from her initial aerial exeriments over Dartmoor, the Aviatrix had swooped upon an escaped murderer, bearing the terrified felon up into the sky and dropping him back in Prince Town Jail.

The principles of Lady Lucinda's winged flight had been explained in learned articles which Catriona understood only vaguely. She had imagined a classical angel—though she knew a human with functional bird-wings ought to have a sternum like a yacht's centreboard to anchor the necessary muscles. The Aviatrix's wings, hardly visible unless sunlight caught them just so, were more like a butterfly's than a bird's. Complex matter seeped from spiracles along her backbone, like ectoplasm from a medium, unfolding into sail-like structures at once extraordinarily strong and supernaturally fine. Extruded through vents in her white leather flying jacket, the wings lasted a few hours. Shed, they liquesced like cobweb, melting to silvery scum. But while Lalla had wings, she could fly.

Like everyone, Catriona was awestruck.

She knew from her father, a country parson, that this was an age of miracles foreseen only by M. Verne and Mr Wells. In his lifetime, the world had accepted the telephone, the Maxim gun, recorded sound, the motor-car, the aeroplane, motion pictures, raised hemlines, world war. But those were things, concepts, reproducible. The Aviatrix was a person, an embodied marvel, a heroine literally above ordinary humanity.

Captain Duell tried to speak. Catriona was concerned for him; how could she explain that he wasn't "seeing things"? Everyone else also saw the woman in the sky. She wasn't an angel come for him.

The Aviatrix hovered, wings beating every few seconds, a rainbow shimmer of facets in sunlight. She was barely twenty feet above the sea, ankles primly together, arms casually folded. With a *whoosh*, she swam through the air, like a phantasmal manta-ray. She flew over the beach, up towards the prom.

All at once, Catriona actually saw the woman with the wings. Lady Lucinda wore white jodhpurs and riding boots, matching her slightly-baggy jacket. An abbreviated yellow leather flying helmet freed waves of pale gold hair that swirled about her shoulders, while tinted goggles concealed her eyes and a long white scarf trailed behind her. A button-down holster hung from her belt, heavy with a service revolver. As insignia on the breast of her jacket and caste-mark on her helmet forehead, she wore the d'Aulney coat of arms—birds and castles.

Catriona realised the Aviatrix was looking through the crowds, checking each upturned face. She was searching for someone. Since doing so well with the jail-breaker, she had specialised in tracking down escaped or wanted felons, like a Wild West bounty hunter—though no d'Aulney would ever stoop to seeking payment for doing his or her duty. Her late brother Aulney Tregellis-d'Aulney, vanquished over No Man's Land by Hans von Hellhund (the so-called "Demon Ace"), had never claimed a penny of his RFC pay.

The outfit showed little of the woman inside—bee-stung red lips and a blot of artificial beauty mark. It struck Catriona that Lady Lucinda painted her face like an actress, so as to give the best effect from a distance. Up close, her mouth would be an exaggerated scarlet bow.

Now the wings hung like a kite, and the Aviatrix held out her arms for balance, gliding on an air current. She seemed to walk on a glass promenade above the general run of humanity, considering then rejecting each.

Catriona recalled that Lady Lucinda had announced that she would hunt down and bring in an international revolutionary known as the Crocodile. The anarchist was behind a series of dynamite outrages on the Continent and reportedly intent upon bringing his stripe of violent upheaval to England.

A chill crept through her. A bomb on the sea-front, timed to go off at the height of a Bank Holiday, would be devastating, resulting in enormous loss of life. With the War so fresh in mind, it was scarcely conceivable that such horrors should resume, and on the mainland. And yet she knew better. Humanity's capacity for beastliness was undimmed even after the mass slaughter of the trenches.

The Aviatrix passed overhead. Catriona had the illusion she could reach up and touch the heels of her boots, though the woman was a good ten feet beyond her grasp. Captain Duell rose from his chair, back creaking, uniform wrinkled around his waist from so long in a sitting position. He was still trying to speak. Floss was back, an arm around the patient, cooing to him, supporting him.

Everyone else—Catriona included—looked to the Aviatrix. At last, Lady Lucinda stopped, as if a gem had caught her eye in a tray of coals.

She stood still, above the entrance to the West pier and looked down at the Punch and Judy theatre. Her scarf streamed like a banner. She slipped her goggles up onto her forehead, disclosing long-lashed blue-grey eyes.

The puppet play continued, but the young audience was hushed, staring at the new arrival, who put a finger to her lips, entreating them to keep the secret a moment longer. The policeman puppet seemed to turn to look up too, truncheon in its arms. A slit opened in the front of the theatre, the puppeteer's eyes shining through.

The Aviatrix smiled and made fists against her chest, crossing her wrists in a pose of concentration, then beat her wings. A humming-bird gust bore down and ripped away the striped fabric of the theatre, revealing a bearded fellow holding up the policeman and covering his face with the crocodile. The stall fell, struts twisting around the puppeteer's legs. Hung inside the stall were the familiar figures of Punch and Judy, their dog and baby. A string of sausages turned out, upon examination, to be linked sticks of dynamite.

The Crocodile waved his crocodile hand, as if warding off the harpy who fell viciously upon him.

Claw-tipped gloves slashed across the anarchist's arm, tearing the puppet off his hand, and hooked into his face, digging deep. A slapstick blood spray spattered the audience.

"You are Mr Lobby Ludd," said the Aviatrix. "And I claim my five pounds."

Catriona felt more than she could cope with—awe, terror, love, disgust. She fainted, unnoticed. When Floss revived her with smelling salts, the show was over, the Crocodile in police custody, the heroine fluttered away. Relieved holidaymakers, only now sensing the peril averted, redoubled their efforts to enjoy their day away from normal life.

In the melée, someone had stolen her purse.

Eight years and many singular experiences later, Catriona Kaye had learned to accept that she shared a world with women who flew. Indeed, by comparison, the Aviatrix was almost a routine marvel. After all, Lady Lucinda was a public figure while her own adventuring usually involved matters which tended to be kept from the newspapers or recorded only as buried, inconclusive items at the foot of the column on an obscure inside page.

In the Bloomsbury flat she shared with Edwin, she sat up in bed, swathed in a sumo-size kimono, fiddling with a Chinese puzzle box. Souvenir of a gruesome bit of business she thought of as The Malign Magics of the Murder Mandarin of Mayfair, the box had defeated her fingers for fourteen months. It held the preserved forefinger of a centuries-dead courtesan-sorceress whose sharpened nail-talon had several times altered the course of history. Or maybe the rattling, lightweight treasure inside the box was a very old twig.

Catriona was no longer primarily a journalist, an *observer*—though she had published books about bogus spiritualists and genuine hauntings. Through her complicated association with Edwin Winthrop of the Diogenes Club, she was a *participant* in a secret life conducted busily just beyond the perceptions of the man or woman in the street. She was still alive and sane; if she thought about it, she was rather pleased with herself for that—such a happy, if provisional, outcome seemed so unlikely for a person in her line.

She slid lacquered panels back and forth, rattling the box, discovering new configurations with each click. The fiddling was at least educational, expanding her knowledge of Chinese characters.

"Still no joy?"

Edwin came into the small bed-room, with a tray of tea, toast and Catriona's mother's marmalade. He wore a cardinal-scarlet, floor-length dressing gown that might have done for a ball-gown, over last night's dress shirt with the collar popped and the tie undone. There had been talk of disowning and a cessation of parental relations when she elected to share accommodation with a man to whom she was not married, but it hadn't lasted.

This was a decade of change.

"It's always three moves away."

Edwin kissed her cheek, took away the puzzle box and poured her a cup of tea, ritually tipping in just the splash of milk she liked.

This morning, he was being especially considerate. He had been out at his club—always *the Club*—last night. She gathered he had not slept.

"You're going to ask me to do something?"

"A brilliant deduction, Catty-Kit," he said, sitting on the bed, legs stretched over the coverlet, pillows propped behind his back. His hair smelled of tobacco; the inner rooms of the Diogenes Club were a perpetual fug, thicker even than the pea-soupers which still afflicted London.

"And it's going to be wretched?"

Edwin rattled the puzzle box next to his ear. He subscribed to the old twig theory. He had also suggested solving the puzzle with an Alexandrine sword-stroke, but she knew he was only teasing.

"It's just a tiny little murder," he admitted.

"That's extreme," she said, nibbling a corner of toast. "Couldn't you just have whoever it is crippled?"

"Not murder as in *committing*, murder as in *investigating*…"

"You may not have heard, ducks, but there's an excellent service for that. Those fellows in the bell-shaped helmets, the ones who always know the time and have those dear little whistles. They don't take kindly to lady journalists getting under their size-eleven boots, or so I've read in the *Police Gazette*."

Edwin shrugged, non-committally.

"Good fellows the 'peelers,' even out in the trackless *terra incognita* that is Heathrow, Surrey. A fine yeoman constabulary excellently qualified for locating missing bicycles, rescuing cats from trees and cuffing apple-scrumpers around the earhole. Maybe just a bit baffled by Murder Most Foul, though. The penetrating intellect and discreet tact of Miss Catriona Kaye would be much appreciated in certain circles."

He marmaladed more toast and chewed it over.

"If Mr Charles Beauregard of the Ruling Cabal of the Diogenes Club wants me to do something," she said, "he could always ask me himself."

Edwin paused mid-mouthful. He always looked naughty boyish when his superior and mentor was involved.

"Better yet, Charles could nominate me for membership, you could second me, and we wouldn't have to go round the houses every time the least-publically-acknowledged of the Kingdom's intelligence and investigative agencies has a task uniquely suited to my abilities."

Edwin scoffed.

"That *would* be murder. A woman member of the Diogenes Club! The ravens would flee the Tower of London. Sir Henry Merrivale would bust a corset. Anarchy in the streets. England would fall."

"Serve it right. This is 1927. We've got the vote. And the Married Woman's Property Act."

This was an old scab, picked at whenever they got bored. The last thing she wanted was to be a member of Edwin's club, but it was still an annoyance that she put herself so frequently at the disposal of an institution that would only allow her into a select few rooms of their cavernous premises in Pall Mall, refusing her admittance to the rest of the place on the spurious grounds of her sex. As it happens, she had seen everything anyway—with the connivance of Charles and Edwin, and disguised as a post-boy, while thwarting the efforts of Ivan Dragomiloff, the *soi-disant* "ethical assassin" and saving the somewhat over-capacious hide of that bloody-minded old reactionary Sir Henry.

"'Sides, *independence* is what makes you an asset," said Edwin, touching her nose. "We trust your objectivity. Diogenes isn't entirely free from the compromises, rivalries and politickings that shackle all servants of the crown. Sometimes, only a free agent will do."

"You aren't making this trip to the country any more attractive."

Edwin smiled, a line of white beneath his clipped moustache. He made adorably sad eyes, like Buster Keaton.

"And that's not going to work either, beast."

He was tickling. Which wasn't fair.

"The problem has features of uncommon interest."

He shifted a facet of the box. It would be just like him to solve the thing without even trying, after she'd spent months on it.

"You mean, it's embarrassing *and* dangerous."

"Not at all. It's probably very ordinary, run of the mill and even, as murders go, tedious. But there's an *aspect* that stands out. Almost certainly an irrelevance, but it needs mulling over. It's something with which the locals have not a hope in Hades of coping. Only you, Catty-Kit, can bring to bear the tact and cunning needed. Hark, what's that? Britannia, calling the finest of her daughters to do her duty…"

She swallowed the last of the toast.

"Aren't you curious?"

He was maddeningly right.

"So, is it a dagger of ice, melted away in an open wound? A beheaded corpse in a room locked from the inside, with the head missing? The venomous bite of a worm unknown to science?"

"None of the above, old thing. Plain blunt instrument, applied to the back of the noggin with undue force. Probably a length of lead pipe. Or a fireplace poker. Mr Peeter Blame, our luckless householder, apparently surprises a burglar in the course of felonious filching, gets badly bashed on the bonce, then left to die on the kitchen floor. Usual portable valuables missing. Cash, watch, minor jewelry. String of housebreakings in the vicinity. Official description of the fellow sought to help the police with their enquiries almost certainly runs to a striped jersey, crepe-soled shoes, a black domino mask, a beret and a big black bag marked 'SWAG.'"

She was being led by the nose. He was daring her to spot what was wrong with this picture.

"Peter Blame?"

"*Peeter*. Pee, double-e, ter. If you ask me, that's an invitation to unlawful killing by itself. The late, lamented had an endearing habit of bringing suit against newspapers who misspelled his name."

"Was he mentioned much in the 'papers?'"

"In the legal notices, which contributed to the problem, really. He had the habit of bringing suit against people for all sorts of things. A stickler for the letter, rather than the spirit, of the law."

She knew what he meant.

"So, Mr Peeter Blame, of the Extraneous E, was one of those busybodies who enjoys dragging all and sundry into court?" she deduced. "Thus scattering motives for murder throughout the countryside in which he lived. Heathrow, you said. I assume he's also been known to, ah, strongly criticise the constabulary currently charged with investigating his demise?"

Edwin barked a laugh.

"They didn't hold an inquest, Catty-Kit. They threw a party. With streamers and funny hats. I'm making that up, but you get my drift. An area of the law in which Mr Battered Blame took especial interest was the licensing of establishments that serve alcoholic beverages."

"Ouch."

"Indeed. Last January, he was successful in ensuring the dismissal of several policemen and the disbarring of a Justice of the Peace on the grounds that they not only allowed the Coat and Dividers, the local pub, to stay open after regular hours but were photographed drinking there."

"Photographed?"

"Another of Blame's hobbies. Flash photography. Neat bit of trickery, done through a mullioned window. All the faces clear and the clock over the bar in perfect focus. Pints in mid-pull, merry coppers in mid-draught, JP rendering the 'sober as a judge' saying inapplicable. Twenty minutes past midnight. On January the first."

"New Year's Eve? Are you *sure* killing Mr Blame was strictly against the law?"

"'Fraid so. Even the smallest, and smallest-*minded*, of His Majesty's subjects deserves full restitution when knocked off by skull-cracking crooks."

Catriona pulled her kimono tighter. She saw the trap closing.

"I'll concede being a killjoy and a bounder isn't grounds for justifiable homicide," she said. "But there's an elephant in the room, something colossal you've omitted mention of. The Diogenes Club doesn't concern itself with page seven stuff, no matter how flagrant the misapplication of local justice. Charles is only concerned with matters momentous. It takes a serious threat to the nation to get him out of his armchair. Even then, he's only *excited* by a serious threat to our plane of existence. So? Perfidious foreigners or supernatural spookery?"

"Maybe both, maybe neither."

She was close to teasing it out of him.

"I give up. What's the feature of uncommon interest?"

Edwin's eyes shone.

"The *address*. The Hollyhocks, Heathrow, Surrey. Mr Blame has...had...unusual neighbours. His property abutted the Drome."

"Ah." Catriona saw it. "The Splendid Six."

"Those are the fellows. And lady. Mustn't forget the lovely Lalla Tregellis-d'Aulney."

Catriona considered the situation.

"When an ordinary everyday unsolved murder is committed *right next door* to the greatest sleuths and saviours in the land, it's a tad awkward."

"Rather."

"So it had better get itself jolly well solved."

"Indeed."

"Quickly and quietly."

"On the nose, admirable girl."

She thought about it.

"But you want *me* to look into it? You're staying out yourself, along with the whole Club?"

"Matter of jurisdiction. Diogenes prefers the shadows, you know. And the Splendid Six...well, they're great ones for the spotlight. We've got by so far on staying out of each other's way. Best all round, really. But Captain Rattray put in a personal telephone call to Charles, on his private line..."

"Captain *Dennis* Rattray. Blackfist?"

"Yes, Blackfist. He asked our opinion. Not something he does often. Rather, not something he's done ever before. The thing is that the Splendid Six are all very well when you want the Eastern Empire saved from a Diabolical Mastermind or need a Royal Princess rescued from the inbred descendants of a lost legion of Roman soldiers maintaining a fief-dom in a hidden Welsh valley, but they aren't who you want to turn loose on a mundane robbery-murder. It'd be like using a team of Derby winners to pull the milk-cart."

"But I'm a suitable dray-horse? Very flattering."

"You have to appreciate our quandary. We can't go charging in mob-handed and take over from the police."

"What you mean is that Charles doesn't like the Club being called in like a tradesman to tidy up a mess on the doorstep of a crew of glory-hogs who won't sully themselves with it. Blackfist didn't ask for your help, he told you to take out the rubbish and lock the gate behind you. So, to get out of the who-can-spit-further contest, you're palming this off on me—because I'm 'independent'. Well, I'm not really allowed to poke into murders. I know there's this craze for amateur detectives, but they're usually so well-connected that the police bite their lips and pretend to appreciate the 'help.' I don't have an ancient title, a chair in advanced cleverness at an Oxbridge college or an obliging nephew in Scotland Yard. I don't think my press card will get much respect. I'm not even eccentric."

Edwin took out a sealed envelope and pressed it into her hand.

"Don't think of yourself as 'amateur,' think of yourself as 'unsalaried.' This will give you all the official status you need. Guaranteed to make any bobby in the land doff his helmet and snap a salute. And, indeed, bite their lips."

She examined the seal.

"Good grief. That's…"

"Yes, and he addressed it personally. Look."

She turned over the envelope and saw her name, written in a most distinguished scrawl. It was misspelled: Catrina Kay.

"You feel like saluting yourself, don't you?" Edwin teased.

Actually, she felt hollow and terrified. Being noticed from on high was deeply discomfiting.

But she had no choice.

"And here, oh my best beloved, is a train ticket."

Rattling out of Paddington Station, Catriona had a compartment to herself. Having purchased the current number of *British Pluck* from the magazine stall, she read up on the latest exploits of the Splendid Six, individually and as a side.

Teddy Trimingham, the Blue Streak, had successfully smashed his own land-speed record, in a bullet-shaped multi-purpose vehicle of his own design, the Racing Swift. Lord Piltdown, the All-Rounder, had just attained his century of centuries in an exhibition match at the Oval, then celebrated by shinning up Nelson's Column and bellowing in triumph from atop the Admiral's stone hat, terrifying the pigeons. The Aviatrix had snatched a fleeing poisoner (and his Eurasian mistress) from a ship at sea just before the absconding pair reached the safety of international waters, and bore the miscreants back to Scotland Yard. And the Six had foiled the Clockwork Cagliostro's grand scheme to seize Edinburgh Castle with wind-up tin soldiers, smashing his ingenious army into scrap metal and springs. Nothing unusual, there.

Since that Bank Holiday in Brighton, she had got used to the Splendid Six and their like. She knew there had always been such unusual individuals, cheerfully eager to turn their talents to the cause of the helpless. Just as there had always been darker fellows, only marginally less gifted, who served only their own interests or flew the Jolly Roger. For every Aviatrix or Clever Dick, there was a Spring-Heel'd Jack or a Wicked William; Edwin had once theorised that the stalemate between these unique persons, clubland heroes and villains, meant that the rest of the world could get on with whatever they were doing relatively unimpaired. Some great battles of Good and Evil turned out to be little more than squabbles: the Aviatrix's continuing campaign to bring Hans von Hellhund to internatuonal justice had more to do with her brother's defeat than the Demon Ace's minor post-war smuggling activities.

Sometimes, though, the rest of the world's business *was* impaired by the doings of superior individuals. Throughout last year's General Strike, the Splendids had been staunch in helping to keep "essential services" running. Something about press photographs of the Blue Streak working as a volunteer driver (joking about the snail's pace of a London omnibus) struck her as comical yet disturbing, while she had very definite feelings about Lady Lalla Tregellis-d'Aulney hovering over union meetings and taking a note of who spoke out the loudest. Catriona's own sympathies had not entirely been with the government in that time of national crisis—she had rowed with Edwin throughout, and he had shown the unexpected decency not to crow at her grief when the strike failed. Many a mine-worker or factory girl, raised on *British Pluck* or the *Girls' Paper*, looked up in awe and admiration, but moderated their opinion when the Six flew what socialist commentators were quick to label their "true colours". Trimingham didn't call himself the "Red Streak", did he? Zooming heroically through certain areas of the country, a Splendid was as liable to be the target of a tossed half-brick as the prompt of a hearty cheer.

At the back of *Pluck* was a helpful article about the Drome. A plot of scrubby flatland had first been turned into a proving ground for Trimingham's pioneering contraptions, where he could whizz and whoosh and go bang well away from the prying eyes of foreign spies or rival inventors. (Peeter "I'll see you in court" Blame must have enjoyed living next door to that racket!) The Splendid Six first convened when the Good Fellows Four put out the call for new recruits to battle the plague hordes of the Rat Rabbi, Norwegicus Cohen, and the Celestial Schemer, Dien Ch'ing. At the successful conclusion of that exploit, the Drome became the Head Quarters of the Six, home to their famed Museum of Mystery. There, surrounded by souvenirs a good deal more impressive than a puzzle-box, the Six sat around King Arthur's original table, each in their appointed place. The round table was recovered from the Shadow Realm of Perfidious Albion during an adventure that had run in *British Pluck* for six consecutive numbers under the title "Against the Nights of the Underground Fable". From the article, she deduced that at meetings the original GFF had the Aviatrix serve the tea, and put the brown-skinned Chandra Nguyen Seth, the Mystic Maharajah, on a stool in the draughty corner.

A fold-out map of the Drome kept her busy turning the magazine upside-down to examine details. The village of Heathrow (and its railway station) was shown, but there was no indication as to which of the adjacent properties had belonged to the late Peeter Blame.

As he saw her off, Edwin had given a final friendly suggestion.

"If you can get this settled without even involving the Splendid Sausages, that would probably be for the best."

That would suit her perfectly.

However, she had muttered "some hope".

She considered the portraits dotted in misty ovals around the map: bright eyes (inevitably blue with silver-grey flecks), forthright chins set against underhandedness, devil-may-care half-smiles eager for adventure, stalwart knotted brows ready for any intellectual challenge, gleaming teeth suitable for biting into a fresh red English apple, dashing signatures (and one thumb-print).

The Splendid Six were heroes. And they terrified her.

◆◆◆

It was fortunate there was little reason for anyone to visit Heathrow. The station was tiny and dilapidated: boards missing from the platform, sign hanging askew. She alone alighted, taking care to avoid jets of steam aimed at ankle-height. The engine came to the boil again and the hissing, clanking train trundled off, picking up speed in anticipation of more interesting stops further down the line.

An old man emerged from a hut. He tripped over someone's left luggage, which had literally taken root. The two suitcases were furred over with moss, weeds sprouting from cracks in the leather.

"You the missy from up Lunnon?"

The toothless apparition wore a battered station-master's cap on the back of his head. He had a white fringe around his collapsed face, thinning hair up top, sparse beard under his chin. He walked bow-legged with the aid of a stick. A single medal hung from his loose blue tunic.

"I'm Catriona Kaye," she said.

"Come about the killin'?"

He gurned something that might have been a smile, making a puckered black hole of his mouth.

"Yes. I suppose so."

"I'm 'Arbottle.'"

"Pleased to meet you, Mr Harbottle."

"*Sergeant* 'Arbottle,'" he insisted.

He snatched off his cap and looked at it with disgust.

"Wrong 'at. Sorry."

Sergeant Harbottle dashed into the hut and came out wearing a policeman's helmet that must have been issued in Victoria's reign. Or perhaps William and Mary's. The chin-strap hung loose under his wattles.

"I'm Station-Master, Post-Master, Captain of Militia and Police Sergeant. Do the milk-round, too."

"Very public-spirited."

"No one else would take the jobs. Not since New Year's Eve."

Catriona understood.

"That might change now."

There wasn't much point coming at this case from the angle of motive.

"Sergeant, please understand I'm here only to offer you assistance. I have full confidence in your ability to bring this unpleasant matter to a neat conclusion."

"Eh?"

"I'm sure you'll bag the culprit."

"Never had one of those round here before. Culp-whatchamacallits. But you're right, missy. Once I put my mind to something, it gets done."

"Should we begin by visiting the scene of the crime?"

Harbottle went cross-eyed.

"'E's been taken away. What with the warm weather, it was best. I'm sure you understand, missy. Deaders gives off a bit of a pong."

"So I understand."

"What for you be wantin' to nose round where a deader's been, then?"

"Clues, Sergeant. Every sleuth needs clues."

"I've never 'ad a clue."

"That, I'll be bound, will change also."

Harbottle's face set in a crumpled version of a determined look. Catriona wondered if she wouldn't be best off on her own.

Then again, she wasn't "up Lunnon" now.

"Lead the way," she invited.

◆◆◆

Harbottle produced a collapsible bone-shaker bicycle from his shed and unfolded it into a shape to delight a Parisian surrealist. He apologised that there was no room for two and told her she'd have to keep up, then began pedaling down a muddy lane away from the station.

She had to drag her feet to let him stay level with her. His conveyance wobbled alarmingly from side to side and his legs were too long, forcing his knees out as he pushed on the pedals. If it hadn't been for the modest slope of the lane, adding gravity to motive power, she feared Harbottle would have made even slower progress. She didn't like to think about his return journey.

A jolly rustic, sat outside the Coat and Dividers, shouted "get off and milk it."

Harbottle spat a stream of brown juice and invective at the fellow, who lifted his pint in salute. Catriona checked the nurse's watch pinned to her blouse. Opening time wasn't for an hour.

"The last sergeant," muttered Harbottle. "Billy Beamish."

She looked back at the celebrating ex-copper. He toasted her too, and showed every indication of having toasted any passerby, human or animal, for the last two days.

"Grieving hard, I see."

"Oh, not him. Billy Beamish hated Pee-ee-eeter Blame worse than poison. Lost his job, see. Lot of them lost their jobs. For drinkin' after hours. Not me, though. I'm temperance."

The Coat and Dividers was in the fork of a Y-junction. A triangle of green with a tree and some small cottages made up the rest of Heathrow. Untended geese muddled about. It was rather pleasant, if dusty.

Harbottle pedaled past a mile-post, then hopped off the bike with a creaking of bones and spokes. From here on, the gradient was against him. He made better time pushing the thing.

"Here's the Hollyhocks."

The cottage was set in its own grounds, very neat and tidy, with regimented rows of petunias and roses. The white filigree gate was set in an arched bower threaded through with pretty red and purple flowers, its picturesque aspect marred somewhat by a superfluity of engraved boards with black warnings: "No Hawkers or Circulars", "Trespassers Will Be Prosecuted to the Full Extent of the Law", "Uninvited Callers Unwelcome", "Keep Off the Grass", "It is Impermissable to Operate a Motorised Conveyance in This Thoroughfare" and "Vagrancy and Mendicancy Are Criminal Offences— The Police *Will* Be Called!". Each board was signed "P. Blame, Esq."

The gate was open. And so was the cottage's door.

"There's someone inside," said Catriona.

"I told you, 'e's been taken away on account of the potential whiff…"

"Not the owner," she said. "Have you ever heard about the murderer returning to the scene of the crime?"

"Why'd 'e want to do a fool thing like that?"

"Hard to fathom, the criminal mind. Even for sleuths such as we."

She opened her purse.

"What's that there?" asked Harbottle, eyes bulging.

"It's a ladylike little automatic."

"It's a pop-pop gun is what it is. A concealed weapon!"

"It's not concealed. I'm showing it to you."

He thought about that.

She ventured into the garden of the Hollyhocks and stepped up to the doorway.

"Knock knock," she said, rapping the open door with the barrel of her ladylike little automatic.

"Who's there?" came a squeak.

"That's what I should be asking," she said.

Little sharp eyes showed in the gloom inside the cottage, one much larger than the other.

"What wight have you to quiz me, madame?"

"I'm with the police," she said.

A little boy stepped into the light. He wore his oiled-down hair cen-tre-parted, and was dressed in grey shorts and a matching blazer. His gaze was resolute, but his chin a touch underdeveloped. The child held up a magnifying glass the size of a large lollipop, which was why one of his watery blue eyes seemed four times the size of the other, emphasising the steely grey flecks.

"You're late," he said. "The clues are getting cold."

There was a sticky black-red splash on the rug. The boy held his glass over it, and peered at the mess.

"Blood, bwains, bits of bone," he said. "Nothing interesting."

Catriona stood out of the way as the boy detective poked about, examining things through his glass. The study where the body had been found was a mess. From the neatness of the garden and the rest of the cottage, it was an easy deduction that the room had been thoroughly ransacked by the murderer. Or else an earlier clue-hunt from one of the too many sleuths on this case.

"Here, a file has been wemoved."

The boy solemnly pointed at a gap in the book-shelves, as obvious as a missing front tooth in a broad smile, between "Oct-Dec "26" and "Apr-Jun "27".

"January to March of this year," he proclaimed.

"Amazing," commented Catriona, drily.

"It's simple, weally," he responded, pleased. "A perspicacious person can tell from the files either side which is missing."

Harbottle scratched his head in admiration.

The boy beamed a wide, not-very-pleasant smile.

This, she knew, was Master Richard Cleaver, "Clever Dick", the brightest eleven-year-old lad in the land. He had taken a double first in Chemistry and Oriental Languages from Oxford last year. Independently wealthy from the patent of a new, more efficient type of paperclip he had twisted out of one of his mother's hairpins when he was seven, he divided his time between solving mysteries that baffled the police and adventur-ing with the rest of the Splendid Six.

She should have brought the Chinese puzzle box. Clever Dick could probably open it in seconds.

"This isn't the first murder I've solved," he announced, somewhat prematurely. "If it weren't for my bwain-power, the Andover Axeman would never have been hanged. Last Whitsun half-holiday, I wecovered the Cwown Jewels. They'd been stolen by Iwish oiks. Served them wight when they got shot."

She reminded herself not to laugh at the child.

His bumps of intellect might be swollen to incredible proportions, but those of humour and humility had withered away entirely.

"I proved Nanny Nuggins was a Bolsheviek spy. Stalin sent her to Sibewia for failing to kidnap me."

She deduced that Stalin had never met Master Richard.

"You must have got on well with Mr Blame," she ventured. "You had a lot in common. An interest in the law."

Clever Dick made a face.

"Ugh! No fear. That common fellow kept saying I ought to be in school. He alleged there were laws about where childwen should be."

Catriona was beginning to sympathise with the unlamented departed.

Clever Dick sorted through strews of papers on the desk.

"I think you'd better leave those alone," she said, mildly.

"I don't think that and you can't make me."

He patted his hands on the papers to prove it, pawing around the desk.

"See. I'm *not* leaving these clues alone. And there's nothing you can do about it. I can identify seventy-eight different types of type-witer letter. I can hold my bweath for four and a half minutes. I have a medal from Scotland Yard."

"So have I," she said. "But it's not done to brag, is it?"

Clever Dick whirled around and looked at her for the first time, applying all his reputed intellect. He was genuinely puzzled by what she'd said, and didn't like the sensation.

"Whyever not? If you've earned something, it's yours. Why shouldn't you bwag?"

"Nobody likes a smart-arse," she suggested, mildly.

The boy waved it away.

"Nonsense. You are a silly person. And a girl, besides. I didn't know they let girls in the police. Or old smelly men without teeth."

Harbottle grunted. "'Ere, you mind your manners, Sonny-Jim-me-Lad."

The brainiest boy in Britain stuck out his tongue at them.

Catriona looked at the papers on the desk. Correspondence with lawyers, courts, newspapers. Blame kept copies of all his letters.

"Those are my clues," said Clever Dick. "You find your own!"

This was becoming tiresome.

"I'm ever so much cleverer than you. I can deduce masses of things about you. You live in a house in Bloomsbury but were bwought up in Somerset or Dorset. You had marmalade on toast for bweakfast with a man who has a moustache."

"It's a flat."

"I *meant* flat when I said house!"

"Somerset."

"I knew it. Your type-witer has a faulty shift-key. You don't spend much money on clothes. That purse was a gift fwom someone Canadian. You have a two-inch scar just above your knee. It's no use pwessing your skirt down. I've seen the wolled tops of your stockings."

She deduced that in a few years' time, Clever Dick was not going to be popular with the ladies.

"You were wecently nearly killed by a Chinaman. (So was I, so there!) You have no bwothers or sisters. And you lied about being a police girl. No, you didn't. You were twying to be clever when you said you were 'with the police' because this fathead is a policeman and you *are* with him. It's no use twying to be clever, because I'll always out-fox you. Do you play chess? I can beat anyone, without looking at the board. You're married but you won't wear a wing."

"I'm not."

"Yes, you are. Your husband is the bweakfast fellow."

She wasn't about to explain her domestic arrangements to an eleven-year-old.

Sweetly, she said "I don't believe you can really hold your breath for four and a half minutes."

"Can so."

"Prove it."

He huffed in a breath, expanding his cheeks and screwing his eyes shut, then began to nod off the seconds.

She looked cursorily around the room, but thought she'd learned all she could for the moment. Later, she would have to spend hours going through all the papers and files, mulling over and rejecting dozens of leads. It was the sort of investigative work the Splendid Six never had to deal with, any more than they cooked their own supper or cleaned their own guns.

Clever Dick's face went red, then distinctly blue. He continued nodding.

She pressed a finger to her lips for quiet and shooed Harbottle out of the room and cottage, following him on tip-toes.

She heard a certain straining behind her, but thought little of it.

Outside, she found a shining reception committee.

◆◆◆

Three more of the Splendid Six were crowded into the tiny cottage garden. Blackfist, the All-Rounder and the Aviatrix. The space wasn't quite suitable for such *big* persons, though only the tall, wide, shambling Lord Piltdown was really much larger than the ordinary.

When her feet were on the ground, Lady Lucinda—Catriona was slightly shocked to realise—was *tiny*, at least a handspan shorter than her own five foot two. From that first sight, she had reckoned the Aviatrix a full fathom of Amazon glory. Without wings, the woman was a petite, long-faced debutante whose jodhpurs wrinkled over thin legs.

Captain Rattray, Blackfist, was a smiling, casual fellow with patent-leather hair and arrow-collar features. On a thin gold chain around his neck hung the famous Fang of Night, the purple-black gemstone he had plucked from the forehead of a pre-human cyclopaean idol discovered in a cavern temple under the Andes. The story was that when the Captain made a fist around the jewel, his body became granite-impervious to harm and his blows landed with the force of a wrecking-ball. Unconsciously, or perhaps not, he fingered his magical knuckle-duster all the time. The fingertips of his left hand were stained black, as if qualities of the gem were seeping into his skin.

He stuck out his free hand to shake hers.

"Miss Kaye, welcome to Heathrow. I'm in the way of being Dennis Rattray."

She shook his hand. He had a firm but not crushing grip.

"Blackfist, don't ch'know? Silly cognomen, hung on me by the yeller press, but have to live with it. This lively filly is Lalla d'Aulney..."

Catriona nodded at the woman, who gave a token courtsey like a little girl presented to disreputable foreign Royalty.

"And dear old Pongo Piltdown. Don't be alarmed by his fizzog and the massive shoulders business. He's the compleat gent."

Lord Piltdown extended a yard-long arm and took her hand with supple, thick, complex fingers. His immaculate cuff slid back over a thickly-furred wrist. He bent low and kissed her knuckles with his wide, rubber-lipped mouth.

The All-Rounder had been found frozen in a glacier under the Yorkshire estate of an aristocratic family whose son and heir had just been lost in the Boer War. The bereaved parents raised "Pongo" as their own, sending him to Uppingham, where he gained his nick-name by captaining the rugby and cricket sides, proving himself nigh-unvanquishable at the bat and nigh-unstoppable as a bowler. He was also the author of several slim volumes of privately-published poetry, favouring as subjects courtly love, English country sports (he was a Master of Fox Hounds) and the superiority of tradition over shallow modernity. His views on the proper place of women made Sir Henry Merrivale seem like Dame Ethel Smythe.

Lord Piltdown gave her back her hand, which was slightly moist. His beetle-browed face was marked by a distinct blush and he screwed a monocle into one of his eyes.

"Pongo likes you," said Lady Lucinda, looking at her sideways. "Watch out, or you'll be showered with rhymes."

The All-Rounder covered his face with his enormous hands, peeking out shyly between banana-fingers. His perfectly-tailored tuxedo would have served her as a survival tent. Two-thirds of his body was barrel torso, supported by bent, spindly legs that gave the impression of powerful, coiled springs. She noted he wore stout, polished leather gloves on his feet.

"It's a shame you should visit in such unhappy circumstances," said Blackfist. "This is an idyllic spot, sheltered in the bosom of Mama England. It's almost sacred to us, untainted by the bloodier businesses for which we are best known. I don't mind telling you it strikes home, such a common-or-garden crime right smack next door. We shall not rest until our good neighbour has been avenged."

Harbottle tugged what little forelock he could find.

"A burglar did it, sir," he said. "We'll feel his collar soon."

From inside the cottage came a spluttering explosion. Catriona checked her watch. Nearly five minutes. Clever Dick had broken his record.

The boy came into the garden. His comrades broke out in identical, indulgent, tolerant smiles. Blackfist patted Clever Dick on the head, mussing his hair.

"We sent our best and brightest to lend a hand," he said.

"Thank you very much," she responded.

"I found a big fat clue," announced Clever Dick. "A missing file."

"Very significant, I'm sure," said the Aviatrix.

"It could be," Catriona admitted.

"The beginning of the year is missing," said the boy. "Wemember what happened then? After the New Year's Eve lock-in at the Coat and Dividers? Old Blamey made a gang of enemies. I'd venture one or more took bloody wevenge on him."

"That's a theory," she said.

Captain Rattray's smile grew. "We've found young Master Richard's theories often have a funny way of hitting the nail right smack on the jolly old head."

"It'll be that Beamish," said Lady Lucinda. "You can tell he's a wrong 'un."

"Frightful rotter," said Blackfist, "drunk as a lord—no offence, Pongo—from noon til Maundy Thursday, and spouting off all manner of resentment against the deceased. That's a throbbing eyesore of a motive."

As he spoke, Rattray grasped the Fang of Night. His hand turned black-purple instantly, skin taking on a rough, gritty texture. A flush of colour appeared at his neck and swarmed up around his jawline, extending vein-tendrils across his cheek, stiffening around his lips and eyes. Inside his Norfolk jacket, the upper left quarter of his body became swollen and lumpy.

"Give the fellow a good grilling and he'll crack, spill the beans."

Blackfist's speech became slurred. He apprehended the change and let go of his jewel. The effect rolled back and he smoothed his face, dabbing spittle from his mouth with his breast-pocket hankie.

"Sorry about that," he said. "No call for the Auld Blackie here."

"When are you arresting Beamish?" demanded the Aviatrix.

Four of the Six looked at her, expectantly, intently. Even Harbottle joined in.

She had never felt smaller, and mentally cursed Edwin for sending her here. He must have known what she'd be contending with. These people were accustomed to purported master crooks who usurped the BBC's airwaves to issue proud boasts about the authorship of atrocities as yet uncommitted, helpfully outlining their wicked plans in good time for them to be thwarted. The Splendid Six specialised in crimes that were vastly complicated but easily solved.

"I'm not strictly supposed to make an arrest. That's Sergeant Harbottle's duty. I'm here to advise him."

"I'll have Beamish in jug before tea-time," said Harbottle.

"I wouldn't advise that."

"Really, I think you should consider it, Miss Gayle," said the Aviatrix. "The fellow has practically been bragging about it. Sitting there drunk and celebrating."

"It's 'Miss Kaye', Lady Lucinda. Before we arrest anyone, we'll need to establish some things. My reading of the situation is that at first everyone assumed Mr Blame was killed during a burglary, robber or robbers unknown being the culprits. Now, general opinion seems to have swung around to indict someone with a grudge against the victim."

"Items were stolen to make it look like a burglawy," said Clever Dick. "It's an old, old twick."

"Absolutely."

"The Mountmain Gang only stole the Cwown Jewels as a distwaction. The weal point of their waid on the Tower of London was to assassinate the Sergeant-at-Arms who shot Aoife Mountmain during the Iwish Civil War. I was the only one who wealised."

"It's the copper-bottomed truth, Miss Kaye," said Blackfist. "We were all haring off after the orb and sceptre, while brainbox Dickie saw the veritable answer to the mystery. Made us all feel proper clods and no mistake. Still, turned out all right in the end. There are two nations who'll be glad never to hear from the Mountmains again."

"See, I'm clever and you're stupid. Now, awwest Beamish."

Catriona's back was literally against a wall, covered in ivy. Through the window, she saw the untidy desk, the missing file.

"It's a mistake to harp on the solution of your last case when dealing with this one," she said. "If a murderer can fake a burglary to conceal his identity, could he not also fake a ransacking for the same reason. If ex-Sergeant Beamish or any of the others who lost their livelihoods after the New Year's party were guilty, why would they take away the file covering their grudge against Mr Blame?"

"To hide their motive, twitty girl."

"But it doesn't hide their motive. The missing file *points directly at it.* Why not take away a file covering something else, say the nuisance suit that led to the bankruptcy of the local newspaper? And point the finger of guilt at *someone else?* In fact, that's what I think has been done. The missing file isn't evidence against Beamish, it's evidence *for* him."

She saw Clever Dick follow her reasoning. His face started to go red, as if he were holding his breath again. He got bad-tempered, which she took as an admission that he, junior genius, was forced to agree with her, a girl.

"But the missing file, which contains nothing of value, also rules out the unknown burglar theory."

"Ah-ha," said Clever Dick, trying to trump her again, "but what if it didn't just contain papers but also something *pwecious*, something *concealed...*"

"Then why take the whole file? If it were a golden pen-knife or the deed to an oil-well or something, the burglar would just have taken it, rather than be burdened with a lot of irrelevant letters of complaint and dry-as-dust writs. No, the missing file is just a distraction..."

"You're rather good at this, aren't you?" said Blackfist, admiring.

Lord Piltdown nodded, bristly chin squashing his four-in-hand cravatte, and—without bending over—fingered the lawn, raising little earthy divots.

"I don't like to blow my own trumpet," she said.

"So 'oo should I arrest?" demanded Harbottle.

Everyone looked at her again. Lady Lucinda lit a cigarette and sucked on a long white holder, pluming smoke through her nostrils. Clever Dick held up his magnifying glass and big-eyed at her.

"I'm not quite ready to stick my neck out yet," she admitted.

There was evident disappointment.

"She's got no idea," said Clever Dick.

Catriona had to admit, though not out loud, that the brat wasn't far off the mark. She'd shot down two theories and it wasn't yet time for lunch, but had no suitable replacement.

Maybe it was natural causes?

Or suicide?

Or one of those fiendish suicides supposed to look like murder so an innocent was hanged and which, therefore, are acts of attempted homicide as much as self-slaughter?

That was ridiculous—the sort of thing she'd expect Clever Dick to suggest.

Her head was beginning to ache.

◆◆◆

At last, she was alone in the cottage. Harbottle had tottered off on his bike to the Coat and Dividers for his lunch, while the Splendids had got bored with watching her mundane sleuthing and gone back to the Drome. Sifting through waste-paper baskets, opening drawers and the like were all pursuits far less exciting than following a trail of burning corpses left in the wake of the Witch-Queen of Northumberland or skirmishing with the terror lizards of Maple White Land.

Catriona sat in a chair with a wonky wheel at the small desk in Peeter Blame's study, wriggling a little in the dead man's seat, trying to think herself back into the crime. One surprisingly useful thing Harbottle had done—prompted, he admitted, by a suggestion from ex-Sergeant Beamish—was employ the victim's own photographic apparatus to take flashlight snaps of the scene of the crime before the "deader" was taken away. Prints rush-developed by a local photographical society, of which the deceased had been a member until he found cause to sue the chairman and committee, now lay before her on the blotter. Though the desk was shoved up against a window—the *moderne* arches and watch-tower of the Drome was visible beyond the forsythia at the end of the back garden—the study was gloomy even in early afternoon. She snapped on a green-shaded reading lamp to examine the snaps.

Blame lay in a huddle, a spatter from his caved-in head on the rug, his chair—the one in which she was sitting—overturned. From the proximity of body to chair, she assumed he had been at his desk when attacked. The thought made her swivel round (the wonky wheel complained) to look at the low doorway through which the murderer must have entered. She had an intuition-flash of a dark, strong shape stepping quickly across the room, blunt instrument raised but arcing down, colliding with Blame's cheek…

A close-up showed a wound where she'd imagined the blow landing.

…and lifting him out of his chair, which caught in his legs and fell with him. She didn't go as far as to tip the chair over, but she looked and judged where the assaulted man would have fallen. There was a stain on the wall and a star-crack in the plaster where his head must have struck. The bloody rug was beneath it, smooth now but wrinkled in the photographs.

One blow had not been enough. The killer had applied the bludgeon many more times, concentrating on the side and top of the head. A panicky burglar, making sure not to leave a witness? A grudge-holding local, exterminating an enemy? That old fail-safe, the escaped homicidal lunatic? She could rule out the last—no reported escapees in the vicinity. Or did it come down to the Splendids? One of their many arch-enemies, frustrated at their untouchability, taking out his or her wrath on their nearest neighbour? Could Blame himself have been the minion of a master villain like Dien Ch'ing or the Clockwork Cagliostro, crushed out of hand for hesitating to follow an order or learning too much of some appalling terror plot? It was tempting to write Edwin's "tiny little murder" into a more satisfying, momentous storyline, to unmask Blame and his attacker as secret players in the great game of clubland heroes and diabolical masterminds. Then, there might at least be the illusion of a point to it.

There was a small fireplace, complete with poker and andirons, all present and correct. A cursory glance around showed other easily-accessible blunt instruments, in their place. The inference was that the murderer brought his own cricket bat or monkey wrench or whatever and had taken it away with him.

She looked back at the photographs.

Under the blood, Peeter Blame looked a sad old man, all dignity torn away. He wouldn't be suing anyone any more. It was difficult to consider the victim as the mean-spirited curmudgeon all accounts made him out to be. The neatness of his garden and the trivial comforts of his cottage made him less a caricature, more pitiable than odious.

She found a droplet of water in her eye and blotted it with her hankie.

A siren sounded, loud enough to rattle teeth and shake every small object in the room. Then, from the Drome, she saw a cloud of white smoke as a large steel shutter opened, lifting a section of lawn to give egress from an underground hangar. A vehicle shot out of the dark, belching flame and crunching gravel. From a perch high above, the Aviatrix—fully-winged—launched herself into the air and followed the flapping pennants of the Racing Swift, her scarf streaming behind her.

The Splendid Six were off adventuring.

Perhaps a personal call from the Prime Minister or an even more exalted personage, and a deadly threat to every man, woman and child in Britain? A human fiend, almost certainly foreign, working some vast, subtle, nigh-unbelievable plot? Again.

In any case, the Blue Streak's latest wonder-wheels whooshed down the lane past the Hollyhocks—Catriona saw the All-Rounder clinging to the roof, huge teeth bared as the rushing wind slipped into his mouth and blew back his lips—and took a sharp turn, spattering pebbles against

Mr Blame's collection of home-made signs ("It is Impermissable to Operate a Motorised Conveyance in This Thoroughfare"), and tearing for the London Road.

It took long seconds for the noise to die down. Even then, Catriona could still feel it in her inner-ear.

No better course of action occurred to her than to examine Blame's remaining files. It would have to be done eventually, and she was in any case stuck.

The first box-file covered the last three months of 1916. It was full to bulging, papers tied into packets and tamped down by a metal spring. A puff of dust suggested the box hadn't been disturbed in a while. She sampled some of the packets—several contained back-and-forth between Blame (Commander Blame, RN, he signed himself) and the Admiralty. She gathered that after having a ship sunk under him at Jutland, he had cooled his heels ashore while agitating for a new command only to be "retired" on the grounds of an unspecified, much-contested injury sustained in action. Blame's letters, then hand-written (and hand-written *twice* if these were copies) foamed with indignation and barely-veiled accusations of dereliction of duty on the part of those bodies who kept him from active service in the nation's hour of direst need. He also had a bee in his bonnet about a particular type of propellor-screw in wide use which he alleged was susceptible to fail under certain conditions and should thus be withdrawn before further disastrous reversals affected the course of the war. There were many, many articles—laboriously transcribed by hand, rather than clipped—on this subject, and an exchange of heated debate in the public forum of the *Times* letters column. The minutiae of stress-points and knot-rates defeated her.

Still, she could add Admiral Viscount Jellicoe and most of the Royal Navy, plus the letter column editor of the *Times*, to the list of suspects. Blame had begun his retirement hobby of bringing suit by naming them all in a massive, still-unresolved private prosecution on the grounds of "high treason."

The next two dozen boxes—four to a year—were more of the same, with a gradual shift as Blame turned his attentions from national to local issues. Mixed in with suits against bird-watchers, a gypsy tribe, the Kaiser (!) and the holder of the patent on a "faster" photographic plate which Blame claimed to have invented first were more innocuous items. Letters of welcome from societies concerned with local history, gardening, photography and the welfare of naval veterans—which gave her the picture of an active, frustrated man casting around for a cause, for some form of companionship. With sadness, she found each of these involvements terminated in quarrel and, inevitably, a flurry of law-suits. At first, he had acted through a London firm of solicitors, then local lawyers—of course, he had ended up suing them too. Finding few professionals willing to bring suit against colleagues, Blame had become an amateur enthusiast, representing himself on the rare occasions his complaints made it before the bench, whereupon they were almost invariably if reluctantly upheld.

She was amazed to find Blame even successfully brought an action for breach of promise against one Maggie McKay Brittles, a barmaid at the Coat and Dividers. An addendum listed every expense he had been put to in his pursuit of a lass thirty years his junior. Maggie's arm, muscled from pulling pints and cuffing drunks, could certainly have wielded a mean blunt instrument.

Peeter Blame's chair was not comfortable. Catriona's back ached and she had only progressed as far as 1922. It was evening outside. Midges buzzed in the pre-sunset summer haze.

A noise alerted her to the return of the Splendid Six.

The Racing Swift almost idled on its passage back to the Drome, probably at a mere 100 m.p.h. A foghorn that might be sounded in Dover and heard in Calais honked as the car passed the cottage.

Everything rattled again. She choked on the dust her investigations had put into the air.

With renewed determination, she opened the first of the 1923 files. Still more of the same. Blame succeeded in proving that the members of a ramblers' association on a walking tour of the district were technically subject to the laws concerning tramps and beggars, and got them jailed until their holiday time was up and they had to go back to office jobs in Bradford. By now, much of her empathy was washed away. She re-imagined the crime as if she were stalking into the study with a length of lead-pipe in her hand and venom in her heart.

The first connection of metal and bone was so satisfying!

The second 1923 file felt different.

It was nothing obvious—though a rough comparison made by balancing each box on her palm as if she were a human set of scales showed that the second box was much lighter than the first. In mid-1922, Blame had purchased a type-writer—the receipt was in the box, along with a writ against the vendor for "price-gouging"—and had switched from making two copies of all documents by hand to using carbon-paper and a flimsy second sheet. She could even see him learning to type—at first, his more impassioned passages (Marked by Use of Capital Initials and Triple Exclamation Points!!!) tended to rip through to the flimsy, which must render the top-copy a stencil. That partially explained the change in weight and bulk.

She tapped her front teeth with a pencil and looked at the type-writer, its case off, on the desk. The letters were worn away from the E, S and T keys.

On the lawn of the Drome, the Splendids—in cricketing or cro-quet whites—were served supper by a deferential staff whose livery included Splendid Six arm-bands. Occasionally, a braying laugh—Trimingham's—could be heard. Between courses, there was a great deal of champagne flute clinking.

Catriona hadn't eaten since an apple on the train. Harbottle had said he'd bring a sandwich back for her, but had never returned.

She stood up and stuck her fingers into the small of her back.

She thought about foraging in the dead man's larder, but that didn't seem right. After being exposed to his personality for hours, she assumed he'd reach out from beyond the grave and sue her for pilfering. He'd probably also sue her for not identifying his murderer in double-quick time, usurping the powers of the police without real legal standing and sitting in his bloody chair.

As a compromise, she decided to make herself tea.

The cottage kitchen was a walk-in cupboard with a sink and a stove, and cupboards that locked. She suspected Blame had duplicated the cramped set-up of some ship on which he had served. A hairpin served to pick the locks, which revealed single items of crockery—one cup, one saucer, one plate, one bowl, etc—and tins of tea, powdered milk, cocoa, sugar and so on. No major clues, though there was something heart-breaking about a man who only had one tea-cup, and disturbing also since she was about to make use of it.

She got a fire going in the stove and set a kettle on it.

The cup was clean, but best to wash it anyway. That done, she decid-ed to do the same for the tea-pot, which was a little dusty.

Dust!

The second 1923 file had produced no dust-puff when opened.

She went back, but it was impossible to check. There was moderate dust in both opened 1923 boxes, disturbed by her thorough search. She lifted the lid of the third 1923 file carefully, as if a live grenade nestled below. No dust-puff. The fourth file, the same. The desk was crowded now with opened boxes. She took a random 1926 file, and didn't get a puff.

Of course, the recent files—in more common use—would have less dust than the older ones, whose business was settled. But that didn't explain what she could swear was a sudden change. It's not as if dust became extinct or radically changed quality at the beginning of April, 1923.

Dust gone. And the boxes lighter. That 1926 file was practically empty when compared with the stuffed earlier boxes. Blame certainly hadn't moderated his habits; if anything, he'd become a more enthusias-tic litigant as the years wore on.

She chewed her lip.

A whistle shrilled in the kitchen. The kettle boiling.

She had finished her tea and her search through the files, and was sunk in a deep dark thought pattern, when a rap came on the window.

She jumped, startled.

Black knuckles pressed against the pane. A white smile gleamed through the glass.

"I say, uh, Miss Kaye, it's Dennis…Captain Rattray, um, Blackfist, don't-ch'know…we were wonderin' if you'd care to join us at the Drome for a bit of a feed. Strawberries and cream, what. Hungry work, this sleuthin', I'll be bound."

It took some work to calm down. She smoothed her hair and her skirt, and constructed a smile.

"That would be most pleasant, Captain," she responded, her voice brittle and fakey inside her head. "I'll just have to wash my hands."

"We're terribly informal, I don't mind saying. No need to stand on the old ceremonials."

"Dusty," she said, showing her hands.

Whyever had she done that! The answer was in the dust!

Blackfist smiled and nodded. He was clutching his gem. His whole hand glistened like a bitumen cactus studded with flint-chips.

She passed through into the kitchen, ran the tap over her fingers, dried herself off, and stepped out into the garden.

"Lovely evenin', isn't it? So bally peaceful."

The Captain smelled the breeze and looked at his ease.

"I say, bit of a scrape this afternoon, don't-ch'know. Frightful business in the fens. Viking skeleton fellers with axes like, well, like big axes. Some sort of a geas, according to Mystic Mary. Know what a geas is?"

"Yes."

"Cor," he breathed admiration. "I didn't."

It was a warm evening, but she felt a touch of chill in the air. Autumn coming. She feared for the petunias and roses of the Hollyhocks when the frosts came. There was no gardener to see them through the next cold snap.

Blackfist offered her his arm and led her down the garden path, towards a small gate—once wired-shut but recently opened by a few judicious snips, she noticed—that led onto the Drome.

◆◆◆

At the white filigree table (oblong, not Arthurian) on the lawn, Catriona found herself seated between Chandra N. Seth, the Mystic Maharajah, and Teddy Trimingham, the Blue Streak.

Seth had piercing blue eyes in a carved teak, fearsomely bearded face, and his large, bulbous turban bore a sapphire to match. He reputedly possessed amazing mesmeric and mentalist abilities and had tought Houdini some of the most dangerous fakir tricks, but he also had a high-pitched voice and a strange way of adding "hmmm" to every sentence that would disqualify him from the talkies. Trimingham was squiffy on champagne and kept "accidentally" brushing her thigh as he described the various crashes he had survived. A matinee idol in photographs, his face close-up was shiny and oddly textured, except for goggle-shapes around his eyes. He was proud of the number of times he had caught fire and put out the flames by going faster.

Though Blackfist still blathered about being terribly informal, Lord Piltdown had dressed for dinner in a tropical white tuxedo with a sunflower in the lapel and a white silk hat that perched steadily on his heavy brow-ridge, and Lady Lucina had exchanged her flying gear for a backless silver cocktail number that cost more than a house in Chelsea. When the Aviatrix turned, Catriona saw the double-row of spiracles outlining her spine, dribbling liquescing traces of wing-matter. The goo was discreetly dabbed away by one of the maids with a towel.

Clever Dick had chocolate all over his face and was explaining how he had known at once the afternoon's phantom horde weren't proper Vikings because they had horns on their helmets.

"Any fool knows it's a fallacy that Viking helms were horned."

"New one on me," said Captain Rattray. "Bless."

Catriona drank good champagne in moderation and scoffed strawberries like someone who had missed dinner. An afternoon in the small and dusty study, not to mention the small and dusty mind, of Mr Peeter Blame made for a shocking contrast with an evening among the Splendids. She imagined the camps eyeing at each other across the forsythia; rather, she imagined Mr Blame glaring fury at the Drome and these fantastical creatures barely noticing him. At first. Their world took little account of Peeter Blames, and barely acknowledged Catriona Kayes. She was their guest now because she was seen as the creature—a step above a servant—of Charles Beauregard, who carried some weight in heroic circles even if he stayed out of the public eye.

"I'm surpwised the Diogenes Club has *girls*!"

She thought Clever Dick might have snuck some champers. Or maybe his brain boiled over on chocolate alone.

"I think they would be too," she said.

"Girls," repeated Clever Dick, eyes wide, sneer eager.

Catriona noticed the Aviatrix's mouth pinching tight as if she were restraining herself from slicing a silver salver across Britain's boy brainbox as if topping a breakfast egg. For the first time, she felt a disturbing kinship with the flying woman. Then she remembered the Crocodile's blood raining down on children's faces and the taloned gloves; this rose had thorns.

"How...hmmm...is your most excellent investigation...hmmm...coming?"

She spread her empty hands.

"As I thought...hmmmm...I shall concentrate my third eye....hmmm...and seek answer on the psychic plane."

"She's orff again," belched Trimingham. "Bloody Mystic Mary."

Seth pressed fingertips to his forehead, shut his conventional eyes and hummed to himself. His gem glowed eerily.

"It's a twick," said Clever Dick, smugly. "A little 'lectric bulb. It's not *weal* magic. Not like Wattway's Fang of Night. That's proper magic. The darkie does it all with *twicks*!"

It occurred to Catriona that she had come across Chandra N. Seth before, under another name, when she was chasing fraudulent mediums.

"It doesn't matter if it's a trick," said Lalla. "What matters is if it works."

"Girls *and* darkies. We shouldn't have them. We could go back to being the Good Fellows Four."

"Of whom...hmmm...you were not...hmmm...one."

"Ho, she's awake now," burbled Trimingham.

"The matter is clouded...hmmm...but truth will emerge, as trueness always does and...hmmm...justice will prevail."

The Mystic Maharajah laid a hand on hers and looked deep into her eyes. Clever Dick was wrong about one thing: he wasn't non-caucasian, but a dyed white man whose name used to be Sid Ramsbottom. His vocal mannerisms were the same, though. Mystic Sid had been on the halls as Woozo the Wizzard.

She laughed the wrong way and champagne got in her nose.

"Sorry," she said.

Seth let go of her hand, and seemed direly offended.

The All-Rounder picked up a bowl-sized tea-cup, little finger perfectly extended, and raised about a gallon to his mouth, which he sucked down in a long, noisy draught. He dabbed his lips with a napkin and excused himself from the table, bowing formally to Catriona and Lady Lucinda, then bounded across the lawn, raising divots at each clutch, followed by a footman who replaced the sods and smoothed them over by hand.

"Pongo puts in an hour in the nets every night," said Trimingham. "Never know when the MCC will call."

As dark gathered, lamps automatically came on, shining columns rising around the Drome, criss-crossing the lawn, playing like searchlights across the grounds.

"One of mine, you know," said Trimingham. "Inventions."

Every few seconds a roving lighthouse beam shone on the Hollyhocks, bleaching the cottage white.

"We have light all night," said Captain Rattray.

"No darkness…hmmm…need apply."

She could imagine.

◆◆◆

"So," said Edwin, springing from his chair as she was admitted into the Strangers' Room of the Diogenes Club, "who dun it?"

"Ha ha," said Catriona. "Who didn't?"

Charles Beauregard was also present, which meant that here at least she was taken seriously. In the end, if there weren't such a horrid business at the bottom of it, her trip to Heathrow would have been ridiculous.

"Catriona, would you care for a light lunch?" offered Charles. "Then, we'll debrief."

"I'm fine, thank you Charles."

She had spent the night at the Coat and Dividers, eaten a proper country breakfast prepared by Maggie Brittles (who, surprisingly, was the first person she had met who even tried to seem sorry that Peeter Blame was dead), bade Harbottle a fond farewell (though overnight he'd forgotten who she was) and taken the train up to town.

"Then, if you'd care to oblige, we'll have your report."

She sat in an armchair, allowing the men to return to theirs. As always with Charles in the room, Edwin was boyish, eager to please the house-captain but also concerned with demonstrating his own brand of 20th Century sharpness.

"Do I need to tell you anything? You must already know."

At her tart tone, Charles's face fell.

"And I can't *prove* anything. You must know that too. Someone told me last night that…hmmm, justice will prevail…"

"Chandra Nguyen Ramsbottom, that's him exactly!" exclaimed Edwin. "Mimickry, another of your talents!"

"Well, justice *won't* prevail, will it? In this case, it *can't.*"

"Please be assured, Catriona, that you have not been used, that there was a real purpose to what we have asked you to do."

Despite herself, she believed Charles.

"As for proof, well…if I thought there was proof to be had, I'd have sent Edwin. No offence, young fellow, but it's what you're good at and if it's not there you're at a loss. Catriona, I wanted you to look into the murder of Peeter Blame because of your capacity for *feeling…*"

"I beg your pardon."

"Nobody could *like* the deceased, I understand, but that doesn't mean he shouldn't be *felt* for. What happened to him was not permissible. Do you understand?"

She was beginning to.

"So, which of 'em was it?" asked Edwin, flashing a grin. "My ten bob is on that Pongo fellow. Long reach, plenty of cricket bats in his kit, super-human strength…"

"In a small room, he'd have done more damage, I think," she said. "See, I can cope with evidence and proofs too. And it took more delicate fingers to go through Mr Blame's files and extract all the relevant documents. That said, I wouldn't rule Lord Piltdown out. My *feeling*, since you set so much stock in it Charles, is that it was Rattray or Trimingham in the study with the blunt instrument, and Lady Lucinda or—and I really mean this—Clever Brat handled the file-filleting to get the Splendids off the hook."

"So you think they *all* did it?"

"If all six can be roped in on a spur-of-the-moment thing, yes."

Charles steepled his fingers and considered the case.

"To sum up," he began, "what's missing from the files?"

"All documentation in connection with law-suits Blame was trying to bring against the Splendid Six, collectively or as individuals. My feeling—that word again—is that there were dozens of them. Just sitting in his cottage for a day, I saw a dozen different ways in which an ordinary person would be infuriated by having clubland heroes as next-door neighbours, and Peeter Blame was far touchier than the average."

"You've ruled out any link between him and their recorded enemies? That Clockwork fellow or the Demon Ace?"

"Edwin, I thought of that. No, this had nothing to do with defending the realm or warding off villains vile. It was about roses shrivelled by passing cars and bright lights shone into the cottage at all hours of the night and people flying overhead heedless of who crawled below and grumbled. It was about the *noise*, and the *view*, and the *commotion*, and the *flaunting*, and the *obnoxiousness*. And frustration, because Blame could sue and sue all he liked, but no court in the land was going to haul in a hero of the age of marvels. Every complaint he lodged would have been quietly quashed. He managed to get rid of a local Justice of the Peace, remember. He must have thought that a victory which would clear the way for a new local bench to sympathise with his complaints. That's how bloody stupid he was; he really thought that getting a JP sacked wouldn't set the county judiciary set against him forever. He believed all that stuff about impartial justice that we're supposed to uphold. My guess is that, frustrated in his usual avenue of action, he took to complaining in person, over the hedge, at every opportunity, nagging, whining, moaning…"

Charles nodded.

"And one of them snapped," he concluded. "Went over, maybe to make a gesture of peace, found Blame resolute, not properly respectful of a national hero. So our Splendid killed him, in a moment. The others clubbed together, tidied up and walked away…"

"And called *you* to get it dealt with."

His face darkened. "Yes, Catriona. They called me."

"That's what annoys you, isn't it? That's why you'll have them for this. Not for the murder—after all, this is 1927, everyone we know has killed someone or something—but for treating the Diogenes Club like a window-washing service."

"I say, Catty-Kit, that's going a bit far…"

"I hope I'm better than that, Catriona."

"I hope you are too."

Charles rose. Above the fireplace hung a portrait of a corpulent man with gimlet eyes, in immaculate Victorian morning dress. One of the Club's founders, and literally a huge figure in the secret world. Charles looked up to him, and thought.

"I'm sorry," she said. "But this business is all about getting angry. Blame was angry, permanently. His murderer lost his rag for a moment. Now it's me and you. This is what appals me the most, the *contempt*. To them, Blame wasn't even worth using their abilities. No black fist or mystic energies or invented contraption, just a plain old common or garden cosh, as used by the dimmest thug. I admit if it were otherwise, we'd have them bang to rights. But it wasn't calculated. Peeter Blame wasn't really murdered, he was *swatted*—like a midge."

Charles turned.

"This, Catriona, is what I will promise. The Drome will fall. A wrong done to the least of the King's subjects is still a wrong, no matter how eminent the wrong-doer might be. The Splendid Six will be removed from the game."

"And the game goes on?"

"Of course. But while I have anything to say about it, rules will be observed."

Charles Beauregard turned again, and looked into the empty, cold fireplace.

Edwin held her arm and escorted her out of the Strangers' Room.

◆◆◆

It happened over months. She perceived the fingers of Charles Beauregard pulling loose ends. Sometimes, she suspected he merely stayed his hand, suspending services that would otherwise step in to protect the Splendids from themselves.

Trimingham suffered a serious smash-up on the proving grounds, and his insurers finally cavilled at the loss, repudiating his daredevilry as a compulsive, nigh-suicidal mania or taking unnecessary risks, which drove his inventing businesses into insolvency. Lady Lucinda, turning thirty, was struck by a debilitating ailment which led to a permanent loss of her power of flight (she could still grow wings but they wouldn't lift her). Clever Dick's investment portfolio went down in flames with the Wall Street Crash and he became a recluse, suffering a serious case of teen-age facial eruptions which led unkind souls to rename him "Spotted Dick". Lord Piltdown, searching for his Northern roots, simply disappeared on a fjord, leaving behind an elegant but empty suit and shaggy footprints that gave out on glacial ice. The MCC missed him dreadfully and she couldn't help but wonder if the Neolithic Nobleman hadn't been the only true innocent among the Splendids. Captain Rattray made an unwise marriage to a mercenary Tiller girl and, fifteen days later, was the first of the Splendids actually to be hauled into court (Peeter Blame, you are avenged!). His divorce action drew mildly mocking then outright critical press comment, as more and more lurid detail spilled out in the dock. Noel Coward penned a witty, nasty revue sketch that made Blackfist impossible to take seriously, especially when the whole truth came out about the long-term physical alterations wrought upon his body by the Fang of Night. Chandra Seth announced to the world that he would perform a fabulous feat of endurance, buried in a glass coffin on the banks of the Thames for a month, but had to be rescued after three days after panicky humming alarmed passersby. In the wake of this fiasco, five women showed up alleging that they were deserted wives of the Mystic Maharajah, who had lived under a bewildering number of names. The line-up and thus the name fluctuated: the Splendid Five, then Three, then it was all off.

The Splendids were eclipsed in popular imagination by the dramatic and headline-hogging reappearance of a dark defender (the original Doctor Shade!) once thought dead. *British Pluck* suspended its serial exploits of the Six, and began to run stories of Shade, who worked alone and struck by night, travelling from his secret lair in Big Ben by autogyro to combat the enemies of decency. Catriona wondered what the point was of having a secret lair but letting everyone know the address?

"Happy now?" asked Edwin, tossing her a folded *Herald*.

They were in the flat, warmed by a nice coal fire as the first January of a new decade brought snow to the city. The puzzle box was on a mantelpiece, undisturbed for some months. There were new matters mysterious, requiring the attention of the Diogenes Club. And Catriona had been freshly accorded the privileged status of Lady Member, prompting a serious blood pressure condition for Sir Henry Merrivale. He was not mollified by the fact that she was obliged by oath not to own up to her status for at least fifty years after her death.

She looked at a foot-of-the-column note in the paper.

"The Heathrow Drome has been reclaimed by HM Government," said Edwin, "set aside for purposes of military aviation."

"That'll gobble up the Hollyhocks as well."

"They'd never have got an airfield sited with Blame next door to file suit against the scheme."

"True."

Though no longer eminent, the Splendid Six were all free. No one had ever answered in court for the murder of Peeter Blame.

"Catty-Kit, you've pursued this hawklike. Were they that bad?"

"They were worse, Edwin. That's what I feel."

He put his arms around her.

"And that's why we value you."

"For having feelings you know you ought to have but can't stretch to?"

"That's a fairly merciless way of putting it."

"But no argument from you."

Charles and Edwin were clubland heroes too, veterans of wars that didn't make it to the history books. They quietly refused the offered knighthoods and would never murder anyone who happened across their way, but they worked in the same arena as the Splendid Six and Doctor Shade, coping with the worst of the world, mulling over intelligence which would cause anarchic panic if it became public knowledge. They had to contain in their minds a big picture, the sweep of an ongoing saga of adventure.

Which was why they needed her. To ground them in the importance of the mundanities, to speak for those in whose name the great struggles were undertaken. Charles understood that deeply—she had been surprised to learn that she was not the first Lady Member associated with the Diogenes Club—and Edwin superficially, though he would grow into a proper understanding.

Without her, they might be monsters too.

I was jazzed when Joe asked me to contribute a story to this anthology. When I was a teenager in high school and playing football, along with trying to figure out girls. I also discovered the paperback reprints Bantam was doing then of the Doc Savage pulp series from the '30s and '40s. I went to many a practice with the latest monthly reprint of Doc and his crew's battle with a conniving evil-doer tucked into my back pocket—trying to keep my defensive tackle plays straight in my head while also worrying about how Doc would get out of the trap the Silver Death-Heads or John Sunlight had set for him.

The success of the Doc reprints led to a revival of the Shadow, the Spider, later the Avenger and, if I'm not mistaken, inspired the late Bryon Preiss to create *Weird Heroes*, a prose series by various writers about then modern-day super heroes that drew on pulp and comic book sensibilities. Which in turn flowered another passion: to write my own stories of adventurers, horror, science fiction and combat. Those latter two categories give you a clue to what "Hill 19" is about. It's firmly set in the '50s, the Korean War theater. Additionally, and not giving away too much, it's a nod to a couple of EC Comics tales as well.

—*Gary Phillips*

Incident on Hill 19

Gary Phillips

"Why can't they put those spades where they belong? Stick 'em in the 24th."

"Yeah, them colored boys get shot at and their eyes get large and they blubber so bad they wind up shooting one of us," his buddy joked.

"Seems to me I seen you shake a time or two when those 82s opened up, Pullman."

"Figures you'd be a nigger lover, O'Neil. I guess up there in New York you had yourself a darkie girlfriend tucked away in Harlem."

Pullman and Hickey cracked up.

"Stow it you mutts," Lieutenant Franklin said, walking up to the three as they greased their M-1s with anti-freeze to keep the parts from icing up. "Keep that kind of talk to yourselves."

"We were, Lieutenant." Hickey responded, stifling a giggle.

Franklin breathed clouds close to the corporal's face. Slowly he said, "You know what I mean, soldier. What you did before you got here and what you'll do afterward does not concern me. What does is this unit functioning at tip-top shape. Understand?"

There was a moment then Hickey managed a "Yes, sir."

"That goes for you too, Pullman."

"I get it, sir."

Franklin walked off and the three exchanged looks.

"Glory boy." Hickey wrung out his rag and wiped down his rifle's breech. "He just wants to be kissy-kissy with the press because he wants to run for office when he gets back to the States."

O'Neil checked the action of his M-1. "What are you talking about?"

Pullman piped in, "You didn't hear our junior MacArthur there talking to that reporter from *Life* who was around last week?"

"I guess not," O'Neil said.

"They were here to take pictures and get stories of how happy us'ins all is to be fighting Joe Chink," Hickey added, smirking. "Like we all sit around the mess eatin' fried chicken and mashed potatoes. Turns out Franklin's father was a senator in Philadelphia or some such. And the reporter asked him was he going to run for his daddy's seat once he got home."

"Yeah, so?" O'Neil inspected his handiwork.

"So he's already running, don't you get it?" Pullman groused. "Last month we had that colored broad from…what's the name of their colored magazine?"

"Jigaboo Monthly," Hickey commented.

"Ebony," O'Neil corrected.

"That's it," Pullman said, snapping his fingers. "All this attention on the integrated front line units because Truman gave in to those loud mouths and Jew trouble makers left over from FDR's time."

"The NK's bullets don't know color," O'Neil remarked. "And a corpse is a corpse."

Pullman and Hickey could only shake their heads as they finished up.

Between a set of Quonsets and across a tuft of frozen ground from the GIs and their maintenance, Lieutenant Mark Franklin entered command's tent.

"Captain." Franklin gave the seated man a crisp salute.

"At ease," Captain Thomas Westlake said. He pushed a pack of Lucky Strikes toward Franklin. "Be my guest."

Franklin lit one and savored the aroma. "What's the skinny, Captain?" He'd observed the prints of aerial shots to one side of the man's ivory inlaid table. An item they'd commandeered along with chairs, canned food, a box of metronomes and a portrait of Pope Pius XII from a bombed out Catholic school.

"Take a gander at this." Westlake's thick fingers shuffled through the prints and arranged three of them for viewing. He held a magnifying glass that Franklin used.

"What am I looking at?"

"That's what G-2 wants to know. These are fresh photographs from our jet jockeys passing over the northeastern section of the Taebaeks less than forty clicks from here. Not far from the border, I don't need to remind you."

Franklin bent again to peer through the glass at the images the Sabers had captured flying over the mountain range. "NKs or Chinese regulars?" Franklin asked, regarding the men marching up a trail in one of the shots.

"One of the details you and a light detachment will find out."

Franklin nodded slightly. The second shot again showed the enemy soldiers along the hill. In this one, they were reacting to something out of frame. Moving the glass onto the third, he regarded an object. "Is it a downed MIG?"

"Doesn't seem to fit that configuration. At least the part that the white coats back in Tokyo can make of it." The captain tapped the third photo. The aerial shot depicted the top of the ridge where an oblong object was stuck in the side of a pyramidal rock formation thrusting up from a portion of the hill's apex. The image was blurry due to the jet's speed, and Franklin couldn't hazard a guess as to its entire shape.

"Maybe it's part of a bubble on some kind of drone spotter plane. Of course there would be debris around and there isn't any."

Captain Westlake held his hands apart, and leaned back to absorb more of the warmth of his portable heater fighting the cold. "You shove off at 04:20. I'd say pick no more than six to go with you. Small enough to move fast, but enough men to handle a situation should it arise." He produced a leather folder and handed that across to the lieutenant.

"There's some exact coordinates delineated on a map, land marks indicated, and notes on what's been troop strength in that area. The brass has designated the hill you're after as Number 19. This is a recon mission, lieutenant, only engage the enemy if there's no back door open."

"Alright, sir." With the toe of his Mickey Mouses, one of his snow boots, he ground out his cigarette and turned to leave.

"And Mark?" Westlake was standing now, rubbing his hands.

"Sir?"

"Do you plan on taking our negro men with you?"

"I planned on taking the dogfaces that can help me fulfill the mission, Captain, why? Is there going to be another reporter waiting when we get back?"

His superior considered the pack of cigarettes then put them aside. "I took you to be a broadminded man."

"I don't follow you."

Westlake came forward, clapping him on the side of his arm. "This is about morale as much as it's about information."

"I see."

"U.N. forces had to cede Kimpo Airfield, and Inchon has been abandoned. Right now ma and pa need to hear how unified our fighting forces are when they sit down to the radio after supper, Mark. How these set backs will be overcome when we regroup."

"This is just a lousy recon mission, sir."

"But one that we can play up a lot of different ways, especially if we can have a picture of smiling black and white faces of our men in an edition of *Stars and Stripes*. This damn police action is getting to be one large mudhole that we can't sink any deeper into. As an officer, as someone looking to build on his war experiences for later, you know what I'm saying."

"And," he continued, "I'm sure you want to put to rest that talk that the colored soldier is only suited for rear guard detail." He paused, smiling, "I believe the negro votes where you come from."

"Very well, sir." Franklin saluted again and left. A bitter wind had kicked up and it matched his mood. He did consider himself a fair man, a man willing to judge another based on what he did and not what he looked like. But when that goofball, that reporter, asked him about his family and his plans, how could he pass up the opportunity? It was sobering to finally realize that he was as ambitious as his father and older brother.

"Sergeant Pickett," Franklin said to the colored man hunkered down with a private by two cans of burning sterno.

"Lieutenant," Dawson Xavier Pickett, snapped to, setting aside his C-ration of corned beef hash. The private also stood and saluted with his cigarette dangling from his mouth.

"Word with you, sergeant."

"Yes, sir." He stepped over to where Franklin had positioned himself next to the fender of the Quad 50 half-track. "What's up?"

"You and a man you choose are with me and three others before sun up."

"Advance patrol?"

"Sort of. We're to do some scouting and report back on what we see in a particular section of the mountains due east of here."

"How about we bring Holmes along?" Pickett indicated the man who'd resumed eating by the low fire.

"Anything special about him?"

"He used to help his uncle, a shutter bug in Detroit. He worked for the local Negro papers and politicians there. Holmes has his Nikon he loves to use."

The officer frowned.

"This nip camera. Pretty good I'm told."

"Why not." Franklin agreed. It couldn't hurt to take some shots." He told him what time to be ready and departed.

"What was that about Ex?" Holmes asked when the sergeant returned.

"Looks like we get to do more than hauling mortar launchers and putting up huts."

Holmes displayed wide teeth. "Maybe it's because the Army has lost so many ofays at Inchon they don't have any choice but to use us too."

Pickett, a sturdily built individual over six-two, stretched, and gulped down an amount of warm water from his canteen. It had been set near the fire to prevent freezing. "Get some shut eye and no apple jack."

"Sarge, you know I—"

"Who you trying to jive, gate?" His bemused expression said it all.

"Okay, chief," the private said and hunkered down to take in all he could from the dying fire.

Before the sun was up over Whitehorse Ridge, the small squad of men moved out. Hickey, a corporal, one of D Company's BAR, Browning Automatic Rifle handlers, had the point with the lieutenant close behind. Private Pullman and Sergeant Pickett were next and the others filled in.

"Eyes front, Hickey," Franklin said, referring to the point man regularly looking back as the soldiers advanced.

"Just want to make sure there's no gooks coming up on my flank, sir."

Franklin pointed ahead. "Keep moving. If the reds show up, we'll send you a telegram."

A little past 09:32, they were walking along the perimeter of a small village called Sohbo-ri. Several scrawny chickens pecked about. The cornstalks the huts were constructed from were like brick, the freezing wind having solidified the last vestiges of the moisture in them from the humid fall.

"Where you going, Pullman?"

He put an index to lips and snuck down to a clay pot suspended in front of a hut. Taking his glove off, he used the back of his hand to feel the pot. He continued on until reaching a hut mid-way along the clearing. He rejoined the others.

"That pot was used recently," he whispered to the lieutenant. Previously, they knew the village had been deserted.

"Pickett, take two over there to cover us and we'll see if we can flush our guests out."

"Got it." Pickett turned and tapped Holmes and Hickey on his way past.

"Hey—" Hickey began but followed the other two, unlimbering his Browning.

Holmes said, "You okay?"

"I'm fine. Just don't get in my way."

"Wouldn't think of it."

As those men went to the left and a slight incline, the three with Franklin converged on the hut in question. There was a crunch of straw and suddenly two North Korean soldiers in heavy coats and fur hats ran from the hut, hands up and hollering in Korean.

"Reds, reds," Hickey shouted and dropped, peeling off rounds from the Browning.

"Hickey, no," Sergeant Pickett yelled. "Stop firing."

"Holy smoke, holy smoke, he's reaching inside his coat," Holmes blurted while he opened fire on the enemy soldiers.

Pickett grabbed Hickey's arm and yanked hard, causing the BAR man to turn with his rifle.

"Look, snowball—"

Both were gritting their teeth, condensed air issuing between the spaces.

"That's enough," Franklin ran up while O'Neil and Pullman went to check on the NKs. "That's enough I said."

To Franklin, Pickett said, "Watch him." And he double-timed over to the two on the ground.

"Who the hell does that dinge think he is?" Hickey's tightening hands made the Browning's casing creak.

"You have to respect the stripes, Hickey."

"Aw, come on, lieutenant."

"This is not some bar or counter at your favorite cafe. This is war, and either there is a chain of command or there's anarchy. It's that simple."

Franklin glared over at Holmes. "That goes for both of you."

"Yes, sir."

Pickett crouched over the bodies. The left side of one man's brain was now splattered on the hut like a hurried paint job. But the other one was gurgling blood, air seeping from the gaping wounds in his chest.

"Haneul eh suh ssol ah ji neun bool," he repeated several times. In his hand was a piece of paper that he shakily held up to Pickett. Their eyes met and then the enemy soldier expired.

"I guess he was praying, huh?" Pullman opined to no one in particular.

"He was saying 'Light or fire from the sky.'" Pickett rose and unfolding the paper, looked at the drawing on it.

"What do you have there, sergeant?" Franklin asked.

"Don't know exactly." Pickett handed the bloodstained scrap to the officer. Holmes got his camera out and captured the enemy in their death poses.

After a moment, Franklin offered, "This supposed to be a meteor?"

Pickett's eyebrows elevated. "It looks like this fireball in his drawing crashed into these rocks. I guess that's where we're headed."

"Yeah, well," the lieutenant drawled, "there's only one way to find out."

"I found their rifles, lieutenant," O'Neil called from the doorway to the hut. "They had them leaning against the wall in here."

Franklin didn't want his men dwelling on the fact the NKs had run out purposely unarmed. "Okay, let's move out," he ordered. Absently, he put the paper in his breast pocket.

After they'd cleared Sohbo-ri, Franklin made a point of walking next to Pickett along the trail.

"Where'd you learn Korean?"

Pickett shrugged. "In Oakland there's a Korean community, actually over into San Francisco too. Of course everybody figures they're Japanese. Anyway, the neighborhood I grew up in I came into contact with them. Even worked awhile at the ice plant with a KA who taught me a little."

"KA?"

"Korean American."

Wind flitted through the trees and they walked on.

"Did you really think that Hickey would shoot you in the back?"

Pickett didn't answer right away. The soft crunch of the packed ground was all that could be heard. "It wouldn't have surprised me. There's been incidents in other squads among the colored and the whites."

"You think that little of your fellow GI?"

"He thinks that little of me."

By late afternoon, the detail had arrived at the foot of the mountains. A light snow had also started.

"Grab some chow. We'll take twenty," Franklin said.

"My dogs are killing me," Pullman complained. He sat down and taking off his boots, massaged his sore feet.

Franklin consulted his map.

"That's it, right?" Pickett was beside him, looking through a pair of binoculars.

"Yes, Hill 19," Franklin said, having put on his rimless glasses for a better look. He regarded Pickett's expression. "I had perfect eyesight before I started getting shot at."

The sergeant chortled and the two puffed on their smokes simultaneously. "Don't see nothin', but of course that doesn't mean anything."

Franklin took a deep drag and exhaled. "Look down from the peak, to the left and there's another small rise. At a kind of valley area between the two."

Pickett said, "That a balloon? You know, like they used in World War One with a spotter to track enemy movements."

The lieutenant asked, "You a student of history?"

The non-com took the binoculars away from his eyes. "Had an uncle in that one. They called him by his middle name, Nefarious—which fit him. He was part of the Harlem Hellfighters who fought with the French." He didn 't supply that was because the black American troops were never allowed active duty by their own country.

"Huh," the lieutenant said, "That's something. Whatever that thing is up there is what we're supposed to find out then hustle back to base to make our report."

In the packet the captain had handed Franklin, there was a brief report from the pilot of the F-86. He wrote that when he made the second pass over the object, his engine stalled and he lost all radio contact but was able to relight his engine. He didn't relay that to the sergeant.

Franklin announced, "All right, men, we keep low and keep sharp. Those two in the village came from somewhere, and G-2 says there might be Chinese troop presence as well. But we need to make that crest." The snowfall was increasing.

"What's up there, lieutenant? Some kind of gook outpost?" Pullman flicked a smoked Chesterfield away.

"You'll know when we get there. Saddle up. Hickey and Pullman, you two up front."

"Those slant-eyes are gonna make us out too easy," Hickey complained ascending the hill. "Those tar babies stand out real good against this damn snow."

"You're too much," Pullman commented.

"I'm just sayin', that's all." And they trudged on.

Ahead were O'Neil and Holmes.

"Can I ask you something, Holmes?"

"What?"

"You enlisted, didn't you?"

"Yeah, so?"

More snow and more walking. "Not much else for you back home?"

"Aw you know, boss man," Holmes began in a Kingfish accent, "we's gots to do what we can for our mamas and babies." He laughed dryly.

"That's not what I meant."

"I'm just having fun with you, O'Neil. Don't take it seriously."

Past the mid-way point, the lieutenant, who'd moved to the head of the line, signaled a halt and the men crouched down on the leeward side of a ledge of rocks. He scanned the terrain ahead.

Hickey leaned close. "I feel it. They're up there, aren't they?"

"Can't say for sure. That's why I wanted to check." The lieutenant considered whether the object was some kind of experimental Russian jet, and were there troops up there guarding it.

"So what should we do, Lieutenant Franklin?"

"We need to—"

"I'll scout ahead. One man should be unnoticed," Pickett blurted.

"You?" Hickey shook his head. "You see how white it's getting out here...sergeant?"

Franklin grimaced. "Got any pineapples on you?"

"I've got one." He tapped a small pouch on his belt.

"Give him yours," Franklin said to Hickey.

"Huh?"

"You heard my order, private."

With a look on his face like he'd swallowed sour milk, Hickey handed over his grenade. "Don't drop it."

Pickett moved off, staying as low as he could to the snow covered earth. He slithered over rocks and through spare stands of shrubbery. It was behind one such outcropping of bush that he peered through the binoculars toward the rise where the object was, then started up again, slowly.

"Come on, Ex, come on," Holmes muttered.

They waited and watched, the snow continuing to fall and crystallize on their lips and eyelids. Pickett got closer until he stopped again, suddenly diving into a natural trench.

"Up at the top, I see somebody," O'Neil said.

"But do they see Pickett?" Holmes said.

The sound of a Tokarev's whine answered that question.

"All right men, let's pour it on," Franklin yelled as he leapt over the ledge, the enlisted men's M-1s cranking out shots around him. He pumped his legs, the soles of his winter boots sinking then lifting out of the snow. Over the top he could see the commies on their bellies shooting down at them.

There was a blur of motion to his right and suddenly Pullman was staggering backwards, his rifle in the air as his heels gave out from under him. The ragged hole in his abdomen was the size of a dinner plate.

Stepping over the body, Holmes aimed but Franklin was too busy scrambling while bullets careened off rock and he could feel a burning in the side of his rib cage. He went to a knee, he was having trouble breathing but he kept shooting. Up there he saw that Pickett was fighting hand-to-hand.

Rifle up, sighting down the barrel, working the trigger, Franklin's father filled his head. It was one of those times the two were out in the thickets hunting quail.

"The men of this family have strived to make our forbearers proud," he said, putting his orator's strength behind the words.

Usually the younger Franklin was tired of hearing about great ancestor Benjamin and the burden of that heritage. But on that cold spare morning in the brush, he accepted his calling.

"I understand, dad," he'd said. And he did.

Lieutenant Franklin looked forward to fulfilling his family's wishes. A bullet cracked and he didn't feel the round that slammed through his five pound helmet and rattled around the back of his steel pot after exiting his head.

Up the hill, the knife in the enemy's hand had carved a chunk out of his shoulder and now it was hovering near Pickett's breast bone. The blade would have been buried in him except he'd crossed his wrists and blocked the other man's thrust. The sergeant then took a step back and the commie soldier assumed he had an opening and lunged forward.

Pickett's fist caught the NK flush just below the cheek, while his other hand grabbed the wrist of the knife hand. And pulling hard, he yanked his opponent off-balance, making him stumble. The sergeant got his sidearm out and shot the other man dead.

More gunfire forced Pickett down into the trench. The enemy was bunched at the top of the ridge, near the object they'd been sent to identify. Whatever that was up there, the communists wanted to protect it.

An NK stuck his head up to get a bead on him but he had to duck down as the whine of M-1s whistled past Pickett. Back on his belly, the sergeant crawled forward inches from his cover, aware that at any second, one of the reds would poke up again, and blast his head off. He pulled the pin on one of his grenades, holding the lever tight so it wouldn't detonate.

There was a scream and he prayed it wasn't Holmes or even Hickey for that matter—they were on the same side, weren't they?

Sucking in air, scared but having no choice, Pickett counted to five. Echoing in his head were his DI's admonishment from basic about the 10 yard killing radius of a pineapple. "Two…Three." That was the explosive part—the shrapnel could fly for some 50 yards or so. "Four…five," and he stood up and threw the grenade into the soldiers clumped together on the ridge. The thing was out of his hand when a bullet pierced his body, driving him down into the snow compacted ground. The grenade exploded and body parts pirouetted in the air and the shooting stopped.

"Ex," Holmes called, "Ex, how bad are you hit?"

"I'm still breathing."

"I'm coming for you, man."

"Hold on, they may not be done."

"They got Pullman and the lieutenant. You're in charge."

"Then do what I say and keep your carcass where it is." He tried to move but it caused blood to seep from his chest wound so he got still again. Moaning drifted toward him from the ridge but that could be a ruse or their buddies were laying low and hoping the anxious GIs would saunter up there and get slaughtered.

"Hey, can you hear me?"

"What is it, Hickey?" Pickett said.

"Since you're also knocked off your pins, that makes me in charge."

"No it doesn't, corporal. You will follow my orders or you will be court-martialed."

"If we get back to base, don't you mean?"

"Don't press it, Hickey. This ain't the time." Grinding his teeth, Pickett turned his body in such a way as to peek over the top of his trench. He tossed a loose rock he'd picked up but that got no response. He settled back and considered what to do next.

"I say we move out," Hickey yelled up to him. "We've done what we can. We need to get you to a MASH."

"We haven't finished the job." He coughed blood and wiped it away with a grimy hand. "O'Neil and Holmes, work your way to me. Hickey, you lay down cover if you see a head pop up. And I'll do the same."

"But—"

"Do it."

There was no answer but soon the two soldiers were belly crawling and running hunched over to the trench.

"You think there's some reds up there paying possum?" O'Neil blew on his hands then put his cotton gloves back on. It continued to snow.

"Between us we must have polished 'em off," Holmes said. "Those two in the village must have been deserters."

"I was wondering about that," Pickett mused. "Could be it was a patrol like ours, small and light sent out to guard their plane or whatever it is up there."

"But that might mean others are on their way," O'Neil added.

"Means we still gotta get up there for a look-see. And this has to be taken care of, soon," Holmes tore off part of his sleeves and pressed the cloth against the wound.

"I'll be all right. Get going you two."

The privates exchanged minimal nods and started their climb.

The pain hadn't let up but that didn't matter because Pickett couldn't allow himself to pass out. He was in charge and he knew what would go around if he couldn't muster up.

"Hickey," he hollered.

"What?"

"Get up here." As he expected, the corporal didn't budge. "Now, mister."

"Okay."

Running in a zigzag pattern, Hickey bowled into the trench and flopped down, his Browning trained on the ridge.

Holmes and O'Neil, moving, halting and listening and repeating that they were almost to the top.

Pickett too had his rifle aimed, but wasn't sure if he could bolt forward if he had to.

Hearing his ragged breathing, Hickey asked, "You gonna make it?"

"You just worry about the men." It surprised Pickett how small his voice sounded.

O'Neil gained the top of the ridge and the sight that greeted him were the insides of a man's stomach spilled over the ground. He retched. As he dabbed at his mouth with his shirt front, Holmes joined him.

Before them were a tangle of three bodies and their disconnected limbs including the one with the missing stomach—this the result of Pickett's grenade. Beyond them was a dead man on his back. Part of his head was shot off and they assumed he'd been picked off by one of them from below. His eyes gazed into the beyond.

Buried in the side of the pyramid-like rock formation was the object. Both men approached it cautiously, rifles in hand.

"It's like a giant metal egg." Holmes reached for the milky gray metal surface but didn't have the nerve to touch it. The thing was at least forty feet tall at its highest point.

"Some kind of bomb?" O'Neil said.

"It's big enough to blow up the whole damn peninsula if it is," Holmes responded. He slung his rifle over his shoulder and taking a few steps back, snapped some pictures.

O'Neil was walking around the other side of the object. "We better," and then he stopped talking. He could only blink and try to process what he saw. "Holmes," he rasped, "come here."

Holmes stepped around and almost dropped his camera. "Holy crud," he exclaimed.

On a flat expanse of snow blotted ground were two more NK soldiers. A dead creature was squatting on one of the soldier's chests, one of its tentacles wrapped around the man's crushed throat, his eyes bulging out of their sockets.

"That egg is a space craft, Holmes."

"That a Martian?"

The alien was about the size of a foot locker though shaped more like an octopus with six tentacles and a gelatinous body. There were two bullet holes in the still creature. A dark fluid had emptied through the holes, and mixed with the snow that now partially covered these two.

The other dead soldier was a radio operator. He was laid out near his instrument, both of his arms had been torn off. Neither GI noticed the transmitter was on.

Holmes took more pictures. O'Neil went back to Pickett and he and Hickey had to carry him up the hill to the sight that awaited them.

"It ain't breathing, that's for sure." Hickey announced after poking the thing with the barrel of his rifle. "I guess we hit the jackpot, fellas. We're going to make the cover of all the magazines."

"Maybe not," Pickett said. He'd managed to stay upright by leaning against a boulder, and had been using his binoculars to look across the other side of the 38th Parallel. "Three jeep loads of soldiers are on their way. Chinese I'd say. And three of 'em are in civvies, serious types."

"Scientists." O'Neil was already heading toward the ledge, the way they'd come. "We've got to move out."

Holmes said, "Not without Ex."

Hickey blared, "You crazy, he'll just slow us down."

Holmes tossed his camera aside and reached to loosen his rifle but Hickey was on him.

"If you want to stay with your colored pal, fine. But me and O'Neil are getting back to base." He pushed him and Holmes fell. Hickey was about to kick him when Pickett yelled.

"That's enough." His .45 was pointed straight at Hickey's heart. "All of you move out, get back and report what you've seen. You've got pictures so maybe they'll believe you and not slap you with Section 8s. I'll keep them busy with me as long as I can. Leave me a few clips for my rifle."

Holmes was on his feet. "Ex, you've got—"

"Get going, soldier, that's my order. And Hickey, stop acting like the peckerwood you are and somebody who is a U.S. Army corporal. Get your men back alive."

O'Neil shoved Hickey's shoulder. "You heard our sergeant."

"I'm not having this," Holmes protested. "Them white boys can leave you, but I'm staying."

"No you ain't. If the reds get past me it's going to take each of you watching out for the other to make it back." Snow flakes dotted his wet forehead. "What we found today is like something out of Flash Gordon. And our side has to know about it 'less we let the enemy use this some-how. You got a duty, Norman, and so do I." He put a hand on the man's shoulder. "We've got to show them we didn't bug out in a fight."

Holmes handed Pickett a couple of extra clips. So did O'Neil. Hickey just looked at the ground. The three made to leave when a portal, where there was no indication of one, suddenly opened like a camera's shutter in reverse in the egg. The hole was in a lower portion of the machine and a being in a silver space suit stepped through it. He was tall, the suit he was in seemed to be of some silken material and there was an oblong helmet covering his head, and affixed to a metal collar. There was no visor, but it was evident he could see from the other side of the helmet.

The being held his hands up to show they were empty to the soldiers and then he, as it was the shape of a muscular man, walked to the dead creature with the tentacles. Hands on his hips, the helmet was tilted down for a few moments. He then put a hand on top of the creature and petted it.

From where the cosmic traveler stood he could see the approaching convoy. Particularly given the vision amplification apparatus built into his helmet, but the earth men didn't know this. Already one of the jeeps had stopped and the soldiers were advancing up the hill.

The space man touched a portion of his collar and a nodule of a peculiar design sprouted from the top of the egg. The nodule, which had no apparent bearings or hinges, undulated like a snake and once in position, a purple ray shot from its nozzle. The nodule repositioned itself and shot another ray blast.

After that, the nodule merged with the casing of the egg. The space man walked back toward his ship.

Holmes and O'Neil looked down the hill.

"What is it? What do you see?" Pickett wheezed. He slumped against the rock.

"He froze them, Sarge," Holmes said. The ones walking and the ones still in their jeeps. It's like they were living photographs."

The visitor from the galaxy reemerged from his ship and came toward Pickett.

"He's going to attack us." Hickey leveled the Browning.

"If he wanted us dead, we would be. Put it down," Pickett braced himself.

Hickey hesitated but complied. The space man, who'd halted, continued toward the sergeant. Facing him, he held up a small rectangular device that had lights of various colors swirling across it. He made a few circles with it around the area of Pickett's wound.

"You all right, Ex?" Holmes asked, worry straining his face.

"Yeah. In fact, I feel much better. It's like he dissolved the bullet. There's no burning anymore." Pickett pulled back his shirt and saw that his wound had been closed as well.

The alien paused before the sergeant, the GI's reflection cast in the helmet's shiny surface. He then turned and went back into his ship. The four watched as the portal started to close. At the space man's feet bounded a creature similar to the dead one. This thing wrapped a tentacle around his leg, much the same as a dog or cat would nuzzle its master.

Just before the portal sealed, the traveler removed his helmet revealing an individual with mahogany colored skin, a wide nose and close cropped kinky hair. Then the egg was once more one seamless piece of milky gray metal.

Speechless, the four were mesmerized as the egg began to vibrate. Large chunks of the stone it was embedded in began to fall away and the men backed up. The egg broke free and was stationary in the air, hovering before them. And then three tail sections shaped like curving spiked heels sprouted in the fat end, equi-distant apart. The ship turned, shook, then zoomed into the heavens.

Holmes took the camera away from his eye and like the others, silently filed down the hill. The snow had stopped.

On the way back to base, they all agreed to say nothing of what they found. The four concluded that the visitor must have crash landed and had to repair his ship.

Sure they had the photographs, but Holmes would have to give the film to the captain who in turn would have to send it off to be processed. Once that happened, who knew what would happen to them? Maybe the brass would hail them as heroes or maybe the G-2 spy boys would want this to remain hush hush. Could be they'd be quarantined or put in separate rubber rooms for who knew how long.

They reported their engagement of the enemy and that the object at the top of the hill was a radio controlled balloon rigged with a camera for tracking troop movements. And that the film that Holmes took got fogged.

A few years later after the war, while walking along Broadway… in downtown Oakland, Dawson Pickett passed a newsstand. The cover feature of *Weird Science Tales* magazine had caught his attention. The story was entitled "The Space Man of the Korean Hills," and depicted an illustration very similar to the traveler in his suit and full helmet. The alien was bending down aiding a wounded GI, while shooting his ray gun at advancing commie soldiers.

Leafing through the magazine the name on the story was credited to a Mark Norman. Pickett bought two copies of the issue. He was going to save a copy for his infant daughter to read when she got older. The Montgomery Bus Boycott was in full swing, and one day, he hoped, she might go to the stars and meet the man who saved his life.

When I sat down to work on "Carrion," I had one goal in mind: I wanted to write the kind of story that Robert E. Howard would have enjoyed.

Howard has long been a favorite of mine. He was one of the first writers whose work I sought out (along with Edgar Rice Burroughs, Ray Bradbury, and Robert Bloch). I still have a few of those old paperbacks, bought at library sales or used bookstores. They're special touchstones for me, and just pulling one of them off the shelf on a summer afternoon can stir clear memories of the would-be writer who first read them a long time ago.

I was twelve when Roy Thomas and Barry Smith introduced me to Howard's work through their *Conan the Barbarian* comic book series. Those stories led me to a slew of Conan paperbacks with great Frank Frazetta covers, and I was hooked. I loved Howard's courageous, stoic heroes. I loved the raw-deal worlds they inhabited. I loved the way they forged ahead despite the odds, willing to go down swinging without complaint once they'd set their course.

All that seems great when you're twelve. But as I grew older, I realized that things were a little more complicated than Bob Howard had made them out to be. Of course, I'm sure Howard knew that all along. And if you know anything about him—if you've read Novalyne Price Ellis's *One Who Walked Alone* or seen the excellent movie based upon it, *The Whole Wide World*—odds are you'll agree.

I'll sum it up by shoveling a cliché in your direction: *the world Bob Howard inhabited was never as easy to navigate as the worlds he created.* Still, there's no doubt that Howard was the kind of writer who took charge when his words hit the page. He stepped right up to the plate and took his cuts. His work was honest. He meant what he said and said it plainly. And that's why I never tire of a tale like "The Fire of Asshurbanipal" no matter how many times I've read it, and that's why I still pull Howard's paperbacks off the shelf on summer afternoons.

I tried to write a charge-ahead story. I wanted characters with backbone—both the good guys and the bad guys—the kind of characters Bob Howard would have liked. And while no character in this story is meant to represent Howard, I wanted to write a little bit about the man himself. The kind of guy he was, and how he dealt with the world. In the end, that's where my characters came from.

The way I see it, Bob Howard was a man who kept too many things locked up inside.

I wish he'd found a way to let some of them go.

I wish he'd found a way to get them down on paper.

—*Norman Partridge*

Carrion

Norman Partridge

PART I

It was quiet and hot—lazy afternoon quiet and desert afternoon hot—and far enough off Route 66 to qualify as the middle of nowhere.

Two guys were heading west in a brand new 1946 Plymouth coupe. Just ahead of them a Mexican girl struggled with another guy by the side of the road, and the girl started screaming, and the guy slammed her against the side of his car and slapped her across the face just as the Plymouth came into view.

The Plymouth's passenger was asleep in the backseat and didn't see any of it, but the driver saw the whole ugly deal. He stomped the brakes, and his door flew open before the car came to a stop. A second later he was running across hot asphalt, straight at the guy, who had his back turned and his hand raised for another slap.

"Hold it, buddy," the driver shouted. "And I mean *right now*—"

He would have said more, but the man who'd done the slapping pulled a gun as he turned around, and the driver froze. Right there in his tracks. Right there on the segmented white line that sliced the road in two.

No one was dead. Not yet.

But high in the sky, above them all, the buzzards were already circling.

◆◆◆

It wasn't the gun that made the driver freeze. Paul Murchison had seen plenty of guns in the last few years, and none of them had stopped him cold. No. It was the guy who held the gun that brought him up short, because that guy wore a county sheriff's uniform. He wore it creased and clean, like a coat of armor, and he stood his ground dressed up in it without apology or explanation, as if the uniform itself explained everything that needed explaining no matter what the hell he happened to be doing, and that's what sent a shiver up Murchison's spine, and that's what stopped him in his tracks.

"Don't try to be a hero," the sheriff said. "What you want to do right now is get back in your car. Pretend you didn't see anything. Start driving."

It sounded like good advice the way the sheriff said it, but it wasn't the kind Paul Murchison could swallow. He stared at the polished badge pinned to the big man's chest and the bruises painting the Mexican girl's cheeks. Those were the kind of things that spoke to a guy like Murchison, and they sent a message he couldn't ignore.

He said, "I think you'd better let that girl go, Sheriff."

The sheriff didn't reply. Not with words, anyway. He only grinned a little as he knotted the fingers of his free hand in the Mexican girl's hair, and then he pulled it back slowly as if he were trying to aim her chin at the sun, and then he yanked it hard…the way you'd yank a dog's leash.

The girl's head whiplashed backwards. She cried out and the sheriff shoved her to her knees, but he wasn't finished with her. He planted a heel between her shoulder blades and pushed her into the dirt, and he did it without a downward glance.

The sheriff's gun was trained on the man who stood before him, and so were his eyes. He took in Murchison top to bottom, and it hardly seemed worth the effort because one look told him that the guy was just a sawed-off runt. But the sheriff was the type who liked to be sure so he eyeballed the guy anyway, and the things he noticed on closer inspection surprised him—starting with a bad regulation haircut that was just beginning to grow out, ending with a pair of scuffed army boots that were poised on a white stripe of hot asphalt.

The sheriff stared at those boots as if they explained a lot.

When he was done staring, he smiled at the ex-soldier who wore them.

The way the sheriff saw it, the time for talking was over. He cocked his pistol. Overhead, the coil of buzzards circled lower, painting the black road with shadows that were blacker still. Veils cast by flapping wings slipped over the men's faces. A frayed rag of darkness enveloped the sheriff's hand and the gun held in it, as if trying to hide the thing that hand and that gun were about to do from the unforgiving stare of the afternoon sun.

Just for a moment, the sheriff glanced down at the shadows playing over his hand.

Just for a moment, because he was about to commit cold-blooded murder.

But that moment was all it took.

◆◆◆

Jim McGraw stepped out of the Plymouth, a Luger clutched in his left hand.

Sergeant Murchison had taken the Luger off a captured Nazi captain in the El Guettar valley. Murchison and his men had presented the pistol to McGraw as a souvenir. The young lieutenant carried it with him the rest of the war, but McGraw hadn't even touched the weapon since mustering out a couple weeks ago on the east coast. He certainly hadn't been thinking about it while he dozed in the back seat of the Plymouth, recovering from a marathon drive that had taken the pair across the Texas Panhandle, New Mexico, and a good chunk of Arizona. Truth be told, he'd never expected to use the pistol stateside for anything more deadly than shooting at rusty cans, but the sight of a sadistic cop pointing a .38 in Murchison's direction had changed McGraw's mind about that PDQ.

He grabbed the Luger from under the seat and came out of the car firing on the run. That surprised the sheriff, who hadn't even noticed that there was another guy in the Plymouth. McGraw's first bullet took the big man dead center in the chest and slammed him back against the county insignia painted on the patrol car door, but the lieutenant didn't leave it there. Places like El Guettar and the Kasserine Pass and Omaha Beach had taught him better than that. So he put two more rounds in the sheriff's chest, and the slugs punched straight through the lawman and blew out a couple of patrol car windows behind him.

Still the stubborn bastard returned fire. Two of the sheriff's shots went wild, but the third bullet trenched McGraw's shoulder. The lanky twenty-six-year-old didn't even notice the wound. McGraw moved forward as the buzzards screamed overhead, but he didn't notice them, either. The Mexican girl stared at him as if she thought he might plug her next, but he didn't spare her a glance. All he could think about was finishing the job he'd started, and the girl wasn't any part of that.

Besides, Murch was watching out for the girl, the same way he'd watched out for countless wet-nosed privates who'd frozen under fire on battlefields from Tunisia to Belgium. The sergeant pulled her out of harm's way, and the sheriff watched him do it. The lawman coughed up a stream of blood as he raised his gun, aiming the .38 in the retreating pair's direction.

McGraw knew that it was time to put an end to things before they really went wrong, and his finger tensed on the Luger's trigger. A scream tore at him from behind, just above his head. Talons raked his wounded shoulder and black wings slapped his tanned face as a buzzard as big as a good-sized cat knocked McGraw off balance. He slapped at the bird's bald head, and the red-faced thing screeched and flapped away as the Luger went off a couple inches from its hooked beak.

But McGraw's bullet didn't hit anything important.

Another bullet did. The wounded sheriff spit blood, laughed, and fired one last shot before falling dead at the side of the road.

The bullet didn't hit Jim McGraw, and it didn't hit the Mexican girl.

It shattered a couple of Paul Murchison's cervical vertebrae as it burrowed through his neck, and it ricocheted off bone and blew out a chunk of his skull the size of a silver dollar. The force of the bullet spun Murchison halfway around, and his eyes found McGraw's for one horrible lingering moment, and in that moment the younger man saw something disappear from the older man's eyes, something rich and bright and good that had been there as long as Paul Murchison had been drawing breath.

McGraw watched that thing glimmer, then watched it go. His friend tottered like a scarecrow freed from its pole. Murch was alive one second and dead the next, and when the clock finished that particularly brutal tick the sergeant's scarecrow legs weren't any good anymore and they went out from under him.

Murchison's corpse toppled through the afternoon heat. His dead jaw cracked against the blacktop like an empty bottle tossed out of a passing car. McGraw winced at the sound, tensing the way you do when you grab a hot skillet by accident. He'd winced like that a hundred times since he'd first seen battle in North Africa, but now he was doing it in a place he'd never expected, on a deserted little stretch of middle-of-nowhere blacktop in the good old U. S. A., and it was odd to discover that the feeling was the same here as it was anywhere. McGraw tried to slam a lid on it as it boiled up inside him but it was stubborn, and it fought him the way it always did, and finally it picked up steam and rolled over him the way those German panzers had rolled over his men in the Kasserine Pass, and it brought other feelings with it, feelings McGraw recognized the same way he suddenly recognized the pain in his shoulder, and once recognized those feelings were as impossible to ignore as a fresh wound carved by a bullet, as inexorable as the steady trickle of blood dribbling from his own torn flesh.

Scarlet droplets rolled down his arm and over his fingers and over his gun. The lieutenant covered the wound with his hand, and still the blood flowed. It splattered his shoes. It dripped onto the roadway. Murchison's blood was down there, too, but it wasn't flowing anymore. It was drying in an angry slash that bisected the road's white line. It was soaking into the cracked, scorching blacktop that smothered the earth, and when all was said and done it would barely leave a stain.

But the buzzards had its scent. Coursing from a fresh wound or dry-ing on the pavement, blood was all the same to them, and they wheeled and capered and screamed in the bright blue sky at the smell of it, and their black shadows danced at the feet of the living and covered the dead men like shrouds.

◆◆◆

The man with the Luger stood in the road for a long time.

Sicorra Rojas didn't want to stand there a moment longer. Not beneath the swirling cloud of black birds. In the last five days she had seen enough of those horrible creatures to last her a lifetime. Nothing would have made her happier than to be far away from the shadows cast by their bristling wings...unless it was putting a good distance between herself and the dead man with the badge, the *cabron* who would have killed her if he'd had the chance.

Sicorra wanted to tell these things to the man who had saved her life, but she did not have the words. She could not speak English, and the stranger could not speak Spanish. So she could not tell him about the birds, or the shuttered house in the desert where she had first encountered them, or the evil things the sheriff had done to her in that place before she escaped.

But she knew that talking made no difference now, and neither did her story. Two men were dead, and one of them wore a badge and one did not, and that was all that mattered. Right and wrong did not enter into it. To stay here would mean death, for surely there were other men with badges who would seek vengeance against those who had slain their fallen *compadré*, no matter what he had done.

That was the way of it. Sicorra could not linger here, and neither could the stranger. Somehow, she had to convince him to go. Sicorra did not have English and the stranger had no Spanish, but in the end she real-ized that both languages shared the only word needed to set their course.

Sicorra took the stranger's hand. She stared into his eyes.

"Mexico," she said.

The stranger did not speak.

He looked down at the dead lawman, at the silver star pinned to his bloodstained shirt.

He nodded.

He understood.

◆◆◆

When the Plymouth was gone and the man and woman with it, the buzzards circled lower. They ignored the corpse with the hole in its throat. That hunk of meat was of no interest to them. Instead, they circled above the dead man who wore the badge.

Since the day two weeks ago when he first stumbled upon the shuttered house in the desert, that man had trod the earth beneath shadows cast by their wings. He was the kind of man the buzzards prized, the kind who had more than a few shadows locked in the red muscle that was his heart.

The man's shadows were dark ones. They had twined while he dwelled within the great wooden beast that gave the birds shelter, setting down roots that burrowed deep in his guts. The darkness within the man had ripened beneath their wings, and the birds had scented his misery the way they now scented his death. They sucked the sweet smell through razored beaks, and they filled their lungs with it, and their knotted hearts beat faster.

The wake of buzzards flew on. The black circle tightened above the dead man's head. Soon it resembled a gigantic funeral wreath rotating above him. The sun shone through the heart of that circle, but it could no longer touch the man the way that shadows could.

The dead man lay on his back, staring up at the circle's changing heart with unblinking eyes. The afternoon sun still shone brightly, but the knot of blue sky contained within the black wings was growing darker.

It grew darker still. The birds watched over the dead man, a swarm of skinned red faces and knowing black eyes.

Hooked beaks parted. Screams tore the silence.

For the birds, and for the dead man, the waiting was over.

PART II

The man stuck to the back roads. To Sicorra, they were little more than bleached scars running across a desert as bloodless as a dead man's skin. That thought frightened her, but she tried hard to bury her fear because she could not share it with the man who had saved her life. Even if she had spoken his language, she could not imagine words that could convey the things she had seen in this desert, at the end of a road that looked so much like every other road that knifed across countless miles of nothing.

Sicorra remembered that road, and the shuttered house that stood at the end of it.

Perhaps that was why she saw that road everywhere.

Perhaps that was why she never wanted to see it again.

Sicorra had traveled north just a few weeks ago. She'd had no other choice. She had two younger sisters, and her mother was dead and her father was old. There was no money. She'd lived in the same small fishing village all her life, and there were many things she loved about her life there—the clean smell of the Gulf of California outside her window, the sharp cry of the white gulls welcoming her father's boat home as the setting sun glowed on the horizon, the taste of the lobsters he caught and the vegetables she grew in their garden each spring.

But time and bad luck had reduced all those simple pleasures to memories. Her father's gaze had grown as dark as an October sky. The old man's vision was fading, though he would not admit it. For months his boat had lingered at the dock collecting barnacles, and Sicorra felt the pain growing inside him as he sat and watched her coax meals from their garden. So when an uncle who lived in Flagstaff wrote that he could help her find a job across the border, Sicorra resigned herself to the move. Leaving her home and family would be better than losing both to the slow grind of poverty. Of this she was certain.

She took a bus north to Nogales. There she hired an American to take her across the border and drive her to Flagstaff. He took most of her money, but that was all right. Sicorra's uncle had warned her that everyone paid to cross the border. More often than not, even the *braceros* who entered the U. S. with legal work permits were forced to kick back a portion of their earnings to their employers. So paying the gringo did not trouble Sicorra. She would make more money in America, where she could live with her uncle's family without spending too much, and she would send the rest of her earnings home to her family.

The gringo had Spanish and a gun. These things made Sicorra feel safe, because the border and the unfamiliar country on the other side of it could be dangerous for a young woman traveling alone. But they had no trouble at the border. Getting across was easy for the gringo, who joked with the guards as if they were his brothers. This pleased the big American greatly, so much so that he insisted on stopping at a roadhouse to celebrate. They ate in a restaurant that was connected to a bar. Sicorra had never visited such a place. She had never been near a bar in her life, and her father would have chastised her for such behavior.

The roadhouse served the best food Sicorra had eaten in months, and despite her nervousness she found herself laughing at the American's jokes. But the sound of her own laughter was a thing that had become strange to her, so she did not laugh long. The man did not seem to notice. He drank a few beers after finishing his meal, and then they drove on, taking back roads. The man explained that it would be safer that way.

The way he said it made it sound like another joke, but it did not seem funny to Sicorra. Nothing in this desert did. As the sun set and the blue sky faded to purple, the American turned off the blacktop and followed a dirt road the color of a bleached scar. The gentle twilight painted the man's white skin, and he began to talk more seriously now, but Sicorra barely heard his words.

Instead, she watched the sunset fading in the distance. Night stole the edges of the sky, spreading shadows across the land, but there were already enough shadows waiting on this road. They played out from the trunks of tall saguaro cacti, and they fell sharply from sandstone ridges that towered in the distance, and they were cast by the wings of great black buzzards that paced the American's car as if it were prey.

And they stirred Sicorra's own shadows. She thought of her father, and she hoped the old man remembered her as more than a silent shadow that tilled sharp stones in the garden. She remembered the way they had laughed together when her mother still lived and the sea shone clear in his eyes and she was only a child, and she remembered the silence that had grown between them when the laughter stopped. And at the same time she remembered the roadhouse, and the easy way laughter had spilled from her own lips in the company of an American she did not really know at all, a man who had given her nothing more than the things she had paid for.

Sicorra was glad her father had not seen her waste her laughter on such a man. She suddenly felt childish, and she was just as suddenly deeply ashamed of her behavior at the roadhouse.

The talkative American droned on. His Spanish was awkward. His words troubled Sicorra. Some of the things he said did not make sense at all. Those things would only begin to make sense later, when she had escaped from the man and the shuttered house that waited for them at the end of that scarred road.

Sicorra would never forget her first look at that evil place, for even then she had known that the house did not belong anywhere this side of hell. Narrow and tall, it was, with an open front door that gaped like a mouth thirsty for the cool indigo wind that blew down from the north. But the door was the only thing that was open in this house. Shutters were nailed over the windows, and scabs of sandblasted wood clung to its sides, and it was crowned with a black roof that looked like an undertaker's hat. Hunched buzzards perched on its rotting cornices, their red-pink heads wobbling on gristly necks like the heads of sick old men. Their black eyes studied Sicorra as she stepped out of the American's car, and their wings unfolded like knife blades from their pommeled black bodies, and their screams stole the desert silence as they took to the air and dove at her.

The buzzards' screams tore through her. The sounds shook the house, rattling shutters against rusted nails that held them tight. Sicorra covered her ears and tried to run, but the American grabbed her.

That was when he hit her for the first time. It surprised her, because she had not yet learned what kind of man he was. She had not yet learned that he was a lawman...the kind of lawman who used his badge to take whatever he wanted. She had not yet watched him murder a man in cold blood on a lonely stretch of desert highway.

But Sicorra learned quickly at the sheriff's hands. She had no choice. He knocked her down with a single blow. Then the *cabron* grabbed her by the hair and pulled her to her feet, and he dragged her through the gaping doors of the dark house, into a wooden throat that breathed indigo wind.

As Sicorra stumbled across the threshold, she knew instantly that the man did not live in that house. It wasn't the kind of place anyone would *live*. The sheriff slammed the door behind them and shoved her down the slivered throat. Even then she knew that this place was not a house at all. It was a *thing*...and being inside it was like being inside a dead carcass that had rotted beneath the desert sun.

The hallway narrowed. The wooden gullet gulped them down. Ahead lay a room with a dozen narrow windows that should have cast no light, for the closed shutters outside bristled with nails driven as deeply as any that speared Christ's hands on a Penitente church's crucifix. But inside, the windows gaped unshuttered. They held no glass...and no world that Sicorra recognized.

Another world waited outside the open windows, a world the young woman could barely believe. Angry clouds swelled in a sky the color of a gutted fish, churned by a wind as hot as a plague pyre. Buzzards circled in that sky, and Sicorra did not know if they were the same buzzards she had seen outside in the desert but it really did not matter, for they ripped through the clouds with talons and beaks, and the clouds spilled red rain as the carrion eaters swooped through the open windows, and they flapped about the gray, lifeless room as the sheriff pushed Sicorra to the floor.

Red rain drummed against the roof of the house. It spilled off the cornices and filled the gutters. The buzzards settled in the great room, roosting on torn furniture stained with their leavings. A foul chill rose from the floor and a shiver traveled Sicorra's spine. Something in that shiver told her that everything that was about to happen here had happened many times before. And then the sheriff reached out for her with his big hands, and the birds stared down with their old man faces...watching...waiting....

◆◆◆

The sheriff lay at the side of the road.

His name was Mitchell Reece and he was dead, but he saw the buzzards well enough as they circled above him in a swirling black knot bordered by too-blue sky. At the center of the circle waited the rich red sky Reece had seen through the windows of the shuttered house. That sky spilled rain like blood, but not one drop made it through the buzzard's swirling funeral wreath, and not one drop touched the sheriff's flesh.

But the rain splashed across his memory. The sheriff had stumbled upon the house for the first time two weeks ago. He'd been chasing an illegal Mex who stabbed one of his deputies before making his getaway in a stolen Ford. The sheriff had wanted the little bastard bad, and he tracked him through the desert, and he found the killer's getaway car parked outside the shuttered house.

Hell, Reece was surprised to find such a house standing out there in the desert. He'd never come across it before, never even heard of a place like that. And that was weird because he figured he *should* have heard of it. It was sure enough odd-looking with all those shutters nailed over like that...and with those damn big buzzards roosting all over the place.

Not that he really gave the house a second thought, given the circumstances. Truth was that Reece was much more interested in the stolen car and the fugitive Mex than a leaning old claptrap that looked like it'd been standing since the Flood.

That's the way it was at first, anyway. Reece made his way up the front stairs and stepped through the open doorway. Once inside, things were different. For one thing, there was a rank smell to the place that seemed to creep right up inside you. Reece got the feeling he was walking into some kind of sewer or something.

But Reece ignored the stink and got down to business. He followed a long hallway that narrowed like an animal's burrow as it twisted into the place, and then he came to a big gray room that seemed all a-jumble—chairs and tables overturned, furniture splattered with bird shit. The windows in the gray room stood open—there were no shutters like the ones he'd seen nailed up outside, not even any glass—and the breeze that blew through those windows made the stink at the front door seem like French perfume. And the sky out there—

That sky was a hell of a sight, and it froze something up inside Mitchell Reece. The sky was *all wrong* out there...and so were the clouds...and those goddamn buzzards—

Those goddamn buzzards made Reece want to turn tail and run.

The sheriff didn't get the chance, because the Mex jumped him then. Straight out of the shadows he came, and he still had the knife he'd used to carve up Reece's deputy. Reece whirled with the .38 in his hand, but the little bastard was on him too fast, and somehow they ended up wrestling on the creaking floorboards and Reece lost his pistol. Rolling around on that floor was like rolling around inside a goddamn stinking clamshell at the bottom of the ocean, but the sheriff couldn't think about that; he could only think about the Mex, and his knife, and the dark fire that gleamed in the killer's eyes.

The buzzards swooped in through the windows as the two men fought. They watched as the Mexican lunged at Reece, his blade slicing a bitter path towards the lawman's neck. Reece dodged out of the way and caught the killer's wrist as it shot past his head, then jammed that wrist into his mouth and bit down hard. The Mexican howled and dropped the knife, and the birds screamed like a crowd at a low-rent prizefight.

The Mex didn't give up easy, though. He kept on fighting until Reece managed to flip him on his back. Quickly, Reece straddled the guy and grabbed him by the wrists to hold him down. The Mex was beat, but he didn't look it. He stared up at Reece, that dark fire still blazing in his eyes.

But he wasn't struggling anymore, and that surprised the sheriff. It was weird—like someone had thrown a switch inside the murderous little bastard or something. Reece just couldn't figure it. The guy wasn't struggling at all, not even a little bit…but that fire still burned in his eyes with an intensity the sheriff had rarely seen….

And then the Mexican did the strangest thing—he started talking. He talked about the deputy he had killed…and *how* he had killed him…and the *way* the man had died. His English was sure enough broken, but the words twisted in Reece's guts like fishhooks, and he began to wish the Mexican still had his knife and was jamming it into his belly instead of talking to him like he was, because nothing could be worse than this.

But the guy wouldn't stop. He kept on talking, and the words burrowed into Reece the same way that narrow hallway burrowed into the house. Reece had the Mex by the wrists, but that wasn't doing any good now, not with the guy's mouth running the way it was. And the sheriff wasn't the only one who knew it—he looked up for a second and saw the buzzards' black eyes blazing in their wizened red faces as they took in the show.

It was as if the goddamn things were laughing at him for letting the Mexican talk like that.

Reece started to go a little crazy. He grabbed a fistful of the killer's hair and pounded his head on that cold floor like he wanted to bust it open, but still the Mexican wouldn't surrender. He wasn't talking anymore, but he did manage to wriggle onto his side, and the next thing Reece knew he was doubled over because the guy had driven an elbow into his nuts.

The Mex crawled out from under him.

Reece tried to get up, but he couldn't make the trip.

The killer ran. He would have made it to the open windows on the far side of the room easily, only the buzzards took him down before he even got close. Reece couldn't believe how fast it happened. The birds ripped into the guy and laid his guts out across the floor like treats torn from some bloody piñata, and then they settled in and really went to work on him.

Reece didn't know for sure what happened after that. He thought that maybe he had passed out for awhile, because the next thing he knew he was sitting on a moldy old sofa, watching the birds finish up with the Mex.

He didn't feel bad about it. Hell, he felt surprisingly good. The birds plucked at the Mex's guts with their sharp beaks, but that was what the bastard deserved, didn't he? He'd killed a deputy, and he'd tried to kill Reece, too, hadn't he? And every now and then the little bastard would twitch a little, and every now and then the birds would stop and stare at Reece for a minute or two, looking down at him with those wizened faces like wise old priests who'd caught a kid smiling at something he shouldn't ought to.

It made Reece feel kind of strange. But he didn't feel bad. The Mexican was getting what was coming to him now, and that was okay because Reece remembered the things the guy had said and the feelings those words had unleashed inside him—the hate and anger and all the rest of it—and how good it had felt to turn those feelings loose.

The sheriff's brain picked that over the same way the birds picked over the Mexican's guts. The buzzards continued their work, but now it just seemed routine. It was as if the Mex didn't have anything they really wanted anymore but they just couldn't help themselves. It was in their nature to finish the job, and that's what they were going to do.

But it was different with Reece, different with those things he'd kept tied up so long in a tight little knot in his gut. Some of those things had come untangled inside him when the Mexican attacked, sure…but there were other things, darker things threading through him just now as he sat there on a shit-stained sofa in a charnel house. Those things were black dreams, and Reece didn't even want to think about them because they were the kind of things a man didn't dare face up to when he looked in the mirror, the kind of dreams that had festered inside him until they rotted like a hunk of meat left out in the sun.

The birds had finished with the Mexican. They were watching Reece now, silently with their old man eyes, and it was as if their beaks were plucking at that tight little knot he hid deep inside.

Pretty soon Reece was damn near crying. And pretty soon he was behind the wheel, driving down to Nogales, chasing after the darkest of the dark dreams that the buzzards had ripped loose.

Nogales was where Reece found the Mexican girl.

The one he brought back to the shuttered house.

The one who'd gotten away.

The one he'd get up and go after any minute now.

Reece lay there at the side of the road. The birds had sure enough stirred things up inside his dead carcass as the desert sun blazed down. His misery had cooked up pretty well. He could almost taste it, and so could the birds. They broke the circle and whipped toward him. Their beaks tore his clothes, ripped through his belly, pecked at his intestines.

Reece jerked on the road the same way that murderous Mexican had on the floor of the shuttered house.

It seemed like every damn one of those buzzards wanted a taste of his misery.

That was all right with Reece.

When it came to misery, he had plenty to go around.

McGraw didn't know where the road would take him.

He only knew it headed south, toward Mexico.

Right now, that was good enough for him. The lieutenant glanced over at the girl. She was asleep. McGraw had slept maybe two hours in the last thirty-six, and he was dog tired. He imagined how wonderful it would feel, just to turn off his brain and let his troubles climb into the backseat of his subconscious for awhile. But he couldn't let that happen. He had to keep moving forward, because he didn't know what was going on behind him.

McGraw ran down the possibilities. Could be that nothing was happening, that the sheriff's corpse hadn't been found yet. Or it could be a posse was already looking for the lawman's killer. Could be there was a radio report out and a statewide dragnet already in place. Could be there'd be a dozen deputies waiting for him at the end of this road, armed with enough firepower to stop a Sherman tank.

In short, it could be that he was making one *mucho grande* mistake, tearing off the way he had, heading south for Mexico when he knew that he and Murchison had been in the right and the dead lawman had been in the wrong. But no matter how he added things up in his head, McGraw couldn't take a chance on that, not out here in the middle of nowhere. Out here he was on the dead sheriff's turf, and he didn't have the lay of the land. Maybe if he was by himself, he might have gambled and turned himself in. But with the girl....

No. McGraw needed to be sure that she was safe before he tried to explain anything to anyone. If Paul Murchison had taught him anything, it was that you took care of those who needed taking care of before you took care of yourself.

That settled it. McGraw decided he'd do this Murchison's way, the way they'd done it in the war. He'd started something, and he'd finish it. He'd take the girl across the border, out of harm's way, and then he'd figure out what to do about the rest of it.

There was plenty of gas in the Plymouth's tank. McGraw clocked another fifty miles. The girl slept through every one of them. To the west, the sun was beginning to set in a pastel smear. Cactus shadows stretched straight and stiff across the bleached desert as the coupe's new tires hissed over a road salted with sandstone grit. It was a quiet, steady sound, like the hollow echo of a seashell, and McGraw began to hear things in it.

Whispers...then voices.

His and Murchison's...easy banter passing back and forth.

The sergeant did most of the talking, of course, because the lieutenant was just naturally the kind who kept most everything to himself. Murchison was tight with a dime, but not with words...not when it came to that new Plymouth, anyway. For him, buying a gleaming hunk of Detroit steel had been a dream come true. He'd saved most of his combat pay during the war, and he'd banked the money he'd earned during a post-war stint he'd served with the lieutenant in Germany. And through it all Murch had rattled on about buying a new car when he landed stateside, until every private in the outfit was tired of hearing about it. But that didn't stop the sarge. Complaints or no complaints, talking about that new car was his favorite pastime.

Only McGraw knew why. Because he knew Murchison. And for Murchison, the new car meant more than he'd ever say.

For Murch, it meant an end to the war.

It meant putting his days as a soldier behind him.

It meant coming home.

And when it came to coming home, and when it came to the new car and most other things, the sergeant was as good as his word. Murch bought the Plymouth on his first day as a civilian, and that was something, because new cars were expensive as hell and twice as hard to come by. The sergeant hadn't cared—he'd peeled off the dough, grabbed a fist-ful of keys from the salesman. "C'mon, Lieutenant," Murch had said. "We're gonna take ourselves a little ride. We're gonna drive this baby across this county, take 66 by storm and rattle every sleepy burg along the way. And when we cross that Golden Gate and hit San Francisco…well, watch out. You'll never forget the time I'm gonna show you when we hit my hometown."

It was quiet in the car. McGraw knew that. There weren't any voices there.

But the words—and the memories—kept on coming. McGraw's grip tightened on the steering wheel. A hissing laughter echoed down there in the wheel wells, but McGraw ignored it and focused on the road. The bleak little strip just kept on heading south, and the Plymouth's engine purred steadily locked up under that big hood as it clocked mile after mile.

McGraw knew that he needed to be the same way the engine was. He just had to drive. He just had to keep moving forward. That's what he needed to do. So he locked up the things inside him, and he thought about the road, and he drove.

To the west, the afternoon pastels were fading. Darker colors were coming on—rich, strong colors that would paint the night. Yawning, McGraw stretched behind the wheel. His shoulder was really starting to ache. The girl had done a good job sewing him up with the first aid kit she found in the trunk, but there was only so much she could do. The wound wasn't bad as gunshots go and McGraw knew he'd been damn lucky…but, hey, a .38 slug had carved up his shoulder a little bit and that sure wasn't going to leave him feeling like he was ready to pitch nine innings anytime soon.

McGraw turned off the road. There was a house up ahead. Out here in the wide lonesome, it was a good bet the place was deserted. Maybe he could catch a little rest there.

The whispering hiss in the wheel wells dulled as the Plymouth fol-lowed a sandstone wash, and pretty soon McGraw got a better look at the house.

Yeah. Had to be that the place was deserted.

The windows were shuttered over.

And the shutters were nailed closed.

◆◆◆

The buzzards flew on, their black wings carving a path through the twilight.

The tattered man drove below them, locked up in a little wheeled box with a star painted on each door. The carrion eaters had taken the best part of him by the side of the road, but they had not taken everything. They had picked him over—just as they had picked over the Mexican and so many others—but they had not picked him clean.

So the birds followed in his wake. They had no choice in the matter. The scent of the tattered man's blood was smeared upon their beaks, and his sins and his flesh lay heavy in their bellies, and the taste of his misery burned like salt in their mouths.

The taste stirred their hunger, but the birds realized that it was no longer a hunger the tattered man could satisfy.

But somewhere out there...up ahead...in the desert....

Somewhere out there...was another man....

PART III

The man with the Luger stumbled out of the house. He tripped down the stairs and dropped to his knees in front of Sicorra, and his breaths came hard and fast above the twilight inhalations that swept through the open door behind him.

Warm desert air washed past Sicorra and up the stairs as the shuttered house drew another breath, but she refused to look at the narrowing hall that waited on the other side of that horrible doorway. She knew better than that.

She turned her back on the house, and she helped the man to his feet and led him back to the car. He leaned against the front fender, clutching his pistol, standing there in the fading light with his eyes closed. His hands were shaking. It did not seem that they could stop.

Sicorra knew why. She had tried to prevent him from entering the house that was not a house at all, but he had not understood her warnings. So he had walked down its splintered throat until he found the gray room where Sicorra had nearly died, and he had looked through the shuttered windows that wore no shutters at all, and he had glimpsed the world that waited on the other side of those windows.

That world was not meant for words. Sicorra realized that much.

She took the stranger's hand. She held it tightly, and soon he was hardly shaking at all.

They stood together in silence. When she first awoke, Sicorra had been terrified to find that fate had returned her to this place. But now...now she was not frightened. Now it seemed that fate was wise, for not one buzzard had flown through the open front door of the house while she stood before it, and none waited perched on the black roof that looked like an undertaker's hat, and not a single bird capered above in the darkening sky.

The house was defenseless. Sicorra was sure of it.

She released the man's hand. His ragged breathing had slowed, and his hands had stopped shaking. Sicorra opened the passenger door and found the man's canteen. She unscrewed the top and gave him the canteen, and, one-handed, he raised it to his lips.

He would not surrender his pistol. That was all right. Sicorra did not need a gun to do what needed to be done; the only thing she needed was locked in the Plymouth's trunk, along with the first-aid kit she had used to sew up the man's shoulder.

Sicorra hoped she would not need the first-aid kit again. The man tipped back the canteen and drank greedily. He sighed when he finished, and he handed the canteen to Sicorra. She had a long drink herself. Then she walked around to the other side of the car, ducked inside, and took the keys from the ignition.

The twilight wind blew down from the north. Sicorra smiled to herself. It was not much of a smile, but she was glad to have it.

She was about to open the trunk when a familiar scream rose in the distance.

Sicorra whirled to face it.

In the gathering darkness, a pair of headlights blazed across the scarred stretch of road.

The sheriff's car was coming fast.

Above it came the birds.

◆◆◆

Reece's right boot was a mess of torn leather, and the foot inside it had been chewed down to gristle and bone, but there was enough of it left to hammer the brakes.

The patrol car skidded to a stop. Its headlights sliced through the purple twilight, spotlighting the Plymouth, the man, and the Mexican girl. And since the idiots were standing there like a couple of deer frozen in the glare, the sheriff didn't waste any time. He popped the handle with his bony left hand and swung open the door before either of them managed so much as an eye-blink.

The buzzards overhead screamed through gore-stained beaks. A pair of birds that had been riding shotgun flapped past the sheriff and took to the air, their wings working hard to lift bellies they'd filled during Reece's trip across the desert. Reece himself came off the leather seat like a big red smear. He stepped out of the car, and the buzzards that had gone hungry during his drive dove straight at him.

Now that the birds had given him a second chance to square things with the guy who'd gunned him down, Reece didn't even care anymore. But he sure as hell couldn't get things done the way he wanted with the buzzards making a meal of him while he tried to do it, so he shook them off, and they damn well must have understood that he meant business because they flapped their shiny wings and got the hell out of his way.

That was the way Reece wanted it. The Mexican girl stared at him with eyes as big as goddamn saucers, but the sheriff didn't care about her anymore, either. He only had eyes for the soldier who'd put three bullets in his chest.

Hate for that bastard burned in what was left of Reece's belly. The sheriff was ready for an old-fashioned showdown, but the man hadn't moved at all. He just stood there, and that surprised Reece. Oh, the guy still had his Luger, all right, but the way he was leaning against the Plymouth you'd have a hard time picturing him using it. Hell, the way he was standing there you'd have figured that someone just finished digging around his guts with a crowbar and he was going to spend a month of Sundays getting over it.

It didn't matter to Reece. The way the sheriff saw it, the guy had it coming and he was going to get it…with or without a fight. Reece had a solid grip on the .38, and he raised it. This time, he told himself, there'd be no surprises, no reinforcements popping out of the Plymouth's back seat.

This time, it'd be strictly *mano a mano*.

Reece took aim. His finger tensed against the trigger.

He tried to pull it, but nothing happened.

He tried again…and found that he couldn't.

His finger wouldn't budge.

Something was wrong.

Something was *very goddamn* wrong—

A wave of buzzards broke from the sky and passed between the two men. They circled Reece in a tight pattern, and within that circle the sound of their flapping wings rattled like a death cadence played on a dozen snare drums. Their screams made his muscles jerk like puppet strings, and the birds circled closer, tighter, plucking at Reece with their beaks, gouging him with their claws, and this time they took everything.

They gorged upon the remnants of his flesh and chased it with the dregs of his hatred, and they tore away the last tattered strips of the tight little knot he had hidden inside for so long, and they swallowed them down gulp by bloody gulp. Reece tottered on bony legs. He couldn't understand what the birds were doing. It didn't make sense, bringing him back to life, bringing him all this way just to abandon him—

Then the last strip of flesh was torn away, and the whole deal came suddenly clear. The black-feathered veil that had ensnared the sheriff evaporated, and a second later the birds were circling above the Plymouth and the used-up man with the Luger. Only the guy didn't look so used up now. It was as if someone had thrown a switch inside him. He stared across the sandstone wash at Reece, and a fire was kindling in his eyes, and to Reece it looked like the kind of fire you put under a skillet when you want to cook up something hot and fast and greasy.

The buzzards' screams hacksawed the sheriff's thoughts. The puppet strings jerked hard. Reece danced like a hunk of bait on a hook. Maybe that's all he was anymore. His finger trembled against the .38's trigger, but he just couldn't pull the damn thing. There wasn't enough left of him to do the job. He belonged to the birds now.

They owned him, and they wouldn't let him use the gun.

They made him use his mouth instead.

They chose his words for him, the same way they'd chosen the Mexican's words when they'd used him to bait Reece in the shuttered house. They were evil words, and they slithered from the sheriff's mouth like snakes that had devoured the memory of a man named Paul Murchison and shit it out, and they cleaved a butcher's path from Jim McGraw's guts to his brain.

Before McGraw even knew it, the Luger was bucking in his hand.

The lieutenant pulled the trigger again and again, and the dead sheriff shut up when the bullets hit him. That was the way it worked. They always shut up when the bullets hit them. McGraw had seen it happen more times than he cared to remember, and the only difference between this time and the others was that the other times the men he'd killed were wearing gray uniforms and speaking a language he couldn't even understand. But they always shut up when the bullets hit them. That was the important part. They shut up, and they never said another word.

Once you start something, you finish it. That's what Jim McGraw learned in the war, and that simple knowledge had brought him home in one piece. Only he hadn't finished things this time. This time the guy he'd killed had come back for more.

That would have been enough to fry anyone's sanity, but the things the dead bastard *said*—

Well, he wouldn't say them anymore. McGraw's Luger was empty now. The sheriff was on the ground. This time he was dead for good, but that knowledge didn't calm McGraw because something inside him had boiled up and boiled over, and there was no jamming a lid on it the way he had back at the road when Murchison bought it.

He clutched the empty pistol in his hand. He stared down at the dead thing on the ground. No human could smell the stink of the thing boiling inside McGraw, but it drove the buzzards crazy, and they dove at him in a black fury. Their talons etched new wounds and opened old, tearing at the stitches the girl had sewn in his wounded shoulder. Their beaks ripped at his splitting flesh. Their screams welcomed his blood, every cell of it alive with things you'd never see under a microscope—the miseries McGraw had endured during the war, the horrors born of wrongs he'd witnessed, his anger at the men who'd committed those wrongs.

But it wasn't so bad to lose those things; it wasn't bad at all, really, because they were the things that burned in your guts late at night and maybe you were better off without them. Only the buzzards weren't going to stop there. They wanted everything McGraw had. They wanted it all. All the things that were buried deep inside him, all the things buried just as deep as the tangled knot of black misery they'd torn from the bowl of Mitchell Reece's pelvis.

But the things inside McGraw were different, because McGraw and Reece were different.

The things inside McGraw had been hidden, certainly, but not from the light.

No. Those things had been hidden from the darkness. McGraw had buried them inside to keep them safe. They were the hopes and dreams and promises he'd made to others and to himself, and he'd protected them the way you protect an ember when you're trying to kindle a fire or keep one from dying. He'd done that for four long years as he and Murchison and the other men marched through Tunisia and France and Belgium, and he hadn't come this far to let anyone or anything steal that ember from him.

But the buzzards had another idea.

Their talons tore McGraw's hide.

Their beaks drilled at him, digging in like picklocks.

For a brief moment McGraw saw himself, bloody and bowed and just like the sheriff—a dead man walking around in a skin sack he didn't even own anymore. That was a vision McGraw could not accept. So the lieutenant fought back with everything he had. He fought back with his bare hands, and the heart and determination that had fueled him for four long years.

He grabbed a buzzard by its gristly red neck, and it was like grabbing a springing rattlesnake but he didn't let go, and he spun the thing's hunched body around and slammed it against sandstone. Feathers exploded from its black hide, and the buzzard went limp in his hands, and a dozen of its brothers took up the fight as soon as McGraw released the bird's corpse. He reached out and caught another, and he slammed it to the ground the same way, but there was no way he could fight them all.

The buzzards rammed into him like medicine balls, and the ones that didn't hit him scored him with claws and beaks as they flew past. Talons sliced his face and arms and tore the shirt right off his back. Jackhammer pecks ripped through his scalp and rattled his skull. Finally the pain tore him down, and he couldn't think straight anymore.

He couldn't think at all—

And he went down.

But it wasn't over yet. Not by a long shot, because McGraw wasn't the only one willing to take up the fight. Through a hail of crashing wings he saw the Mexican girl running toward the shuttered house...running up the stairs....

A road flare blazed in her hand.

The two-legged creature stepped into the wooden thing's mouth. The house sucked a ragged inhalation and scented the creature's determination, and something else...something that smelled like the red world outside its windows.

The clapboard beast would have screamed had it had the ability. It would have called to its little brothers for protection, and they would have turned on black wings and carried the two-legged creature down its wooden gullet and through the maze of its gray corridors, and they would have spilled its blood in the house's great belly and strewn its bones in the red world.

But the house that breathed was a voiceless thing. It could not utter so much as a whisper. And so it stayed silent as the little creature's feet scurried across its throat, and it remained still as the fire from the stick the creature carried touched its splintery gullet.

The flames spread quickly, racing across the great beast's timbered ribs and climbing its stairwells, roaring beneath its eaves while the house stood mute. And soon the roar was joined by the groans of swaying frames and jams, and the anguished barks of exploding balusters and stairs.

Dry lumber crackled as studs and rafters burst aflame.

Nails screamed as the walls began to shudder and twist.

The two-legged creature ran free. The house's shutters rattled like coffin lids on Resurrection Day, and at last they exploded from the windows, and the windows blazed red, and the color flowed across the sandstone and tinted the gleaming wings of the buzzards below.

The birds rose from the wounded soldier like a cloud.

They wheeled through the air and flew toward the unshuttered windows.

The light in the windows blazed as red as the world from which the buzzards had come.

They swept through the open portals.

But no world waited there.

All they found was fire.

PART IV

Sicorra thought of many things as she stared out at the gulf waters late at night. The moon in the sky and its twin on the water, and the white birds that rode the evening breezes between the two. The man who lay sleeping in her bed, and the easy, soft sound of his breathing as he passed a peaceful night. The promises they'd made to each other so many months ago, and the promises they'd kept.

At the beginning they had shared a single word. *Mexico.* Since then Sicorra had learned his language, and he learned hers, but for them it was never really about words. McGraw was not much for words, in any language.

They had other things, of course. Some of them she saw in his eyes. They were the things she treasured most, and they glowed like banked embers that would survive a long winter's night. She saw them when he woke her in the soft glow of morning, and she saw them as he worked repairing her father's fishing boat in the harsh afternoon sun. And she saw them most often in the evening, when his eyes gleamed in the sunset as her father taught him the ways of the Gulf, and he spoke to her with smiles that the blind old man could never see.

Still, Sicorra never forgot the first time she saw her husband's eyes. How frightening they had been, ablaze with wild fire as he crossed a strip of desert highway with a German pistol in his hand. That fire had been kindled deep in his soul. It too had grown from an ember that flared inside him, but it was a fire and not an ember, and Sicorra had learned the difference between the two.

She had learned the difference in the shuttered house, with a burning road flare in her hand.

And now she thought that fire itself was a strange thing, and the fire she'd seen in her husband's eyes on the day they met seemed the strangest of all. Sicorra knew that fire had saved her life, just as she knew that it had saved her husband's. But while she never said it, she also knew that a man could not endure with such a fire burning inside him, for a fire like that could consume everything a man held dear.

A fire like that could destroy dreams, and hopes, and promises.

Sicorra believed that men needed such things, even if they would not speak of them.

In truth, she believed that men who would not speak of them needed those things most of all.